Disguise

by

Candice Kohl

LionHearted Publishing, Inc.
Zephyr Cove, NV, USA

With special appreciation to
Robert and Elizabeth Cook

This book is a work of fiction. Names, characters, places and incidents are products of the author's imagination or are used fictitiously. Any resemblance to actual events or locales or persons, living or dead, is entirely coincidental.

LionHearted Publishing, Inc.
PO Box 618
Zephyr Cove, NV 89448-0618

Copyright © 1996 by Candice Kohl

Cover art by Cathryn McClelland

All rights reserved. No part of this book may be reproduced or transmitted in any form or by any means, electronic or mechanical, including photocopying, recording, or by any information storage and retrieval system, without permission in writing from the publisher. For information contact LionHearted Publishing, Inc.

ISBN: 1-57343-006-4

Printed in the U.S.A.

To my husband—he knows who he is—and to every friend—you know who you are—who said: "Don't quit. You're going to make it!"

Chapter One

✧ ✧ ✧

Gwyneth stood in the drafty outbuilding considering the iron pots and wooden vats in which her ale was brewing and her mead and mulberry wine fermenting. She turned to her servant and said, "Jean, you'll be sure to keep the fire through the night?"

"Aye, milady. If the draughts don't push through the chinks and cracks, blowin' it out altogether."

Gwyneth nodded in understanding, pulling the hood of her cloak up over her cinnamon hair as Jean tucked her own arms beneath her woolen shawl. "What's that?" the serving woman asked, cocking her head. "The wind, is it?"

Both of them fell silent, straining to hear. Suddenly Gwyneth's emerald eyes widened, and as she bolted through the doorway she exclaimed, "It sounds like Gwendolyn!"

The hems of her bliaut and cloak swirled as she raced into the yard. The chickens pecking among the stones flapped their wings and fluttered away at her intrusion, like ripples in a pond. Gwyneth ignored the fowl as Jean joined her and they peered into the gloomy, gray dusk of the blustery, autumn evening.

"There!"

Gwyneth turned to where Jean was pointing and spied the girl running toward them, her long, red braids flying out behind her. Gwyneth opened her arms and the girl ran into them, clinging to her tearfully.

"Gwendolyn, what is it? What's happened?"

"The—the baron's men. They—they're sacking the village! Ethel's cottage has been fired, and—and little Robbie, Alice and Willie's son... Oh, Gwyneth, he was trampled to death by horses' hooves! I saw it, Gwyn! I saw it!"

Gritting her teeth, Gwyneth stroked her sister's head and tried to comfort her. But her eyes remained on the path Gwendolyn had taken up the hill. Just beyond, an unsettling orange glow brightened the smoky sky giving credence to the girl's report that the house belonging to the cottar James and his wife, Ethel, was indeed aflame.

"The baron?" Jean repeated, putting a hand on Gwendolyn's shoulder. "Elwood of Eye?"

Before she could reply, thundering hooves pounding up the path from the village below interrupted. Reacting instinctively, Gwyneth shoved Gwendolyn and Jean behind a full haycart, where the three of them hid in its shadows. Within seconds two warhorses galloped into the yard, prancing and pawing the air as the knights astride them sawed on their reins.

"Arnulf! Arnulf, prepare to pledge your fealty to Lord Elwood, or lose your village, its people, your house and your kin this very night!"

Gwyneth could feel Gwendolyn's continued shaking, though she held the girl firm. But her eyes never left the yard or the intruding knights until the door to the manor house opened, and Arnulf appeared.

He stood on the top of the steps at the second story

entrance. He was garbed in full armor, as the knights on horseback were, but he looked, Gwyneth realized, almost foolish. Arnulf was old and frail; it appeared as if he might crumple under the weight of his mail and helmet. Yet he spread his bowed legs in a fighting stance as he gripped his lance firmly.

"I've sworn my fealty to the baron," he announced, his voice not nearly as sure as it had been thirty years ago.

"*Only* to the baron!" Elwood's man clarified.

"I cannot do that," Arnulf insisted, shaking his head, though it was apparent his protest was futile. The baron's knights knew full well the circumstances the village of Sherborne found itself in. Yet the lord of the manor continued, as if there were some hope of reasoning with these intimidating and unwelcomed visitors, "My allegiance is dual, to both Elwood of Eye and the earl of Farleigh. I've done nothing for one and against the other."

The knight on the lead horse laughed, and his steed's front hooves pawed the dirt. Gwendolyn uttered a startled cry, but Gwyneth silenced her by placing a hand none too gently over her mouth.

"There is no earl of Farleigh! Old Hugh and his son went on crusade and died there. It's been years, old man, and we've a new king now, Henry, Count of Anjou, and a new queen, Eleanor of Aquitaine. And you, Sir Arnulf, have only one lord, Elwood of Eye, baron of all this shire!"

"No!" Thunder in his eyes despite his squawky voice, the old knight, Arnulf, pounded the shaft of his lance on the stone stoop. "Hugh has a son who's the earl now! I've not heard our new King Henry declare otherwise."

"God's teeth, you blithering fool!" the second knight swore in exasperation. "The longer you stand there arguing, the more of Sherborne is lost to you."

"If it's lost to me, it's lost to the baron as well. Methinks your lord shan't be well-pleased if you plunder and burn to the ground one of his richest holdings!"

"There's no earl," the other insisted again. "Old Hugh's sons are dead, either beside him in Jerusalem or felled by fever here at home."

"Not all," Arnulf snarled. "John still lives."

"Are you a seer?" the knight fired back sarcastically. "The youngest has not been heard from since he went to foster in Maine at the end of old King Henry's reign! He will not be returning, and you are not bound by your oath to that house where only a seneschal rules. Your only loyalty is to Elwood of Eye!"

"He's witless," that one's companion declared impatiently, pulling his horse up alongside the other's. "Kill him, be done with it. There's wenches still to be had—"

The baron's man never finished his sentence, except with an explosion of air that blew past his lips at the impact of an arrow piercing his back and splitting his chest. The remaining knight turned quickly, twirling his mace, but he had no chance to defend himself. He, too, was killed by an archer's arrow.

The women remained hiding until the long bowmen appeared. They were Arnulf's men-at-arms, and they were on foot. The old lord climbed awkwardly down the steps, clanging like a ghost bound with chains, and joined them in the yard. "The village?" he asked as his womenfolk crept out of the shadows and several servants emerged from the house above and the stable below.

"There are fires what still need putting out," one explained. "The baron's men slew several of the town's folk, including children who had the bad luck to stumble into their way. And I fear a few maids were used badly. But we put an end to the lives of a number of Elwood's men, and the rest rode off quickly enough."

"Go!" Arnulf barked to his people. "See what you can do to put out the flames before all the village is reduced to ash and rubble."

Obediently, everyone save the youngest children ran off down the path; the archers who had saved their lord's life and manor trotted briskly after them, their weapons still at the ready. Even Jean headed toward Sherborne town, leaving only Gwyneth, Gwendolyn and the manor servants' babes behind with the old knight.

"Father!" young Gwendolyn sobbed, looking as if she longed to embrace him, though she was restrained by his scowl, or his armor, or both.

"In the house, you two."

"Come, children," Gwyneth ordered, lifting two toddlers and carrying them up the stone steps into the house. She followed the old man and the young girl, while the little children followed her like ducklings trailing their mother.

There was only one large room in the manor, with an open bower loft extending a third of the way beneath the vaulted roof. A decent blaze roared in the large pit at one end of the main room but, Gwyneth noticed, despite her best efforts to keep the floor clean, bones had been strewn among the rushes. Setting the children down, she began picking up the remnants of past meals as she told Gwendolyn, "Bring blankets from the chest in our bedchamber. I'll settle the babes down close to the fire so they can sleep 'til their parents return."

Obediently Gwendolyn climbed the narrow, wooden staircase. As she ducked between the heavy curtains that separated the women's sleeping room from Arnulf's, she was hidden by the velvet wall that afforded those above protection from any prying eyes below. When she returned to the lower floor, she spread the blankets near the hearth and tucked the children in as Gwyneth, her cloak now removed, assisted Arnulf in shedding his knightly garb.

When both the ladies' tasks were done, Gwyneth poured methagline from a flagon into three pewter goblets. The drink was laced with herbs designed to ease the old man's aches and pains, but all three of them drank it that evening, sitting on benches at the long, trestle table, Gwyneth and Gwendolyn hoping to still their trembling fingers and pounding hearts.

"The bodies—in the yard—" Gwendolyn muttered, her green eyes locked on Gwyneth's, so much like her own.

"The men will remove them before dawn," she assured her and then, without pause, she spoke her next words to Arnulf. "They were right. Elwood's men were right. You should have renounced your oath to the earl and sworn your fealty to the baron alone. There's no lord in Farleigh Castle; there hasn't been for many a year. If the young Henry, in the two years' time he's been king here, has not seen fit to reward one of his loyal barons with the earldom, it is still no reason for you to keep your oath to a ghost."

Arnulf's rheumy green eyes widened, and more quickly than it would seem possible for a man of the knight's many years, he raised his bony hand and cuffed Gwyneth soundly. She, however, barely flinched, having received many blows in her lifetime as daughter and wife.

Scowling, Arnulf sat back and took a long gulp from his goblet, the red liquid dribbling sloppily down his chin and into his stringy beard. For an idle second, Gwyneth wondered if the red streaks in his gray whiskers were remnants of its former color, or simply accumulated wine stains.

"You dare gainsay me?" he snarled, scowling angrily. "Nearly a hundred years ago my grandsire fought beside the Conqueror, and in reward this fief, this manor house and town, was bestowed upon him. From poverty he rose to landed knight, and he held to his heart his duty to protect this place and its people."

"But as the town lies 'twixt the lands of the baron and the earl, the Lord of Sherborne has always owed dual allegiance to the two. Forty days service he gives to each, and the fruits of the fields he shares with both," Gwendolyn recited by rote.

"Damned right, girl!" Arnulf swore, slapping his palm on the table so that the child jumped. Then he turned his eyes to the woman. "So it has ever been, and so it will ever be."

"But with only a seneschal managing the earl's estate, Lord Elwood will soon take it over. It's his plan, as everyone knows," Gwyneth pointed out. "When he makes himself earl, he'll rule all the lands surrounding Sherborne. Why do you refuse to see? There is no way for it but, without an heir to Farleigh, the baron will one day be your only lord. Save for the king," she added.

"Save for the king!" Arnulf shouted. "It is he who rules England, not the land-lords who make war upon each other. You'd best remember that, woman."

"I do remember it," she admitted grudgingly. "But this new King Henry is little more than a boy. Has he any wit, or might, or vision? I think not, or the house of Farleigh would have a lord to rule and protect those beholden to it."

For a moment the old knight stuttered and stammered, and the women thought he might collapse in a fit, or worse, dead. But when he found his voice it was still a bellow: "How dare you speak with such contempt for our sovereign lord! No wonder females must be guarded, instructed and beaten into submissiveness! You haven't room for a single intelligent thought between your ears!"

Arnulf's shouting had wakened one of the servant's babes. Glad for the distraction, Gwyneth stood, picked up the child, and brought her back to the table. Concentrating on quieting the little girl, she jiggled and rocked her, cooing softly in her tiny, pink ear.

"What is fact," she pointed out as she returned the child to its makeshift crib of rushes and swaddling, "is that Lord Elwood will one day be the earl of Farleigh. If you do not give up your stubbornness, you'll see us all in graves alongside the old earl to whom you once swore fealty."

When Arnulf stood, his bench did indeed topple. Young Gwendolyn, who had been sitting on the end of it, tumbled off and was, therefore, unable to stop him as he lunged for Gwyneth. She did manage to grab the hem of his tunic, which fell to mid-calf, but that only caused her father to fall against Gwyneth. He grabbed his older daughter by her shoulder and slammed his fist into her face more than once before she managed to push him off.

"Cease! Father, please!" Gwendolyn begged, scrambling to her feet and putting herself between the two of them.

Spittle clung to Arnulf's whiskers and his eyes were narrowed to dangerous slits, but he paused long enough for the girl to help Gwyneth stand upright. "She didn't mean what she said, surely she didn't," Gwendolyn apologized. "It is only—Elwood's a cruel overlord, and should you defy him, he will see us all brought low. Besides, there has been no earl at Farleigh since the last one died nearly three winters past. Why do you think another son lives?" she asked anxiously. "Where is this man, John, whom you wait for?"

It was Gwyneth, as stubborn as Arnulf, who replied, "In heaven, with his father and brothers, no doubt."

"No!"

Gwendolyn intercepted another blow Arnulf intended for her sister. He seemed upset to have missed his mark. "Get up," he growled. "And do not interfere again."

This time it was Gwyneth who helped Gwendolyn to her feet. The two leaned against each other for support as the man deigned at last to answer his younger daughter's question. "John, Hugh's youngest son, the last alive and the present earl of Farleigh, is on his way here. He'll be returning—soon."

"How do you know?" Gwyneth demanded skeptically, despite Gwendolyn's pleading look that she remain silent.

"Because the blind old witch what lives on the edge of the forest told one of the lord's villeins. Word reached my ear just this morning: John of Farleigh is on his way home."

Gwyneth was inclined to scoff, but this time she heeded her sister's baleful look and remained silent. Let the old fool believe what he wishes, she decided, that a man who was absent all through King Stephen's reign is alive and well and on the road home.

Chapter Two

✣   ✣   ✣

Sirs Lionel and Bruno trudged at a slow pace on their palfreys as they followed the ambling dirt road. "God's teeth, but it's damnably hot in Gascony this autumn!"

Lionel was a thick man in his middle years while Bruno was youthful still, having been knighted only a few years earlier. Yet it was Bruno who was complaining as he pulled back the hood of his hauberk and wiped his sweat-stained brow.

"Homesick for the cold, damp winds of England, are you?" Lionel asked, turning to look at his companion.

"Aye, I am," the younger man admitted. "We've been on this quest for nearly three years, now. I'm tired of wandering." As they came around a bend in the road, their pack horse trailing behind them, Bruno peered up at the walled fortress that suddenly loomed ahead. "What if he's not here?"

His friend looked at the castle, too. "He's here," Lionel declared with certainty.

"*The Dane* may well be here, I'll grant you that. But there's no guarantee he's the man we seek."

"He must be," Lionel insisted. "Our lord was dubbed The Dane while he was still fostering, a mere squire. It must be he."

Bruno spat in the dirt as they continued at a walk. "All of Henry's lands are peopled with the descendants of Danes. Who's to say the one we search for is the only one called that?"

"We'll know soon enough," Lionel said reasonably, kicking his mount into a trot that Bruno's horse quickly mimicked.

"But if he isn't?"

"Then we'll keep looking."

"I think not," Bruno countered. "I think, if our information has once again led us to naught, that we should return home and declare the man dead."

"With what proof?" the older warrior demanded, his bushy brows knitting together into a frown.

"Why should we need proof? After all these years, he is certainly dead. How can we be expected to supply any proof, except for the stories we've been told and the conclusions we have reached?"

Sir Lionel did not reply. They had reached the access road that meandered like a river up the motte to the gate in the keep's outer wall. With a sudden burst of determined speed, Lionel urged his horse up the narrow road at full gallop; his companion and the pack horse were forced to keep pace. Only when the guards appeared above the parapet did Lionel slow down to a walk and then halt completely.

"Who are you? What business have you here?" a sentry shouted down to them, and Lionel explained who he and Bruno were and why they had come to Hubert de Tusaine's barony.

The gate was opened, and when they were inside the outer bailey the two knights dismounted, slapping the road dirt from their chausses and tunics. "The captain of the guard!" Bruno shouted up to the man on the wall who had allowed them admittance. "Where might we find him?"

"Right here."

Bruno and Lionel whirled around to face the captain. After introductions were completed, Lionel explained their purpose there. "Does the baron employ the services of a knight called The Dane? He would be new here; he's not been too many months in Gascony, we don't think."

"Why do you want him? He's not an outlaw, is he?"

"No." The knight shook his graying head. "If The Dane is the man we think he is, he's a landless knight no longer. He has come into an inheritance of some substance."

"I'd hate to lose him, if that be true. But I'd wish him well," the captain admitted. Standing aside, he pointed. "He's there, on the practice field, leading a training exercise."

"He answers to 'The Dane?'" Bruno inquired.

"If you need to call him out, yes. But there'll be no need, I suspect. You cannot miss him."

The English knights strode toward the practice field where the baron's men were parying and thrusting their broadswords. The dozens of men were paired in twos, pretending at mortal combat, all except for one who stood alone in the center of the melee, thwarting haphazard attacks with apparent ease as he shouted directions. He stood head and shoulders taller than the rest, but with his hooded mail hauberk and conical helmet complete with nose guard, it was impossible to discern his features.

Patiently, curiously, Lionel and Bruno waited for the exercise to end. When it did, and the baron's knights began to leave the yard, Bruno hailed The Dane, not by name but with a wave and a shout. "Yes?" the tall soldier said, pausing distractedly as his eyes followed the others making their way to the inner baily.

"You're the one called The Dane?"

"Yes, but I've no time—"

"Please, milord. We've been on the road more years than months, tracking you."

The Dane removed his helmet and pulled back his hood, revealing a wealth of unfashionably long, golden hair that glinted red in the sunlight despite the fact it was disheveled and damp with sweat. "Tracking me?" he repeated, scowling at Bruno. The expression made his bright, cerulean blue eyes darken, and the scar on his left cheek, which disappeared into the neatly trimmed beard on his chin, look deep and black. "Who sent you after me? That fool, Von Riggins? His daughter's babe wasn't mine. I never touched her though she appeared, more than once, naked on my pallet."

"Gerald sent us," Lionel explained quickly.

"Gerald?" The Dane's eyes went from Bruno to Lionel.

"You don't know him, then," Bruno surmised, giving his friend an I-told-you-so glance.

"He wouldn't know Gerald," Lionel informed his young companion. "He's been gone too many years."

"That's true enough. I know no Gerald, and I must be off. If you'll grant me leave," The Dane said, about to move away.

But Lionel stopped him by asking, "Are you John? John of Farleigh?"

The man pivoted on his heel and faced his two visitors again. His expression changed so completely even Bruno would have had to admit that the battle-scarred warrior, who had surely celebrated forty natal days if he had celebrated one, was a handsome man. The hard, impatient edge to his voice was gone, too, when he replied, "Aye. I'm John, John of Farleigh. My father, Hugh, is—was—the earl. I'm sorry," he apologized quickly. "It's been so long since anyone has called me by my birth name, it caught me unaware."

"I knew it." Lionel cast a smug smile in Bruno's direction.

"Is the Gerald of whom you speak Penworth's son?"

"He is, indeed, and he himself has been seneschal of Farleigh Castle since Penworth passed on more than fifteen summers past."

"Good God." John shook his head and stared at the dirt at his feet. After a moment his head snapped up and he asked, "Gerald sent you to look for me? When? Why?"

"We have been on our mission the best of the last three years. We began at Maygenne, where you fostered," Bruno explained, "and have since been following you throughout the kingdoms of France, Germany—the entire Holy Roman Empire, or so it seems!"

"Why?"

"You, my lord," Lionel informed John respectfully, "are now the earl of Farleigh. You have been since your brother Robert died on the fourth day of Christmas in the year 1153."

"Robert was earl? And you say he is dead?"

Though the knights on the practice field had been unable to fell him, this news seemed to knock the wind from John. Turning his back on Bruno and Lionel, he ambled to a bench and sat. The other two men followed him but remained silent until he could gather his thoughts.

At last he looked up. "My father died on crusade and my brother, Garwin, with him. I received word of that. But that would have made my elder brother, Vincent, earl. What of him? How did Robert come to be earl?"

"Lord Vincent did inherit the earldom," Lionel explained. "He ruled the estates for some four years, and during that time Robert returned. But in the year of our Lord, 1152, a sickness swept through the land in the south. Vincent of Farleigh succumbed, as did his wife, Evelyn, who was some months with child at the time of her death."

"God's tears," John mumbled, his Adam's apple bobbing visibly as he swallowed hard. "Now Robert's dead, too, I surmise."

"Aye." Bruno nodded. "The sickness of which Lionel spoke began to wane in the summer. Robert, as earl, went searching for a bride to ensure heirs. Late the following year he became betrothed to one Lady Ardyth, whom he was to wed after the new year. But suddenly he fell ill with the fever as the sickness reared its ugly head once again, and he passed on before taking his marriage vows."

For several long minutes no one spoke, the three knights ignoring the chatter and commotion going on around them in the outer bailey. "The entire house of Farleigh is gone," John whispered finally. "All my family dead."

"Nay, not all, milord," Lionel argued gently. "You're still among the living, and by God's hand destined to rule and defend Farleigh's holdings and people."

John shook his head and Lionel continued. "It's true! God's chosen you, surely He has, for 'tis a miracle we've even found you, as you've been gone so many years and hired on to serve so many masters."

"It is what the youngest, landless sons must do," John reminded him, cocking one fair, arched brow.

"Yes. But no longer. You are the earl, and Farleigh needs you more than you can know."

"How so?" John came to his feet again.

"Elwood of Eye has been busy making war upon his neighbors, all in an effort to expand his domain. But what he yearns for most is Farleigh, for yours is an earldom that has been handed down from long generations of Saxons and Danes, while his own barony is, in comparison, of little consequence."

"He was in favor with Stephen," Bruno explained, "but not so with the new king. Never has Henry called the baron of Eye to his council."

John tucked his helmet under his arm. The hard look of the warrior had returned to his face. "Come," he said simply, "I will see you fed. Then we will be off."

He strode ahead of the two English knights, and Bruno paused to smile at Lionel. "I thank the sweet, holy mother of Jesu! We're going home at last and for good."

"Aye, that we are. But I fear the last years will seem like a May Day romp compared to what we will find for ourselves serving our new lord, John."

"Why?"

"You told him yourself: Elwood of Eye wants Farleigh for his own. The new earl will fight hard and long to prevent that. And we, as his loyal defenders, will fight right alongside him, unless death takes us from his side."

The smile disappeared from Bruno's handsome, young face. Still, he was eager to return home to England.

Chapter Three

✣   ✣   ✣

The sisters were in their bedchamber, which was brightened only by the starlight shining through the small window they had not yet covered for the night, and two thick candles. There was an obvious similarity between them. Despite the considerable difference in their ages, they shared the same coppery red hair color and green eyes and their slim figures were much the same. But Gwendolyn's eyes were wide and round, her nose dusted with faint freckles, and her bosom as flat as her hips were narrow, while Gwyneth's dark-lashed eyes were slanted like a cat's, her smooth skin creamy, and her curves more voluptuous.

"You shouldn't provoke Father so," Gwendolyn advised from her perch on a three-legged stool as Gwyneth ran a comb through the length of her locks. The girl knew that in spite of the fact there were no marks yet, tomorrow Gwyneth would be swollen and bruised where Arnulf had struck her this evening. "He's old and short-tempered, and the results are always the same."

"I'm old, too," Gwyneth replied. "Too old to accept his ill-advised arguments. Look what happened today! Elwood slaughtered a dozen of our own sheep—and for what purpose? A portion of their wool would have been his. He ordered it simply to frighten the old man into obeying his command. And why shouldn't Arnulf oblige him, I ask you? There is no longer any Earl of Farleigh he must serve."

"Father believes there is."

"His brains are addled."

"Even if that's true—that there is no living heir to Farleigh, not that Father's brains are addled," Gwendolyn explained as she spun about on her stool. "Even if it is, the earldom of Farleigh still exists and Sherborne owes allegiance there just as we do to the barony of Eye."

Gwyneth looked down at her and shook her head. "A man gives his oath to another man, be he king or baron or knight. Arnulf and the people of Sherborne town do not owe their loyalty to a castle or a plot of land, no matter how many hides it is."

"You are as stubborn as Father."

"That isn't so." Gwyneth set the comb down. "I simply do not wish to see you hurt, and I fear the worst at Elwood's hand if Arnulf does not submit."

Gwyneth waited for Gwendolyn's reaction. She had no wish to frighten the girl, who was only fifteen and more innocent than most her age. But Gwendolyn's response was unexpected. Raising her chin almost haughtily, she stood and announced, "I fear neither Elwood nor his men. Thomas will protect me."

Surprised, Gwyneth recovered quickly. Stepping to the rail, she pulled back the edge of the heavy fabric hanging that served as the chamber's second wall. Peeking through the slit, she could see the floor below. As usual it was dark and smoky, and at this late hour nearly everyone who lived in the house was asleep. Sprawled on pallets among the rushes were Arnulf's men-at-arms, several servants, and the lord's young squire, Thomas of Brandywine. He had come to Sherborne to foster at the age of seven. He was now nigh on eighteen years, and a handsome lad with sandy hair and twinkling brown eyes.

Gwyneth dropped the curtain. "So that's how it is, is it?"

Immediately, Gwendolyn was defensive. "He's a good man. He attends mass every morning, he's honorable, chaste, and—and he will defend me with his own life."

"Go to bed," Gwyneth urged indulgently, pulling back the coverlet on the bed they shared.

Obediently the girl crawled in, but still she continued with her praise for Thomas of Brandywine. "He is a wonderful soldier, skilled in all the knightly arts."

"I am sure he is."

"He's brave and strong."

"I am sure that's true as well."

"He loves me."

With a sigh, Gwyneth sat down on the edge of the mattress. "How was he born?"

"Second son. So he may marry."

"His father's estate?"

"Grunwald of Brandywine's fief is not too very large," the girl admitted. "But Thomas assures me he will inherit something."

Gwyneth said nothing. Grunwald of Brandywine's holdings could be no bigger than a fly's dropping if he'd sent his son to foster with Arnulf, who was only a landed knight with no castle, no keep.

Gwendolyn seemed to read her thoughts. "When—

if—we wed, I'll have my dower lands."

The girl forgets the order of things, Gwyneth thought. There's little enough here and she must share it with me. She gets none of it 'til Arnulf dies.

But Gwyneth did not speak her thoughts. Instead she covered the window opening with the oiled skin nailed above it and blew out one candle, leaving the remaining one burning to keep the night pixies at bay. Then she snuggled in beside Gwendolyn and closed her eyes, trying for sleep.

After long minutes Gwendolyn whispered, "Gwyn, do you wish things were as they used to be? Are you never lonely for your husband, Ector? And do you not miss Matthew and Rodney and Richard?"

"Aye," she whispered back, "I miss my sons."

Not more than a few minutes later, Gwyneth recognized Gwendolyn's even breathing of sleep. Not so much as drowsy herself, she sat up, pulled felt shoes on her bare feet, and wrapped her woolen cloak over her lightly clad shoulders. Then, lighting the cold candle from the one that still burned, she slipped out of her bed chamber past a snoring, raspy Arnulf, asleep on his own fur-covered bed, and down the stairs into the main room. Picking her way through the prone, sleeping bodies, she gave a quick nod to the one alert sentry posted inside the door, and went outside.

The cold of the stone stairs penetrated the cloth soles of her shoes, but Gwyneth ignored the discomfort. Moving quickly, she crossed the yard and hurried between the outbuildings. She did not head toward the daub and wattle cottages that made up the town of Sherborne, nor did she run into the common fields. Instead she made for the river. There on its bank she sat, huddling beneath her cloak as if it were a tent, and cried.

Gwyneth was a strong woman who rarely cried, no matter how brutally she was beaten, how frustrated she became, how fearful she was, or how bitterly her heart was breaking. But now she cried, alone where no one could see her except for the sprites that lived in the wild and the stars in the uncommonly clear night sky. She cried because Arnulf was an honorable but stubborn old man who would see his family and the whole town destroyed before too many months were out. She cried, not because she feared for herself but because of sweet, young Gwendolyn's dreams, which would most certainly be crushed. She even cried for Gwendolyn's love of Thomas, because that sort of love was so precious and rare, and something she herself had never known.

But mostly Gwyneth cried, not for Ector, who was cold in his grave and good riddance, but for Matthew and Rodney and Richard. Mattie, Roddy and Richie, she had called them when they were children. Was it really only months ago, she marveled, that they'd returned from fostering in the northern shires—men, all of them, at eighteen and nineteen years—informing her they'd outgrown their childhood nicknames? She had called them by their Christian names then, to humor them, but in her heart—which was bursting with her love for them—they were children still. It was how she saw them in her mind's eye: sticky-fingered, bow-legged little boys, with bright eyes and giggles spilling from their rosy lips.

But they were babes no longer, that she knew. Each had earned his knighthood; all had faced danger and, so far, survived. She wondered, as she wiped the tears from her thick, sooty lashes, if she would see them again before they all were in heaven. That hope seemed dim.

Yet at that very moment, in the dark, lonely night, Gwyneth happened to glance skyward to glimpse a shooting star. It shot across the glossy heavens, leaving a glittering tail in its wake before disappearing as if it had never been.

She sucked in her breath. Perhaps it was an omen. Perhaps it portended good fortune. Perhaps the future was not so black, after all.

Three trail-weary knights approached the gate of Farleigh Castle as the wayward star shot across the inky sky. All the men noticed it, but only two thought it a timely and prophetic heralding—John was too world-weary and cynical to believe heavenly bodies manipulated or reflected upon the circumstances of earthly men.

The castle guard shouted out, "Who goes there? Identify yourself!"

"Odo, it's Lionel and Bruno, back from our mission at last."

"Lionel?" the guard repeated before shouting a quick order over his shoulder that resulted in the bridge being lowered over the moat and the portcullis being raised.

The knights did not dismount in the outer bailey. They left their pack horse in the care of a sleepy stable boy, but continued across the second bridge that led to the inner bailey and keep. The three of them dismounted finally in front of the keep's main entrance and trudged up the steps to the door.

Not surprisingly, the great arched and timbered hall

was littered with bodies of servants sleeping on the rush-covered floor. Torches and a low fire in the hearth glowed dimly through the gray haze as the smoke took its time seeking the outdoors through narrow windows and chinks in the thick stone walls.

Lionel and Bruno smiled at each other, delighted at having returned home. But John, as he removed his head gear, had a strange look on his face. He appeared both stunned and confused, and not a little sad. Farleigh Castle seemed the same as the day he'd left it nearly a quarter century earlier, yet he could feel the emptiness herein. They were all gone, his family, every one of them. It was not right, it should never have happened. Yet he, the youngest son, forced by tradition and law to be landless and unwed, had returned to assume the title of earl, a position he had never expected thrust upon him and, therefore, had neither coveted nor trained for.

Some of the sleeping servants stirred and peered at the intruders through slitted eyes. Bruno grabbed the shoulder of one man lying near his feet and barked in his ear. The servant's eyes suddenly bulged, staring at John as if he were seeing a ghost. Jumping to his feet, he ran off.

Minutes later, from the stairs that led to the small rooms in the gallery that ringed the great hall, a small, slim man appeared. It appeared he had been wakened from sleep and had quickly pulled on a rumpled tunic, for his feet were bare and his dark hair disheveled. "John?" he said, his voice questioning. "Sweet mother of Jesu, is it you, John?"

With a nod and a grin at last, John opened his arms and approached the seneschal, Gerald. Quickly they embraced, clapping each other on the back, and laughed happily.

When Gerald pulled back, he shook his head. "It's almost impossible for me to believe it's you. Last I saw you, you were a gangly lad of fifteen with arms and legs too long and awkward to suit you. But I see that you've gained enough height and girth to justify your ungainly limbs."

"But not you!" John countered. "What were you last I saw you—ten or twelve years? If you'd not been an only child, you'd have been the runt of the litter. Have you grown a hair's breadth or gained the weight of a flea?"

"It may surprise you, my lord, but I have." Gerald smiled. "Yet compared to your mighty stature, I'm afraid my growth has been negligible." The seneschal considered his friend and master critically, his eyes roving from the toes of the earl's muddy shoes to the top of his leonine head. "No wonder I've heard it said you were known far and wide as The Dane. Though it never showed itself in your father or brothers, you seem to have inherited every drop of Viking blood that ever flowed through your ancestors."

At the mention of his family, John's smile faded. Immediately, Gerald glanced at the two knights who had escorted the heir to Farleigh Castle home, and they departed to seek their individual comforts. Next he looked to the servant that had roused him, who stood off to one side, eagerly observing the homecoming of the new earl, and ordered him to wake the cook and see that victuals were quickly prepared and served. Lastly, he motioned for John to precede him up the stairs. Only on the gallery landing did Gerald join him at his side and lead him into a small chamber with a window overlooking the interior hall below.

"Sit," Gerald beckoned, motioning to a sturdy, carved chair beside a small table. As he poured wine into a pewter mug, which he then offered to John, he urged, "Tell me of your life since last you resided at Farleigh. I've had little news of you the past fifteen years; none the past ten."

Sipping the mulbery wine thoughtfully, John told his friend, his seneschal, of his years as a mercenary knight. It did not take long. John was not given to eloquent talk, and he detailed neither the bloody battles he had fought in, the festering wounds he had survived, the close comrades he had lost, nor the trysts with pretty village girls that had no doubt resulted in more than a few bastards growing up fatherless in the lands beyond the Channel.

"And here?" he asked when he finished his tale, already halfway through the array of foods that had been brought up for him to sup on. "Tell me all that has happened here, and why."

"Lionel and Bruno did not explain?"

"They did. But I wish to hear it from your lips."

So Gerald told John of his family's tragedies. He paused after mentioning the nearly three years' search for the last heir to Farleigh Castle, its demesne, and all its holdings.

John's meal, by that time, had been consumed, the trencher pushed aside. Now he leaned back in his chair and sipped from his full mug of wine. "Why hasn't the new English king rewarded some vassal of his with this estate?"

"Your father was loyal to Henry and then supported his daughter, Matilda. Henry II is aware of this, I know, and has been generous enough to wait a fair while until you, the rightful heir, could be found. But..."

Gerald, too, leaned back in his chair and tented his fingers together.

"Yes?" John's golden brow arched curiously.

"Your men told you about that foul cockshead, Elwood of Eye?" Gerald asked, and his lord nodded. "All his life, in as much as I've heard, he's been a lazy sluggard, willing to cheat and mistreat his villeins so that he could have the best in life while they went cold and hungry and sick to early graves. You know his keep is still a wooden one erected in King William's time? And that he's outlived three wives—killed them all, I've no doubt, by accident or design. As well his one living son, Walter, is a sorrier man than his sire, a drunk and a gambler with neither enough brains nor wit to keep his ears apart."

"Aye," John said a little impatiently. "But what's his threat to me? He wants Farleigh for his own? Little chance of that, I think, now that I'm here to defend it."

"True," the seneschal agreed, "except, since Stephen's death, Elwood seems to have gone a little mad. If not close to our late king, the baron was at least tolerated and thought to be in royal favor. But such is not the case with our young Henry, and being shunned by the present court seems to have sent Elwood into a furious rage. The last two years he's ordered his men into wild, seemingly purposeless warring, most frequently in border disputes with his neighbors."

"But he has never attacked Farleigh?"

"No. Only the town of Sherborne, which serves two masters, both Farleigh and Eye. He has been trying to coerce Sir Arnulf, Lord of Sherborne Manor, to disavow his oath of fealty to your house, and pledge his loyalty to Eye alone."

"Has he done the town much harm?"

"Elwood's men have made sporadic raids on it. Some dwellings have been fired, some women raped. I've heard, less than a fortnight ago, Elwood's knights trampled to death a small boy with their horses' hooves."

"Damn!" John swore, making his callused hand into a large, clenched fist. "I've seen much of that kind of horror in my time away. War drains men of their humanity, and the first to lose it are always the soldiers ordered to wreak destruction and death. Never before, though, has it been mine own who are victims."

"Sherborne was vassal to the baron, too. Eye's turning against the man and his people in this way is unprecedented and unforgivable."

"Arnulf would not give in?" John asked, and Gerald shook his head. "Good God, Arnulf! I would have thought he'd been dead years ago. He must be nearing a hundred."

The seneschal leaned forward across the table. "My lord," he said softly, "you must make Sherborne your own. To have a manor and town divided between two barons has never worked well. Now, for Sherborne, it has become impossible."

"You want me to emulate Elwood? You're saying two wrongs make a right?"

"No. I suggest you protect the people of Sherborne as a father does his children, by enveloping them in the folds of his cloak."

"How?"

"Marry Sir Arnulf's youngest daughter."

Chapter Four

✣   ✣   ✣

Gwyneth was supervising the monthly laundering. Though the servants and villeins washed their clothes infrequently—some, she thought, almost never—she was adamant that once a month all the manor house's linens and the family's clothes be washed.

The steaming caldrons, where the woolen garments were boiled not once, but thrice, were set outside between some outbuildings behind the manor house. There, now, Gwyneth leaned over one, stirring its contents with a wooden stick. Unfortunately she stepped on a large stone that pierced the sole of her cloth shoe and she stumbled, inadvertently grazing her hand on the edge of the scalding pot. Crying out, she backed away into her servant, Jean's, steadying arms.

"Are you all right, my lady?" Jean asked worriedly.

"'Tis nothing," Gwyneth insisted, blowing on her injured hand, which showed a red, puckered streak.

The servant shook her head, frowning at her mistress. Though the lady had not plaited her waist-length hair, allowing it to fall freely over her face with every turn of her head, and though she wore a long, flowing head covering that, despite the metal circlet keeping it in place, swooped forward to cover her features as well,

Jean could see the marks that marred Gwyneth's comely face. One eye was swollen and cut, and her cheekbone below the other was puffy and purple. Gwyneth's lower lip was disfigured, too, a cut in the center breaking open constantly to seep fresh blood.

"Why don't you go inside, my lady?" she suggested. "You should lie down. You don't... look well. Besides, I know how to do the wash, I do. 'Twas I who taught you, after all."

"I am quite all right," Gwyneth insisted. "But Gwendolyn should be helping. One day she'll be chatelaine of her husband's keep, and she—"

"Lady Gwendolyn!" Jean called out, interrupting as she caught sight of the girl in the yard. "Lady Gwyneth wants you here!"

"Gwyn!" the girl cried breathlessly, rounding the corner of the house to join the women by the wash kettles. "Someone is coming!"

"Who?"

"Knights. I know not whose. I was returning from the town, and at the top of the hill I saw—"

The girl broke off as the sound of horses cantering into the yard reached her ears. Immediately Gwyneth pulled her farther back, out of sight of the riders.

"Do you think they're Elwood's men?" she whispered to Jean.

With a shrug of her shoulders, the servant moved close to the outside wall of the house and, clinging to it, peered around the corner. When she returned she said, "I think not. They seemed peaceful enough."

"How many are there?"

"Three. Two have already gone inside the house."

"We'll take no chances," Gwyneth declared. "Gwendolyn, if I signal you, run as fast as you can into the forest and hide there. You know the place—the hollowed trunk. Do not come out 'til someone comes to fetch you."

She nodded obediently, falling in beside Gwyneth and Jean. For many long minutes they waited curiously, anxiously, until a man's voice called out, "Lady Gwendolyn! Has anyone seen lady Gwendolyn about?"

"That's Thomas," the girl whispered excitedly, and before Gwyneth could stop her she scampered off into the yard, shouting, "I'm here, Thomas! I'm coming!"

"Your father wishes to speak to you," Gwyneth heard the young man say. When she looked, she saw the handsome squire escorting Gwendolyn inside.

"I'm going in to find out what this is all about," she informed Jean. And before the servant could stop her, Gwyneth had climbed the steps and slipped inside the manor house.

Despite the uncovered windows and fire in the hearth, the dwelling's interior was dim with shadows. This suited Gwyneth, who had no desire to display her bruises to outsiders. Slipping into deeper darkness beneath the bower stairs, she was able to observe without being observed. What she saw was Arnulf, his squire, Gwendolyn, a servant, and two unknown knights. Both knights and Arnulf were seated at the trestle table near the fire. They were drinking ale from cups the servant kept refilling. Thomas of Brandywine stood behind and some distance away, while Gwendolyn, standing also, remained near him.

There was conversation, but Gwyneth could make out none of it clearly. She saw, however, that Arnulf was in unusually good spirits. His papery cheeks were flushed as he smiled, nodding his head vigorously at his guests. The guests, though, appeared formal and stern, and when the larger of the two glanced over his shoulder at Gwendolyn, she noticed the girl take an involuntary step backwards.

Gwyneth peered at the large knight again, scrutinizing him. Who is he? she wondered. Sweet mother Mary, he was huge—a veritable giant. He was so tall and so broad, he was like a stone wall. His yellow hair was ridiculously long for one who, more often than not, had his head encased in metal, and his blue eyes were hard and piercing. He was scarred like a devil, for despite the distance and the shadows, Gwyneth could see a deep, black line running beneath his left eye, down across his cheek and into his red-gold beard. God's teeth, he looks like an ancient Viking warrior, she thought, and then it came to her: The knight was the earl, John of Farleigh!

Before she could digest what she had just discerned, Gwyneth witnessed a happening that first made her heart sink and then made her blood boil. The big knight twisted a signet ring off his little finger and passed it to his man, who then passed it to Arnulf. In turn, Arnulf barked at his younger daughter and when she came forward, he passed it to her. Frail, little Gwendolyn hesitated for a second, glancing surreptitiously at Thomas. Then, with obvious reluctance, she slipped the ring onto one of her own fingers.

John of Farleigh did not speak to her. In fact, he did not even bother looking at her again. Instead he swilled down the contents of his mug before raising it to be refilled once more by Arnulf's servant, and resumed conversing with his host. Gwendolyn, painfully aware she was being excluded, gave her beloved squire another woeful glance before backing off and slipping up the bower stairs to her bedchamber.

Still standing in her shadowy hiding place, Gwyneth raged silently. Damn them all to hell! she thought. John of Farleigh has just betrothed himself to Gwendolyn! But he cannot wed her— I *will not* allow it to happen! How dare he and Arnulf even consider it? Gwendolyn of Sherborne is a lady, not a piece of property to be haggled over, bought and sold. Yet that is what they have just done, as if she were nothing more than a horse to be ridden home by her new owner.

Ridden. That word, though only a thought, made Gwyneth shudder. She could not help but think of her own wedding night and how she was ridden by her new husband, her lord, her master. So young she had been and so frightened, and not a soul in the strange household had come forward to offer a word of advice or comfort. No, she recalled, grinding her teeth. At the wedding party they had eaten like pigs, danced lewdly and laughed raucously, and drunk so much wine and beer many had vomited. Most had not reached the outdoors or the jakes before heaving up their insides, either.

Later, a few women had escorted her to the bedchamber, and there they had stripped her of her wedding costume, offering no linen shift or bed robe to replace it. Instead they had tossed Gwyneth naked into bed, refusing her a sheet to cover that nakedness. They had laughed wickedly, telling her vile stories of men coupling with women and men coupling with beasts.

Gwyneth closed her eyes now, trying to block out the memories. But instead they came to her more clearly. She could almost hear Ector's footsteps as he and his friends ascended the stairs. She could envision, precisely, the door swinging open and the lord standing there, his body still muscled, then, despite the fact he had long before reached his middle years. With a leer he'd thrown off his clothes and to her horror, Gwyneth had seen his staff standing rampant. Ector had been proud of himself, displaying his raging manhood to the men who had accompanied him upstairs and the women who waited, crowded around the marriage bed. Though Gwyneth had closed her eyes years ago even as she was doing now, she had heard the bawdy revelers complimenting the bridegroom on his prowess and making jokes about the sport to come. The echoes of all those obscene comments continued to ring in her ears, and she hugged herself to combat the sudden shaking of her limbs.

Still her memories raced along as she recalled that though the guests had left the bridal chamber after her husband had joined her in bed, the humiliations continued. Ector was neither gentle nor considerate, and had leaped upon her, straddled her, and thrust his rod between her virgin thighs. Oh, the pain, the searing, tearing pain! Gwyneth had thought he was killing her, had wished she would die. But she lived—she lived through the mortification of his shoving her out of bed as soon as he had spent himself, ripping the linen from the mattress, and racing outside to stand at the top of the stairs, displaying the bloody flag of victory to his drunken guests below.

Gwyneth's cat-like, emerald eyes now flew open. Staring at Arnulf across the hall, she hated him with a burning rage that was too hot to cool.

She would *not* allow him to force Gwendolyn to suffer what he had once forced upon her. She would not!

The men at the opposite end of the room were still drinking and talking. Stealthily, Gwyneth crept out to the foot of the stairs and made her way up to the bower. In the curtained chamber she shared with Gwendolyn, she found the girl prone on their bed, her shoulders quaking as she sobbed.

"Hush, don't let them hear you crying," she advised.

"B-b-but—"

"Not a word," she whispered, stroking Gwendolyn's forehead. "We'll speak when they've gone. And I promise you, sweetling, you won't be forced into the earl's bed anymore than you would be forced into the baron of Eye's."

They remained as they were, the girl prone, the woman sitting, while Gwyneth stroked her sister's hair and Gwendolyn did her best to control her ragged crying. In a short while it was clear from the sounds below that the visitors were leaving. Several minutes after that Arnulf shouted for Gwyneth. Obediently, she went downstairs.

"I saw you spying," he sneered, "so you know Lord John has returned as I said he would. Best of all, he's going to wed our little Gwen."

Gwyneth kept her face impassive. "When?"

"Sunday next. Ten days."

"Where?"

"The castle, of course. No reason to wed in a country manor, or the village church, when the earl of Farleigh has a castle that would be the envy of any king!" He chortled and belched, reaching for his mug again, gulping the last of the beer it contained.

Out of the corner of her eye, Gwyneth saw Thomas was still in the room. He was trying to be inconspicuous, standing in the shadows. She turned more fully and their eyes met and held for a moment; suddenly, the wild fury she had been trying to contain fused into an intense, white heat that gave her purpose.

"Is it to be a large affair?" she asked Arnulf. "If they're planning to marry so quickly, there'll hardly be enough time for the banns to be read—"

"The banns be damned!" the old knight barked, slamming his mug down onto the table. "These nuptials are not to be announced until they're completed, and I'll see you whipped if you or that one upstairs utters a word about them outside this house. There'll be few in attendance, either, I can tell you that."

"Why?"

"Because the earl has no wish for Elwood to get wind of his plans! Ach, you stupid wench, must everything be explained to you?" Arnulf sat down heavily in his chair. "Once your sister is wed to the earl, Sherborne, her dowerlands, will be fully under his protection. The baron of Eye will have no choice but to cease his attacks on my town and to give up any plans he may have had to attack Farleigh Castle."

"Why?" Gwyneth asked again.

Arnulf's head jerked as he stared up at her. "Why? What kind of a fool question is that?"

"I don't think it is a fool question," she said reasonably. "Simply because John of Farleigh has wed the lord of the manor's daughter does not mean Elwood of Eye must forego his plans. He can still sack and burn the town, murder you and me in our beds, and attack Farleigh Castle. What's to stop him? Who is to stop him?"

"John of Farleigh, that's who!"

Gwyneth did not pursue the topic further. Instead she asked, "When do you plan to knight Thomas of Brandywine?" Without looking directly at him, she saw Arnulf's squire pull himself erect and cock his head curiously.

"What? Why? I've no idea," the old knight replied,

turning to the young man with a scowl. "What difference?" he demanded, looking back at Gwyneth.

"Before the excitement of today, it occurred to me that the time for Thomas' knighthood has probably come. I expected you to announce it shortly, so that the ceremony could be performed and Thomas could return to Brandywine before Christmas."

"Aye, yes, I'd been thinking that, too," he declared with another sidelong glance at his squire. Gwyneth knew immediately no other thought had been further from his mind. "Would you like that, lad?"

"Yes, milord, I surely would," Thomas announced, stepping forward.

"You could do it this Sunday," Gwyneth suggested.

"Sunday! But that's only three days' hence!"

"If you fear you cannot arrange it…"

"I can arrange it!" Arnulf jumped up out of his chair as nimbly as an old man can jump. "No banns are required," he added sarcastically.

"As you wish," Gwyneth said evenly. "I'd best go up to Gwendolyn now. There's much we must do in preparation for her wedding."

"Such as?"

"Why, she must have a new tunic and bliaut, and all her belongings need be packed and made ready for cartage to the castle."

"Ah, oh, yes." He nodded and stroked his beard. "Get to it then, you lazy wench," he ordered, shooing her away before turning to Thomas. "Come, sit," he urged his squire. "We have our own plans to make, now, don't we?"

Chapter Five

✧   ✧   ✧

Gwyneth was plotting like one of the king's own entourage, yet she was certain Arnulf suspected nothing at all. He would never entertain the idea she might object to Gwendolyn's marrying the earl, let alone try to thwart him. Thus, he was completely unaware she was doing exactly that, and as well had made him an unwitting accomplice to her schemes.

Now, two short days before the earl of Farleigh was to join in wedlock with Gwendolyn, the lord of Sherborne's daughter, Gwyneth deemed the time right to enlist three more willing accomplices.

It was mid-afternoon; the manor house was empty save for the ladies of Sherborne and their servant, Jean. Gwendolyn was standing on a stool while her older sister marked her pale blue bliaut, trimmed with gold threaded embroidery, for hemming. She kept clenching her fists and staring up at the beamed ceiling above. Finally she looked down, and in a furtive hiss demanded of Gwyneth, "If I do not have to marry John of Farleigh, as you keep saying, Gwyn, why then are you fitting me for this wedding costume? Besides," she added petulantly, grabbing a fistful of the ample fabric that covered her chest, "there is not enough of me to fill it up. My breasts are too small, or this gown is too large—"

"Hush!" Gwyneth ordered sternly, rising from a crouch. "Get down from there, now, and I'll explain."

Scowling but curious, she stepped down and sat on the stool she had previously been standing on.

"The tunic is for me, not for you."

"What?!" Gwendolyn gasped, and even Jean's mouth dropped open, as if her jaw were poorly hinged.

"I will not allow you to marry a crude, uncouth knight who has spent his life battling and whoring from one end of the Holy Roman Empire to the other. Not a man old enough to be your father—indeed, almost old enough to be your grandfather."

The girl and the servant continued to stare at Gwyneth.

"I will marry him instead."

"But, Lady Gwyneth!" Jean exclaimed.

"That's impossible!" Gwendolyn squeaked. "How could you hope to fool everyone, from Lord John to Father to the priest? Even if you could, it would not be lawful—"

"You let me worry about what is lawful and what is not. And don't worry about me being able to fool them all. I can. Except for your bosoms," Gwyneth teased, allowing herself a small smile, "we're near enough in figure, height and coloring. Garbed in the gown Arnulf expects you to wed in, my face covered with a veil, I doubt any shall notice the discrepancy until it is too late."

"But won't the union be invalid? How—"

"Keep still," Gwyneth warned, glancing toward the door. To Jean she ordered, "Find Sir Thomas. Bring him here. Now." When the servant was gone she continued, "The marriage shan't be invalid. I'm a widow, after all. Thus, it will take a little while for the earl to undo it. By then you'll be gone, you'll be safe."

Before Gwendolyn could comment, the door opened and Thomas strode in, swaggering a bit with his new status as knight. But he faltered a little when he spied his young love in her wedding gown, and Jean, behind him, had to prod him forward by pushing against his back.

"My ladies," he said with a quick, knee-jerk bow.

"Sir Thomas," Gwyneth greeted him in turn, nodding. Gwendolyn remained silent, staring up at her handsome, youthful swain.

"Sir Thomas, do you love Lady Gwendolyn of Sherborne?" Gwyneth asked him abruptly.

Startled, the young man's eyes widened as he tore his glance from the girl and settled it on the woman. "Yes. Of course. With all my heart."

"Gwendolyn? Do you love Sir Thomas?"

"You—you know I do," she whispered, her voice a creak.

"Sir Thomas, are you wed or even betrothed to another?"

"No."

"Would you like to take Lady Gwendolyn to wife?"

"Aye!"

Gwyneth could swear she saw the young knight's heart pounding beneath the fabric of his tunic. She decided not to keep him or Gwendolyn in suspense any longer.

"Then you may wed her, if you heed what I say."

Without asking leave, Thomas sank down onto a stool beside Gwendolyn's and took one of the girl's hands in both his own.

"Tomorrow evening," Gwyneth explained, "we plan a special supper to celebrate your recent knighting ceremony and Gwendolyn's pending marriage to the earl. Following, you will take your leave of Sherborne to ride home to Brandywine. But, Thomas, you shall not ride off alone; rather, you shall take Gwendolyn with you."

"How?"

"When you leave the manor, make for the hollow tree in the forest, the one where I and Gwendolyn have been instructed to hide if there is ever an attack on Sherborne. My own palfrey and a pack mule carrying Gwendolyn's belongings will be there already. She will come to you on foot."

"And?" Thomas' dark eyes locked on Gwyneth's.

"And you will ride off together!" she exclaimed impatiently before adding, "I know my sister will be your true and wedded wife before you arrive at your father's house."

"Without question!" the young man agreed quickly.

But Gwendolyn looked doubtful as she asked, "How can we manage that? Marriages are arranged, ceremonies planned."

"Not always," Gwyneth assured her. "Many's the priest who will overlook the necessity of banns if you fill his pockets with silver. There are no impediments; neither of you have spouses, alive or dead, nor are you related in any way, let alone to the fourth degree."

"But—but the earl of Farleigh!" Thomas sputtered, abruptly realizing the part that formidable lord played in all of this. "He shan't be well-pleased to find himself alone at the altar on his wedding day."

"He shan't be alone," Gwendolyn told him. "Gwyneth intends to marry him in my stead."

"What!" Thomas stared first at her, then at Gwyneth. "You, milady? But you cannot. 'Tis impossible!"

"'Tis very possible," Gwyneth countered. Folding her arms over her chest she explained patiently, "The methagline Arnulf drinks during tomorrow eve's supper will be heavily drugged. He should be unconscious before the feast is done, Thomas, and I do not expect him to rise in time for the wedding ceremony. I will also plead illness upon the morn but, when the time comes for the bride to be escorted to the castle for the ceremony, it shall be I riding there, posing as Gwendolyn."

"The ruse will not work," the young knight insisted sadly, shaking his head. "The earl has already seen Lady Gwendolyn. And you, Lady Gwyneth, are not she. You are too—" Thomas fell silent, unwilling to insult her by mentioning her age.

Gwyneth understood, and made it easy for him. "True, I've more than twice Gwendolyn's years. But garbed in her wedding finery and shrouded in a veil, I doubt that oaf of an earl—who hardly glanced at the damsel he deems to take to wife—will notice I am not she until after the vows are said. And as I am a widow, the marriage will take time to undo even after he realizes he's been played the fool."

The young man seemed torn between hope and doubt. "But Lord John will demand the wrong be righted once he knows," he pointed out. "Then he will insist again Lord Arnulf give him Gwendolyn to wed."

"He can insist all he wants." Gwyneth shrugged, unconcerned. "But he will be unable to wed Gwendolyn if she is already wed to you." Arching a fine, dark brow she eyed Thomas sternly. "You understand your marriage must be consummated immediately."

The youth and the girl faced each other, sharing a

look that brought color to their cheeks. When Thomas turned back to Gwyneth, it was apparent he had accepted her scheme. "Aye, I understand," he promised soberly, as if pledging to slay dragons.

"Might your father object to our marriage?" Gwendolyn asked hesitantly.

And Thomas responded, "Nay. He and your sire are old friends. 'Tis why he sent me to foster here. Grunwald would never reject Arnulf's daughter."

"Good." Gwyneth considered the two before her seriously. "Mind you both hold your tongues and keep our plan to yourselves. Thomas, pay no undue attention to Gwendolyn, and be sure to keep your wits about you tomorrow night. Spill your mead and your beer more often than you drink it. When she makes good her escape, Gwendolyn will need a clever husband to escort and defend her, not a dizzy lad in his cups."

The sound of a horse riding into the yard intruded. A moment later, Arnulf's crackly voice was heard giving orders to the stable lad. Instantly, Thomas was up and out the door while Gwendolyn leaped back up onto the stool so that Jean could resume the fitting of her gown.

And Gwyneth could resume her desperate plotting.

"Lord John?"

"Gerald, is that you? Come in."

The seneschal entered the earl's room at his master's brusque beckoning. The chamber was high up in the keep and its window tall and wide. Uncovered this morning, a wash of yellow sunshine splashed inside, lighting John and making him appear golden as he stood in the center of the chamber in his wedding finery: a white tunic of the softest wool, an over tunic of a shade that matched the day's cloudless sky, both edged with a wide trim of gold as glittering as the heavy, round medallion hanging on a thick chain around the earl's neck.

"I see you are ready for the ceremony, milord," Gerald observed conversationally, trying to ignore the ominous scowl on his master's face.

"There will be no ceremony today."

"What?"

"She's not arrived yet, has she?"

"No, milord," the seneschal reluctantly admitted. "But she'll be arriving shortly, I'm sure of it. Bruno and Lionel are part of the guard sent to escort her here. Nothing untoward has happened. They'll see her safely here—"

"She's not coming," John announced with such certainty Gerald began to wonder if he'd received a message. "It is nearing Terce. The ceremony's set to begin shortly after. If she were coming, she would have been here long ago."

Impatiently, the earl strode to the window and paused before it, looking out. Gerald stepped up behind him. "She's a female," he said, excusing the bride's tardiness with her sex, "and frivolous, no doubt. Surely she has been fussing and primping, and that is why she is later that we'd expected."

"We've had no word that Elwood's men attacked Sherborne, have we?" John inquired, his back still to his seneschal. When Gerald replied in the negative John continued, "Then certainly Lady... Gwen, is it? Then certainly Lady Gwen has come to her senses and, being more determined than I to avoid this ridiculous alliance, is refusing to appear for the ceremony."

"Lord John!" The seneschal was aghast. "This is a most crucial alliance."

"But she appeared to me as little more than a child!" the earl complained, rounding on his man, towering over him. "Why I let you persuade me in this matter, Gerald, I do not know. Yet I do know I can deal with that cockshead, Elwood, on my own terms. I've no need to hide behind a girl's skirts to do it. Why, he's not even dared send his men into Sherborne since I've returned home, let alone made a move toward Farleigh Castle. Mayhap my troubles with the baron have ended before they've begun. So I do not need marriage, most especially not to a terrified, timorous girl only a few years out of the nursery!"

"My lord, your betrothed is not that young, nor do I believe she is timid. Having had contact in years past with a lady of that house, I deem it impossible," Gerald admitted. "I am sure, too, she understands the importance of this marriage and is on her way here— yet not for you to hide behind her skirts, as you put it. The baron of Eye has turned on his own. Now Sherborne and its people have turned to you. The lady realizes you must annex the town and its fields to Farleigh through this marriage in order to protect them. And when Eye attacks your demesne—which he will," Gerald promised soberly, "you will need Sherborne's men-at-arms at your disposal."

John exhaled a loud sigh and crossed the room again. This time he sank down into one of two ornately carved chairs. "Just the same," he insisted stubbornly, "if Arnulf's daughter—Guinevere? Gilda? If she is reluctant in this marriage, I'll not force her."

"You also need heirs, milord," Gerald reminded him.

"Aye. But I'd prefer to get them on a wife who looked on me kindly."

"The lady does not look on you unkindly," the seneschal insisted, though his scowl matched his master's as he turned to gaze out the window at the bailey below. It was devoid of commotion, of arriving guests. His smile was forced when he turned back and suggested, "What say you we have a game or two of draughts to pass the time until your bride arrives?" At John's non-committal shrug, he opened the heavy-timbered door. "I'll bring up the board and pieces myself. And I'll have Cook send up another plate of victuals, since it's been hours since you first broke your fast."

Gwyneth had not been to Farleigh Castle since the summer before she had wed. In her mind, through the years, it had grown smaller and softer around the edges. Now it jutted up from the countryside, immense and hard and formidable, like a great a mountain. Her heart beat furiously.

Everything had gone as she had planned it. Gwendolyn and Thomas were safely away, and old Arnulf was so deeply unconscious that this morning the servants had feared him dead. Jean had been forced to pinch his nose until he started snoring to convince the others he was alive.

Jean had also announced that she, Gwyneth, was ill. Upstairs in her bedchamber, the faithful servant had dressed her in the gown so many had seen being fashioned for Gwendolyn: a deep blue under tunic and a pale blue bliaut, both trimmed with gold embroidery. About her waist was a jewel-studded girdle and on her head was a gauze veil also edged in gold and held in place by a thin gold circlet, a gift to her from her first bridegroom on that long ago—and ill-remembered—wedding day. On her finger was the lord of Farleigh's signet ring.

As Lord John's men escorted her to the castle, Gwyneth dared to raise the flowing veil from her face. But when they neared the gate in the curtain walls she let it fall again so that it covered her eyes and the bridge of her nose. She could not fool anyone into thinking she was a girl of fifteen, so Gwyneth hid her features to disguise her identity, her years.

None of the six knights surrounding her dappled palfrey announced themselves as they approached the castle guard, yet the bridge was dropped immediately upon their arrival and all seven walked their mounts purposefully into the inner bailey.

There were servants and serfs everywhere. Gwyneth had forgotten how many people lived within a large barony's castle walls. Her heartbeat did not slow as a new thought occurred to her. Perhaps she knew some of the people here. Perhaps she had encountered them in Sherborne town, or perhaps they had been sent on errands to Arnulf's manor. If someone knew her for her true self—

No, she told herself sternly as she was led across the second bridge and into the inner bailey. No one would recognize her so quickly. Besides, only a chosen few would have been advised of today's nuptials. Certainly none of these people would suspect she was a bride at all.

Determinedly Gwyneth calmed herself so that, by the time she entered the great hall of the keep, the shaking of her hands was nearly unnoticeable.

"My lady."

The seneschal strode across the room and before her, fell onto bended knee. Gwyneth almost smiled. Never before had she been the recipient of so courtly a gesture.

When he rose he snapped his finger at a servant and said, "Your cloak."

More nimbly than she would have thought herself able, Gwyneth unfastened her long, white wrap and handed it off to the servant. Through the dim distortion of her veil, she studied the seneschal. When recognition dawned she gasped, though she swallowed the sound in her throat and prayed the man had not heard it. He was Gerald, son of Penworth, and a lifetime ago, during her childhood, he had been her friend. Gerald!

"My lady Gwendolyn, we were concerned for you. Where...?" He looked beyond her shoulder. "Where is your family? Your father?"

"My... My..." Her thoughts were a jumble of confusion. She had to close her eyes for a moment in order to focus. "My father was ill this morning and—and he bade me go on without him."

"'Tis nothing serious, I hope?"

"I don't think so. Arnulf of Sherborne will probably outlive us all."

"No doubt." The seneschal smiled and turned, looking over his own shoulder.

"Lord John?" Gwyneth asked. "Is he also tardy?"

"No!" Gerald spun back to face her, his color heightening as if she had caught him in some mischief. "He has been waiting for you since dawn."

"I apologize for my lateness. My father's illness, you understand..." With a sharp sigh she announced, "Terce is past. Perhaps we should proceed to the chapel in order that the ceremony may be said before Sext?"

"Not if you do not wish it."

Gwyneth jumped at the sound of the unfamiliar voice and her eyes flew to the stairs where the earl had suddenly appeared. Though her heart was hammering in her chest, she was a little awed by his presence. He was such a giant of a man and still scarred like the devil, but today he looked splendid. With a royal blue cape edged in miniver tossed casually over one broad shoulder, John of Farleigh looked rather princely as he approached her.

Only his expression looked ominous as he reached Gwyneth and frowned down at her. "Do you?" he demanded sternly.

"Do I—what, milord?"

"Do you wish to marry me?"

"Lord John," Gerald tried interrupting, but he was ignored.

Gwyneth glanced at the seneschal and then at her—at Gwendolyn's—intended. "Why do you ask?" she inquired in a voice so small, she hardly recognized it as her own.

"Why?" John's scowl deepened, making his scar seem to recede even more darkly into the flesh of his face. "Because this marriage would have a small something to do with you, I assume. Does it not?"

"Yes, but…"

"Do you wish to marry me or not?" the earl asked impatiently.

"My wishes do not matter." Purposely, Gwyneth bowed her head so that, in spite of the veil, the earl of Farleigh would know her to be demure, docile and obedient. "As a maid in my father's care, it is his decision whom I'm to wed."

"I am not interested in custom, mistress. Tell me now

you wish to marry me, or this wedding shall never take place. I'll not wed a woman who despises or fears me."

John's voice was low but keen as a knife blade, and suddenly Gwyneth was more frightened than she had been since conceiving of the ruse she was now playing out. She did not fear the earl of Farleigh, no. She had no great like of him; she suspected him of being, as most men were, hard, cruel, uncaring and selfish. But she was terrified that he would not take her to wife and that, before Gwendolyn and Thomas could escape through wedlock and miles traversed, her sister would be caught and returned.

Clearing her throat, Gwyneth raised her head and looked squarely at John, though he could not see the hard spark of determination in the green eyes that locked on him. "Aye, I wish to marry you, Lord John of Farleigh," she announced. "If I wished otherwise, I'd not be here."

"Her father is ill," Gerald hastened to inform his lord. "The lady Gwen came despite the fact Arnulf remains bedridden at home."

"Did you?" John asked softly, more a spoken thought to himself than a question posed to the damsel. "Then come."

He offered his arm to Gwyneth and led her back outside to the stone chapel near the keep. Before the ceremony began two knights entered, two of the same who'd escorted her to the castle. They remained by the door, as if their main purpose was protecting rather than witnessing. The seneschal also joined them, and though he stood not far behind the bride and groom kneeling on tapestry cushions before the priest, his presence did not much bother Gwyneth. He—as childhood friend or keeper of the earl's castle—could do nothing to thwart the nuptials once they were said. Quickly, the priest began the sacrament.

In truth, Gwyneth of Sherborne began to relax as the litany of Latin flowed over her. Besides the Father's words, the chapel itself was comforting. The virgin Mary's countenance and Jesus' own dear face seemed to smile down on her from their honored positions above the altar, sweet incense filled her nostrils with a familiar scent. Even the flickering candles brightened the otherwise gloomy structure with a pleasant and soothing light. Most importantly to her, though, with every passing minute Gwyneth came closer to her goal of becoming the earl's wife in Gwendolyn's stead.

Until he said her name. When the priest intoned, "Gwendolyn of Sherborne," her heart leapt into her throat. It was all she could do to correct him, and when she muttered, "Gwyneth," her voice was little more than a croak. It took a second for the cleric to understand her meaning, but he did repeat her true name and as he did so, she turned warily to the bridegroom beside her, prepared to see John come to his feet and demand an end to the ceremony.

To her surprise the earl seemed undisturbed, if not oblivious to, what had just occurred. So the ceremony continued as she returned the earl's signet ring to his finger and he replaced it on her hand with a delicate wedding band of wide, filigreed gold. It ended as the priest declared them man and wife.

It was done, yet Gwyneth dreaded the earl's response when he raised her veil and discovered her to be someone other than the young girl he was to have wed. Her hand shook when he took it to help her to her feet, yet the expected unveiling and kiss did not take place. At that moment the chapel door banged open as another of the castle knights entered hurriedly.

For a brief second the intruder took stock of the situation. If he was privy to what had just taken place at the altar, he made no comment on it. When his lord asked, "Odo, what is it?" the man strode forward to explain:

"A score of Elwood's men have been spied on the road leading to Farleigh."

"Are they armed for battle?"

"Reports vary," the knight admitted.

"Lionel, Bruno," John commanded the other two, "mount up a force large enough to deal with the baron's men, should it come to that. I'll join you shortly."

"Wait!" Gerald held up his hand and the knights hesitated. "Milord, you, your lady, and your men must sign certain documents immediately."

"Oh, aye." John looked back at Gwyneth distractedly, as if his seneschal's words had only just made him aware that he'd taken a wife. "Odo, you organize the men that will be needed. We three will join you shortly."

The messenger left and those remaining put their names or marks to the Bible and the register. Gwyneth, a little surprised by the earl's abrupt and pending departure, remained silent when she was finally escorted outside. It was Gerald who spoke up.

"Your men cannot see to this matter without you to lead them?" he asked his lord.

"They could," John replied gruffly, already unpinning his cape as the three of them strode toward the keep. "But I've no intention of letting anything to do with the baron escape my own eye."

"But your guests! They'll be arriving soon."

John stopped, forcing the others to stop as well. "If

there's less than a dozen men on the road, I hardly think Elwood plans to attack me. I simply wish to make sure my guests' journey here is safe. I will be back in plenty of time for the festivities." He paused and his glance fell on his bride. "Though they think they come only to welcome me home to Farleigh, I've invited some of my neighbors here this night. At supper we'll announce our wedding, my lady wife. In short order then, Elwood of Eye will know to keep the peace in Sherborne." Brusquely, he took Gwyneth's hand again and brushed his lips across her knuckles. "'Til later," he said before striding away, leaving his seneschal and bride alone together in the yard.

Chapter Six

✥ ✥ ✥

They lingered until the lord of Farleigh and his knights rode off. Then Gerald growled, "We must talk, Lady *Gwyneth!*" as he grabbed her elbow and propelled her toward the keep. Once inside, he fairly carried her up the stairs to one of the little rooms in the gallery. Though the servants in the hall stared, disconcerted by the seneschal's rough handling of this unknown but certainly noble lady, Gerald was oblivious to their gaping. He was too furious to notice.

As soon as they were alone, he closed the door to the room and drew closed the tapestry curtain that covered the inside window. Whirling around, he did what John should have done. He drew back Gwyneth's gauze veil.

"I cannot believe it!" he hissed. "I'd no idea you had returned to Sherborne with Gwendolyn, and when I heard you correct Father Peter, giving your name as Gwyneth…!" Exhaling loudly, he shook his head. "I nearly stopped the ceremony then and there, 'til I decided you must have just cause to do what you did." Sternly, he pointed to a stool and bade Gwyneth sit. When she dutifully lowered herself, he pulled up another and sat facing her. "Explain your reasons to me now, my lady," he demanded.

Defiantly, she raised her chin and locked on her old friend's dark eyes with her slanted green ones.

"I think none of this concerns you, Gerald. We're no longer children playing in the king's forest or the earl's fields. You cannot bully me—"

"Bully you! God's teeth, Gwynnie—*Lady* Gwyneth—when did I ever bully you? 'Twas you who put a burr beneath my pony's saddle so that he threw me and I cracked my skull on a rock! 'Twas you also who put rabbit turds in the raisin tarts I'd planned to eat on a summer's outing. Bully you? I doubt any man's ever forced his will on you. Certainly, I never did."

Gwyneth's face lost its hardness and her eyes their spark; as Gerald watched, she seemed to fold in on herself. Turning away from him she muttered, "Little girls can be as stubborn and devilish as little boys. But only men can be masters, and women must be subservient." She turned her head slowly to look at Gerald again. "It's been a long while since I was a little girl. Don't doubt in the time since I've not swallowed bitter gall to force myself into doing some man's bidding."

"Why?" he asked, his voice softer now. "Why did you marry Lord John in Gwendolyn's stead? Surely your father did not demand you do it."

"Surely not! If Arnulf knew..." Gwyneth glanced about distractedly before explaining, "I had to protect my sister, Gerald. I raised her from infancy and love her like a daughter. In truth, I'm the only mother Gwendolyn's ever known. How, then, could I be a party to her marrying an aging lord who wants her only for her dower lands and as a brood mare to birth his babies? Please, understand. She loves a young knight who fostered with Arnulf. I married the earl to allow them a chance to wed and find happiness together. Besides," she added thoughtfully, "Gwendolyn could never have endured a union tied to John of Farleigh. She is too young and has lived too sheltered a life. But I..." Her eyes locked on Gerald's, "... I know only too well how to endure."

Gerald covered his face with his hand and shook his dark head. Abruptly he stood, drew back the curtain and called to a servant in the hall below. He returned to his stool, and both waited silently until the servant arrived bearing the wine and cups he had ordered. Only when the servant was gone did Gerald ask, "Why do you think marriage to the earl of Farleigh will be such hell, Lady Gwyneth? My lord is a good man."

"Ach!" She slapped at the air. "A good man from another man's point of view, aye, I don't doubt that. But from a woman's? No. There are few enough such men about. Hopefully, my young Gwendolyn has found one and they are wed by now. And I—I can deal with a brute like John of Farleigh."

"A brute!" Gerald exclaimed. "Lord John's no brute. He's as big as an ox and he's lived a hard, lonely life, it's true. But he's strong and brave, fair-minded and loyal. He's no brute." With a flourish, the seneschal filled the two cups with mulled wine, raised one to his lips, and drank it down in a single gulp.

"There's no need for you to defend him to me," Gwyneth said, sipping from her own cup. "I've already wed him. He's my husband."

"Is he?" Gerald questioned, one dark brow arched questioningly as he refilled his cup. "How valid is this marriage in the eyes of the Church?"

"As Ector of Durningham died, making me a widow, it's valid enough, I suppose."

Cocking one dark brow the man observed, "Except for the impediment of your deceit?"

"Aye, except for that," she agreed, her mouth a grim line. "Yet, if the earl chooses to undo our wedlock, it will take him some time to do so. Long enough, in any case, for Gwendolyn to be safe from ever having to wed him herself."

Gerald drank more wine and set the empty cup aside. "I cannot believe you've done this, milady. First, that you believed your sister's life would be a misery if she were wed to the earl. Second, that you would sacrifice yourself for her, believing what you do. Third, that you expect Arnulf, your father, to accept what you've done. And fourth, that you can think to deceive Lord John for any time!" He stood and frowned at her. "Lady Gwyneth, you're a beautiful woman still, but you're no child. The earl will return before nightfall, and at this evening's festivities your veil can no longer cover your face. You think he will not see you for what you are?"

"Will he, this very night?" Gwyneth asked in turn, rising also to face her old friend squarely. "I noted that his bride's sudden change in name caused him not even to blink. I suspect he is as familiar with his wife's face as he is with what she is called." Reaching out, she touched her fingers to Gerald's bearded jaw. "I do not need much time, only a little. Enough to spare my sister's life and ensure her a future with the man she loves."

The man exhaled loudly and placed his hand over Gwyneth's. "You think Lord John a churl, but you cannot think him witless, too."

"I don't think him witless. Only a man." Her look was grim, and Gerald moaned, removing her hand from his face but keeping it clenched in his fingers.

"You insult me, too, milady, for am I not a man? God's wounds, you've not changed! I cannot believe any man has ever tamed you."

"You're right. No man's tamed me. Only sent me into hiding and forced me into secrets and deceits."

"Lord John doesn't deserve that. He deserves a wife who cares for him."

"I don't want to hear that!" she shouted suddenly, pulling away from Gerald. "How many husbands truly care for their wives? Yet all wives are expected to dutifully care for their husbands? Why is it so, when it is at their husbands' hands most women are beaten?"

She had turned away from Gerald, but now she turned back to him. "Gwendolyn would not have cared for your lord. Nor could she have run his household as his chatelaine." She took a step toward him. "But I can. And I will endure both his beatings and his mountings as long as he has enough interest in me to do either.

"Keep my secret for me, will you, Gerald? Please. In memory of the happy times we shared in childhood."

"Sweet Jesu," he whispered softly, crooking a finger beneath Gwyneth's chin to raise her delicate, heart-shaped face to his. "What was done to you all those years you were away?" When she did not reply he asked, "And what will Arnulf do when he learns of the trickery you've hatched on his liege lord?"

Gwyneth shrugged. "I'm no longer my father's to do with as he pleases—I am the earl's. Whatever Lord John decides to do about me—*when* he learns the truth—I care not. He can kill me, even, and I'll be victorious as long as Gwendolyn is spared."

Again Gerald sighed as he dropped his hand to his side. "I'll keep your secret, milady, though I doubt I'll have to keep it long. Just promise me one thing."

"Anything."

"Do not think of your husband as your enemy. He is not."

"As you say," she agreed, following him to the door.

"Now I will show you to a room where you can rest," he informed her, opening the door. "I'll have a meal brought up to you."

"You're very kind."

"I only hope I'm not a fool."

Gerald kept his own council for the next several hours. He greeted the arriving guests, made them comfortable, and gave excuses for the earl's absence. None knew of the recent nuptials; therefore, he had to make no excuses for the earl's absent lady wife.

The sun was well into its descent when John returned with his men. Gerald went out into the yard to greet him. "Did you find the baron's men?" he asked as the earl swung himself down off his destrier.

"No. Methinks it was Lord Neville's party headed here." John gestured to the additional knights dismounting with his own. "The baron of Kurth brought a large escort and no ladies. Perhaps they were spied and mistaken for Elwood of Eye's men."

John removed his gauntlets and strode toward the keep. Neville of Kurth, the baron under discussion, joined him and Gerald as they stepped inside the hall. As soon as a servant was beckoned to show the earl's guest to a room upstairs, John turned to his seneschal. "Is my lady wife..."

"The lady Gwyneth."

"Ah, yes, Lady Gwyneth. Is she here, Gerald?"

"Where else?" the seneschal frowned as they, too,

headed upstairs.

"You're right, of course. A foolish question. Yet if you'd told me she'd run off during my absence today, I can't say I'd have blamed her."

The two men reached John's door, and from nowhere, it seemed, John's squire, Miles, appeared to open it. As soon as they all had entered the room the boy set about removing his lord's armor. Gerald and the earl continued their conversation as if he were not there.

"I cannot understand why you feel Arnulf's daughter did not wish to wed you. Until this morning," Gerald said, leaning against a wall as John raised his arms overhead in order that his mail could be removed, "you were a very eligible man. Any one of scores of women would have been delighted, had you asked for her hand in holy wedlock."

"Harumph!" John snorted as he sat on his bed so that Miles could pull off his shoes and his chausses. "Scores of women, you say? I doubt that. But were it true, why did I not wed one of them instead of a child who had no say in the matter?"

Gerald looked at the floor. "Perhaps she's not so young as we assumed, milord," he suggested. "Just the same, it's apparent she's a woman who knows her own mind. She did come here this morn of her own volition, her father too ill, it appears, to even accompany her."

"Perhaps she was cowed into doing what she was told is her duty," John argued. He was naked now. Turning to his squire he said, "Fetch me water to bathe—I'm covered with road dust. And green hazel and a cloth so I might clean my teeth."

When the aspiring knight left the room to do his lord's bidding, John sat naked in his chair and poured himself a goblet of wine. He gargled and swallowed and looked up at his seneschal. "I am not going through the wedding night ritual, Gerald."

"What? You don't mean to bed her?"

The earl's bright blue eyes squinted with thought. "My intent, Gerald, was not to allow my bride to be readied for bed by my lady guests, nor I to be brought to her, naked, by my comrades. Neither did I plan to prove my wife's virginity with the flaunting of our bloodied bedsheet. I'm too old for such nonsense," he explained, "and she's too young.

"But now that you've spoken of it," he continued as the door opened and two servants dragged a tub over the threshold, "I think delaying the breaching of her maidenhead may well be for the best."

"But, milord!" Gerald protested. "The marriage won't be binding if you do not consummate it. Besides, the purpose of your marrying Gwyneth of Sherborne was not only to protect her father's holdings from Elwood, but to get yourself heirs for Farleigh."

The earl's face broke into a lopsided grin. "Good God, Gerald! I didn't say I would *never* bed her, only that I would not do it tonight. I've seen too many women, peasants and high-born alike, used ill. But no one can say that The Dane ever took an unwilling woman." He rose as the servants began spilling buckets of hot water into his tub. "Despite what you think, I sense my new wife somewhat dislikes me. When I take her, I wish her to be a willing participant in my bed even though she is my lawful spouse."

"Aye, milord," Gerald nodded, "I understand, now. But still, your new lady wife may feel slighted if you shun her bed on your wedding night."

"I doubt that," the earl disagreed. "I think she'll be relieved."

"I suspect," the seneschal ventured thoughtfully, "you understand the lady you wed this morning even less than you think you do."

Chapter Seven

✧　✧　✧

Gwyneth sat in one of two tall, ornately carved chairs at the center of the long dais table. The chair beside hers was empty, but she was flanked on each side by several noblemen and women. Since Gerald had escorted her there and promptly deserted her, Gwyneth had not dared look at the others. She kept her gaze lowered, intently studying her empty trencher, yet she could feel the earl's guests looking at her curiously and could hear their discreet whispers.

While the other trestle tables in the great hall filled with the barony's many knights and men-at-arms, Gwyneth grew anxious. He—John of Farleigh, her husband—would join her soon. And Gerald was probably right. The man was no fool. He had no need to be familiar with Gwendolyn's features to see she was not the young girl he knew Arnulf's daughter to be. He might well cry foul and denounce her. Gwyneth knew she could bear that humiliation, but she would be devastated if Gwendolyn and Thomas were caught and separated before a wedding of their own provided her sister with the protection she required.

There was a little stir—Gwyneth felt it more than heard it—and she looked up to see Lord John nearing the foot of the staircase that curled its way from the hall to the very top chamber of the keep. As he had been that morning, he was again dressed in the fine clothes he'd worn for the wedding, and despite a hard day's riding he looked fit and not at all tired. Gwyneth watched him nervously as he strode between the tables, approaching his guests with smiles and courteous nods, when suddenly his gaze settled on her own person. She stopped breathing for that moment, waiting for his amiable expression to cloud over. But instead, to her surprise, he smiled broadly at her and gave her a quick, conspiratorial wink. Her breath escaped in a rush as he resumed walking toward the dais.

When he mounted it at one end, he began greeting his guests personally, kissing the ladies' hands, clapping the lords on their backs. He passed by Gwyneth's chair once, making his way to the opposite end of the long table, but when he returned to the empty chair beside hers, he did not sit. Instead he bade her rise and as she did so, with his assistance, he whispered, "Don't be nervous, milady. I realize they are all strangers to you, but they're strangers to me also." He looked at her—her exposed face—not with consternation but with kindness. Gwyneth could not have replied if she'd wished to—words failed her.

Fortunately, John continued on. "Lords and ladies," he began softly. Repeating himself more loudly, he added, "And all my castle guard and loyal staff…" He squeezed Gwyneth's hand and took a deep breath. "I should like to present my bride." There seemed to be a collective gasp, but John continued quickly, "Lady Gwyneth of Farleigh."

She had been certain he would call her Gwendolyn, if a name came to his mind at all. That John knew and spoke her true name nearly bowled her over, her knees giving way just a little. Seeing her sway, John grasped her fingers hard and put his free hand beneath one of her elbows to support her. Suddenly, and surprisingly to her, Gwyneth felt most grateful to her husband.

"A toast to my lord and his new lady wife," Gerald proposed, rising from a bench where he had been sitting, unobserved by Gwyneth. The entire hall's occupants, save for the servants, raised their mugs and goblets in salute. Politely, John handed Gwyneth hers. She glanced away at Gerald, but she could feel her husband staring at her as she took a small sip. She feared that now the delayed dawn of recognition, the obviousness of her deceit, was registering in the earl's mind. She dared not face him, but she saw his goblet had been emptied when he set it down on the table.

No storm broke over her head. John helped his bride to sit again and took his own place beside her. Gwyneth's wary relief was, however, tempered by her dismay at her new husband's over-indulging. For, after that initial toast, he raised his empty goblet for his steward to refill. When it was refilled he drained it, and this ritual repeated itself dozens of times during the course of the evening. Gwyneth could not believe that even a man as large as John of Farleigh could hold so much grape without collapsing in a stupor.

They did not speak to each other during their wedding feast. That the earl had not recognized her as an impostor seemed not so important to Gwyneth any longer. His heavy drinking explained much. He had probably been drunk the day he'd come to Sherborne to ask for Gwendolyn's hand. Surely he'd no more recall of her age than he did her looks or name.

Gwyneth's thoughts instead wandered uneasily,

exploring the hours that still lay ahead of her. She was resigned to bedding the knight; it was a final and a most necessary element to her plan. What she dreaded was the crude and public ritual that would precede the mating act itself.

As the after supper entertainment of minstrels and jugglers came to a close, Gwyneth risked a sidelong glance at John. She worried he might be too inebriated to attempt his husbandly duties that night. To her surprise, though, he had not yet slid off his chair. In fact, he was engaged in earnest conversation with the man seated at his other side.

Shortly after the troupe of entertainers was led from the hall, John stood and announced that he and the new lady of Farleigh would be retiring. Gwyneth braced herself for the onslaught of females who would drag her upstairs, strip her, and hold her down, if need be, until her husband was brought to her. But again the earl surprised her. Standing, he took her hand and led her from the dais and through the hall. Together—alone—he escorted her up the stairs.

At first she did not know which surprised her more—that he was foregoing the crude wedding night rituals or that he could walk. Before she could sort that out, though, he did something that shocked her. He deposited her at the door to the room where she'd rested that afternoon.

"Sleep well, my lady wife," he whispered thickly, raising her hand to his lips. "God be with you 'til the morn," he added, turning away before he could see her numbed expression.

Gwyneth remained rooted to the landing, her mouth agape, as she watched her new husband disappear up the stone steps. He climbed heavily, a bit unsteadily, so she knew he was not as sober as he wished others to think. But was he really so dizzy with drink he had no desire to bed his new bride? That *couldn't* be, and yet—

She turned into her room muttering, "God be with me? My *husband* is supposed to be with me! Sweet mother of Jesu, this marriage *must* be consummated..." She paused and gazed up at the ceiling as if peering into her husband's room, far above. "But what can I do if he has no interest? Probably, his rod would not stand straight if I tied a switch to it! Am I that decrepit, that uncomely?" Indulging in self-pity, Gwyneth threw herself onto the bed and considered the irony of her situation. She *had* to mate with the earl, it was her desire and intent to do so. Yet he left her to her own devices. "Would that Ector of Durningham had done the same," she muttered bitterly, her first husband's hated countenance briefly swimming before her eyes.

Her glance happened to fall upon her trunk. Rising, she went to it and threw back the lid. There on top lay her finest garment, a samite bed robe made from fabric the boys had given her when they returned after earning their knighthood. It had been her intention to wear it to please her new husband. "All husbands be damned," she mumbled and, stripping off her wedding costume, she slipped her naked body into it.

Gwyneth unbraided her hair and brushed it free of snarls so that the long, russet waves flew out about her face like a cloud and tumbled down her shoulders and back like a mantle. Then she climbed into her solitary bed, yanked at the curtains surrounding it, and shut her eyes.

Yet sleep would not come. Gwyneth's mind raced as she reviewed every step of her plan to spare Gwendolyn from a forced marriage to the earl, each thoughtfully conceived and executed detail. Yet the most critical one still loomed before her, and as her wedding night stretched to a close with her husband sleeping in some distant chamber, she knew that detail would not be realized if she did not take some drastic action.

"I *cannot* fail!"

Exasperated, Gwyneth threw off her covers and padded, barefoot on the cold floor, to the window. This one, being far below the one in the earl's chamber, was shorter and narrower, to thwart any intruder who might be able to gain the wall at this height. When she threw back the skin covering it, crisp, damp air hit her full force.

Inhaling deeply, ignoring the gooseflesh that prickled her arms, she looked up at the sky. A new day was not many hours behind, though the sky was still dark and starless. Clouds had thickened above, though the night's darkness hid them, and would successfully bring to an end the false summer days they had recently enjoyed. Gone were the blue skies and warm breezes. From now until spring only cold and damp, wind and snow, would greet the Norman Saxons when they rose from their beds.

Rose from their beds. The words in her head repeated themselves, and suddenly Gwyneth knew she could not let her husband rise from his bed—not until she had joined him in it, anyway. If he would not come to her, she had no choice but to go to him.

Before she could lose her courage, she tied the sash about her robe more securely, grabbed her solitary lighted candle, and pulled open the chamber door. There was about as much light on the stairs as there was outside; her flame brightened the gloom only a little. But at least the tower, with its narrow steps and dim corridors, appeared deserted.

Gwyneth made her way up. She might have gone still farther, to the solar at the very top of the keep, except that she recognized John's squire curled up on a pallet in front of a door that seemed wider, taller, and stronger than any other.

Crouching, she passed the candle above the boy's face. Except for squinting and waving his hand weakly in the air, as if trying to shoo away a fly, he did not rouse. She stood again, leaned across him, raised the latch, and held her breath as she pushed the door in. Fortunately it did not creak, and she lost no time stepping over the sleeping servant, tiptoeing inside her husband's room and latching the door again.

The hangings about the bed were closed. For a moment, as she surveyed the typical furnishings of a lord's private chamber—the enclosed bed, the metal-hinged clothing trunks, the small hearth in a pit near the outside wall and window, the stool, the high-backed, carved wooden chairs—

Gwyneth blinked. The second chair was a twin to the first. It was meant for the lord's lady, for her own self. Why, she wondered, glancing surreptitiously toward the bed, had the earl furnished his room with a wife in mind, and then put his bride elsewhere?

Because, she decided, reaching the only conclusion she could, he was in no hurry to bed her. But bed him she was bound to do, so, with grizzly determination, she set about the business that had brought her here.

Putting down her candle, Gwyneth confronted the bed she would soon have to enter. John was asleep or in a drunken stupor near as deep as the one she had left Arnulf in. How could she expect him to perform his husbandly duties? Ector was the only man she'd ever lain with, and he had always done the work when it came to taking his ease. She herself might have been nothing more than a knothole in a plank, the oiled neck of a wide-throated vessel, a dumb sheep in a pasture. Ector had never taken much notice of her except for the cleft between her legs. Always she had lain still on her back with her eyes closed as he climbed above, pushed himself in, heaved and thrashed about a bit, and then left her. If John did not do the same, if he lay there as limp as a swaybacked gelding, how could she join their bodies in the marriage ritual?

Feeling foolish and nearly defeated, Gwyneth closed her eyes to consider. It may have been many years since Ector had visited her bed, but she was not an innocent virgin like her sister. As chatelaine of Durningham's small and crowded keep for most of her life, she had seen enough of others' matings to know there were ways a woman could make a man's rod stiff. She herself had never done such things, but at night when some errand sent her tiptoeing through the great hall's rushes, she had glimpsed certain acts being performed. True, it would have been easier had John been awake. A man's root hardened quickly, she knew, from the littlest contact with a hip or a hand. Sometimes it bulged in response to a whispered, wicked word or a flash of ample bosom; even a coy look or a flick of a tongue wetting parted lips. But John was not awake.

Gwyneth knew she had no choice but to resort to the lowest tactics to make him rise to the occasion. With a determined sigh, she parted the hangings on one side of the bed and found her husband naked. It was the manner in which all who were afforded private accommodations slept, but it startled her to find him so because... he looked... magnificent.

Stepping closer, her thighs hitting the side of the raised mattress, Gwyneth studied John. He was lying on his back, legs and arms splayed carelessly, as if he were floating on the most deliciously comfortable cloud. He was scarred, as she'd suspected, several times over. A puffy red rose blossomed at the juncture where his left arm met his shoulder; a wide ribbon of discolored flesh ran a hand's length down the side of his right calf. A thin, pink line curved across his chest beneath his right nipple. It swept across his ribs and belly, below his navel, and ended just above the thatch of red-gold curls in which his manhood nestled. Quickly Gwyneth glanced at that masculine appendage— Whatever had cut him had stopped before injuring him there. Considering the size of him, the earl's new lady wife deemed him capable of performing still.

If she could rouse him—not to wakefulness, necessarily, but to randy lustfulness.

Impulsively, Gwyneth blew out all but her own candle before climbing cautiously into bed beside her husband. Despite his years and the marks they had left on him, she thought he looked rather like a little boy in his sleep. With his red-tinged hair, he reminded her of Matthew; with his parted lips and gentle snoring, he reminded her of the twins, Rodney and Richard, who had, in sleep, sounded like trumpeters.

Experimentally, she leaned forward and brushed her lips across his bristled cheek. Like the young man asleep in the hall, John simply twitched and tossed his head without awakening. More confidently, she tried it again, finding it very strange to kiss a man so leisurely. In fact, to kiss a man at all. She had no memory of ever having done such a thing before, yet now she found that it was not unpleasant. At least, kissing John of Farleigh was not unpleasant. Since she was fairly certain the quantity of spirits he'd consumed had put him in so deep a sleep he would not fully waken and catch her at what she was about, Gwyneth grew bold. She ran her lips along the dark scar on his cheek and across the golden foliage on his jaw until her mouth met his.

Oh, my, how different this is! she thought. Not like a mother's tender buss, or a child's sweet slobbering. Her heart skipped erratically, but the pounding was not enough to scare her off too quickly. She lingered—

Too long. John's arm snaked around her. How he did it she had no time to figure. But Gwyneth found herself suddenly clasped to his side as he kissed her back, slowly and sensuously, his tongue actually winding its way into her own mouth!

With a frightened gasp she pulled away. She expected to find her lord's blue eyes wide and glaring when she looked at him again. But when she did extricate herself from his grasp and risked a peek, they were still closed. And as she scrambled off the bed he turned away with a stuporous snort, flinging his arm over his forehead.

"Fool," she muttered to herself as she made her way to the foot of the bed, the hangings against her back. "This is no time to dawdle. You've work to do, so do it!"

As if admonished by a stern taskmaster, Gwyneth got down to work. This time she climbed up onto the bed between John's still-splayed legs.

If her imagination was not deceiving her, his root had thickened considerably. Longer now, it lay against his right thigh. Good God, she thought excitedly, did I manage that with but a few kisses? What if…?

Timidly she leaned forward and touched her lips to the earl's manhood. The shaft was firm but the skin was soft and loose. Did it taste like his cheeks or his lips? she wondered. To find the answer, she touched the tip of her tongue to it.

John's legs jerked and Gwyneth jumped. She watched frightenedly as his head tossed against the pillow, but he did not open his eyes in spite of a low moan emitted from deep in his throat. Cautious but desperate to bring this business to a successful conclusion, Gwyneth rubbed her hands briskly together to warm them before reaching out and lifting John's manhood from the cushion of his thigh.

It sprang to life so quickly, so unexpectedly, she almost let go of it. If she had, it would have stood of its own accord, but that was not the full purpose of her ministrations. She needed to make it—to make John— one with herself, not merely to have his shaft point skyward like some bearer's standard.

"You must... be one... with me," she whispered to herself, not to John. "Then no one... can... gainsay... our marriage."

As she spoke, Gwyneth climbed over her husband's thighs and straddled his hips. When she did this, the royal purple silk of her robe parted below the sash at her waist, exposing the swell of her belly and the thatch of tight, copper curls at the apex of her thighs. She looked down. The long, thick appendage in her hand was directly in front of the cleft both custom and law required it to pierce if she and the earl of Farleigh were to be deemed true man and wife. Inhaling a deep, courage-building gulp of air, Gwyneth raised herself to her knees, scrambled forward, and eased John's maleness into her own femininity.

To her surprise she took him whole and effortlessly. With Ector there had always been pain, searing pain. Never had it ended. Each time it was like the first terrible, shameful time. But though John was captured snugly within her—he was a large man and Gwyneth was virginally tight—his entry had been easy and smooth.

She smiled and thought: How wonderful to do this all in secret! To ride the steed rather than being ridden. And—such—pleasure! was her last coherent thought as she began to ease herself away and against her sleeping mate, slowly, purposefully. Where they were joined it was moist and warm; like a pestle fitted into a powdering jar, they seemed perfectly molded to each other.

Gwyneth forgot why she had come to her husband, how distasteful her purpose had seemed, even how imperative she knew it to be. All she was aware of was the heat, the itch, the burning in her loins. As she bucked to and fro, trying with her increased motion to satisfy some longing she could not identify, she threw her head back and closed her eyes. The wealth of her thick, wavy hair fell dark and wild over her shoulders as her robe opened, revealing her bouncing, pert-nippled breasts. Perspiration glistened like dew on her alabaster flesh, but Gwyneth was unaware, even as she was oblivious to John's muffled groans, of the reciprocal thrusting of his hips and his long, strong fingers, which had threaded through her own and held her surely.

Her actions reached a fevered pitch before two things happened: She felt, deep inside her, John's release as he spent his seed. Quickly following, a great wave of sensation unlike anything she had imagined and could never describe washed through her thighs and that private place where they joined, culminating in an explosion that sent vibrant colors ricocheting through her brain. All movement ceased then, both in her and in him, except that the lady collapsed upon her husband's chest, her hands still locked in his.

She lay there some minutes before she recalled her circumstances. Raising her head, she again expected to find John of Farleigh's blue eyes peering at her accusingly. But when she looked they were, as before, closed. His breathing, too, was gentle, as in sleep.

Awed by her experience, grateful for her good luck, Gwyneth slipped off the man and the bed, securing her robe again. Before grabbing up her candle and departing, she intended to close the bed hangings. But first she lifted the furs John had long ago tossed off and covered him gently.

Chapter Eight

✥   ✥   ✥

The lord of Farleigh woke without opening his eyes. Stretching, he rolled onto his side and reached out, unconsciously exploring the empty space beside him with his open hand.

"Milord? Milady?"

Abruptly his eyes flew open at the sound of Miles' voice coming from immediately beyond the bed curtains. He scowled for a second at discovering himself alone in his bed, but realized immediately his squire assumed such was not the case. Clearing his throat he barked, "Aye, Miles, I'm awake."

"Ahhhh..." The young man hesitated. "I presume Lady Gwyneth desires her privacy," he said to the hangings between him and his lord. "I've brought in towels and a ewer of warm water. Do you need me to attend you, milord? And does the lady require a maid?"

John coughed again. "No, lad. We'll manage on our own, thank you."

"As you wish, milord. But there's not much time before chapel."

"I'll—we'll be there."

"I'll wait for you beyond, then."

"No, boy. Run down to the kitchen and steal yourself

an early morning meal. If I need you, I'll send for you."

John waited until he heard his chamber door open and close again.

Kicking open the curtains, he swung his well-muscled legs over the side of the mattress and reached for his bed robe, hanging on a peg. As soon as he'd shrugged himself into it he left the room, heading to the nearest garderobe. It took him some while to empty his bladder of the quantity of liquids he'd consumed the evening before, but he was still scowling thoughtfully when he returned to his room. Not even bothering to close the door, he yanked the bed curtains wide and explored the sheets first with his eyes, then with his hands.

"There can be no evidence of your having mounted your bride if you did not even take her to your bed."

"Gerald!" the earl exclaimed as he spun around to find his seneschal standing inside the doorway. "God's wounds, you should have been a spy in the king's service, man. You're quiet as a cat. Do you know you nearly stole ten years of my life just now?"

"I'm sorry. I hadn't meant to startle you, milord, but your door was standing open." Gerald closed it. "Were you looking for something in particular?"

"No. Yes. I don't know," John admitted as he sat down on the edge of his mattress. "I had... the strangest dream last night. In truth, I would have sworn upon waking it was no dream it all. But it must have been."

"May I ask what it was about?"

"A woman." His blue eyes were locked on Gerald's face, but the seneschal doubted the earl was seeing him at all.

"What of this woman?"

"What, indeed," he said on a sigh. "She was comely and well-formed. Damn, she was a goddess! In my dream she came to me while I was sleeping. I awoke to find her riding me with wild, lustful passion. I swear, had she been real I could have fathered another full generation on this isle with the seed she drew from me into her womb."

John looked away, down at his splayed fingers resting on the mattress beside him. Curiously, Gerald inquired, "What did she look like, this dream lover of yours?"

"I could not see her features," he admitted, his head snapping up so that his gaze met the seneschal's again. "I know she was beautiful. What man would dream of mating with an ugly crone?" he jested, his lip drawing up into a crooked smile. "But because of the hangings about the bed and the thin candlelight, all I recall is that her hair seemed dark. It shimmered a little, in the light that there was. It was long and heavy, and rippled with waves.

"Ach!" He came to his feet and slapped at the air as Gerald thoughtfully considered what his lord had said. "I'm speaking of her as if she were flesh and blood, and of course she was not. I'm glad of it, too," he added, "or I'd be forced to be unfaithful to my new wife. No man could know a female like that and then give her up—that is, if she truly existed."

He strode to the table and poured warm water into the basin there. As he washed himself Gerald asked, "What of your bride?"

"I did as I said I would: I left her untouched last evening. She's in the chamber you provided for her yesterday afternoon."

"She didn't object?"

"Of course not! What virginal bride of tender years would object to being released from her wifely responsibilities the first night of her marriage?"

"Surely there are some."

"Not the damsel I married," he declared as he toweled himself dry.

"You don't dislike her?"

"What!" John's face appeared above the linen cloth he held in his hands. "No, of course I don't dislike her. In truth, once she removed her veil, I found her more attractive than I'd recalled."

"But not as comely as the woman in your dreams?"

"Ah, Gerald. No earthly woman could match my— what did you call her before? My dream lover. But Gwyneth of Sherborne can certainly turn men's heads."

"Still, you intend to put her off?"

John was now naked and pulling on his clothes himself. "Aye, indeed," he replied. "I don't think she's quite the child I was led to believe, either, but she is still very naive and definitely wary of me. I sensed her unease all last evening."

"Is that why you put away enough drink to keep a shipful of men happy?" Gerald asked casually.

"No!" John stopped in the act of belting his tunic.

"I don't suppose it is my place to inquire exactly why you consumed so much wine last night?"

"Nay, 'tis not." Brusquely, the earl began yanking on his shoes.

"Then I suggest only that you accompany your new lady wife to chapel. Young Miles believes your bride shared your room last night. Surely your guests and your servants do, too. If you leave Lady Gwyneth to her own devices during the day, I fear it would humiliate her."

"Thank you much for your advice, Gerald," John snapped, anchoring his cape at the shoulder. "Rest assured I've no intention of ignoring my bride. I wish to win her over, do I not?

"Now, unless there is business you need to discuss with me, you may go."

"Yes, milord," Gerald said quickly, and before the earl's temper could explode full blown, he bowed and backed out of the room.

In the small guest chamber below, Gwyneth had wakened as lazily as John. She felt as contented as a cat full of cream until a knock at the door was quickly followed by a young serving girl Gwendolyn's age bursting into the room.

"Good morning, milady," the raven-haired wench chirped as she set on the table a jug of warm water and a soft, folded towel. "My name's Bess, and I'm here to serve you."

Gwyneth's bed curtains were open. She sat up and hugged her samite robe closed tight across her chest. "Did the earl send you?" she asked hesitantly.

"Aye, milady," Bess replied, "that he did."

Gwyneth felt her face flush and a tremor of anger ripple through her limbs. That oaf! she thought heatedly. That boorish, insensitive oaf! How she had ever managed to carry through her scheme last night with such a cockshead, well... "It was a miracle!" she whispered beneath her breath.

Bess was looking pointedly at her trunk. "Do you need me to help you dress?"

"You may as well, long as you're here," she grumbled irritatedly, climbing from her bed.

"What is it you wish to wear today?"

"The black tunic and the green bliaut."

"Oh, they're fine garments, milady!" Bess said admiringly as she unfolded them and held them up.

"Fine enough for the earl's lady wife."

"Thank you so kindly," Gwyneth ground out in stilted syllables.

"You've seen her, no doubt?"

Gwyneth, pouring water into the wash basin, nearly dropped the jug. "What?"

"You've seen our new mistress, Lady Gwyneth, at the festivities last night?" Bess continued as she laid Gwyneth's clothes out on the bed. "Most everyone of the castle staff did, too. Except me. I was confined to the kitchen the whole night. By the time I was free, the lord and his lady had retired." She picked up a towel and waited patiently for Gwyneth to finish her ablutions. "Such news it was to us all, Lord John taking a wife! They say no one was advised aforehand, that even you guests were unaware of the reason you were invited here. Word is he kept the wedding secret so that the evil Elwood of Eye would bring no harm to Lady Gwyneth before the event took place."

The servant had no idea who she was, Gwyneth realized. That John had gone to bed alone last night was not common knowledge. With a deep breath, her anger cooled and she recovered herself. "You shouldn't gossip like that, Bess. Not among your own, and not with your betters," she advised, splashing water on her face before patting dry with the towel.

"Oh, I'm sorry, milady. I know my tongue runs away with me sometimes. But could you tell me, please, is she as comely as they say?"

Gwyneth blinked. "Who?"

"Lord John's lady wife, of course."

"No, Bess. I mean, who says she is comely?"

"Why, everyone who's seen her! Everyone who works at the castle, that is."

"That can't be true."

The girl looked insulted. "I may carry tales, milady, but I don't tell lies. That's what they say, that she's beautiful."

"I myself am not much good at such judgments." Dropping the subject, she turned away. "Please help me to dress, now. It must be nearing time for Lauds."

"It is, milady." Cheerfully, the servant helped Gwyneth into her clothes. "Your husband must be an early riser," she observed as later she helped to braid her hair.

"What!"

"Your husband, milady, was gone before I arrived. Is he an avid falconer? So many lords are, rising in the dark of winter's night to see to their hawks."

"Ah—" Gwyneth stood and glanced at the large, rumpled bed. Of course the girl assumed she was wed; men might have accepted the earl's invitation and arrived companionless, but a lady would never have come to the castle without her husband as escort. "Yes, I suppose he is."

"There, now." Bess stood back and appraised the lady. "Except for your head piece, all's in place. If there's nothing else, then, I've others to see to."

"I'm fine. Please go on. I will leave immediately for chapel."

"Do you know where it is?"

"Aye." *I was married there only yesterday,* Gwyneth thought to herself as she arranged a veil and circlet over her cinnamon colored braids.

The door had not yet swung closed behind the departing Bess when Gwyneth grabbed it and pulled it full open again, intending to hurry to chapel. As if the image of her husband conjured him up in the flesh,

Gwyneth now discovered John in the hallway. With a gasp, she took a quick step back.

"My dear lady wife," he said, his voice sounding a trifle bemused as he considered her face unblinkingly.

"My—my lord."

"Please." The earl reached out and took her hand, bringing it briefly to his lips. A tickle, like a flutter of butterfly's wings, ran up her arm to her bosom before nesting in her belly. "We are man and wife. 'Twould be best you called me John and I called you Gwyneth."

"Yes—John. It would be best."

"May I escort you to chapel?"

"Please."

He did not simply hold his wife's hand as he led her down the stairs, but wrapped one strong arm about her waist as well. "The stone steps are narrow and steep," he explained when she glanced at him sidelong. "I shouldn't like for you to fall and break your neck."

"Nor would I."

"Nothing of that sort will happen to you while I'm about," he promised as they reached the great hall. He chuckled when she turned to gaze up at him with questioning eyes. "You disbelieve me?"

"No, I…" Gwyneth turned away, flustered. Though the earl was fully clothed, when she looked at him she saw him naked—scarred but glorious. To rid her mind of the image it contained and the sort of thoughts that were suddenly cluttering it, she shook her head.

"What, then?"

She looked up at him again. Though they had descended the stairs safely, his arm was still about her. "'Tis only… No man's ever made such a promise to me."

John cupped Gwyneth's chin in his palm, causing

her flesh to tingle where he touched her. "That is only because you are so young and were sheltered by your father, too, no doubt. Had you more time to enjoy May Days and fairs, many the young swain would have made all sorts of promises to protect you."

In battle were you wounded in one eye or both? Gwyneth wished to ask him. Why cannot you see me for what I am? Yet she wanted to believe his promises just as Gwendolyn did Thomas' vows.

While she mused about these things, John studied her, the creamy complexion and slanted, black-lashed, emerald eyes. Yet he ended his contemplation abruptly, and with a cough released her. Offering only his arm he said crisply, "To chapel, now, Gwyneth. Come."

Out the keep's door and into the gray light of dawn, he escorted her to the stone chapel where the priest and their guests were already gathered for the morning's service and where, less than twenty-four hours earlier, they had been wed.

Afterwards, the lords and ladies returned to the keep as a group. The tables were again set up in the hall, and as the knights of the castle settled down at those in the center of the room, the nobles ascended the dais and seated themselves at the head table. John, however, stayed in his chair but a moment before pacing up and down behind the others' benches, pausing frequently in order to speak to the neighboring barons. Alone in the ornately carved chair beside her husband's empty one, Gwyneth ate more heartily than she had the night before. In fact, the quince tarts were so tasty she gobbled two and beckoned Bess when she saw the girl, requesting still another.

"Of course, milady, but—"

"Yes?"

"Where's the earl's lady wife, if I may ask? I've been looking to see her all morning. Why are you in her chair?"

Gwyneth sighed uneasily, but before she could think to reply, John returned and sat down heavily in his chair. "Is there a problem, wench?" he demanded of Bess. The servant's eyes grew round and she shook her head vehemently. He turned to Gwyneth. "Did you need something?"

"I—ah—"

"If it's in my power to get it for you, I will," he said with a smile. "Another promise," he added, with a wink.

Gwyneth turned aside, flustered again. The earl was so gentle with her, and he did not even know they had been intimate. *That* caused her to blush, though she managed to explain, "I—I simply asked for another quince tart."

"A task I think even you can handle," John said, turning to look down at Bess. "Be off, then, quickly, and bring my lady wife her tart."

Bess' mouth fell open and her eyes darted from the lord to his lady. Gwyneth's heart sank as she watched the girl's mind fit the pieces of the puzzle together. Knowing she had the full picture now, she also knew that within minutes everyone employed at Farleigh Castle would be advised that the earl's bride had slept alone on their wedding night.

God, no! the voice in Gwyneth's mind cried as a far worse realization struck her. John did not know of their shared intimacies because he'd been too drunk to be aware of his wife's seduction. That, coupled with everyone knowing the bride and groom had spent their wedding night in separate rooms would give weight to the notion their marriage was still not consummated. God's wounds! she swore silently. Only she knew the truth, and she was without the proof to back it. There was even no bloodied bedsheet, for she'd lost her virginity with her childhood at the hands of Ector of Durningham, not John of Farleigh.

Clenching her teeth, Gwyneth's chin quivered. Then her name on her husband's lips caused her to turn her face toward his.

"Gwyneth—" John began.

Her eyes, so close to his, were bright with unshed tears and framed with spikey, damp, black lashes. "What—?" he began to inquire until, as if pulled by a magnet, his lips and hers drew closer. When they were but a hair's breadth apart, John abruptly pulled back, muttering, "Excuse me, madam." Shoving out his chair noisily, he left the dais and crossed the hall, where he determinedly engaged several of his knights in earnest conversation.

Gwyneth stared at John's back, willing the tears welling up in her eyes not to fall. She was at a loss to understand either her husband's actions or her own reactions, but she knew her cheeks were flaming and her pulse was racing.

"Here you go, milady," Bess announced with a quick curtsy as she set a plate of half a dozen tarts before Gwyneth. But the earl's lady wife did not touch even one of them. Her appetite had fled with her husband.

Because John was so near the arched entryway to the great hall, when a messenger appeared there he spoke directly to him. There was no need to hail Neville of Kurth; he saw his man and came forward immediately. Soon the other barons joined them, and when all had heard the messenger's tale they collected their wives and men-at-arms, making haste to depart.

"You intend to go with them?" Gerald asked,

breaking his silence as soon as Lionel and Bruno had hurried off to obey their lord's harshly barked commands.

"Of course," John replied distractedly.

"But, why, milord?"

"Because Neville asked for my help."

"Surely he meant the aid of your knights, not your own lance."

John's blue eyes narrowed to slits beneath his golden brows. "Also," he continued, scowling at Gerald, "because I've no wish to allow that devil, Eye, to get away with naught. Certainly not while I hide, sniveling and cowardly, behind my castle walls!"

"But, milord," the seneschal persisted, "if you remained here to protect your own, no one would construe your actions as cowardly. Surely the others are not hurrying off to fight alongside the baron of Kurth! They are only returning to their own demesnes to protect them from Elwood's men.

"They do what they must," John replied curtly. "I do what I must."

"But your lady wife!" he hissed.

"My lady wife," John repeated softly, turning to look at the place where he had left Gwyneth. To his chagrin, he found her no longer seated at the table but instead making her way across the hall, toward him.

"Milord?" she said questioningly as she approached.

The earl looked to his right and his left, as though for escape. Finding none he replied, "I've no time for talk now, Gwyneth. I must go."

"Again, so soon, and so abruptly?"

Her words were not accusatory; she spoke gently. But John was gruff as he replied, "I fear I've not always time to explain my every action to you, my lady wife. You must understand that a lord's business takes him away. In any case," he added, glancing toward Gerald, "I assumed my seneschal would provide any explanations you required."

With that and a curt nod, John turned and sprinted up the staircase.

Gwyneth bit her lower lip as she watched her husband go. In as even a tone as she could manage she asked Gerald, "What news takes him off?"

"'Tis Elwood."

"I thought as much. What's he done?"

"His men attacked the village of Kurth on Lord Neville's lands."

"Jesu!"

Gerald nodded. "They burned it to the ground and killed many."

"May Elwood himself burn in everlasting hell," Gwyneth cursed. "Are the earl's guests returning to their homes?"

"Aye."

"And the earl—my husband?"

"Lord John is accompanying Lord Neville, who requested his aid."

Gwyneth took a deep breath. This was good, his going. The earl's absence, however long or short, would allow Gwendolyn and Thomas more time to marry. And yet—

She frowned. Gwyneth needed still to consummate the marriage. Or did she? As long as her sister was safe from him, did the validity of her own wedded union matter at all?

"Do not worry for him, Lady Gwyneth. Lord John will return to you."

"I am not worried."

"Nay? You looked to be fretting, to me."

"Well, I am not. I was only thinking how disturbed Gwendolyn would have been had she been the bride he so easily deserts."

Gerald considered Gwyneth thoughtfully. "'Tis the troubled times," he explained. "Elwood is a very real threat to all who reside in these parts."

Her eyes on the staircase, she muttered, "Did the baron threaten the earl's own bed?"

The seneschal's eyebrows danced. "Nay," he said, smiling a little as he shook his dark head. "There was no chance Elwood would intrude there. But another did."

Gwyneth's eyes grew round, though she did not voice her question.

Still, Gerald answered it. "My lord was visited by a damsel he calls his 'dream lover.'"

She blinked. Then, recovering, she scoffed, "Mayhap if he'd had his bride in his bed, John of Farleigh would have had no need to dream of other ladies."

"Lord John attempted—" he coughed purposely— "to sleep alone on his wedding night to spare his virginal bride's sensibilities."

"His—his vir—virginal…!" Gwyneth sputtered.

"My lady, 'tis what you've led him to believe you are—a sheltered, innocent damsel. And I would think that in light of the secrets you keep, you'd have been as relieved that he kept his distance as any frightened, child-bride would have."

She took a deep breath, and leaned closer in to Gerald, keeping her voice low. "You know I must validate this marriage by sharing the earl's bed."

"Oh?" The seneschal cocked his head, looking skeptical. "For your sister's sake, or for yours?"

Gwyneth could not even respond. She stared at her old friend and then, with a "harumph!" raised her chin and the hem of her skirts, and strode haughtily from the great hall. She did not see that Gerald's amused smile had returned to his lips as he watched her go.

Gwyneth stood in the bailey exchanging pleasantries with the guests as they departed. Graciously, she spoke to each lady in turn, extending an open invitation and wishing them God's speed. But while she did this, she kept an ever-watchful eye on the keep's open door. Before even half the guests had emerged from that portal, John of Farleigh strode through it dressed for battle.

The sight of him took her breath away—he looked both fearsome and magnificent in his mail and helmet, his shield in one hand, his sword on one hip. Yet when she saw him, Gwyneth thought of how he had looked at her when he first saw her face—with pleasure and kindness. She thought, too, of his conspiratorial winks, designed to reassure her. And the thoughtful way he had assisted her down the stairs. But mostly, Gwyneth remembered how he had responded to her awkward efforts at love-making. Even more asleep than awake, he had brought her pleasure—something Ector had never even tried to do.

She hesitated, debating whether or not to approach him, and in that moment Miles appeared amidst the throng of people, horses and carts, leading his lord's black warhorse. John mounted it quickly, swinging himself easily into the saddle despite his heavy mail and armor.

"John!" Gwyneth called out, her heartbeat quickening irrationally. "My lord!" But she was too late.

Miles was now mounted on his own horse, and together he and the earl maneuvered their steeds through the cluster of mortals and beasts.

"John!" she called again, ignoring the woman beside her, to whom she'd been speaking only moments earlier. It was suddenly imperative that she speak to her husband before he left her, so she shouted his name again in a voice that had, years ago, always brought Roddy and Richie, Mattie and Gwendolyn back to her no matter how far afield they had run. But her husband did not have an ear trained to hear his wife's call as children did their mothers'. He continued toward the gate connecting the inner courtyard with the outer one, joined along the way by his own men and Lord Neville's.

Gwyneth broke into a run. "JOHN!" she shrieked and finally he heard her. Turning his steed he rode against the tide of men and animals until he was beside her. She felt embarrassed, then, because she'd been shouting like a fishwife and in truth she had naught to say to her husband. When he halted beside her, she simply stood with her hand on her head as if anchoring her veil against the breeze. She wished she had let him go, and yet a part of her was glad she had not.

It took the lord a few scant seconds to realize his lady wife was not going to speak, despite her efforts to call him back to her. On an impulse of his own then, he swooped low, wrapped his arm about Gwyneth's waist, and hauled her up beside him. "Christ," he muttered as he gazed into her emerald eyes, "I've bungled this husband business from the start, have I not?"

She did not reply, so he continued, "I thought you did not want to wed me, milady, and though you did, I've been giving you good reason to change your mind. Gwyneth." He jerked her closer to him so that they were nearly nose to nose. "If you vow to remain here until I return, I pledge to be a better husband to you."

She did not speak still, but she blinked her thick

lashes and nodded her head. John kissed her, then, hard, as if he was pressing his seal onto her. In the next instant, he set her down and rode away.

Chapter Nine

✜ ✜ ✜

When nothing was left of the guests and their entourage but dust in the air and footprints in the dirt, Gwyneth went inside the keep again. As she entered the great hall to ascend the stairs, she heard a tittering. An arrogant glare was enough to silence the serving maids, but she knew why they had been whispering and that they would begin again once she was out of sight.

"If you've so little to do that you have time to stand about making merry, I shall find some chores for you that will not only keep you busy well into the night, they'll bring tears to your eyes!" Gwyneth announced. Immediately, the girls scattered.

"You!" she called to a burly scullion on his way to the kitchen. "Hold off a moment. I need you to carry something for me."

"Aye, milady," he said, nodding his head agreeably.

"Come with me."

Gwyneth climbed the narrow stairs and when she reached her room—the one she'd slept in—she pushed open the door. "That trunk. Please be good enough to take it up to Lord John's chamber."

"Yes, milady," the man said, grunting as he hefted the weight of the large, wooden, iron-bound trunk.

Quickly Gwyneth preceded him up the remaining stairs, not wishing to be behind him if he took a tumble. "Over there," she said, pointing when they'd entered the earl's private quarters. With another grunt, the man deposited the trunk where she told him to.

"Anything else, milady?"

"No... I'm sorry. What is your name?"

"Paddy's what they call me, milady."

"Paddy. Well, thank you for your assistance." Nodding his head once more, the thick-set peasant turned to leave. But Gwyneth stopped him. "I just thought of something else, Paddy, that you can help me with. Please pass the word that I wish to see all the castle staff in the hall at... Nones. I know there's been no chatelaine at Farleigh since Lady Evelyn, Lord Vincent's wife, passed on some years ago. But I am here now, and as Lord John's lady wife, I intend to see that the keep is run properly. To that end I wish to speak to everyone, from the cook to the stable boys, this afternoon. Can you do that for me, Paddy?"

"Aye, milady, I can do that."

"Please close the door on your way out."

Another nod and the man was gone. Gwyneth turned around to survey the room in daylight that she had seen before only in the dimmest candlelight—not that her concentration had even then been on the chamber's contents.

The bed. She blushed, simply looking at it. What she had done there, she had done nowhere else and with no other man, not even Ector. She had felt passion and had willingly succumbed to that compelling force. It had all been for naught, for none save she knew of that intimacy shared with her lord husband—not even her lord husband! But... Gwyneth frowned thoughtfully.

It had been worth it, to understand what it was that compelled most of mankind to pursue it. All her life, Gwyneth had only dreaded the act of mating and had not, before, comprehended why others, wedded or not, sought out bed partners.

Now she finally understood.

"I must lure him into taking me again," she muttered aloud. Silently, her thoughts continued. True, if the earl remains away long enough, 'twould not be necessary to officially consummate the marriage in order to entangle John in the machinations of the ecclesiastical courts. Surely Gwendolyn and Thomas will already be wed and, mayhap, expecting an heir. So if—*when*—he is determined to cast me out, it shall not matter if the process is slow or swift.

"Yet, to be safe, I should try and make him bed me again," Gwyneth decided, her eyes straying once more to the heavy oak bed.

It was not nearly so intriguing without her warrior husband lying naked in it. It was, in truth, in sorry shape. Though the heavy wooden frame appeared sturdy enough, the hangings and coverlets— God's teeth! Gwyneth thought, they looked to be from William's time!

Crinkling her nose, she approached and shook one of the curtains. In the sunlight the dust she set free was visible, as well as the streaks of rich color in the folds of the cloth that made the faded hue elsewhere more noticeable.

"So, he took what was left him," Gwyneth deduced, "without even looking at what it was that he had. Foolish man! If only I'd ever had the power and wealth to make my life more comfortable..." she muttered until the realization struck her. "God's tears! I *shall* make things pleasant for the while that I'm here," she declared and, tugging fiercely with both her arms, she pulled on one bed curtain until it tore free and she went sprawling, covered by a tent of heavy wool so thick with dirt she would have suffocated had she not been able to get free.

During the next days, Gwyneth was so busy setting the keep to rights she nearly forgot the one person who had the power still to foil all her carefully wrought schemes: her father, Arnulf.

As she stood in the great hall, supervising the rehanging of the thoroughly aired and dusted boar heads and stag antlers, Gerald came up behind her and said, "One would think you found me lacking in my duties as seneschal."

"Oh, no!" she countered, turning around to face him. Even when she saw that he was smiling and knew he'd been teasing her she explained, "Your duties lie in more important matters than dusting and mopping and sweeping. As seneschal you're required to deal with tender and law, and to represent your lord in the earl's absence. 'Twas never your responsibility to see that the linens were laundered, the ale brewed with fresh water instead of that from the moat, or to replace the old rushes on the floor with those green and fragrant."

"That's true enough. But I had a steward who was supposed to see to all those things and more."

"Did you? Where is he now?" Gwyneth inquired.

"Gone some time, and not much missed. In truth, as I noticed no changes after he departed, I thought we could get on well enough without replacing him." Gerald looked about the room, bustling with activity. "I see now that I was wrong."

"Are you planning to replace the steward, then?"

"And waste my lord's money by adding still another to his staff when he has a fine chatelaine in his lady wife?" he asked. "I think not, for the earl would probably decide to replace his seneschal to make up the difference in coin."

Gwyneth gave her friend a look and was shaking her head when one of John's men called from the entryway: "Pardon the interruption, but there's a messenger from Sherborne to see the lady." She blanched at the unexpected news and stood deathly still.

"If there were trouble, Lady Gwyneth," Gerald reminded her in a low voice only she could hear, "it would be one of Farleigh's men come to tell us, not one of Arnulf's."

"Shall I send him in?" the man beyond inquired.

"No!" Gwyneth replied too quickly. Leaning close to Gerald she explained in a whisper, "Surely the messenger expects the earl of Farleigh's wife to be Gwendolyn, and surely the messenger will know I'm not she. After all, I am acquainted with most everyone from both the town and the manor. I can't see him, Gerald!" she hissed plaintively. "What shall I do?"

"Run up to the gallery and hide yourself in one of the rooms," he told her. And he instructed the guard, "Send Sherborne's messenger in here to me. But give me a moment first."

The man nodded and departed; Gwyneth had raised her skirts and was running up the stairs before he was even gone from sight.

She turned into the first room and though the curtains were open, allowing a clear view of the hall below, she stood back, afraid to risk a look, afraid of being seen. Shortly, Gerald joined her.

"It's all right," he said, closing the door. "The

man's gone."

"What did he have to say?"

"Arnulf's not very well; he's confined to the house and unable to visit."

"Thank God!"

"He hopes you—Gwendolyn—are serving your new husband well." Gwyneth made no comment, but arched one fine brow and pursed her lips. "He also wishes to advise you that your sister—that you, actually—are missing."

Crossing her arms over her chest, Gwyneth turned aside. "I wonder how long it took the old man to realize that?" she mused, more to herself than to Gerald. "Well?" She looked over her shoulder at him. "What message did you give him in return?"

"I told him we'd no word of any abduction. I did not say outright that I'd no knowledge of your whereabouts. Eventually, Lady Gwyneth, it will come out that you've been here all along, that it is young Gwendolyn who's missing."

"No doubt. Was that all you said?"

Gerald shrugged. "I added that I did not think the baron of Eye had anything to do with his daughter's disappearance. If he had, he'd have contacted Arnulf, certainly."

"That was it?"

"Aye."

Gwyneth exhaled a long sigh. "I can only pray that whatever ails my father keeps him house-bound for some time yet. In the meanwhile, my sister can settle more surely into her role as wife of Thomas of Brandywine."

"And you?" Both the seneschal's dark brows rose in question. "Are you settling more surely into your role of wife to John of Farleigh?"

"Aye, and well I should!" she exclaimed. "I told you I'd do what was expected of me without crying in my ale. Managing this household is my responsibility."

"As it's your right to sleep in your husband's bedchamber."

Gwyneth blushed to the roots of her hair. "The servants were beginning to gossip, and as the earl is gone, I did not think he'd object."

Gerald smiled. "I do not think he'd object were he here." He paused before suggesting, "When Lord John returns, milady, I advise you to tell him the truth."

"The truth!" she gasped. "Nay! I cannot risk it. John mustn't learn who I really am, not for a while yet. And you, Gerald, must remember that you promised to keep my secret."

The seneschal shook his head. "I do not like this business, milady. I should never have made such a promise."

"But you did," she reminded him.

"I don't wish to see my lord hurt—"

"I would never hurt him!" Gwyneth blurted, and her pronouncement caught not only Gerald but her own self by surprise. Swallowing visibly she lowered her eyes and explained softly, "My only intent has been to allow my sister to marry the man she loves. Never did I wish to do the earl injury." She raised her eyes to meet Gerald's again. "I told you at the first I would do my duty by him. I am performing the duties of chatelaine, am I not?"

"Aye, you are," he agreed thoughtfully. "You've gone beyond that, too, by putting yourself in his chamber. As well you have—"

"I have what?" Gwyneth looked wary.

But Gerald responded kindly, "We both know what, milady. 'Twas no dream my lord had on his wedding night."

Chagrined, she turned and hurried to the chamber door so that the seneschal would not see the pink staining her cheeks.

As Gwyneth put her hand to the latch, she declared, "You speak foolishness, Gerald, son of Penworth." There was little force behind her words. "But know that when I must, I will tell the earl the truth. 'Til then, I'll see to my wifely duties—whatever they may be. Right now I must go belowstairs and show the cook how to use a few more seasonings when she poaches the fish and roasts the venison."

"By all means," the seneschal said, smiling at Gwyneth's back. "Do not let me keep you."

Chapter Ten

✢   ✢   ✢

The lord of Farleigh returned late into the night, entering the great hall not a little noisily with his men close behind him. Immediately the servants and the castle guard, who were asleep among the rushes, woke. Moments later the seneschal, summoned to confer with his lord, appeared on the stairs.

"Have you requested food and drink?" he asked John before anything else.

"Aye, I have," the earl replied as he sat down in his chair before the fire and Miles began tugging off his sollarets. "How goes it here?"

"No trouble from Eye, if that is what you mean," Gerald said, joining him at the table.

John scowled. "Trouble from elsewhere, then?"

"Oh, no, milord! We had one messenger just today, from Sherborne. There's no trouble there, either. It seems Sir Arnulf is still feeling poorly, but he sent his man to inquire after his daughter and to apologize for not being able to visit."

John rubbed his face tiredly before turning his eyes to the trencher of food and flagon of wine a servant placed before him. "And... my wife—How is she?"

"Quite well, milord. Lady Gwyneth has taken the

castle servants well in hand."

"How so?"

"She gathered them all together, learned their names and their duties, and set about instructing them on how better to do their tasks."

"They weren't doing them correctly before?" John asked, chewing on a leg of roasted fowl.

"It would seem not. I fear moat water, rather than that taken from a fresh stream, was used for brewing ale. Lady Gwyneth assures me that much of the stomach ailments so many suffered will now be relieved. And Cook's fare has improved substantially under your lady wife's tutelage, wouldn't you agree?"

"Indeed." John wiped his lips on the sleeve of his tunic before casting his eye about the room. "I hadn't thought the keep was run so poorly, had you?"

"Nay." Gerald, too, looked about. "But Lady Gwyneth has shown me otherwise."

"Good." The earl smiled and gulped a healthy swig of wine. "'Tis odd, though."

"What is?"

"That Lady Gwyneth is so skilled a chatelaine. Her sire is, after all, simply lord of a manor and his house is little bigger than this hall. Where'd she learn such skills, do you think?"

Clearing his throat, Gerald said tentatively, "Milord, Lady Gwyneth's not so young and inexperienced as we assumed she was. As well, she's not spent all her years in her father's house."

"Nay?" John finished off his cup of wine and mused, "So old Arnulf thought to deceive me by wedding me to an aged daughter of more than a score of years, eh?" He chuckled. "Well, Gerald, truth be told, I'm glad Gwyneth is no child. A man needs a woman as a wife, not a babe." His blue eyes slanted toward Gerald's. "Do you think she schooled with the nuns and was taught her skills at the monastery?"

"Mayhap." The seneschal looked down at his knees before changing the subject. "What of your ride with Neville of Kurth? Did you encounter Elwood's men?"

Exhaling noisily, John nodded. "What he did to that village was a blasphemy, Gerald. Such carnage, and for what? He's as evil as they say. There was no purpose in it. Kurth had no quarrel with him, and he'll not bring in his borders."

"You said you encountered the baron's men."

"Aye. They were returning to Eye when we attacked them. A mangy lot, but fearless—mercenaries to a man. Yet they did not fare so well when fighting trained knights rather than defenseless cottars and villeins."

"You slew them all?"

"Nay, not all. But many. Still, the one I wish to slay is Elwood himself." John stood, running his fingers through his mussed hair. "We'll talk in the morning, Gerald. Now all I want is a bath and my bed. Will you send someone up with hot water for my tub?"

"Yes, milord, but—"

The earl squinted at Gerald, who had come to his feet when he had.

"Nothing, milord. I'll do as you ask."

With a nod, John strode to the stairs and slowly climbed them.

Gwyneth woke with a start; there was noise and confusion downstairs in the great hall. For a moment she, too, was confused. Though it was obviously late into the night and all the candles in the chamber had burned down low, none had guttered out yet. She was still dressed as she'd been all day, except for the absence of her head veil. When Gwyneth looked down at her lap, she saw her sewing there and recalled she had settled into her chair to do some embroidering. She must have dozed off immediately, for she was still in the chair and her needlework had not progressed a stitch.

Curiously, she opened the door and stepped into the hallway, peering down the staircase. It was impossible to see beyond the bend as the stairs spiraled, but she could hear voices and knew the earl was home.

"Sweet Mother of Jesu!" she whispered beneath her breath as she fled back into John's chamber and closed the door again. All day she'd been thinking about Gerald's advice. By day's end she had decided he might be right—she should confess. But it was too soon, John had returned too soon. She was not prepared and, mayhap, if Gwendolyn and Thomas had met with any difficulties, they might not yet be wed. Nay, she told herself, she had to consummate the marriage again, if only to protect her sister. There would, she knew, be time enough for confessions.

Gwyneth heard John's footsteps on the stairs and had barely turned to face the door when it opened again and her husband stood there. "Milord," she greeted her husband respectfully.

"Milady!"

The earl was surprised to find his wife in his room. He glanced at her briefly before surveying the chamber.

"What have you done here, Gwyneth?" he asked, finally crossing the threshold and moving toward the bed where he fingered a covering of thick, silver wolf fur where, when he'd left, there'd been only a balding rug of pelts.

"Your room needed some improvements, milord."

"John."

"John." Gwyneth swallowed her anxiety and spoke surely. "The—the bedclothes were worn, faded and dusty, hardly fit for an earl. Men may not notice such things, but a woman does. I felt it my duty to make your private chamber pleasant and comfortable."

He opened his mouth to reply, but at that moment two servants appeared in the open doorway, dragging with them a tub and several buckets of hot water. John's squire, Miles, trailed behind them.

"Milady." The boy bowed courteously to Gwyneth, and, turning to his lord, he asked, "Do you wish me to finish helping you undress, or will your lady wife assist you?"

"You, Miles," John informed the youth quickly. "My thanks for your efforts here, Gwyneth. If you'll excuse me…"

Custom required the lady of a keep to bathe visiting guests. That the earl would urge his own wife from the chamber during his bath was shocking. Yet Gwyneth followed the servants out into the hallway where, on the other side of the door, she considered her dilemma. It took no long thought for her to reach the same conclusion she had on her wedding night. She had to get both inside the earl's chamber and into her husband's bed.

When John's squire quit the master's room and proceeded down the stairs as the other servants had, Gwyneth took a deep breath, opened the door, and boldly stepped into the chamber again.

John was standing in the middle of the room, quite naked. For a second the sight of him took her breath away. She stood as still as he, staring, while memories of her wedding night came flooding back. Desire flamed in her with a rush of heat, and though it embarrassed her to feel so, Gwyneth stood her ground.

Quickly covering himself with his bed robe, John demanded, "Gwyneth, why are you here?"

It was like being doused with a bucketful of cold water. "I am your wife. You are my husband. Why should I not be here?"

John frowned and studied Gwyneth curiously. "I did not know if you wished to live with me as man and wife, yet," he admitted. "I thought, now that I am home again, we might talk."

She took a tentative step toward him. "We are newly wed, milord. I would not think most couples recently married would spend much time—ah—talking." She swallowed hard, but held his gaze.

John took a step toward Gwyneth, which brought them close enough to touch. Thoughtfully, he reached out and traced the line of her jaw with one finger. "I don't wish to rush you, lady wife. Answer me truly, now: Are you saying you wish to share my bed?"

Gwyneth tried to answer. But only a little sound emerged from her throat, so she was forced to nod silently.

It was all the earl needed, though. His hand dropped to her waist and he drew Gwyneth to him, holding her tightly as his lips pressed hungrily to hers. The passions she had tamped down ignited abruptly, like an explosion of fire. A primal urge to explore him, to rip his robe from his body so that she might stroke him, fondle his manhood until she made it ready to plunge deep into her, churned within her like a stormy sea. She was ready to melt into him, to cleave to him, to offer herself up—

Gwyneth stiffened. She could do none of those

things, she realized with belated horror. John was not now in a drunken sleep. This time he would be aware of her behavior, and it would not do to show wild abandon or any hint of expertise. He thought her a virgin; she had to display a virgin's reluctance. God's wounds! she cried silently, her thoughts growing frantic. She ought also to display a virgin's blood—but she had not considered it, and had made no arrangements. Suddenly her passions cooled again, and her quandary at being in her husband's arms was not feigned.

John released her. "So, you are not so sure what you want of me," he said. It was a statement, not a question. "Or is it you only wish to be with me, in this room, to silence any gossip among the castle staff?"

"Aye. Nay." She shook her head, her fist pressed to her lips. "Milord, I do wish to share your bed, only I—"

"Don't worry." His voice was kind as again John reached out to touch Gwyneth's cheek. But this time the gesture was paternal. "I should like you to share the master's chamber and the master's bed. But I vow I shan't take you until you are a willing partner."

"I'll go," Gwyneth muttered, stumbling backward toward the door. "You are exhausted, you need your sleep..."

"Stay." He grabbed her arm. "I am not as tired as you might think," he admitted with a rueful smile. Yet he shrugged as he assured her, "The bed is large enough for two—even when one is the size I am—so that we can lie side by side without touching. I shan't touch you, Gwyneth," he promised. "Not until you wish me to."

Reluctantly, Gwyneth climbed into bed beside John. Though he threw off his robe and settled naked beneath the covers, she remained dressed, except for her shoes. He noticed, but made no comment.

He seemed to go off to sleep immediately, too, while Gwyneth lay rigid as a tent pole staring at the canopy above. She was miserable, uncomfortable, and it was all her lord husband's fault. He was so damnably thoughtful and generous, patient and kind, gentle and—Gwyneth forced herself to stop naming the earl's higher attributes. He was supposed to be an oaf, a crude, self-centered churl. Why was he not? And why did he rouse the feelings in her that he did? Lust, that's what it was. Lust, which no lady admitted to and few more indulged in. Yet she, Gwyneth of Sherborne, Durningham and Farleigh, was rattled by the intensity of her lust for her husband.

Sneaking a slant-eyed look at him, Gwyneth gently eased herself off the bed. Stripping down to her linen shift, she uncovered and unplaited her hair, running an ivory comb through her heavy, russet tresses until the thick waves billowed wildly about her head and shoulders. Then she turned and looked over at the bed.

That bed. Jesu, that bed disturbed her. And now, again, her massive, hulking husband was sprawled naked upon it, just as he'd been on their wedding night, the night she had seduced him.

Gwyneth knew she should take a fur rug and sleep in her chair, or on the floor. If she wanted any sleep, that was. And yet... she considered the bed with longing... it was so comfortable. And it was chilly in this chamber with walls of stone. John of Farleigh's massive form would generate more heat to warm her than a blazing fire.

There was no point in further debate; Gwyneth gave in to her desires and crawled again into the massive oak bed beside her husband. Carefully she eased the furs up over her body; cautiously she kept a few inches between her shoulder, her leg, and his. But this time the tension fled fast, and in no time Gwyneth was asleep, in bed beside her husband, where she belonged.

Gwyneth did not waken fully when the carefully measured space between her and John disappeared. Vaguely she was aware he had turned to her and enfolded her in his arms. But her mellow mind sounded no alarm; it felt deliciously good to be pressed to the length of his strong, hard body. Even his sex was long and hard as the length of it nestled in the curls below the swell of her belly. Instinctively, she wriggled her hips to bring the pressure of his rod more heavily against her pelvis. With a groan, she slipped her arms around him. In turn, he pressed his hands against her back and nuzzled his bearded face into her hair. "My dream lover," he whispered, "you've returned. I'd feared you would not."

Gwyneth finally came fully to her senses. Her lashes fluttered and she opened her mouth to speak. But before she could utter even the softest sigh, John's mouth found hers and he plundered it with his tongue.

His kiss made her mind blank to all but the sensation of his mouth on hers. Her fingers twined through his hair as he rolled over, bringing her with him so that she lay against him. Gwyneth threw back her head, gasped for breath, and then she kissed him in return, on his forehead, his bearded chin, his stubbly throat, his furred chest. Again she squirmed against his root, making him slick with the juices of her own need. John responded by tumbling her, not a little roughly, onto the mattress beside him. Pinning her there, he tore off her shift, nudged her thighs apart with his knees and found her cleft with the head of his throbbing cock.

Blindly, Gwyneth reached for him and pulled him down to her by encircling his neck with her arms. She bucked against him, straining until she took all of him inside her. Then she kept him there by wrapping her slim calves about his waist, allowing him only enough freedom to move in the manner she wished him to move.

John obliged. Stroke after powerful stroke he made her his until, with a shudder, he spent himself. And still he was not finished; collapsing neither from exhaustion nor sleep on top of Gwyneth. No, he eased himself from her and came to his knees, and while she lay still beneath him, her hair streaming out across the pillows, her black lashes thick against her cheeks, he slipped his fingers in the musky, moist hollow between her thighs and stroked her heat.

Gwyneth, eyes still closed, moaned with joy and passion, giving herself up to this entirely new and exquisitely delightful experience. Her breasts heaved with every breath. She made little, kitten-like sounds in her throat as her husband's fingers explored the place his shaft had been, and his thumb rubbed the swollen nub that was the core of all her wildest sensations.

"Sweetling, give in to it. Ride it like a stallion or the crest of a wave," he crooned, stroking her forehead first, her breast second. "You're almost there. Come to me. Come to me—"

Crying aloud, Gwyneth spasmed and twitched with her release. Only when she was done and his fingers fell still but remained cupping her woman's flesh, did she open her eyes. Unlike her wedding night, she discovered her husband's eyes wide and thoughtful as he contemplated her face.

"Your hair," he whispered, a note of surprise in his

tone. "In the shadows it's dark, except where it glistens, reflecting the candlelight." With his free hand, he grabbed a fistful and gently stroked it between his fingers and thumb. "It was no dream, then, but you who came to me on our wedding night. You, Gwyneth, my lady wife."

Caught, more embarrassed than fearful, Gwyneth clamped her thighs together, rolling onto her side away from John. She did not consider the tempting view she presented to her husband—a wealth of hair, a slim, narrow back, and lush, rounded buttocks that were enough to make any man's limp cock thicken and stiffen again.

But, though his manhood was willing to rise to the occasion once more, the earl did not begin to make love to his bride again. Instead he settled down beside her and covered them both with the fur rug. Propped on one elbow, he leaned close to Gwyneth and lifted a heavy tangle of hair off her shoulder, exposing one small, pink ear. Dropping a tender kiss there, he whispered, "Sweetling, whatever it is you think that I'm thinking, you are wrong. I'm very well pleased to find it was you."

"You... are?"

"God's tears, yes, I am! I'd thought you a drunken fantasy, and wished by some magic you'd become flesh, warm and real. I'd thought, too, I was married to a shy, frightened wench who would force me to wait long weeks before she'd be willing to share my bed." Placing one callused hand on her shoulder, he gently forced Gwyneth onto her back again so that she had nowhere to look but up at him. "Believe me when I tell you I am pleased my bride is not what I thought she was, and better, she's what I dreamed she might be."

Gwyneth licked her dry lips. "And... and that is?" she asked tentatively.

"A chatelaine who can run my keep and spare me the expense of a steward."

"Oh!"

John laughed a deep, rumbling laugh. "I was only teasing you, my sweetling," he assured her before lowering his lips to those he could no longer resist.

Gwyneth was breathless when John raised his head some long moments later. Trying to gather her wits she admitted, "John, there are things I should tell you. I'm not who you think I am."

He frowned. "You're not Arnulf of Sherborne's daughter?"

"Oh, aye, I'm that, but—"

"You're not my true and wedded wife?"

"I'm that, too, but—"

"Whatever else you may or may not be, Gwyneth, I do not care." With a tired sigh he rolled onto his own back, yet he reached between them and took her hand, threading his fingers through hers. "I am simply relieved that of all the women in the land it was in my best interest to wed, you were that woman." He glanced at her sidelong. "You've no regrets?"

"Nay. None."

"Then if you are happy with this marriage, so too am I. Sweet Mary knows I've enough other concerns. I'll be glad not to have a burdensome wife to worry about as well."

Gwyneth felt numb, but her numbness was buoyant. "John. John?" she whispered his name in the darkness. But he did not reply, and the sound of his even breathing gave her to know he was sleeping. Content, she gave herself up to sleep again, too.

Chapter Eleven

✣   ✣   ✣

When Gwyneth woke, the sun was already ascending. Though the sky was overcast, she knew by the light streaming through the uncovered window that it was well into the morning, and her first thought was that she'd missed chapel at Lauds. Her second thought was that she was alone, her husband gone.

But when she turned away from the window to peer through the parted curtains on the other side of the bed, she saw John seated in his chair. "Good morning, Gwyneth," he greeted her before taking a sip from his pewter mug.

With a start she sat up, oblivious to the fallen coverlet exposing her naked breasts. "You're not drinking beer, are you?" she demanded. "'Tis poison, the stuff you've had around here, and the new batch I'm brewing is not yet ready to drink."

She noticed not only John's purposefully lowered gaze but his smile. Realizing what had brought both about, she immediately covered herself with the sheet.

"Well," she pressed, as if unaware of what had just passed between them, "is it?"

His blue eyes were twinkling as they met hers again. "Beer? Nay, not beer. Watered wine, is all. And here," he gestured to the table beside him, "is fresh bread and cheese and cold beef to break your fast."

"We did miss chapel!"

"Aye, that we did," he nodded. "And the morning's meal as well. At least the one served in the hall.

"Now, don't get up, there's no reason to hurry," he informed Gwyneth quickly when he saw her beginning to scramble off the bed. He also came to his feet and, in a flash, was beside her. Thwarting her exit, he bribed her with a thick slab of warm, fresh bread lathed with sweet honey.

"No reason to hurry! John, the day is half done, and I've much to do. Surely you have, too. I must be—"

Gwyneth was effectively silenced by the wad of bread and dripping honey that her husband popped into her open mouth. Having no choice, she began to chew until she could tear off the remainder.

"I've had few leisure hours in my life," John sighed, "but those that I've had I've taken advantage of well. Since we've lost the best of the morning, let's lose the rest of the day together, what say you?"

Still chewing, she shook her head.

"Listen, lady wife" he said sternly, grabbing her chin between his thumb and finger. "I'm not one for using women badly, and I've never approved of husbands who beat their wives into submissiveness. But I'm the earl here, and wife or no your duty is to obey me, is it not?"

An old anger began to smolder within her, and John saw the fire in Gwyneth's eyes. He was almost tempted to grin, though he thought better of it.

"Don't fight me, woman," he warned, cocking one golden brow. "A man has a right to be lazy and slothful the first few days—nay, weeks—of his marriage. No one thinks the worse of him or his bride for it, either. Beggar or baron, they all understand. So I intend to make today a holiday, for you and me, in any case."

Swallowing, Gwyneth stubbornly shook her head again. "I simply cannot. You've got no one spinning your wool or weaving the cloth or sewing new clothes, and it must be done, milord. I ferreted out among your serving women those with the skills, and informed them that today they would set to work as spinsters. The chamber below the solar is in readiness. I—"

Again, the husband silenced his wife by grabbing the last of the bread she held in her fingers and stuffing it into her mouth. Gwyneth's green eyes widened in annoyance, not only because he'd used the ploy twice but because this time a glob of sticky honey had dropped onto her chest and was running between her breasts.

Before she was free to speak again, John yanked down the sheet to watch the slow progress the golden nectar made as it slid slowly through the valley between Gwyneth's firm, white breasts. "I apologize for that, milady," he said not very sincerely, with a wicked gleam in his eyes. "Let me attend to you immediately."

No fool she, Gwyneth caught the double meaning of his words the moment he uttered them, but it was still too late to escape John's ministrations. In a thrice she was on her back, pressed firmly into the mattress, and he was above her, straddling her, his head tucked down as he tongued up the honey. And tongue it thoroughly he did, like a cat lapping the last drop of cream from the dish. Before he freed her his attention was diverted, and though there were no spills there, he licked her pink nipples until they were standing taut, like little mountain peaks, and Gwyneth herself was sighing.

It was daylight, it was shameful, but her husband's expert lips and fingers made Gwyneth forget all she'd ever been taught and all she'd ever learned from her own experience. Within a short minute she was yielding to him, fairly begging him to take her.

Yet he did not. He threw off all her covers, leaving her naked and exposed and completely his to do with as he wished. He did not throw off his tunic and use her as Gwyneth wished him to. Instead, with killing slowness, he traced the outline of her lips with his tongue, nipped her earlobes and nibbled her neck. He kneaded her breasts gently and swirled his palm over her belly in never-ending circles. He sucked her toes and kissed her instep and then ran the tip of his tongue from her ankle to her calf and up the inside of her thigh until...

Gwyneth's dreamy eyes flew open in shock and she tried to squirm away. But by the time John's tongue began exploring her woman's flesh, her wrists were manacled by his strong fingers and her legs pinned beneath his muscled forearms. Trapped, she could not escape his boldly intimate scrutiny, and unable to avoid his attentions, her body could do naught but ignore her mind and succumb to the exquisite sensations he created. Soon he'd no need to keep her imprisoned beneath him. She opened her legs to him wider and clutched at his fair hair with her fingers. When she breached the wall of passion he was helping her to scale, she cried aloud with her victory, her release.

"Husband," she whispered throatily, her eyes limpid with passion, "come into me. Fill me up. Please."

John's successful attempt to see his bride fully satisfied had not left him unmoved. At her husky beckoning, he tore off his clothing at last and mounted her. With his ram he battered her, though there was no barrier keeping him at bay. Gwyneth took all of him easily, straining to meet him thrust for thrust until, with his own release, he clasped her to him.

The lady held her husband 'til his shuddering ceased. Then she kissed his damp brow and considered trying to explain to him all that he had shown her in the relatively few, short hours they had been together since the morning they had wed. Marriage to the earl, to... What was it she'd heard him called? The Dane. Yes, marriage to this descendant of Viking warriors was not at all as she'd imagined it would be, for her sister or herself. She wanted to admit she was glad it was she who'd become his lady wife, not young Gwendolyn.

But words failed Gwyneth because so much else was still unsaid between them. She had yet to confess her ruse, her deception. As she wondered where, if any place at all, she could begin, what had just transpired between herself and her husband in the past hour made her blush. Suddenly she was ashamed by both her feelings and her actions. Words like depraved, wanton and whore came to mind as she sought to describe herself. Dear Lord, she cried silently, what was it about her battle-scarred husband that made her so changed? Ector, despite his neglect and his cruelties, had never made her forfeit her dignity. But with John—tender and kind as he often was to her—she'd sunk to depths of depravity Gwyneth had heretofore never imagined.

"Sweetling?" John whispered tenderly, seeing her tears when at last he raised his head from her bosom. "Did I hurt you? I did not mean to—" He reached down and pulled the covers over her, for Gwyneth had begun to shiver in her nakedness. "I was crazed with desire, I... What is it?" he demanded as she turned her head away, covered her face with her hands, and began to sob in earnest. "Gwyneth, please."

She shrugged off his attempt to hold her, and, resigned, John waited some moments for her to give vent to her emotions and then to compose herself. But the longer he waited the harder she cried until finally he insisted she explain herself. "What ails you?" he asked sternly. "Tell me now, or I'll send for a midwife."

"I am the midwife of Farleigh, you fool!" she snapped, attempting to dry her damp face on the edge of the linen sheet. "The lord's wife always provides healing herbs to the serfs, attends the serving women's birthings, and sets the knights' broken bones after battles and tournaments. Surely even you know that!"

"Who attends the lord's wife if she's ailing?"

"No one! She drops dead in her tracks!" Gwyneth exploded.

And John grinned. "Nay, I won't let that happen to you, sweetling. I'll attend you myself, if need be."

"You've done enough attending to my person!" she protested, wriggling her rump so that she put the distance of a couple more inches between them. "How could you?" she asked in a reed-thin voice. "I'm your wife, not a scullery maid from the kitchen, or a camp follower, or a village whore! I am your *wife!*" she repeated emphatically.

Though John's smile had been replaced by a frown, now the wrinkles in his brow smoothed. Reaching out, he sought to catch Gwyneth's chin. When she eluded him, he grabbed her jaw purposefully, forcing her to look at him. "You think that what we've done in bed is shameful, is that it? Answer me, wife."

"Not all of it, no," she hedged.

"Where was the wickedness in it? In the wanting or the act?"

"John, please!"

"Answer me."

Gwyneth took a deep breath. "Wanting is natural enough..."

"Aye?"

"Last night. Our wedding night, too. That's the way of it, I suppose, between men and women—when it's good between them," she added as John strained to hear her almost inaudible words.

"But?" he prompted, still holding her chin.

"But today! What you did to me, what I begged from you—No God-fearing woman of noble birth would dare submit—"

"Gwyneth." John grabbed her shoulders and shook her not very gently. "Listen to me and listen well.

"What went between us this morn, in this bed... the first of it, I mean, not the latter... I did because I wished to pleasure you. There is never anything wrong with a man pleasuring his woman. It brought me nearly as much pleasure as it seemed to bring you, as did your telling me of your need for me. A man likes to know that his wo—that his wife—desires him."

He paused, pursing his lips thoughtfully. "Do you understand now?"

Gwyneth chewed her lip. She neither spoke, nodded nor blinked her eyes.

"I'm much older than you, Gwyneth," he continued, "and though some men lie to their women, I tell you true. What went between us each time we bedded was good. I'll not have you feeling shamed or abused because of our love-making. I wish you only to enjoy it and to look forward to joining with me."

"But—"

"But what?"

"You have lived so long as a knight errant, from lord to lord, kingdom to kingdom, battle to battle. Surely you've known many women in your lifetime, most of them—common." Gwyneth blurted out the last word as if it were distasteful. "I can't help feeling that you've made me common," she explained, swallowing hard.

And that made John's bright blue eyes darken as a sudden cloudburst darkens a summer's sky. "Don't be a stupid wench," he ordered through gritted teeth. "I'll forgive you, knowing the sort of tales your mother must have told you, and the ignorant teachings of the nuns who certainly schooled you. But do not continue with such foolish thinking. What man would explore a female's body as I have yours, if she were a dirty, lice-infected peasant? None, I promise you! Only ladies true born and bred receive such attention from their lovers. Damn, woman! I wished to treat you as young Henry surely does Eleanor of Aquitaine!"

With that he leaped out of bed and pulled on his discarded tunic.

Gwyneth watched him, realizing she had tarnished a most rare and golden moment in her life. Worse, she had wounded the only man who had ever put herself and her feelings before himself and his own. Abandoning her covers, she scrambled out of bed and touched his shoulder with her hand, as his back was to her. "John."

He turned around, his face impassive.

"Forgive me. I—" She looked down at her bare

feet, unable to gaze up at his scarred but still attractive face as she confessed, "I have never known a man like you. You are not at all what I expected. I'm confused and a little stupid about such matters as... love-making." She said the word as if it came from a foreign language. In truth, it was a term she'd never heard until her husband spoke it. All her life, matters of mating between men and women were referred to with coarse vulgarities or the very same words used to describe the mating of beasts. Love had never entered into it.

Before she could look up at John again, she felt his arms encircle her waist as he lifted her up to him and kissed her surely. "Let's begin again, you and I, what say you?" he suggested, smiling again. "I'm new to this marriage business, and you're new to everything, I'd imagine."

A notion struck her, but Gwyneth decided to let it go. Now was not the moment to try and remove her husband's misconceptions about her. "Aye," was all she replied, nodding her head for emphasis.

He set her down on her feet and kissed the top of her head. "Then let's have a day of leisure as I suggested earlier. Do you like hawking? We'll go out to the mews and choose a fine falcon for your own. Then we'll go hunting and perhaps have a picnic, if the weather's not too crisp. Later..."

"Yes?"

"We'll repeat some of what we were at a few minutes ago, and perhaps make a babe in the bargain."

Nodding again, Gwyneth smiled. But her smile felt tight because John's comment reminded her of the main reason he'd wed Sir Arnulf's daughter—to get his heirs upon her. That was, of course, the main reason every man wed. Almost never was it a woman's.

Chapter Twelve

✦ ✦ ✦

Miles, John's young squire, did not attempt to intrude on them, so Gwyneth helped her husband with his dressing. In turn, he helped her a little, too, by pulling on and fastening her leather shoes. He made certain she wore a cloak with a warm, fur-lined hood and that she took with her a pair of leather gloves. Then he assisted her down the narrow staircase.

They did not descend all the way to the great hall, however. On the level above the gallery John stopped, knocked, and entered a room that proved to be lined with scrolls and ledgers. In the center was a wide table and at it, seated on a stool, was Gerald. "Good morning, milord, milady," the seneschal greeted them, coming quickly to his feet.

"No need for ceremony, Gerald," John informed him, waving him back onto his perch. "Gwyneth and I stopped by only to inform you that we'll be out most of the day."

"Out?"

"Aye, we're going hawking, and perhaps we'll have a picnic lunch, and then—I know not what." He winked at Gwyneth.

"A picnic lunch? At this time of year, milord?" the

seneschal said, his surprise apparent in his voice. "Well, the weather is not too cold for it, I think," he added upon reflection, smiling at his lord indulgently.

When his dark eyes moved to the lord's lady wife, his smile broadened as he noticed her furious blushing.

"Speaking of picnic baskets," the earl grumbled and, turning away, leaned out into the hallway to shout for his squire. As always, at his lord's beckoning, the boy materialized seemingly from nowhere and the two conversed in low tones just beyond the door.

Gerald came to his feet again and rounded the work table. Softly he said to Gwyneth, "You seem to be getting on well with your new husband."

Chewing her lower lip, she looked at everything in the room but her friend. "As well as can be expected."

"Better than *you* expected, though, is that not so?"

She looked at him sidelong, arching one fine brow. "John—the earl—is not the man I thought him to be," she whispered.

"Nor are you what *he* thought, Lady Gwyneth, of that you may be assured."

Before she could respond to Gerald's comment, John strode back into the room. "I've sent Miles to the kitchen to fetch us a basket," he informed his bride. "Gerald," he went on, "have there been any messages this morning?"

"No, milord. If there had been, you'd have been notified."

"Then we've no reason to believe the baron of Eye is wreaking havoc on my or my neighbors' estates?"

"Nay. We've heard no such thing, though there was a traveler through here sometime before dawn."

"Aye?" John perched on the corner of the table and without looking at her, reached for Gwyneth's hand, which he clasped in his own.

She stared hard at her husband, and the gesture did not escape the seneschal's eyes as he continued: "A monk on his way to the abbey sought to exchange his lame horse for another. As the stable men saw to his needs, he said in passing that King Henry has returned to Anjou. That word reached the keep by way of the servants' prattle not more than an hour ago."

"Hmmm. Interesting, but of no great import to me." He stood and placed his arm possessively across Gwyneth's shoulders. "Then there is naught that requires my immediate attention, Gerald?"

"Nay, not at all, milord. Go, enjoy the day."

"I fully intend to." John winked at Gwyneth, causing her ears to burn. "Good day to you, Gerald," he said cheerily, unaware of his wife's discomfort as he ushered her through the doorway.

Gwyneth could not even look at Gerald as they left his work room.

As soon as they were outdoors, she freed herself from her husband's grip and put some distance between them, though they still walked side by side.

"What's wrong?" John asked her. He came to a halt, forcing her to stop also.

"Nothing," she informed him, looking down at her shoes.

"Something," he insisted.

Slowly, Gwyneth raised her eyes to meet the earl's. "You... you lied to me."

"What!"

At John's loud exclamation, a number of people hurrying about their business in the bailey turned to look at the lord and his wife. Gwyneth felt her color heighten again. Reluctantly she moved closer to her husband in order to whisper, "You deem me as common as any whore."

John's brow knit in confusion. "You're daft, woman! I took a vow to cherish you."

"Words!" she scoffed. "I was right to be ashamed by how you used me in your bed. Yet I expected you to feign respect for me before your seneschal. Instead you treated me as a soldier does a slut."

"God's teeth! How did I treat you so?"

John's voice was as loud as Gwyneth's was soft. Again she glanced about at the others in the yard. Though she found no one bold enough to be blatantly staring, her mortification grew. Beneath her breath she informed him, "You fondled me, your looks were lewd, you pawed—"

Before Gwyneth was quite sure what had happened, her husband cut her off by grabbing her about the waist, lifting her off her feet, and carrying her into the shadows. There he pressed her against the stone wall of the keep. When he set her down, she was pinned on both sides by his muscled arms and virtually enfolded in the wealth of his cloak. "Pawed?" he repeated, his voice low, now little more than a growl. "I'll show you what it is to be pawed, my prissy little wench."

Before he was done speaking, John had reached one hand inside Gwyneth's cloak and slipped his fingers into the V-neckline of her bliaut. With only her thin under tunic between them, he began to knead first one breast, then the other. Gwyneth's eyes grew round, but nearly all she could see were her husband's own eyes, so close was his face to hers.

"This is pawing," he declared. "And this."

Immediately, he reached both his arms around her, hitched up her tunics, and began to squeeze the fleshy curves of her buttocks.

"This, too."

With the speed of a viper he pulled one arm back around and thrust his hands between his wife's legs.

Gwyneth squeaked, having purposely strangled an outraged cry. From a lifetime of experience she knew to keep her humiliations secret. Besides, though his handling of her was anything but tender, it was not hurtful, either. In fact, John's expert stroking was making her moist.

She'd barely had a moment to recognize that development when John raised his head. "Lewd glances? Is this how I looked at you?" he asked, his lids drooping sensually to all but cover his cerulean eyes, his lips parting as he ran his tongue over them salaciously, hungrily, and his mouth curling up at one corner in a wicked, predatory smirk. Without warning he descended, crushing his mouth to Gwyneth's. It was all she could do to breathe—If he'd not been cupping her bottom from both front and back, she might have crumpled to her knees.

All at once he released her completely, letting her tunics and cloak fall back into place as he stepped away. "I felt protective and possessive of you, my lady wife. Every male, be he beast or man, behaves the same toward his mate. 'Tis a pity you feel compelled to twist a man's natural instincts until they seem depraved."

He turned and strode away, and she watched his back with narrowed eyes and a set chin. If John of Farleigh had been any other man, she would have lost sight of him as he approached the lowered bridge that spanned the moat, connecting this yard to the outer bailey. But John of Farleigh was no other man; he stood a head taller than all the rest. His burnished gold hair was like a beacon, and she could not take her eyes off him, until she forced herself to. Then she walked, with forced casualness, back to the keep's front portal. She was just about to go inside again when she turned, her eyes straining for a glimpse of her husband. When she did not see him she found herself running not away, but after him.

Gwyneth caught up with John at the mews. His back was to her; he seemed not to know she was there as he spoke gently and sweetly to a peregrine perched on his forearm. She hesitated, wondering whether to stay or to go. But just as she turned to leave, John spoke.

"Are you satisfied, milady, that I have never demeaned you by my actions, whether in the privacy of our chamber or the company of others?"

Turning back, Gwyneth stood still, her eyes taking in all the birds in their cages as if studying them was her intent. She did not immediately reply, and her husband set about securing a little hood on his falcon's head. Only when it seemed he might stride past and abandon her again did she speak.

"Forgive me, milord," Gwyneth whispered. "Apparently my knowledge of marriage... of the ways of husbands and wives is... is limited. I appear to have misunderstood, misinterpreted—"

"Which of these hawks might you like for your own?" John interrupted softly, settling his falcon on a perch before closing the distance between himself and his wife.

Grateful for his apparent understanding and thankful for a change in topic, once again Gwyneth looked around at the powerful birds, each bearing the distinctively curved beaks and talons that marked them as hunters.

"I—don't know. Mustn't one train a hawk from the

day it is hatched?"

"These are all trained," John explained, feeding a few from his gauntleted hand. "Mine—Baron, I call him—I've had but a few short months. But we made friends from the first and Odo, one of my guards, had raised and trained him well.

"Pick one," he urged, and though she was reluctant, Gwyneth finally pointed to a small, delicate-looking bird. "Ah, a little sparrow hawk," he smiled, lifting it from its perch. "Put your gloves on, Gwyneth."

From her belt she removed the pair of leather gloves and slipped them on her fingers.

"Hold your hand out."

She did as her husband instructed and he laughed.

"Not like you're begging for alms, sweetling. Like this." He showed her and then set the bird above her wrist where the cuff of her glove protected her flesh and her clothing from the animal's claws. The sparrow hawk's wings fluttered and Gwyneth jumped, her arm flailing in the air. The bird flew off and returned to its perch.

"What do you know of hawking?" John asked patiently, frowning curiously at his wife.

"Nothing."

"Nothing! But not a lady in the land, on this or the other side of the Channel, does not go hawking! Even yeomen and priests go hawking. Surely Arnulf—"

"Of course my father enjoyed the sport. At least he did before his age caught up with him. But I did not live long in my father's house."

"Ah, the convent." As he spoke, John busied himself again with the birds. Gwyneth felt less confused and intimidated when he was not studying her so intently. For a mad moment, she actually considered that this might be the opportunity to admit to her husband the truth of their situation, their marriage. To begin by explaining where she had spent most of the years of her life would be reasonable.

But then the possibility that he might walk away from her for good seemed an unreasonable risk. She had felt awful when he'd walked away from her for a moment. So she said simply, "Aye. The convent."

"Which one?"

"Abingdon."

"What did the nuns teach you?"

"Mostly to pray. Nothing about hawking."

"Or men and marriage."

John uttered the last as he rose from a crouching position and spun about to face Gwyneth again. He so startled her, she backed up and hit her head on a timber.

"Sweetling," he sighed, pulling her into his arms and caressing her uncovered head with both gentle stroking and light kisses. "I forget how young and innocent you are. You've a great deal to learn. As I do," he added, releasing her a little so that he could look into her eyes, "about being a husband. You know, of course, that as youngest son, I never expected to wed, let alone become earl." His gaze wandered and for a second he stared off into the darkened space above the rafters. "Now my life is unlike anything I'd ever dreamt it might be. I live nearly every moment by my instincts and my wits." His eyes settled again on Gwyneth as he admitted, with a smile, "Sometimes I make mistakes. I hope, as my lady wife, you will forgive me."

Sweet Mary, mother of Jesu! Whatever made and shaped a man like you, John of Farleigh? Gwyneth wondered. She could fathom no explanation, but she felt sure there was no one like him anywhere, not even Gwendolyn's young Thomas.

But when she replied, her tone was light. "A lord never needs forgiving, sir. Not an earl, in any case. Your word, like the king's, is law, and your actions, like the Pope's, divinely inspired."

John considered her through narrowed eyes. "I believe you are jesting with me, milady."

"A wife's privilege, is it not?"

"Do not abuse your wifely privileges, or I may enforce my husbandly rights at times and places you will not deem suitable." He glanced quickly about the mews. "Here, for example."

"I think not." She dared to smile light-heartedly, something she'd done infrequently in life. As she backed up through the doorway she reminded him, "You promised me an outing, and I intend to hold you to it!"

"But I thought hawking was the first of our plans."

"Must it be?" She frowned as John followed her into the yard.

"No. A ride and a picnic will suffice, if we don't find other diversions." He stopped and looked around; as Gwyneth followed his gaze, he found what he was searching for. "Here comes Miles, with our mounts and our provisions."

"You are coming, too?" she asked the boy as he climbed onto his own horse after his lord and lady were seated.

"Of course, milady. A squire follows his master everywhere."

Gwyneth looked to John for confirmation, half-hoping he would release the young man from his obligations. He must have read the message in her eyes, because he said to his squire, "I think I can ensure my lady's safety, Miles. Why don't you take the rest of the day for yourself and see what amusements you can find here about?"

"But, milord!"

"No arguing, lad. There are some duties a man must perform unassisted," he explained, and his comment elicited a blush not only in his bride, but on his squire's downy cheeks as well. Still, young Miles obediently turned his horse around and walked it back to the stables, allowing John and Gwyneth to ride through the gate in the curtain walls completely unattended.

The sky was overcast with heavy, wintry clouds, and the wind was brisk. But galloping across open fields kept the riders warm enough. When they settled on a place to take their meal, they did so in the forest where the trees sheltered them and kept the little fire John built from blowing out.

"Cook's food is more palatable," John commented as he licked his greasy fingers, "since you've come to Farleigh. Not that it was inedible before," he went on as he burrowed into the basket looking for some other dish to feast upon. "Still, it's definitely improved."

"Thank you. It's my recipes, I think."

"Yours or your mother's?"

"Mine. My mother died when I was barely out of swaddling."

"I'm sorry. I knew my mother and loved her well. I've fond memories of her."

"She died though, too, when you were gone to foster, did she not?"

John, sprawled on a rug with his head propped up on one hand, glanced quickly at Gwyneth, who sat cross-legged beside him. "That's true enough, but how would you know? Surely you were not yet born."

"Oh, I was born," she assured him, recalling that she'd attended the funeral mass for Hugh of Farleigh's lady wife. She'd been about twelve years old at the time.

"Well, no more than a babe, then," John persisted.

"You flatter me," Gwyneth said shyly, anxiously, turning her head away. When she dared to look back she admitted, "I'm not so young as you think, milord. In fact, an unmarried woman of my age would most likely be called a spinster."

As was his habit, John reached out and held Gwyneth's chin between his thumb and finger. He studied her purposefully. "Lady wife of mine, you're neither unwed nor do you spin thread, so that term cannot apply to you. And if you've lived a few more than a score of years it bothers me not. I'd rather a woman for a wife than a child."

Gwyneth bit her lower lip, hesitating. Finally, though, she gave in and asked, "Have you lived much among women, John? Young or old, or even children?"

With a shake of his head and a smile, he pushed himself up so he sat as Gwyneth did, directly across from her. "I understand if you wish to know more about your husband, sweetling. But 'tis an odd question to ask."

"You don't have to answer if you don't wish to."

"I'll answer." He shrugged. "Girl children, no. I only had brothers, you know, and they were all older than I. I suppose there were girls in the castle, but when you're a child, you don't think of your friends as children. You're all the same, except for your elders who are simply, to your mind, quite aged."

Gwyneth nodded, understanding him exactly.

"As a knight I lived on my own during my travels,

and with other knights when I was bound to service. Though I've briefly known a comely wench or two," he admitted, grinning sheepishly at his wife, "I've mostly lived a man among men.

"Why?" he asked. "Is there something you feel I should know about the fairer sex, in order better to serve you?"

Gwyneth quickly shook her head, fighting the flush that crept up her throat at his double entendre. "No," she said. "I just wondered."

"I wonder about you, too."

"You do?" Her lashes fluttered. "What do you wonder?"

"Why a maid as beautiful and talented as you did not find herself wed as soon as she was able to bear children."

Gwyneth closed her eyes and inhaled deeply. When she opened them again she promised, "Someday I will recount my childhood for you. But not now, please." She stood and held out her hand to him, and when John took it, rising, she looked up into the trees. "I think if we were out of the forest we would find that it was snowing. What say you?"

"I say you may be right. Let's go and see."

Gwyneth packed up their basket and John helped her mount. When they rode out from cover of the trees, they found her prediction to be correct. Already a thin carpet of snow lay over the stiff grass in the meadows.

"I love the first snow," Gwyneth confessed. "It makes the whole world so pretty and clean. It sparkles in the sun and the moonlight, and it hides all the mud and the filth.

"I know where a stream runs close to here," she pointed. "I'd wager it looks pretty as a tapestry right now. Would you like to see it?"

"You're not too cold?"

"I'm fine."

"Lead on, then. But stay close to my side. We've only one sword between us."

Gwyneth paid no heed to John's reference to Elwood of Eye. The crazed and hateful baron had no place in the world in which she was now living. That world, in which the snow fell in flakes as big as daisies, was a beautiful place untouched by either pain or danger.

The stream was delightful to see. Clear and gray, it ran through the white snow blanketing its banks like liquid silver. They allowed the horses to drink from it before following it along, chatting of nonessential things.

Suddenly Gwyneth reined in her palfrey. "John, no! We shouldn't have come here."

"Why not? I thought it was your intention."

"Nay." Shaking her head, she turned her horse and trotted away from the water's edge. "I wasn't thinking. 'Twas habit."

"But, Gwyneth, the manor's just beyond that rise. You can even see the town if you look hard." As he spoke, John shaded his eyes and peered in the direction of Sherborne.

"No, please!"

She turned her horse completely around and kicked its sides until it lurched forward at a brisk jog. Immediately, John on his destrier was beside her. Grabbing her reins, he forced her to halt. "Gwyneth, what is the matter? Come, let's go visit your father now. He missed our wedding; he's been unable to travel to Farleigh. Surely he'd like to see you."

"I'm cold!" she complained. "I wish to go home."

"Home lies directly over the hill, and I'm sure

there's a warm fire blazing."

"Not Arnulf's home, *our* home. Farleigh. I wish to return to Farleigh."

John's displeasure showed on his face. "This is foolish nonsense, milady. I won't have it. Now we're here, we're going to pay your father our respects."

"Nay."

The word hung in the air, more brittle, more icy, than the wind blowing their capes about them. Gwyneth saw the look in her husband's eyes, surprised that she would resist him so emphatically. She hated doing it, she truly had no wish to thwart him this way. If it were possible she might have explained, but it was not so she made no attempt.

Yet she would not be swayed. John could give her honeyed words or brutal blows, but Gwyneth would not bend. For suddenly, by her very proximity to Sherborne Manor, she had become her old self again. During the past few days she had felt naive, confused, helpless, and even a little smitten in the company of her new husband. But no more. Not now. At this moment she felt her years and knew her purpose, which was solely to protect her sister, Gwendolyn.

"No?" John leaned in his saddle, bringing his face closer to Gwyneth's. The wind had picked up and the heavy, swirling snow made it difficult to see. "You dare defy me, Gwyneth?"

"I fear I must, milord."

"Woman!"

She shook her head adamantly. "I will not go there. Nothing you can do will make me go there."

"We'll see about that!"

Digging her heels into her mare's sides, Gwyneth bounded off. But her little palfrey was no match for the earl's steed, and in seconds he was upon her, dragging her from her mount onto his. Gwyneth struggled fiercely, finally escaping when John halted and began to dismount. But it did her no good. Few could win a footrace against a man with legs as long and powerful as her husband's. She certainly could not, not with her skirts whipping about her ankles as she ran and the snow beneath her shoes as slick as oil.

In seconds John was upon her again. Grabbing her about her waist they tumbled to the ground together, there to grapple and roll, kick and squirm until the man had his wife firmly trapped beneath him, his knees straddling her hips, his hands pinning her arms in the snow above her head.

"I will humor you as best I can, Gwyneth, but you dare not defy me in this manner," he informed her, not at all winded.

And she replied breathlessly, but with a cold determination that surprised him, "I've already defied you! It is done! And I care not for being humored. 'Tis worse than being shown your true feelings."

"I did not say I lied to you."

"It matters not if you have! What matters is that I *will not* return to my father's house, not now, not ever!"

Gwyneth's face was flushed with emotion and pink with the cold. Her green eyes sparkled, too, and though it may have been anger or hate or perversity that made them so, the result was the same: She looked beautiful. John, seeing her thus, hesitated. At first that uncertainty simply fueled his rising ire. As Gwyneth glared up at him, she noticed that the scar on his cheek seemed to darken and recede even deeper into his flesh. But then he let his anger go, and he let her go with a movement that left both his hands suddenly high in the air.

Instinctively Gwyneth cowered, rolling onto her side and covering her head with her arms. If John had not been straddling her, she'd have curled up into a ball.

"Beat me!" she shrieked, still hiding herself as best as she was able. "Beat me 'til I'm black with bruises, my eyes are swollen shut, and my arms so sore I can't lift them. Beat me, I do not care. My father will not see me this day unless you carry my corpse to him!"

"Sweetling." Despite his need to talk above the wind, John's voice was low. Rolling onto the ground beside Gwyneth, he raised her up, pulling her into his lap and cradling her against his broad chest. "Is that what Arnulf did to you? Did he beat you 'til you could neither see nor walk?"

She made a sound like a laugh and nearly choked on it. "Nay, my father never beat me bad enough to send me to my bed. He needed me to work, you see, and a slackard daughter he'd not tolerate. No, your loyal knight and vassal, who kept his oath to you when all thought you were dead, beat me just enough to bend me to his will, never enough that I could not serve him."

"God's wounds!" John swore as he rocked Gwyneth gently to and fro, like a babe in her mother's arms. "Why didn't you tell me?"

"What?" Tears streamed down her face as she looked up at her husband. "That my father beat me? Is that of some import to anyone in this realm?" She laughed again, a dry, mirthless laugh. "I think not. Besides, I did not live with him much of my life, only as a child and now of late. But he—"

"What? Gwyneth, tell me."

"He... gave me to one who used me ill, and I hate

him for it."

"Who? Who was it? The abbess of the monastery where you were schooled? Who hurt you?"

She shook her head, tucking it beneath his bearded chin. "I cannot speak of it now. Besides, you do not really wish to know."

"I do!"

"No, you don't. The day that you do know, you'll also know I was right in this. It's something you'll wish you'd remained ignorant of all of your days."

"You're speaking in riddles."

"Aye."

"You're shivering."

"I was not lying when I said I was cold."

"And you spoke true when you said you wished to go home to Farleigh Castle?" he asked and felt her nod again against his chest. "Then that is where we will go, right now."

"You're not going to try to force me to visit the manor?"

"Sweetling, I'll never force you to do anything. It's not my way."

"Then you'll be a popular but very poor earl," she said, attempting a joke as they came to their feet.

"Being an earl is not the most important thing to me."

"What is?" Gwyneth asked as he led her back to their horses.

"I think I'm just beginning to discover. When I know for sure, I will tell you of it."

"Now, though," he said, cupping his hands so that she could hoist herself up into her saddle, "let's get you home to bed. You need a fire and hot broth and mulled wine. Perhaps, too, the heat of a man's body beside you to take the chill from your bones." He stood a moment beside her palfrey and looked up at Gwyneth hopefully. "Perhaps?"

"Perhaps," she agreed, and she could not help smiling.

Chapter Thirteen

✥ ✥ ✥

Gwyneth was perched in a window seat, keeping an eye on the women who'd been set to spinning thread and weaving cloth of the wool that had lain in storage since the spring shearing. In her lap she had a length of the first fabric which, though neither dyed nor bleached, she was fashioning into a shirt for her husband to wear beneath his armor. She liked listening to the gossipy chatter of the spinsters who, though tradition held they should all be old and virginal, shared confidences among themselves about their husbands and lovers. For the first time in her life, Gwyneth could appreciate their jokes and their stories. She might have had one or two to tell herself, except that she would never say anything that might reflect badly on the earl. Besides, she considered herself privileged to know her husband's personal quirks.

"Milady!"

She glanced up from her sewing to find Bess standing in the doorway. "Yes? What is it?"

"A message, milady."

"If you're looking for Lord John, he's certainly not here. In truth, he's in the bailey below, working with his men." She glanced out the window behind her to verify that fact. She could see him, in helmet and mail, leading his knights in practice combat.

"Nay, milady," Bess continued, making her way through the wheels, the looms, and the women working them. "The news the messenger brings is for you."

"For me!" She jumped up, tossing her sewing onto the seat. "Who is he?" she asked, forcing the girl to turn around and following her quickly out into the hallway. "What does he say?"

"I've no idea who he is or where he's from, Lady Gwyneth. Only that he asked to speak to you, not Lord John."

"To me?" she demanded as they began scurrying down the stairs. "Did he refer to me by name?"

"I wouldn't know that," Bess admitted, giving her mistress a sidelong, curious glance. "One of the guards caught me in passing and begged me to fetch you. He told me to tell you a messenger brings you news, and that he must speak only to you."

Gwyneth stopped on the landing one short flight above the great hall. "Send him in here," she ordered, opening the door to one of the little rooms in the gallery. "Now."

Bess nodded, raised the hem of her bliaut higher above her ankles, and headed down the remaining stairs at a run. Gwyneth remained in the doorway, and as soon as the messenger came into view, she ushered him into the room.

"What news do you bring me? Is it from Arnulf of Sherborne?"

"Nay, milady." He shook his head. "'Tis from Thomas of Brandywine."

"Thomas!" Gwyneth pressed a fist to her bosom and sank down onto a stool. "Has something happened? Is there trouble?"

"Nay," the messenger said again.

"What is it, then?" she demanded.

"He said to inform you, the earl of Farleigh's lady wife, that he and his new bride have completed their journey. Both are safe and well."

"Thank God!" She waited expectantly. "Well? Is there nothing else?"

"Nay, milady. That's all of it."

For a moment Gwyneth was disturbed until she realized there was little else Thomas could tell her. It was too soon to know if Gwendolyn was with child, and certainly Arnulf had neither been told nor discovered the fate of either of his daughters. At least the young man had been thoughtful enough to advise her of her sister's circumstances. Gwendolyn was with Thomas, they were wed, and they had made the journey safely to Brandywine.

"That's enough, then, I suppose," she decided aloud, smiling graciously as she came to her feet. "Let me escort you down to the hall and I'll see you're fed and have a place to rest before you are on your way again."

"Thank you, milady."

No sooner had Gwyneth collared Paddy, sending the messenger to the kitchen in his care, than John burst into the hall surrounded by a cluster of his men. She watched him for a moment—he'd removed his helmet and tossed it to his squire—and she thought how handsome he was with his touseled golden hair and striking blue eyes. She also thought of the past two weeks they had shared together. He had treated her gently, as if she were a delicate, fragile thing, and tenderly, as if she were the love of his life. It had been almost as if he were courting her as he had not done before their marriage.

He began to move off and she called to him. Glancing about the room, he saw her and nodded distractedly. When Gwyneth approached he said, "What is it, lady wife? I must make haste."

"Why? Where are you going?"

"There's been news, and I must act swiftly."

"News? What kind of news? The baron of Eye has not sent his men marauding again, has he? There's been no trouble at Sherborne?" she asked, clutching his arm.

"No. The opposite, in fact," he told her before turning and barking quick orders to several of his men, who quickly hurried off to do his bidding.

"What is it?" she pressed, forcing John to look at her again.

"There's been a message."

Gwyneth gasped. So he *had* heard the news Thomas' man had brought her. Was he suspicious? Where did he—

"Elwood of Eye's been seen in Southampton, set to sail the Channel," John explained, interrupting her thoughts. "We think he's following King Henry into Anjou."

Exhaling her relief she said, "That's good, is it not?"

"Aye. It gives us a little time, if we act quickly and together."

"I don't understand," she admitted, frowning in her confusion.

"Together, all the landholders in the vicinity of Eye intend to fortify their estates against future attacks by Elwood's men."

"What?"

Taking her elbow, John led Gwyneth to a corner of the hall, away from the bustle of activity that was growing all around them.

"I haven't time for this, Gwyneth," he said impatiently. "Listen quietly, and I'll explain what I'm about."

"Where are you going?"

He silenced his wife with a look. "To aid my fellow barons."

"You were simply going to leave, without a word to me?" she asked as she deduced the truth of it.

Sir Lionel came up behind John and coughed until he gained his lord's attention. For a few seconds they conversed before Lionel went off again.

When John returned his attention to his wife, he seemed not only distracted but irritated. "Elwood is gone, and we crippled his forces some in the battle a fortnight past. Do you remember that?" he asked, and she nodded. "Surely now there will be a lull in his attacks against his neighbors and mine."

"But—"

"Gwyneth, please!" he said, his tone short. Immediately, she fell silent. "Neville of Kurth has proposed a plan— 'Tis he who sent me the message I only just received. If all of us with demesnes in these parts prepare ourselves for a full scale siege by Eye's men, we'll be better able to defend ourselves when he resumes the attacks."

"Mayhap he won't. Mayhap he'll stay in Anjou, or wherever he's off to."

John sighed. "Don't be foolish, Gwyneth. He'll return. After all, Walter, his son, remains here."

"Then how do you know Walter won't lay siege to one estate or another, even though the baron is away?"

"I don't. No one can know that. But from what I've learned, it seems the son does nothing without the father's blessing. We are hoping he'll lie low as a dog in the grass until his father returns."

"And if he does? What do you intend to do meanwhile?"

"As I said—help fortify my neighbors' estates."

"Personally." Gwyneth crossed her arms over her chest and pursed her lips together. "You are personally going to carry oil for boiling up to the top of the parapets, and boulders for the catapults, and—"

"Be still, woman," her husband warned.

"I won't be still!" She uncrossed her arms and balled her hands into fists. "You are bored with being a husband, with having nothing to do but manage your own estate! You intended to sneak away like a fox from the chicken pen, without a word to me, your own wife. And all to play soldier!"

"I cannot believe I am hearing this."

"Men!" she cried exasperatedly. "As children you play with wooden swords almost before you've learned to walk, and you keep on playing with your weapons 'til you're too old to seat a horse—or you're dead, whichever comes first."

Uncharacteristically, Gwyneth seemed oblivious to the curious looks of the servants and men-at-arms in the hall; her husband was not. With a hand on her shoulder he pushed her against the wall and held her there. Leaning his head close to hers he whispered harshly, "You are behaving like a shrew, my lady wife, and attempting to shame me in front of my own people. Behave yourself, or I'll be forced to punish you."

"Punish me!" she hissed, her green eyes flashing. "You *are* just like all other men!"

"I think not," he said quietly.

"Then why are you running off when it is so unnecessary? Your castle is battle-ready; no force could penetrate its walls. Why must you, a lord—an earl descended of Danish jarls—put your life in danger to aid other barons who were not clever enough to prepare their homes for siege?"

"You've answered your own question, Gwyneth. My home is a castle built long before King William's time. All within are as safe as any can be.

"But my neighbors' baronies are small and vulnerable in comparison. Many are no more than a keep upon a motte. Those whose lands border on Eye's have endured many raids and skirmishes; they've lost property and men. And there are the towns, too, many like Sherborne, completely open to attack. They all need better defenses. The more men there are to help with the preparations, the faster all will be completed. We don't know how much time we have, Gwyneth."

John's voice had lost its edge as he explained the situation to his wife in greater detail. When she spoke again her voice, too, was gentler. "But why must *you* go? Cannot you simply send some of your men? Surely Bruno, Lionel and the captain of your guard understand what needs to be done. The others would follow their directions."

"*I* am their lord."

"But you are my husband!"

"I do not see how that creates any conflict."

"Nay?" Gwyneth's voice was a whisper against John's cheek. "I suppose you would not." Determinedly, she pushed his hand from her shoulder and strode away. "Go, then," she called back to him airily, waving one hand in dismissal. "But you'll have no one but yourself to blame if, in your absence, Eye's men attack and Farleigh falls to them." She paused and glanced back at her husband. "What will you be called then?

Not John of Farleigh. John of Nothing? John of Nowhere? Oh!" Gwyneth donned an exaggerated, wide-eyed expression and exclaimed, "You'll be The Dane—the wandering, landless knight you always were—and wish to be again!"

With that parting comment, Gwyneth ran fast up the stairs, all the way to the top of the keep where she entered the solar and bolted the door behind her.

Still below in the hall, John ran one hand over his flushed face before slamming the other against the wall. If it hurt, he made no sign.

"Miles," he barked, stomping toward the staircase, "I need your assistance. I intend to be gone from here as quickly as I'm able."

Gwyneth sat in the solar's window seat. Though she wished not to, she was drawn to watch the ground below where her husband and a sizable force from the castle's complement of guards were mounting their destriers and riding away.

"Damn you!" she muttered, her hands clenched in anger. "There's no need for you to do this, none at all. But you like the risk, you thrill to the danger. And I know, John of Farleigh," she informed his small figure as it disappeared from her sight, "you are hoping Eye's men find you so that you can battle them. Ach!"

In disgust she turned away from the window. She was thinking he might just as well attach a pennant to his lance that read, *I am the earl of Farleigh; come, try to slay me!* For with his height and his bulk, even among a thousand other knights, he would be recognizable to any of Eye's outriders.

"Ah!" Gwyneth winced and doubled over as a painful cramp clutched at her belly. Bringing her knees up to ease the pain, her thoughts rushed ahead nastily. I would be better off, she told herself, were my husband dead. Not only would Gwendolyn be safe from him, I, too, would be free—and one of the richest ladies in the realm!

A knock at the door interrupted her mean musings. "Lady Gwyneth? May I speak with you?"

"Aye." She eased herself up and crossed the floor. As she unbarred the door, she attempted to ignore the rising and ebbing cramps in her belly. "What is it, Gerald?"

The seneschal entered the solar as Gwyneth hobbled back to the window seat. "Lord John asked me to speak with you."

She snorted and looked away. "What of?"

"He wished me to assure you that he's left the castle well-armed. He wants you to know you'll be quite safe here until he and the men who ride with him return."

"I know that."

"He also bade me tell you…"

As Gerald paused, hesitating, Gwyneth turned to peer up at him. "What?" she demanded testily. "What else did he tell you to say?"

"Ah… The earl suggests you learn the more docile, obedient ways of a good wife, mayhap by conferring with a woman who's been wed far more years than you. He would be reluctant, he told me, to have to punish you until you learn your rightful place."

"My rightful place!" she exploded, her eyes growing round as a cat's in the dark. "That arrogant oaf can take the high road to hell!" she swore, her face flushing with anger. "I've had two decades of being married—the earl's had but two weeks! What does he know of good wives? Better yet, I ask you, what does he know of good husbands?"

For a minute Gerald stood silently, his hands folded in front of him, his eyes cast on the floor. Then he raised his head and said, "Lady Gwyneth, you may not think it my place, but... I've known you since we were childhood friends, and I feel... I feel I must defend my lord to you."

"I'll not hear it."

"But I shall speak it, nonetheless." He took a step forward as Gwyneth turned her face away. "Lord John has lived a hard life, wandering hither and yon, always alone, sleeping on stone floors and rushes or on rocky ground in the wind and the rain, the snow and the cold. Though gently born, as a man he's known little comfort and little tenderness. Yet I am surprised by how good a husband he's been to you these short weeks."

"How good a husband!" she repeated, her head snapping back as she turned again to Gerald.

"How good a husband," he said again, nodding. "He's no experience at it. But I think, Lady Gwyneth, even you must agree he's made every effort to be considerate and caring toward you. He has no example to follow, no one to advise him, and I believe—" Gerald straightened his shoulders and raised his chin— "I believe my lord's done an admirable job."

"Oh, you do, do you?"

"Aye, Gwynnie," he insisted, using the name he'd used for her in childhood, "I do. He's a good man and he's been fair to you. Admit it. He's done naught for you to be displeased about."

"But I am displeased," she insisted stubbornly, "for every time he takes himself off, he tries to do so without bidding me farewell, let alone advising me of his plans."

Gerald frowned. "I suppose Ector of Durningham always came to you and coddled you before riding out?"

"Of course not. But I did not care—"

Gwyneth stopped herself, but she'd already said too much. Besides, her tear-bleary eyes were enough for the seneschal to see through his lady's shrewishness.

"So that's the way of it, is it?" Gerald surmised. "You care for your lord husband and you fear for his safety."

"Well," Gwyneth sniffed, "I should like to have him around, since I took great risk to wed him in the first place. But..." She looked down at her lap. "... He does not seem content with being lord of his demesne. I think, mayhap, he misses the mercenary life."

Shaking his head, Gerald came closer, fell to one knee, and looked up at Gwyneth. "Milady," he said gently, "trust me when I tell you your husband cares for you as much as you do he. Lord John would certainly rather be in your bed at night than enduring the elements. He's no longer an impulsive youth, Lady Gwyneth. He has seen it all and done it all, and surely he has no desire to be anywhere but here at home.

"As for the business that took him away now, 'tis not war, you know. He is merely aiding his neighbors who are threatened by a mutual foe. There's no danger in it. Think of him not as a warrior out to do battle, but an architect designing fortifications."

Gwyneth wiped her nose on the back of her hand. "Very well," she agreed. But as Gerald stood and turned to leave she added, "He must think I'm a witch, considering how I behaved in the hall."

"Nay, I'm sure he doesn't," he assured her, turning back with a smile. "But may I suggest, milady, that when Lord John returns to Farleigh, you tell him the truth. All of the truth."

"I can't."

"You can. Your mission, as it were, is accomplished."

Gwyneth's eyes widened. "What do you know?" she demanded.

"I know that your sister is well and truly wed, and residing with her new husband on his family's estate of Brandywine."

"You spoke to the messenger!"

"Aye." He nodded his head slowly. "As seneschal of Farleigh, it is my duty to know all that goes on here, especially if it involves intrigue."

"I'm not involved in any intrigue!"

"Nay? Well, you are certainly not being honest with your lord husband, and as he wed you in good faith, I think you owe him the truth now."

"I will think on it," Gwyneth promised, her words clipped.

"Very well, milady," Gerald said, and this time he did quit the room.

When she was alone again, Gwyneth doubled over in pain. She knew her monthly flux was upon her, and she surmised, based on years of past experience, that her hellish temper was due far more to her woman's complaint than to anything John had either said or done. She wished she did not have this cursed discomfort to deal with every month, not only because of the unpleasantness, but because if the flux did not visit her it would mean she was with child. Were she with child, Gwyneth was more than half certain John would not annul his marriage to her when she confessed her deceit. But as long as she remained barren, the chance was very real he would cast her out.

Gwyneth did not want to be cast out of Farleigh or the earl's life. A few weeks earlier, she realized, it would not have mattered to her at all; in truth, she expected it. But now it mattered very much and she feared the prospect more than she would ever have admitted.

Chapter Fourteen

✥   ✥   ✥

Gwyneth was in the kitchen, not just supervising but up to her elbows in flour as she helped prepare the sweets that were the Christmastide tradition. It was only a few short days 'til the celebration of Christ's birth, and already Cook had broths simmering and meats roasting in anticipation of the feasting to come.

But the lady of Farleigh worried that there would be no great feasting, with so many of the castle's soldiers, including the earl himself, still away. Her husband had been gone long weeks now, and not a word had been sent to her. The few short messages carried to the castle were directed to Gerald, and if there were more to them than the sparse facts he in turn related to her, Gwyneth knew not. All she did know was that there had been no trouble, no sightings, even, of Eye's men, and that the men of Farleigh would try to be home by Christmas Day.

Perspiring in the hot kitchen, Gwyneth wiped her brow. Bess, beside her, glanced her way and laughed. "Milady, you look like a spirit, you do! Hardly an inch of you is not covered in white."

"You're little better," she pointed out, shaking her uncovered head so that the flour, settled like a layer of dust in her hair, puffed out in a great, white cloud.

Bess sneezed and shook her own head. "But I'm just a lowly servant. You're a great lady."

"A great lady covered in flour—which I would not be if Paddy had not dropped the sack as he pulled it from the shelf above me," she added, turning pointedly to the scullion working beside them.

"I apologized, milady."

"That you did and I forgave you. You're just lucky it's the Christmas season and the spirit of forgiveness is heavy all around. Bess—I need more honey. And Paddy, where are those baskets of apples I told you to bring up from the stores?"

Both servants had just disappeared to get what their mistress asked for, when Gwyneth felt two arms snake about her waist. Startled, she gasped and whirled about within her captor's arms only to find it was her husband embracing her. "Milord."

"Milady," he smiled.

His beard was long and his hair unwashed; he smelled of his horse and of his unwashed clothes. But Gwyneth was thrilled to bursting at finding him home again.

"I did not know when you'd be returning, if even you would."

"You don't think I could leave you too long, do you, sweetling? For the unfortunate truth of the matter is," he leaned closer and whispered in her ear, "my lover no longer comes to me in dreams. I must, instead, attend my lady wife if I'm to see her at all."

When John pulled back, Gwyneth was blushing furiously. Fortunately no one could tell, coated by a dusting of flour as she was. "You shouldn't say such things in front of the servants," she admonished him.

"Oh, aye! As if you ever give a care for what you say to me in front of my staff!" he chided gently.

"I'm sorry for that. I should never—"

"—Have spoken thusly to my husband?" he finished for her.

"No," she informed him, shaking her head so that flour flew again all about her shoulders, and this time onto John's chest, too. "I meant to say that I should never have spoken thusly except in the privacy of our chamber."

"Oh, Gwyneth, I have missed you sorely," he laughed good-naturedly. Stepping back, he brushed the flour from the front of his cloak. "You need a bath," he informed her.

"You stink like a stable, and need one worse than I!" she countered, holding her nose with her fingers.

They both heard the kitchen staff's chuckling at the same moment; each glanced quickly about the room at the suddenly idle workers, and then back at each other. Like a schoolboy attempting to elude his priestly teacher, John grabbed his wife's hand and led her at a run into the great hall and on up the stairs.

In their chamber servants were already filling the tub with hot water. "Get out, Miles," John ordered his squire bluntly. "If I've need of you, I'll send for you. Otherwise, be about your own business the rest of this day."

Bobbing his head obediently, the young man quickly departed. As soon as the tub was readied, the other servants disappeared, too.

"Dear lady wife, help me out of these foul clothes," he begged, extending his arms to her. "I think it best they be burned when I'm free of them."

"At least you'll have new ones to wear," she

announced as she unfastened his cloak and then, as he bent forward, pulled his tunics off over his head.

"You've been busy then?"

"Aye, I have. The women have been spinning and weaving and dyeing fine cloth of the softest wool. Others have been sewing garments for the castle staff but I, I have been making some things especially for you."

As John was naked except for his chausses, which he began pulling off after first removing his shoes, Gwyneth turned away and opened her trunk. From it she retrieved a handsome outer tunic the blue-green color of the sea.

"'Tis supposed to be a Christmas gift for you. But I've another, so you may have this one now."

"Good God, Gwyneth! You made this?" Unconcerned with his nakedness, he reached for the garment and felt its smoothness between his fingers and thumb. "Such a brilliant hue! However did you create it?"

"From berries and leaves. I found the combination by chance years ago, and I thought…" She hesitated, afraid to look at his body or his face, but finally deciding on his face. "… I thought the hue would do you justice."

"Gwyneth." He whispered her name and looked down at the tunic in his hands. "No one has ever…"

"You'd best get in that tub before the water's cold," she interrupted, taking the garment from him and setting it aside before steering him, as a mother would her child, into the bathing tub. "Let me do that for you," she urged, taking the sliver of sweet-smelling soap he grabbed just before climbing into the water. She lathered his hair and washed his shoulders, his back, his arms, his chest, his…

The lord's voice was husky as he grabbed her wrist. "Join me, lady wife. As I mentioned earlier, you, too, need a bath."

"I can bathe when you're done."

"Now."

She obeyed his order as quickly as Miles had the one given him. In an instant she was out of her dusty, stained clothes. Naked, she climbed over the rim of the tub and stood in the water, her feet planted between her husband's knees.

"Turn-about's fair play," he said softly and, taking her hands, pulled her into the water with him. Because of the smallness of the tub, she was forced to wrap her thighs around John's waist, and he was forced to do the same. "Give me the soap."

She found it in the water and handed it to him, as nervous as a virgin bride. As she had him, John washed Gwyneth's hair, her shoulders and back, her arms and her chest, her...

"Your belly is so flat, there's only the slightest swell to it," he observed, his hand making swirling motions below her navel as his eyes held hers. "I'd hoped, perhaps, you'd be showing signs of being with child."

Her eyes did not leave his; she did not even blink. "I'd hoped so, too, milord," she admitted. "But conceiving a child takes time, in many cases."

The swirling motions of his hand moved perceptibly lower, into the nest of curls hidden by the opaque water. "And in all cases, a very particular activity," he added, watching as Gwyneth's eyes closed, her damp, black lashes spikey against the roundness of her cheeks. "Activity that begins like this." Releasing the soap, his fingers found their way between her legs and she moaned as he stroked her. "And this." With his free hand he grabbed one of hers and led it gently to his rigid sex. With no assistance, she grasped it and pulled on it rhythmically.

It was John's turn to groan before abruptly untangling himself from his wife, rising, and pulling her up with him. "I've been too long away from you, woman," he growled, grasping her to him as he drank hungrily of her lips.

Already beside herself with need and wanting, Gwyneth raised one bare, damp leg and wrapped it around her husband's waist. Following her lead, he cupped her buttocks in his large hands, raised her up slightly, and penetrated the hot core of her sex with his throbbing manhood.

It took but seconds of thrusting before the lord spent himself and the lady convulsed with the spasms of her own release. For a minute they clung to each other, kissing noses and brows and throats. Then John retrieved the soap to cleanse Gwyneth of his spendings, while she, in turn, rinsed away the residue of their love from him.

"God's teeth, but it's cold in here!" he declared suddenly, jumping from the tub and lifting Gwyneth from it, too. "Where are those towels?" Finding them, he wrapped his wife in the largest before using another to blot the water from his skin and hair. "Let me stoke the fire," he said, throwing wood into the little pit that served as a fireplace in his chamber.

"I only hope the smoke can find its way out the window before we suffocate."

"Uncover it some," Gwyneth suggested, turning back the covers on the bed. "Join me here and I'll close the bed curtains."

"I'll join you gladly, wife." With a grin he tied back the skin that served as a window covering before jumping into bed beside her and yanking the blankets and furs up over both of them.

"Let me up!" she giggled as he grabbed her and pressed her backside to his front. "I must dry my hair. It's wet and cold and heavy."

"Let me do it."

Swaddled in bedclothes, Gwyneth took the towel from her body and handed it to John, who rubbed her lengthy tresses briskly. "You're better than the sun or a swift breeze," she complimented him, noting how quickly her hair was drying.

"Such flattery! Next you'll be saying I'm stronger than Hercules or more seductive than Pan."

"I will not. You're already a giant of a man, John of Farleigh. I wouldn't want your head swelling up any larger than it already is."

"Is it only my head you don't want swelled?"

"What?"

Her back had been to him; now Gwyneth pivoted around to face him. "You don't mind if this swells, do you?" he asked, taking her hand and guiding her fingers to his stiff cock.

"Oh!" she gasped, a little startled, but then she laughed. "I missed you, husband," she admitted as he pressed her down against the pillows.

"Not half as much, surely, as I missed you."

John stretched out against his wife and soon had her writhing beneath him. Still this time he took his time, and only when she was fairly screaming her needs, her wants, her desires, did he satisfy both her own and his.

Later they snuggled beneath the covers together, comfortable in each other's arms. "Perhaps this afternoon we've made a babe, what say you?" he suggested.

"Mayhap," she agreed, a little chord of fear thrumming in her bosom. What if, she wondered, she could no longer conceive? What if her time was past, she was too old? How disappointed John would be. Nay, worse than that, she thought, for he *needed* heirs to carry on the lineage of Farleigh. If she could not give him children—male children—even if he did not wish to, he would have to seek to annul their marriage in order to wed a younger, fertile woman. A younger woman like Gwendolyn, who had decades still ahead of her in which to bring forth babies; a younger woman like Gwendolyn who would have known a happy life married to this man.

"What is it?" John asked softly, playing with a tendril of damp hair that curled loosely over Gwyneth's forehead. "You wish to have children, don't you?"

"Aye, I do. But what if... what if I'm barren? Some women are."

"Nay, it's the men who are at fault in childless unions, of that I am sure. And I won't disappoint you there, sweetling, for I confess to having left a few bastards behind me in my travels abroad."

"You have children?" She raised her head up and rested it in her hand in order to better look at John. When he nodded she asked, "Don't you miss them terribly?"

"No." He seemed surprised by her question. "I hardly know of them. I don't even know their names."

"How can you be so callous? You've no love for your children at all?"

He shrugged, searching for words. "Gwyneth, men aren't like women. They've no instinct for nurturing, as you do."

"So you only wish to have children to carry on your name and the title that comes with your land. You won't love them or care for them or even lend a hand in rearing them—"

"Hold on, there! A moment to explain, please," he begged, smiling indulgently. "Of course I will love our children, because they will not only be my heirs, they'll be my bond with you. Sweetling, the mothers of my bastards were naught to me but a tumble in the hay. There was no bond between us even at the start, and the children are only bastards resulting from some minutes' passion."

"How many have you?" she demanded.

"Just two—nay, three."

"And you've left them to live as peasants, scorned in their own villages for being fatherless?"

"They are not scorned. You've been too sheltered, Gwyneth. In the villages and towns a great many know not their fathers. It is no shame. And I settled as much money as I could afford on each of their mothers. In fact, after I returned here as earl, I settled quite a princely sum on them, since now it is in my power to do so."

Gwyneth was not pacified. Falling onto her back again, she stared at the canopy, recalling how Ector had treated his own sons—taunting and bullying them when they were mere children attempting to emulate his knightly skills. Oblivious to their illnesses that kept the household awake through long and fearful nights. Never sharing a joke or a laugh or a game with them until they were too old to wish or expect him to. Would John be such a father, despite his protests to the contrary? Were all noblemen distant sires with no feeling of love for their offspring, only knowledge of the obligations due them from their children?

"Sweetling, what troubles you?" John persisted,

touching his finger to her chin to turn his face toward his again. "I will be a good father to our children, I promise you that. My father was a good father. The man who fostered me was, too. I know more about fathering than I do about husbanding, and I don't think I'm doing too poorly in that role, do you?"

"As a husband? My answer depends on what time of day you ask me."

"Oh, you saucy wench," he smiled, leaning forward to kiss her quickly on the lips. "You'd best watch your tongue. If I hadn't had to leave so hurriedly the day you made mincemeat of me in the hall—before most of my household—I'd have lingered long enough to have throttled you. I'm not going anywhere soon," he added pointedly.

Gwyneth could not remain in a dark mood for long, not with her husband naked beside her in bed—before the sun had even set—all cozy and warm and contented. "Can you tell me now about your adventure? Are Kurth and Sherborne, all the other fiefs and towns, ready to defend themselves against Elwood of Eye?"

"Better than they were," he assured her. "I saw your father, Gwyneth, when we built a wall around his town."

She stiffened. "When? When did you do this?"

"A month past, perhaps less. His health is better, but I fear he'll never recover completely. His end is most certainly near."

God rest his soul, she thought silently.

"He inquired after you."

"Mostly he inquired if I was serving you well, I'd wager," she corrected knowingly.

"Aye, mostly it was that. But he told me something, Gwyneth, that I've put off telling you."

"What is that?" she asked warily.

"Your sister is missing."

Gwyneth pounced on John, figuratively with her words and literally by rolling over, looming above him. "What, exactly, did he say to you?"

"Well, the old man is confused. His wits are addled in his old age. He kept calling you Gwendolyn and your missing sister by your name. But I take it your sister—she's older than you by some years?—disappeared about the day of our wedding." His eyes narrowed thoughtfully as he peered up at his wife. "Did you know of this?"

"Aye, I knew," she admitted, dropping back down onto the mattress beside him. Her pounding heart began to still as she realized her deception was still undetected. "Gwendolyn ran away from him, from Arnulf. I helped her to do it, actually. It made me late for our own marriage ceremony."

"Why?" John raised himself up on his side, propping his head in his hand.

"You can't imagine how it was, living with him— being a daughter in his care."

"I think I can," he countered gently, tracing the outline of Gwyneth's jaw with his fingertip.

"Then if you can, know that it was more than a man could bear—certainly more than a woman should have to. When Gwendolyn found the opportunity for happiness, she took it—with my blessing. I helped her go and I'll not help Arnulf find her. When he's dead she may return, but not before."

"Shouldn't you put your father's mind at ease?" John suggested. "Tell him where she is, that she's safe and well?"

"He doesn't care about her!" She sat up abruptly. "He only wants someone to order about, someone to see to his every need. I'm never going back to Sherborne, and neither is my sister!"

"Very well, I agree with you, no one will force either of you to return." Reaching up, he pulled her back down into his arms. For several minutes they remained that way, John cocooning Gwyneth in his embrace as he ran his fingers up and down the length of her bare arm.

"It's rather nice lazing about midday, sharing idle chat and confidences," Gwyneth admitted. "I never thought marriage could be like this."

"Nor I. Not that I ever thought much about marriage."

"Oh, yes. Knight-errant extraordinaire."

"You mock me, woman?"

"No." She kissed the tip of his nose. "But my hour of idleness is done. There's supper to be readied."

"Cook can do it."

"She can do it better with my supervision," Gwyneth declared, hopping from the bed and pulling on a clean tunic.

"And what am I to do while you are gone?"

"Trim your beard and comb your hair."

"Ach!" He tossed a pillow at her. "Now I know why I never thought of marriage—I was glad believing I'd never be chained to a woman. Wives are always giving orders to their husbands."

"But wives are always there to give their husbands ease," she reminded him, tossing the pillow back.

John cocked one brow and leered at Gwyneth. "Oh, yes, I like that part. Come back to bed."

"Not now." She scampered about, retrieving her shoes. "Tonight."

"Do you promise?"

"I promise," she smiled.

Chapter Fifteen

✥   ✥   ✥

Gwyneth could not believe she was dancing. It was only early evening, but this Christmas had been a long day indeed. It had begun with mass at dawn, and had been followed by incessant feasting and merry-making. Gifts had been exchanged midday. She and John had presented all the castle servants with shirts or tunics of the newly made cloth. Gwyneth had gifted her husband with the soft undershirt to wear beneath his mail. He had given her a hair ornament—shaped like a skull cap, it was a web of gold wire as intricate as her filigreed wedding band.

Now, though she felt she should be collapsed upon her bed upstairs, she was dancing with Lionel while those who could played their instruments—their flutes, their lyres. She was laughing as the heavy-set knight invented steps she was forced to follow, and so concentrating, she did not notice when the keep's guard announced visitors. Gwyneth was surprised, then, when one of the little pages now fostering in the earl's care beckoned her to join her lord and greet the new guests standing in the archway to the hall.

There were three of them, all knights, and she was only a little curious as she approached. But she felt like swooning when she recognized them, and they her.

"Mother!" they chorused, as shocked as Gwyneth, and then, in a burst of youthful exuberance and maternal love, all four ran to each other and embraced en masse.

"God's tears, Mother, have you been here all along?" Matthew demanded. "We came to speak to Gwendolyn."

"I feared you were dead!" Rodney admitted.

"Where is Gwendolyn, if not here?" Richard asked.

"Let me see you, let me see you, sweet mother of Mary, I thought never to see any of you again," Gwyneth cried, clasping each of her son's faces in her hands before kissing their cheeks soundly.

But suddenly Gwyneth saw her husband's face in the corner of her eye, and she realized then the great hall had gone very quiet except for herself and her own. "John," she said evenly, trying to grasp and maintain some composure, "these are my sons, Matthew, Rodney and Richard, all late of Durningham. Boys, this is my husband, the earl, John of Farleigh."

There was a stunned, silent moment during which John cast his wife a hard, accusatory glance. Then, very cordially, he greeted each of the young men in turn. Gesturing to the dais table he said, "Please, join us in a repast. Girl," he ordered Bess, "have trenchers, mugs and some trays of victuals brought out for our new guests."

"We've only just come from Sherborne," Richard explained. "We spent the day with Grandfather, and he fed us there."

"Oh, you've always room for something more to eat," Gwyneth chided him, glad to look away from John as she led Richard and his brothers to the table. "Besides, I've had all our family favorites prepared."

"You don't have to convince me," Matthew laughed, wrapping his arm about his mother's shoulders. "Oh, to have Christmas with you again, Mother. I hadn't expected that, not with all that's happened in the past year."

"What's happened, then?" John inquired, for he had followed them all to the table and gestured for his steward to pour fresh wine.

"You don't know?" Rodney responded with another question.

"He's knows much of it," Gwyneth put in quickly, "but my husband's been busy with urgent concerns of his own, so I've not bothered him with it all." She risked a quick glance at John.

"Explain to us how you happen to be wed to Lord John, when we thought it was Gwendolyn the earl took to wife," Matthew urged.

And Rodney and Richard chorused, "That is what Grandfather told us."

"Do tell them the story," John urged also, his eyes hard as he considered Gwyneth.

She squirmed under his scrutiny, glanced away, and ignored the request. "The twins have always done that—spoken as one," was her only comment.

"Twins, yes," he said thoughtfully, "I see it now. Like mirror images you are, yet there's not a trace of your mother in you."

"'Tis true enough," Richard agreed cheerily, swigging back a healthy swallow of mead. "Matthew, the carrot-top, is the one who wears his Sherborne blood like a crown, while Rodney and I have the less than good fortune of resembling our late and unlamented sire."

"Nay, that's not true," Gwyneth countered, unable to stop looking lovingly at the sons she'd not seen for so long. "You may have black hair and dark eyes, but you're handsome lads, the two of you."

"And I'm not?" Matthew asked, as if she'd slighted him.

"Oh, you're the handsomest of all," she teased.

Though the young men had filled their trenchers with the food Bess had brought out from the kitchen, their mother hovered over them. Her reason was twofold: She had missed them and she wished to visit with them, but she also wanted to delay the private conversation—the confrontation—she was doomed soon to have with her husband.

"Why were you at Sherborne?" John asked conversationally. Still at the front side of the table with Gwyneth, he was resting one foot on the platform and leaning on his thigh with one arm. "Simply to visit your grandsire?"

"No, milord, he sent for us. To look for Mother," Rodney explained.

John's golden head turned ever so slightly, and his blue eyes slanted toward Gwyneth's. She smiled quickly and too brightly, and immediately turned away.

"Mother, Grandfather's losing his wits. How can he not know you've wed the earl of Farleigh? He thinks it's Gwendolyn living here," Matthew told her.

"He's not very well, and Jean makes him methagline that could put a horse to sleep, which he drinks all day long," Rodney went on.

"He dirties himself and he babbles nonsense a lot. It's sad, Mother, to see a man as Sir Arnulf once was reduced to such a sorry state," Richard elaborated.

"But why haven't you visited him?" Rodney wondered aloud.

Before Gwyneth could reply, Matthew exclaimed, "God's blood! If you're the earl's lady wife, Mother, then it is our dear sister Gwendolyn who's missing!"

"Your sister?" John snapped, startling both his wife and her sons as he leaned forward, as if to pounce.

"Nay, milord, Gwen's not really our sister at all. But as she's some years younger than we and she grew up in our house, my brothers and I all think of her as our baby sister. In truth, she is our aunt."

"And my sister," Gwyneth declared, her eyes meeting and holding her husband's for the longest moment since her family had so unexpectedly arrived.

"You're not to worry about Gwendolyn," she informed Matthew. "She's gone but not missing. I assure you, too, she's happy and safe and well."

"But where's she gone to?"

"I'm not able to tell you that, Matthew. Not yet, anyway."

Gwyneth realized the noise in the hall had resumed, though not quite to the rowdy level it had been. When she turned halfway and surveyed the room, she discovered only Gerald curiously watching the group at the head table. Their eyes met, and he made to stand. But, almost imperceptibly, she shook her head and he resumed his seat.

When she turned back she grabbed her own goblet, which she had left on the table sometime earlier. It was more than half-filled, but she drank it all down. As she set the empty goblet down again, she noticed her husband watching her steadily. His visage was calm, but his eyes sparked with fury.

"How did Arnulf find you?" she asked her sons quickly. "Even I had no idea where you were."

"We've been none too long in any one place, that's a fact," Rodney told her before he stuffed a piece of succulently greasy pork into his mouth with his fingers.

"'Tis fair near impossible for three unseasoned and landless young knights to engage an army."

"Aye," his twin agreed, stabbing a piece of baked apple with his eating knife. "We may as well resign ourselves to attacking Terrence on our own with nothing but rocks to throw at the keep."

"But how did your grandfather find you?" she asked again, pointedly attempting to keep their conversation from veering to other topics.

"He sent one of his men to Becknock Keep."

"Harold, your foster father!" Gwyneth exclaimed. "I'd never thought of that. Besides, I always felt not knowing what had become of you three was better than learning you'd been killed."

"Tell me," John interjected, "why is it you wish to raise an army? Surely the baron of Eye is not threatening your estate as he is those in this territory."

"Nay." Matthew shook his head. "I don't even know this baron of whom you speak, except that Grandfather mentioned him frequently during our visit. The servants explained the wall was put up 'round the town to protect the folk residing there from that lord.

"No, our enemy is Terrence, now calling himself Terrence of Durningham since he attacked our keep, killed our father, and claimed my inheritance for his own."

"By what right?"

"None." Gwyneth's handsome, eldest son looked years older as he continued, "Terrence was some cousin to Ector, our father. Our great-grandfather, who'd lost his own sons, disinherited Terrence for some cause, leaving Durningham to our father. It would seem he spent all his life attempting to get back what he thought was owed him. He's old now, nearly three score in years, surely. Yet it took him that long to raise the money and men to attack our home. And he succeeded."

"But he spared your lives?" John asked, looking from one young man to the next.

"It was arranged for Mother and Gwendolyn to slip away and return to Sherborne before the battle began. We," Matthew said dryly as he looked to each of his brothers, "escaped to fight again so that I might have my inheritance in the end."

For a long moment Gwyneth, her sons, and her husband were quiet, thoughtful and reflective. Then she said, "If you'll excuse me," and turned to leave.

But John grabbed her wrist and demanded in a low voice, "Where are you off to?"

His fingers hurt her arm, but she did not struggle for release or even flinch. "I've some gifts set aside for my boys. I was only going to retrieve them. It is Christmas, after all," she explained as he released her. She wanted to rub her wrist, which was red with the imprint of her husband's fingers, but she did not. And when he nodded, in effect giving her permission to leave the hall, she went slowly, back stiff, head high.

John's eyes were on her when she came down the stairs later, and they stayed on her as she crossed the room again. She did not look at him, though, as she stepped up onto the dais platform and leaned across the table, pressing into each of her son's hands a medallion on a chain.

"Mother, how wonderful! I shall treasure it," Matthew exclaimed, coming to his feet and leaning forward to kiss Gwyneth.

"As will I!" the twins chorused, likewise kissing their mother before dropping the chains over their heads so that the small, gold medallions rested on their chests.

"They're from the holy land," she told them, "or so the peddler from whom I bought them said. I hope they are. They're supposed to bring the wearers good fortune."

"They will, Mother," Rodney smiled.

"If only because you gave them to us," Richard added.

"We didn't bring you anything," Matthew apologized.

Gwyneth took his hand, so hard and callused already despite his youth, and squeezed it. "No matter. I've got everything I want in you three—my Mattie and Roddy and Richie."

"Oh, Mother!" all three wailed in unison, so that Gwyneth almost laughed. She certainly would have if she had not felt the stern glower her husband was giving her.

"You know we hate those childish nicknames," Matthew reminded her.

"But you know they are dear to me, as you are." Again she turned halfway to survey the room. Some had resumed their energetic dancing, while a few of the serving maids, Bess included, were eyeing the young knights on the dais rather hungrily.

"Why don't you lads join in the merriment?" she suggested. "There are a few unattached females in this hall who I'm sure wouldn't mind putting you through your paces on the dance floor."

"Oh, no, Mother. We'll stay here and visit with you and Lord John."

"Perhaps my husband is up to conversation, but I've had a long and tiring day," Gwyneth admitted. "I'm up to bed, now."

"The same is true for me," John announced, stretching a little as he straightened himself. "Enjoy yourselves, lads, it's Christmas. We'll talk again."

"If you insist," the twins said together, pushing out the bench on which they'd been sitting. Both had their eyes on Bess, who was smiling at them as if they were one.

Gwyneth, seeing this, wondered if the girl could, indeed, handle two randy youths at once. Deciding Bess probably could, she said over her shoulder, "Confine your entertainments to dancing, my sons. More could prove costly to you later on."

"Aye, Mother," they promised. But the moment her back was turned, the twins winked at each other and together shared a chuckle with their brother, Matthew.

Gwyneth was no longer thinking of them, however. John, beside her, was not even touching her let alone assisting her up the stairs. She felt cold as the dead, yet she could feel the heat of his anger as they climbed the steps to their room.

As soon as the door was shut behind them, he rounded on her. Surprisingly, his voice was even, though his words were clipped. "What say you, woman? Explain yourself."

Inhaling deeply, Gwyneth turned away, fingering the arm of her chair. "I am sorry, John."

"I want no apologies. I demand explanations."

"Where do you wish me to begin?"

"At the beginning!"

She spun about and swallowed hard. "I changed places with my sister so that she'd not be forced to wed you."

John looked as if he had been poleaxed. "Forced! God's wounds! When you arrived here on the morn of our wedding, did I not ask you if marriage to me was your desire? Did I not give you every opportunity to decline?"

"You did." She looked away, her eyes darting about nervously, guiltily.

"I thought I was allowing your sister to act upon her own inclinations."

Gwyneth's eyes met John's. "How did I know you would make her such an offer?" she demanded. "She's so young, Gwendolyn is, not yet sixteen. and she's in love with another. I could not be party to a plan to tear her from her beloved and force her into wedlock with some crude and aging knight well old enough to be her father."

"A crude and aging knight?" John eyes bulged. "And what of you, Lady Gwyneth? Obviously, you have more years on you than you led me to believe. You must have known that as the last living heir to the earldom of Farleigh, I need heirs of my own, heirs you cannot give me. When I offered you, or the girl I thought you to be, the chance to forego the marriage, why did you not then tell me who you really are and what you two had done? Neither she nor you would have had to enter into this sham of a marriage, and I'd not be tied to a woman beyond the age of childbearing. Why did you not speak up then?"

Gwyneth tried to be calm. Wringing her hands she admitted, "I don't know. I was not concerned for children that might or might not be conceived. I was concerned only with protecting my sister."

"You willfully deceived me!"

"You were easy to deceive! You knew not what your betrothed looked like, nor did you remember her name."

John muttered a string of oaths, closed his eyes, and shook his head. "Damn you," he said at the last, looking at Gwyneth again.

"Be damned yourself, milord," she cursed softly.

But when John suddenly leapt forward, closing the distance between them with two long strides, she backed up to a far wall where she was trapped when he reached her. There he pulled off her gold cap and grabbed fistfuls of her heavy, wavy, gingery hair in his hands. "What are you, woman, a witch? Did you put a spell on me so that I would not see you for what you truly are? How do you hide the white threads in these red tresses?"

At that remark, Gwyneth reacted much as the earl had to being called a crude and aging knight. "There is no white in my hair!" she protested. "Is there white in yours? I see none, yet you are far older than I!"

"That cannot be! It is not true!" He released her and turned away. "Your children are grown men."

"Are none of yours?" she asked his back.

Again he turned. "My eldest cannot be more than ten or twelve or…

"Twenty?" she sneered.

"My children, my age, are of no matter here," he announced righteously, puffing out his chest. "Yours alone are."

"Well, your age was a matter to be considered when Arnulf decided to wed Gwendolyn off to you. A girl—a child—of her tender years should not have to endure the marriage bed with a brutal, selfish, uncaring lord of your advanced age. I could not be a party to that, so I sacrificed myself on her behalf."

"Brutal? Uncaring?" John shook his head incredulously. "How dare you say that of me, The Dane?"

"Oh, The Dane, The Dane, The Dane," Gwyneth repeated contemptuously. "Are you some sort of legend? Do minstrels sing of your heroic exploits as they do of Cuchulain and Sigurd?"

"Nay, they do not. But I am an honorable lord in my dealings with all, both men and women alike, and I've a reputation for such. For you to say marriage to me is a sacrifice... Sweet Jesu, one would think you were a martyr!"

Gwyneth flinched as if her husband had slapped her. Yet she explained, "Marriage for a woman to any man is a sacrifice, save for those few who marry for love. But marriage of a girl-child to a doddering old warrior is God's own hell on Earth."

John's steely jaw was clenched, the muscles twitching. "I am no doddering old warrior, lady wife, any more than you are a child."

"You're quite right," she agreed quickly. "At least you are not to me. But then I'm an old crone with white hair and blackened teeth, am I not?"

"I did not say that."

"You said as much!"

"My point was only that you deceived me by pretending to be what you are not."

"I never said I was a maid—that, you assumed. Did I not ask you if you'd spent much time with children and women? You were the one who looked upon my face and saw an innocent girl there. I never claimed that I was one."

"But you covered that fair face of yours, Gwyneth, throughout the wedding mass. Why, except to keep me from knowing you were not the daughter of Sir Arnulf's I had met the day I asked for her hand?"

"Asked for her hand?" With a snort, Gwyneth

began pacing the the length of the room. "I was at the manor. I witnessed the arranging of the marriage contract between you and Gwendolyn. She was cowering in fear in a corner, and you glanced at her but once. You could not pick her out in a crowd of three!" She brought herself up short directly in front of John. "You ought to have wed my father. You spent the most time courting him!"

Before he might strike her or grab her sleeve, Gwyneth resumed her pacing. "You lied to me," he insisted, watching her walk to and fro.

"I did not! Did you marry a woman called Gwendolyn of Sherborne? No. You married me, Gwyneth of Sherborne. I did not hide behind my sister's name. And you, goodly knight, were not the least perturbed when I corrected the priest during the ceremony. God's blood, you did not even know what your bride was called!"

The scar on John's face had receded deeply; it looked drawn in black ink. "The fact remains," he growled, "that you deceived me, that you tricked me into taking you as wife."

"Aye, that I did," she admitted. She had reached the table between their two carved chairs and she stopped there, resting her open hands upon it. "But I did not trap you. Now that my sister is out of this web of intrigue, safely away and happily wed to another, you may have your freedom back, John of Farleigh."

"What say you now?"

Slowly she turned. "Seek to have our marriage annulled, milord. Surely my deception will be accepted as an impediment. Then find yourself a wife of tender years who can serve as your broodmare for as long as you have need."

John did not move, but he nodded his head slowly. "I will, milady. Be sure of that."

As if neither was willing to be the first to turn away a final time, both stood for a long moment facing each other. It was John, finally, who tore his eyes from Gwyneth's and left the chamber, securing the door behind him.

Chapter Sixteen

✥   ✥   ✥

Gwyneth's heart was filled with trepidation as she came down the stairs the next morning. When the hall came into her view, even before she had reached the bottom step, she scanned it, both afraid and almost hoping she would see her husband there. He was not. But what disarray there was! Many of the Christmas Day revelers, both male and female, were still snoring, asleep on their pallets, curled among the rushes, or sprawled on the floor with limbs thrown over their bedmates. Gwyneth groaned inwardly at the work that lay ahead in order to set the castle keep to rights. She also sighed in relief at not finding any of her sons in tawdry dishabille.

"Bess!" She shook the serving girl's shoulder until she roused from her stupor. "Paddy!" She kicked the scullion in the rump with the toe of her shoe until he swore in complaint and sat up. "Up, you two! It's nearly Lauds and time for chapel. Up, now!"

As the maid and the man were separated by a little distance, each thought their mistress spoke to them alone. Almost as one they stood, nodding their obedience.

"Wake everyone and get them about their duties before the earl comes down and sees what a slovenly pack of servants he employs. Bess, clear everyone out. Paddy, have the tables set up for the morning meal."

With that, Gwyneth pivoted on her toes, her white cape swirling out around her, heading outdoors to the chapel.

Services were not well attended that morning. She noted that neither her husband nor her sons were there. She intended to speak to Matthew and the twins about their dereliction. They might be grown men, but it was her duty as a mother to see to their souls.

Yet when she returned to the keep and encountered Matthew almost immediately, reprimanding him for missing morning mass was not the first thing on her mind. "Where are you going?" she asked. "To Sherborne to tell Arnulf you've found me?"

"No!" Her eldest looked surprised that she would think such a thing. "Mother, we can't return to Sherborne so quickly. Grandfather expects us to be gone weeks, perhaps months, in our search for you. Were I to tell him you're so nearby and living at Farleigh Castle, he'd expect you to return. Then, addled wits or no, I'd wager he'd begin asking questions you'd not care to answer. Am I right?"

"Aye." She nodded, a little surprised at how discerning Matthew was. Despite her fond memories of telling him tales at bedtime and tickling him until, flushed with his giggling, he begged for mercy, her son had left childhood far behind. More than a knight, he had grown into the role of lord to which his birthright entitled him. "Where are you headed, then?" she inquired. "You look dressed for hunting."

"I am," he smiled, nodding his head. "Rodney and Richard and I are joining Lord John for hawking, at his invitation."

She felt a painful prick, as if she'd stuck herself with her eating knife. She was certain, too, her husband had intended her to feel it, for he'd been teaching her to hawk in recent weeks. Nearly every day, after the morning meal, they had ridden out together into the woods.

"That was kind of him," she said evenly. "Where are your brothers?"

"Gone to the mews with the earl, I'd imagine, to choose their falcons for the day. I'd best join them, Mother, before they think I've changed my mind about going with them."

Kissing her quickly on the cheek, Matthew hurried out the door. Alone, Gwyneth turned into the great hall where she was pleased to find, at least, Bess and Paddy had obeyed her orders. The trestle tables were up, and many of the Farleigh knights were breaking their fast.

"May I join you, milady?"

She had filled a trencher and was seated at her place on the otherwise empty dais. But as she had no real appetite, she'd been staring at her food. Now she looked up at Gerald, beside her, and nodded.

"If I may be so bold," he said as he sat, "Lord John seems to have accepted your sons well enough. I heard they are heading out to the forest to go hawking."

Gwyneth said nothing. She kept looking down at the victuals before her as if she expected them to do something extraordinary.

"How goes it with you? With you and your husband?"

"It doesn't." Her throat was tight.

"You told him all?"

With a sigh, Gwyneth turned to her friend. "Nay, not all. Only what he needed to know."

"Which was?"

"That I changed places with Gwendolyn to spare her from marriage to him."

Gerald raised his dark eyes to the ceiling. *"That's* what you told him? That's all? That you thought him so vile, so wicked, you sacrificed yourself on your sister's behalf?" He shook his head. "No wonder it does not go well between you two."

"It is the truth! He deserved the truth!"

"But not a half truth, Lady Gwyneth." He glanced about the room. "Perhaps, if you wish to continue this conversation, we ought to go somewhere more private."

"There's no need—"

"There is."

"But—"

"Gwynnie, think of me as your old friend, not your husband's seneschal," he urged, and finally she acquiesced, following him up to his work room.

Gerald sat on a stool beside the table laden with parchment and counting sticks. Gwyneth declined to sit, meandering about the room and idly fingering the items stored on the seneschal's shelves.

"You don't think Lord John a crude oaf any longer, do you?" he asked her, trying to resume the conversation they had broken off.

"Of course not."

"Did you tell him that during your confession?"

"I think so."

"You think so?"

She shot Gerald an impatient look. "Well, when he pointed out that the day I arrived here to wed him he gave me the chance to decline, I told him I'd no way of knowing, beforehand, that he would be so fair-minded."

"A less than forthright compliment, milady."

"It was the best I could do while he was shouting at me that I had deceived him!" Gwyneth stopped abruptly and stood, glaring at Gerald.

"You *did* deceive him."

"But as I tried to explain to him, not to cause him harm. Only to protect Gwendolyn."

Gerald nodded understandingly. "You must remember, Lady Gwyneth, that though your husband is a toughened knight he is still a man with feelings. You hurt him doubly, not only by your deception but by the reason for it. You believed he would be a cruel and harsh husband who would crush your young sister beneath his hard hand."

"Of course I believed that! Why wouldn't I?" With an exasperated, hopeless sigh, Gwyneth finally collapsed onto a stool near Gerald's own. "My father was a husband twice, and in between he used me as if I was his wife, to run his house and cater to his needs. He beat both my own and Gwendolyn's mother, and always he beat me. Not a kind word do I ever recall him uttering."

"And Ector of Durningham?"

"God's wounds," she swore softly, shaking her head and wiping an errant tear from her lashes. "If you only knew what I suffered at my first husband's hands."

"Tell me," Gerald urged gently.

With a sniff she raised her chin and looked away, into the past. "You know my own mother died when I was little more than a babe. Arnulf did not remarry 'til I was ten and two. Miriam was sweet and gentle... I liked having her there at the manor. But my father did not like having me there any longer. I think he felt the place was too small for the three of us. Besides, he had Miriam to do the work I'd done since I was old enough to manage it."

She shifted her weight on the stool. "He sent inquiries to the noble houses to find a lord who would marry me. I had no great dowry, but I was not uncomely and still very young, young enough to breed a household of heirs for anyone who would take me to wife. Ector needed heirs badly. He'd sired none but sons in his first marriage, yet all were dead from one cause or another. He accepted Arnulf's offer and I was sent off to marry him."

"I remember that, milady." Gerald's words were hardly more than a whisper. "I remember thinking that, if I were far too young to take a wife, how could you be old enough to take a husband? Yet none of our friends seemed concerned by it. Some of the girls, I remember, seemed to envy you."

"Ha! Envy me. I pray God none knew marriage as I did!"

Gwyneth's lip was trembling. Another stray tear streamed down her cheek before she could wipe it away.

"I knew nothing, Gerald. I was but fourteen when I wed him, and Ector hurt and humiliated me on our wedding night. You know the customs—Sweet Mary, but I hate them! I felt so exposed, so shamed..."

"And Durningham keep, what a sty it was. But I knew about that, I knew about running a household. So I did that, just as I'd done for my father in the years before he married Miriam. Ector treated me as my father had as well, beating me when he was drunk and feeling surly or when he was sober and feeling mean. But there was something he did to me my father did not." She raised her green eyes to meet Gerald's. "He mounted me every night until I conceived Matthew. And though Mattie was born before the first year was out, Ector resumed his assaults, for assaults they were, until I conceived the twins."

Gwyneth came to her feet and walked away from Gerald, her head hanging. "I don't know if you ever thought of me after I'd gone, but I thought of you and the others who were our friends. Not that I'd had much time to myself as a child, but those hours I stole away to go riding in the meadows or fishing in the stream or playing hide and seek in the woods, God, how I longed for them! A few moments of carefree idleness." She turned around. "But I was by then a mother of three, Lady of Durningham, chatelaine of Durningham keep. And I was still younger than Gwendolyn is now."

Gerald opened his mouth as if he would speak, but remained silent. Pacing again, Gwyneth resumed her tale.

"Fortunately, I could not accommodate my husband in the months after the twins' birthing, and in that time he turned to others—serving wenches in the castle and girls from the village. By the time my health was restored, Ector no longer took an interest in me. Perhaps he felt three sons as heirs were enough. Or, more likely, I had filled out into full womanhood after bearing my babes and he no longer found me the least appealing." Pausing, she leaned toward the seneschal to share a confidence.

In a whisper she admitted, "I suspect Ector had a preference for very young girls. Children, actually. It came to my attention during the endless years I resided at Durningham that several of the servants' young daughters bled to death before they were old enough to have experienced a woman's monthly courses. Therefore, I purposely kept Gwendolyn out of his sight."

"How did Gwendolyn come to be with you at Durningham?"

Gwyneth strolled around the table, running her fingertips along its edge. "Miriam died in childbirth. Word came to me that my father was acting deranged. He resented that his second child was female, especially when it had taken so long for his wife to conceive. He was blaming Miriam for dying, too, because there was now no chance for a second babe, a son. But what frightened me most was that the servants who were caring for Gwendolyn feared she would not survive.

"So I came and took her. I thought I would have to fight Arnulf to get her, and Ector to keep her, but neither paid any mind. My father seemed not to know she was gone, or so my old friend from the manor, Jean, told me. And my husband seemed not to know she was there because his interests lay everywhere but with his wife and her children.

"She was a blessing to me." Gwyneth took a deep breath and smiled. "I had them all for a while, my boys and my daughter—I have most always thought of Gwendolyn as such. But the years flew quickly by and then my sons went off to foster. Matthew was eight and the twins only seven. I had no one save Gwendolyn then, to raise and to love."

"You love her dearly," Gerald observed.

"Aye. More like a mother than a sister, that's true. It's why I couldn't force her into marrying a man I believed would treat her as Ector treated me."

"All men are not like Ector," he pointed out, placing his hand familiarly over Gwyneth's.

She did not take offense. She left her own enclosed by his. "They seemed to be, Gerald. If not black-hearted and cruel, then simply indifferent and cold."

"Yet you did not send your sister away to take the veil and join a convent," he observed. "You helped her to run off to wed a young knight. Did you not fear that she might suffer at Thomas of Brandywine's hand?"

"She loves him. He loves her. And both of them are young, Gerald, unlike those marriages I'm most familiar with, where the husband is aging and the wife still in the bloom of her youth. I thought—" she shrugged, slipping her hand from Gerald's and turning aside, "—perhaps there was a chance for them if they could begin together and grow old together, especially as they already loved each other." She turned back. "But now…"

"You have doubts about the match?"

"No, it's only…"

"What?" Gerald came to his feet, rounded the corner of the table, and though Gwyneth gave him her back he put his hands on her shoulders.

"I know now marriage to John of Farleigh is not what I presumed it to be. You were right when you defended your lord to me the day of my wedding. He is a good man. Gwendolyn would not have been unhappy being his wife. Oh, she'd have been frightened a little, at first. She'd have longed for Thomas, I don't doubt. But despite his formidable appearance, his size and his scars…" Gwyneth turned around to face him. "He's gentle and tender and he's rarely ever thoughtless. Oh, Gerald! What have I done?"

She threw herself into her old friend's arms and he held her comfortingly. "What are you saying?"

"I've ruined everything. Perhaps Sir Thomas is not old enough to be a good husband to Gwendolyn. The earl may have been a far better match for her. Who—who—who was I to think I knew what was best?" she sniffed. "John deserves children. My sister could have given him dozens."

"You can give him children, milady."

"Oh, aye!" she scoffed, still wetting Gerald's shoulder with her tears. "He thinks I'm of an age with the old witch in the forest, that I should wear a wimple to cover my graying hair."

"I'm sure my lord thinks nothing of the sort."

"He does. He said as much."

"What else did he say?"

"That he—intends—to have—the marriage—annulled."

Gerald was silently thoughtful for a moment. "Lord John announced this, or did you suggest it to him?"

"I... may have suggested it," Gwyneth admitted, leaning back her head and blinking to release still more tears. "But he took up the idea with relish, I assure you!"

The seneschal shook his head slowly. "You love your husband, don't you, milady?"

"What!"

"You love John of Farleigh."

She inhaled a ragged, noisy breath. "Oh, aye, Gerald. I think I do," she confessed, and again she leaned her head on his shoulder as great sobs racked her body.

For long minutes the man held her thus, waiting patiently for her crying to subside. Her breathing was finally becoming even and regular when the door to Gerald's work room flew open without a knock or a word from without.

The earl's huge presence took up the entire portal, his expression quickly hardening to an icy glare. "What's this?" he demanded, and at the sound of his voice Gwyneth flew backwards out of her friend's embrace.

She had no words with which to reply. Even Gerald seemed at a loss. Finally he muttered, "Nothing, milord. Lady Gwyneth was upset. I—I was trying to comfort her. She—"

"Comfort her?" John sneered. "I've heard it called many things, but—"

"Milord, I must protest!" Gerald stepped forward and straightened his shoulders. Gwyneth, watching the two men, thought her friend looked rather like David confronting Goliath. "There was nothing untoward in what has passed between me and your lady wife. I know it may appear improper, your seneschal and the lady of the castle, but..." He turned and glanced over his shoulder at Gwyneth. When he looked back to his lord he said, "Gwynnie—Lady Gwyneth—and I are old friends. Friends from childhood."

If he thought his explanation was going to soothe the earl of Farleigh, Gerald, son of Penworth, was very wrong. John's eyes narrowed to blue slits, his scar receded and blackened, and his face grew ruddy with rage.

"Gwynnie?" he repeated, as if the name were offal on his tongue. "You dare to call the lady of Farleigh by so familiar a name? You must know her well indeed, Gerald."

"Milord, as I said, I've known her since childhood. There is nothing improper—"

"I heard you before, Gerald," John interrupted, stepping into the room and slamming the door behind him. "So, you betrayed me, too."

"Nay! I am trying to explain, milord, that there is nothing between us save for an old friendship."

"I heard that, too." His hard, hateful glance darted to Gwyneth and back to Gerald. "And I take it you recognized her when she came to Farleigh Castle posing as her *much* younger sister. The sister I'd contracted to wed."

He paused, waiting for his seneschal to reply. Gerald did not speak, however. He merely nodded.

"Yet you said nothing to me?" John took another step forward and grabbed the man's shoulder, shaking him angrily. "You let me marry the wrong daughter of Sir Arnulf's, knowing full well the consequences?"

"He was going to tell you!" Gwyneth at last found her tongue and came forward, grabbing John's wrist and tugging at his arm so that he finally freed Gerald. "He did not realize who I was 'til after the ceremony, but still he would tell you except that I begged him nay! John, Gerald's secrecy was not his doing. I begged him to stay silent. I am completely responsible for all the wrong done you. Do not lay even partial blame at Gerald's feet."

"No." Gerald spoke to Gwyneth. "Do not defend me, milady. I knew what I was about, and I should not have done it."

"You did it for me!"

"My loyalty should have been to my lord, none other." He turned to look at John again. "I will remove my possessions and be gone before nightfall, milord. I cannot beg your forgiveness in this matter. I've dishonored my position in this castle by abusing the faith a baron puts in his seneschal. But know this, milord. I meant you no ill, nor did I feel any would come from your marriage to lady Gwyneth. I mistakenly assumed you would be pleased with her as your lady wife."

Gerald made to move past the earl, but John grabbed his shoulder again. "You cannot go."

"What?"

"You owe me for your part in Gwyneth of Sherborne's deception, and now you must give me my due. I am leaving here and I need you to keep order at Farleigh just as you did during the years between my brother's death and my return."

"Leaving?"

It was Gwyneth who spoke—John ignored her and directed his comments to Gerald.

"Elwood of Eye's men attacked Neville of Kurth's demesne. A messenger caught up with me a short while ago as I rode out to go hawking."

"They're laying siege? How many men are you taking with you to help defend the keep?"

"Eye's men are no longer laying siege," John responded to his seneschal's question. His tone was level but hard-edged. "They've overtaken it."

"What!" Gerald's response was indicative of his surprise. "But I thought all the barons in the region had fortified their estates against just such an attack. May I ask when Eye's men made their move, and how Kurth was lost?"

"They attacked Christmas Day."

"Only yesterday?" Again it was Gwyneth who spoke, unable to restrain herself. "How could the lord of Kurth have lost his lands so quickly?"

"They kidnapped his eldest son." John's eyes moved slowly to meet and hold his wife's. "He was returning home for the holy day from Cherburg, where he was fostering. The lad was only sixteen."

"Was?"

His confirmation was a slow blink. "Eye's men attacked him and his companions before he drew close enough to home to see the battle being waged. Recognizing him, they held him hostage and sent an ultimatum to Neville."

Both Gwyneth and Gerald held their tongues, waiting for the outcome of this tale.

John continued quickly, "Of course, Neville surrendered. But they cut the boy's throat nonetheless."

"Sweet holy Mother Mary!" Gwyneth gasped, covering her mouth as her eyes widened in horror. "His mother must be beside herself with grief."

"Perhaps his father's shed a tear or two of his own. Do you think that possible?" John asked irritably.

"This could not be a ruse, a trap?" Gerald asked in concern.

"Nay. It was one of the freemen from the village of Kurth that rode here to advise me and beg my support. With him rode one of Lord Maynard's knights. I sent one of my own men with them to warn the other barons in these parts and to solicit their help. We must form a large army in order to take back Kurth for its rightful owners."

"Where are Lord Neville and his lady wife?"

"As far as anyone knows, being held prisoner within their own keep." John turned on his heel. "I've no time to discuss this further. Those who are going with me are readying themselves for battle and so, too, must I."

"John." Gwyneth stepped forward and reached out, but before she dared touch his sleeve she retracted her hand quickly. "God go with you."

Again his eyes narrowed contemptuously. "A crude, old, aging warrior has no need of God's assistance, milady. My life's been well-lived and is probably nearing its end. Better you save the well-wishing for your sons who are young and have much still to live for."

"My sons?"

"They've volunteered to join the fight."

Chapter Seventeen

✣   ✣   ✣

John quit the room and for a moment Gwyneth remained rooted to the spot where she stood, like a tree. Then she grabbed up her skirts and ran after him, catching up to him on the stairs above. This time she did not hesitate in taking his arm. She lunged for him and forced him to turn, to look at her. "Where?" she demanded. "Where are they?"

"Come," he said casually, and continued climbing.

She followed her husband to the next level and when he nodded toward the closed door before them, she knocked quickly and entered before anyone within could reply. Finding her sons in full battle gear, she kicked the door closed behind her, not giving a thought to the earl.

"What in the name of all things holy are you doing?" she asked them, her voice shrill. "You cannot be going to war in a fight that's not your own!"

Matthew smoothed down his hauberk and met his mother's glare with eyes so like her own. "The fight for justice is every knight's fight."

"Don't give me that damnable chivalrous rhetoric," she warned. "I want to know why you are doing this thing. Have you gone mad?"

"Mother." Stepping forward, he touched her arm respectfully. "Men like this Elwood and Durningham's own Terrence must be stopped. It is well nigh impossible for a victim of such men to revenge himself on them. Look at me, Mother. Look at Richard and Rodney." He glanced over his shoulder at his brothers standing silent and watchful. "Without aid, we shall never get back what is rightfully ours. Neither will the baron of Kurth be freed if righteous men do not rescue him and help him regain his estate."

"An eye for an Eye," Rodney quipped, and his mother's eyes flashed their fury at him. As he'd done as a child, he hung his head apologetically.

"This is no game, Rodney," she informed him sternly. Looking back at Matthew she went on, "How do you intend to retrieve your inheritance if you're killed on the field fighting another's battle?"

"My brothers will continue our fight," he said simply. "Durningham will be their legacy if I'm gone."

"What if you are *all* killed?"

"Then Terrence may remain the lord of Durningham. You and Lord John have no need of it. Farleigh is vastly superior in size and wealth and beauty when compared to Durningham's demesne."

That comment brought Gwyneth a moment of pause. Her son assumed she would be living out her life in Farleigh Castle; she herself would not risk estimating how many weeks she had left to live within this fine keep's walls.

"I care not about keeps or common fields, bushels of barley or bails of wool. Property means nothing to me. You are my children—I care for your lives!" she cried, tears welling up in her eyes again.

"Mother," Richard said gently, stepping forward

quickly and hugging her close. "Mother, Matthew speaks of this business as if it were some holy crusade. But in truth we are being practical by joining your husband's cause."

"Aye, Mother," Rodney put in. "Your husband has offered us generous wages to join his men-at-arms. And if we help avenge this lord of Kurth and put down the wicked Elwood of Eye, the earl assures us the barons in this region will reciprocate by providing soldiers to help us regain our home."

"We need help," Richard continued. "We could get nowhere with the lords in our own region. Their demesnes are all protected by thanes who serve only their required forty days before returning to their own fiefs. None are willing to risk their lives for our fight. But here the barons and their knights are joining forces to protect one and all from a common evil. If we aid their cause, they should be willing to aid ours."

"What my brothers say is true," Matthew confirmed. "Besides, it is good for us to serve your husband. Instead of wandering the Holy Roman Empire as mercenary knights, instead of hoping to recruit loyal comrades-in-arms to help us take back our birthright before we're old men, we will be serving our own kin. The bargain we struck with Lord John is a good one, Mother."

"Oh, sweet mother of Jesu," she whispered, leaning against the door. Gwyneth felt like collapsing. How her world had changed since yesterday! How it had changed since Michaelmas! Yet she could not explain to her sons what she felt sure was true: Because she had done the earl a grievous wrong, this was his retribution. "In trying to spare Gwendolyn," she muttered beneath her breath as she hung her head, "I've sacrificed my sons."

"What say you, Mother?" Matthew asked.

She raised her head to look at him. "I say you three are too young to know you are not invincible. Did you not see your father die at Durningham? Do you think he lost his life's blood because he was old? Nay, he lost it because an arrow pierced his heart!" She stuck her fingers through some of the metal rings that, sewn into his leather shirt made up Matthew's mail. Then she jerked him toward her. "Your heart—all your hearts—can be pierced as easily as his was. When they stop beating you may know no more pain, but give a care to mine! I shall not be able to live with the agony should I lose you!"

The brothers glanced at each other uneasily. "Please," the twins begged, but Gwyneth shook her head and groped for the latch on the door behind her.

As she pulled it open a few inches she sniffed and squared her shoulders. "Until I was old I'd known no joy in my life save for you, my children. Yet I endured for your sakes and all I did—everything I did—I did for you. I understand why you feel you must fight, but if possible I would forfeit the small happiness I've lately found if I could but sway you from this course. If you should fall, so young, upon this battlefield—" she eyed each of her sons in turn— "my life shall have been for naught. And I should have nothing to live for anymore."

Again the brothers exchanged looks of concern. Then, as one, they looked at their mother again. "You are worried for nothing," Matthew assured her. "Please, do not be so distraught. We'll return, whole and healthy, and one day Durningham will be ours again."

"Damn Durningham!" she cried. "But I pray God

go with you, since you are so determined to go."

Gwyneth turned and stumbled through the portal, nearly slamming into John, who stood beyond. As the door behind her swung closed she said bitterly, "I deserve your full wrath, milord, for what I've done to you. But I'd rather you'd cut out my heart than lure my sons into harm's way."

Before he could respond, Gwyneth ran up the remaining stairs to the solar, and there she barricaded herself within. Alone again, she collapsed on the floor to shed the sorriest tears of her life.

Gwyneth stood in the tall, wide window of the solar, holding closed about her shoulders a heavy fur rug. The damp, icy wind cut her cheeks and made her red, chapped knuckles burn, but she was oblivious to it. She had stood in this window long hours, scrutinizing the barren landscape beyond the crenellated walls of the bailey. And barren it was, for though in the near distance stood the dark green pines of the forest, those trees were not in her view. All Gwyneth could see were the snow-dusted fields, most of them brown with dead grass, and the mottled, muddy road leading to the castle. The road was untraveled; she saw no men returning.

"Lady Gwyneth, open the door, please!"

She turned from the window and considered the barricaded door hostilely. She did not reply.

"Lady Gwyneth, you must open the door—now!"

"Go away," she ordered at last, with little emotion.

"I will not."

"Gerald, go away!"

"I cannot do that, milady. I must speak with you."

"We are speaking now." Still clutching the rug about her, Gwyneth stepped down from the window seat.

"This will not do. My lady, I beseech you, let me in."

Again she did not speak for some long seconds. When she did she sounded tired. "I am still, for the moment, the lady of Farleigh and you are the seneschal, subject to my command. Obey me, Gerald, and go from my door."

"You are not quite correct in your assumption, milady," he called back to her through the heavy oak timbers. "As seneschal of Farleigh Castle, I follow my lord's commands. It is on his behalf that I come to you now."

Gwyneth had padded softly into the center of the chamber. Now she paused. More animated than she had been in days she asked, "Have you word from Lord John? Do you know of my sons' fates?"

"I will speak to you of this when you let me inside the solar, Lady Gwyneth," Gerald promised.

She hesitated only a moment longer before going to the door and removing the beam from its bracings. She had felt secure in this room designed to be the last hold-out in the event of invasion by hostile forces. It was the highest in the keep, with one of the strongest doors. But Gwyneth felt vulnerable again, having opened it to Gerald, so she did not undo the latch. She stood still, watching as the handle was moved tentatively from the outside. And she took several steps back when, finally, the door creaked open and she saw her friend standing alone on the landing.

"Lady Gwyneth!" he gasped, giving in to his shock. "Jesu in heaven, are you all right?"

He hurried into the room before she could change

her mind and slam the door shut on him again. He considered his mistress more carefully, but what he saw eased his mind not at all. In the week she'd been secluded in the solar, Gwyneth had lost weight. It was obvious even in her face, which seemed unusually gaunt. Her slanted green eyes were bright, but they were sunken and shadowed as if bruised. Her flesh was pale, except where her cheeks were wind-burned an unnaturally rosy pink. Even her hair, uncovered and unbraided, was wild and snarled in disarray.

The seneschal swallowed visibly, his adam's apple bobbing up and down above his collar.

"Milady, 'tis awfully cold in here. Cold as it is outdoors."

Gwyneth shrugged, so he passed her and went to the window where he tied down a skin to cut the wind whistling into the chamber. When he turned around, he glanced at the cold pit where only ash remained from the last fire that had burned there. "Have you no wood?" he asked, knowing full well she did not. No servant had been allowed inside these past many days with kindling or candles, food or drink.

"Tell me what you've heard," she demanded, ignoring his question.

The seneschal glanced through the open doorway at the burning torch mounted on the wall beyond. He considered calling for wood and lighting a fire, but immediately decided against it.

"Let's go downstairs to your chamber or my work room, Lady Gwyneth. You could warm yourself by a blazing fire and perhaps drink some mulled wine, eat some fresh bread—"

"I care not about warming my limbs or filling my belly, Gerald," she interrupted. "I care only for my children. Now tell me, what have you heard?" She stepped toward him and grabbed his tunic with one hand. "Are they wounded? Dead? Tell me!"

"Neither, milady," he informed her quickly, wary of the unnatural glint in her eyes.

"They are well?" she asked hopefully. "You've had word?"

He considered lying, but gave up that notion, too. "Nay, milady," he confessed gently, placing his hand over hers on his chest. It was cold as a corpse and rough to the touch. He could not help wincing, though he squeezed her fingers comfortingly. "There's been no word of your sons. But there would have been word, had something grave happened to any of them. You know that, Lady Gwyneth, surely you do."

She frowned, digesting the information. "So there's been no messenger sent here in all the days they've been gone, and you know nothing of the situation at Kurth."

"Ah, but I do," he assured her, and she cocked her head like a little bird. "The combined army of the local barons attacked the keep at Kurth only yesterday. The battle to free Lord Neville and his family has just begun."

Gwyneth straightened, sighed and turned away. "Then my sons have been safe this past week. Only now are they facing danger." She looked at Gerald over her shoulder. "You lied to me."

"I did not, milady!"

"You did. You told me you came to speak to me as the earl's own voice. Yet, by your own admission, you've not heard from him."

"That is irrelevant. I know my lord's wishes and intentions."

"His wishes and intentions are irrelevant to me."

"That, milady, is quite obviously a lie," Gerald said wisely. Coming around to face her squarely, he continued, "Lord John would not have you behave as you've been. 'Tis unfitting for his lady wife, chatelaine of Farleigh's keep and the earl's representative in his absence, to seclude herself as you have done."

"*You* are John's representative in his absence," she corrected. "You hold the highest office in his household."

Gerald shook his head and flexed his fingers. "My lady, listen to me. In matters of business, what you say is true. But as his lawful spouse you must, in the earl's absence, welcome any guests."

"Guests!" Gwyneth responded with a snarl. "I've no wish to entertain guests of any kind. Besides, you could handle such tedious duties yourself, Gerald. Certainly you did as much before the earl was found in Gascony."

"There were few visitors to Farleigh in the years no lord resided here, and those what came were of no consequence—"

The lady frowned, detecting an odd nervousness in Gerald, son of Penworth. Arching one brow, she shrewdly inquired, "Who of importance is coming here now?"

"The king," he confessed abruptly, seemingly relieved to have said it. "King Henry II himself."

"What!" Gwyneth scoffed. "Why would the ruler of the largest kingdom in the world come to Farleigh?"

"I do not know his purpose."

"How do you know he is headed here?"

"There was a messenger, a royal messenger, who arrived at the castle early this morn."

"I did not see him," Gwyneth said suspiciously. "And I would have, had one come. I've stood in that window for hours, day after day, and no man rode in through the gates this day."

Gerald shook his head, but there was relief in his sigh and a hint of a smile pulling at his lips now. "Come below with me," he suggested, urging her toward the door. "We'll talk elsewhere."

"Why? What is wrong with this chamber?"

"It's damned cold, that's what is wrong with it."

"Nay." Widening her stance in defiance, Gwyneth crossed her arms over her chest. "I know you, Gerald. You are trying to trick me into going downstairs and resuming my duties."

"I admit I would, if I deemed it necessary, to get you from this frigid chamber. But the truth is what I'm telling you, and I believe it shall move you to action."

"I intend to remain here 'til my sons return or I've word of them, at least."

"Lady Gwyneth, you are no mad woman as the servants here are beginning to think. Nor are you grief-stricken, either, for your sons and your husband are alive and well."

"As far as we know!"

"Aye, as far as we know. Neither are you a fool, milady; you know when the message you wait for comes, it will be carried through the front portal, not through the window in this, the highest room of the keep. Below, you'll receive any word more quickly than you would locked away up here."

Gwyneth scowled thoughtfully but did not relax her posture. "You speak truly when you say a messenger from the king arrived?"

"I do." Gerald nodded emphatically. "He arrived in the dark hours before dawn. No doubt you were sleeping."

She pursed her lips. "Mayhap."

"Then, please, Lady Gwyneth, let us go downstairs. There's a warm fire in my work room, and while we speak I'll arrange for a bath to be readied in yours and the earl's private chamber."

With a curt nod, Gwyneth agreed to accompany Gerald down the stairs. On the way they passed two spinsters returning to the weaving room who lowered their eyes and scuttled by without meeting their mistress' gaze.

"Do they all think I've gone mad?" she asked softly when they turned into the seneschal's chamber.

"Let us say there's been more than a little gossip. Now that you've come out of the solar, it should cease quickly enough."

Gerald motioned for Gwyneth to take a stool at one end of his table. As she sat she noticed the bread trencher, the platters of victuals, and the flagon of wine. "Don't you usually break your fast in the great hall?" she asked casually. "Or were you simply so sure of your persuasive tongue?"

"I was hopeful, that's all," he explained, sitting down opposite his lord's wife. "Hopeful you would come to your senses."

"Let us assume that I have," Gwyneth continued, beginning to nibble on a quince tart. "Tell me when the king is coming here, and why."

"I've no idea why, except, in answer to the question you posed earlier, John of Farleigh is the greatest lord in these parts. He's no young upstart, granted a fief by Stephen or Henry's grandfather. His demesne is not so young even as your father's, bestowed in King William's time. Nay, Lord John's family has ruled this shire seemingly forever, since his ancestors were Danish chieftains. He is one of the few earls in

England, Lady Gwyneth; his power and his influence are great."

She licked crumbs from her fingers but set her mouth in a grim line. "He influenced my sons," she said quietly, "to fight a battle that is not their own, a battle wherein they might easily be maimed or killed. I suspect his motive is to take my children from me even as I, with my old, barren womb, am keeping him from siring children of his own."

Gerald frowned and snapped, "Lady Gwyneth, gather your wits! 'Tis because you feel so guilty you expect even God to smite you with a bolt of lightning. But realize Lord John would never do what you suspect. You learned quickly to care for him. How could you care for a man as cruel as you imagine him now to be?"

Suitably chastised, Gwyneth realized her old friend spoke true. How could she, indeed? she asked herself silently. Aloud, she inquired, "When is King Henry expected?"

"In a fortnight."

"You have notified John?"

"Aye. But he may be delayed. Even if he is not, you must be at his side, Lady Gwyneth, to welcome the king."

"You think so?" she asked, breaking off a piece of warm, partridge pie and stuffing the morsel into her mouth.

"Of course I think so!" Gerald leaned forward, his palms on the table, and brought his face close to hers. "You are no longer Gwyneth of Sherborne or Gwyneth of Durningham, but Gwyneth of Farleigh, the earl's lady wife."

"Not for very much longer," she said calmly.

"What are you saying?"

"This is not news to you," Gwyneth informed him. "I told you before the earl declared his intent to annul our marriage as soon as he learned I was not Arnulf's youngest daughter, but an old dame with grown sons."

Pushing himself off the table Gerald recalled, "You told me *you* suggested an annulment to my lord, not the other way 'round."

"No matter." She finished the wedge of pie and filled a cup with wine. When she'd sipped from it she reminded him, "I tricked the lord of Farleigh into marrying me and, as I always expected, he will rid me as his wife as soon as he is able. Thus, I doubt he would care to have me at his side when he entertains the king—I would be an embarrassment he will have to explain after I'm gone."

"Well, he is not here and someone at Farleigh must host our royal visitor. 'Tis your duty, milady. You owe John that much."

"Very well. I'll not shirk my duty so that he has even more grievances against me. But if my husband returns to Farleigh before our sovereign arrives, I shall make myself scarce."

"Where would you go?" the seneschal asked curiously.

"Mayhap to my son's graves."

Chapter Eighteen

✣ ✣ ✣

Gwyneth waited. She was not waiting for King Henry but the earl of Farleigh, her husband, whom she believed would be the first to arrive at the castle. When he returned it would be her time to go. But in the meanwhile she ate as if she had just discovered food, putting back on the weight she had lost. She smoothed balms into her wind-roughened skin until her hands and face were no longer red and cracked. She slept until she felt rested and fit again. In between times she ordered the servants about, ignoring their unease around her until it disappeared altogether. The keep was cleaned to sparkling, the guest rooms readied for overnight visitors, and there were always extra meats roasting and sweet delicacies cooling in anticipation of additional mouths to feed.

"You've done an admirable job, if I may say so, Lady Gwyneth," Gerald complimented her one afternoon. It was a week to the day since she had emerged from the solar above. "The earl will be well pleased."

"I hope so."

Gerald cocked a brow curiously. "Oh? You still care that he looks upon you favorably?"

"I do, but not for the reasons you suspect. I've done

what I have not so that he can impress our sovereign, but so that he can never say I was derelict in my duties or worse, a mad woman."

"My lady." The two of them were standing on the stairs just above the level of the gallery, and Gerald put his hands on her shoulders. "I know, after the men left to join forces against Eye, that you were distraught. But you cannot still believe Lord John means your sons harm."

"Perhaps not. But I can't know, once he returns, what my husband means for me."

The seneschal removed his hands from her. "As a knight the earl is hard, but as a husband was he so?" he asked her searchingly. Though Gwyneth did not answer, an image flashed in her mind of John still lying abed, patting the empty space beside him and urging her to return to that warm spot she had just vacated. She could almost feel the soft pillow in her hands that she tossed at him with a promise that when her chores were done, she would do as he asked.

There was a commotion below, a rush of excitement. Gwyneth and Gerald sensed it more than heard it. Together they hurried down the few stairs that took them to one of the rooms in the gallery. Entering it, they hurried to the window overlooking the great hall below and looked down.

"Master Gerald! Lady Gwyneth!" one of the men-at-arms called out, seeing them there. "He's come! He's been spotted on the road to Farleigh!"

"Lord John?" Gwyneth asked.

"No." The knight shook his head. "The king. King Henry II, lord of all England!"

"He's early, by a sennight," Gerald pointed out as he and his mistress retreated again into the small room. "Lord John believes he still has another week before he need return."

"Look at me!" Gwyneth wailed, feeling a flutter of nervousness in her belly at the thought of the king coming to dwell in her home. "I must change out of these rags and comb my hair." She was out on the stairs again before she had finished speaking. Knowing Gerald was right behind her she turned and begged, "Send Bess to me, will you? In my husband's absence, I'd best be at the door to greet the king when he arrives, and I'd rather not look like a serving wench when I do."

"Immediately," Gerald promised, hurrying down the stairs as Gwyneth hurried up them.

In the chamber she shared with John, Gwyneth stripped out of her dun-colored tunic and chocolate brown bliaut, which she often wore when doing messy or menial chores. By the time Bess knocked on the door and entered, she had pulled out every tunic she owned and strewn them on the bed as she attempted to decide on the appropriate ones to wear in the king's presence.

"Your wedding costume," the girl suggested helpfully, and Gwyneth nodded in agreement.

"'Tis the best I own; I suppose the king of England deserves to see me in my best."

Bess had a little trouble doing up the side laces of her lady's bliaut, and she apologized with a giggle. "I cannot believe King Henry's almost at our door! Some day I'll be able to tell my children of it."

"Aye," Gwyneth agreed, trying to help her with the ties, but only making matters worse as sixteen fingers and four thumbs were far too many to do the job correctly. "I give up!" she exclaimed, raising her hands to her head and beginning to unplait her braids. "Get me into my clothes, Bess, or I shall have to appear before his majesty naked!"

"There, there, I have it now. It's done." Bess urged Gwyneth onto a stool and took over the combing of her hair. "I wouldn't think you'd be as nervous as I, milady. Surely you've visited baronies where old King Stephen was holding court."

"Ha!" Gwyneth scoffed. "Surely I've not. And yet, I did not expect to feel quite so... so excited at the prospect of entertaining our king."

"You wish the earl were here, eh?"

"Aye," she replied softly, "I suppose I do." Picking up the gold web hair ornament John had given her at Christmas she ordered, "Braid only the locks framing my face. Let the rest of it flow freely. And I'll wear this with the sheerest veil I own."

"Very good, milady."

Gwyneth looked very good indeed, when she went down to the hall to await the king's arrival. Gerald complimented her profusely on her appearance, and she knew he was relieved she no longer looked like the deranged woman he'd found in the solar just a week ago. But he, too, was put out in his most splendid finery, a gray under tunic topped by a black one, both edged with intricate, silver embroidery.

"He's here!" a man called from the door of the keep. "He's in the outer bailey and about to cross the second bridge!"

Without either suggesting it to the other, the lady of Farleigh and Farleigh's seneschal moved to the arched entryway leading to the great hall.

There they stood, awaiting the arrival of King

Henry. It took a full minute for Gwyneth to realize a goodly number of servants were hovering in the shadows on the stairs and in doorways. "Out!" she hissed, making shooing motions. "You'll see the king when you serve him! Don't loiter about, or you'll be dismissed!"

There was a flurry of scurrying and shuffling. A minute later the keep seemed deserted, except for its mistress and castle-keeper. Then there was a noise at the keep's entrance. When they looked, Gwyneth and Gerald first saw two of Farleigh's castle guards, both in full knightly garb, standing at attention on either side of the opened door. Next a man appeared between them as he strolled leisurely inside. It was Henry, son of Matilda and Geoffrey Plantagenet, now ruler of nearly all the land on both sides of the Channel.

The Farleigh guards clicked their lance poles smartly on the stone floor as King Henry passed them. When his eyes fell on them, Gerald bowed and Gwyneth curtsied. Her heart was pounding; she wondered if everyone—noble, merchant and peasant alike—felt such awe in the presence of their monarch.

"Your majesty," she managed to say when she saw his legs come to a stop before her.

"Welcome to Farleigh, your highness," Gerald said quickly following.

"Rise."

At his command the two stood. Because the king was directly in front of Gwyneth, for a moment she gazed at him and he at her.

He was not what she'd expected.

She'd grown up with stories of this king's grandfather, his own namesake, and grand and glorious tales they'd been. Also, though many felt Stephen of Blois had been a failure as a ruler, those who'd known him insisted his shortcomings resulted from his kindly and placid nature. Of course, every Briton knew of this young king's mother, Matilda, Empress of Germany, who had fought all her life to ensure her son's ascension to the English throne. Because of these stories of courage and kindness, strength and daring, Gwyneth had expected to sense a special aura surrounding this sovereign lord.

She did not, and she was immediately disappointed.

This King Henry, standing before her, did not look so very young. He was of medium height, yet though he wore fine clothes and shoes, heavy gold rings and medallions, and had a rich, ermine cloak tossed back over one shoulder, his costume did not disguise the fact that he was painfully thin. One shoulder, too, was a little lower than the other, as if he'd had rickets. And his face! Though his features might not have been unpleasant, his watery blue eyes protruded as if the sockets were not quite large enough to accommodate them, and there was a cruel—and permanent—smirk to his mouth. But the most unattractive aspect of his appearance was his hair. Everyone knew Henry had red hair, but surely no one had ever referred to him as a carrot-top. Beet-head was the term that came to Gwyneth's mind, and she had to swallow a laugh that almost choked her. Yet it was true. Henry's hair was not the dark, russet hue of her own and Gwendolyn's, or the lighter, brighter shade of Matthew's, or even the red-tinged gold of her husband's. It was near the color of wine, and more precisely the color of beets.

The lady's nervousness disappeared as abruptly as a dream upon waking. "This way, your majesty," she invited, gesturing him into the hall. "I must apologize for the absence of my husband, but duty has called him away." She led him to the table on the dais, and his full complement of guards—ten in all—joined him there. The wine steward had already made himself available, and she bade him pour the finest from the cellar for her guests. "Would you care for anything else? Are you hungry from your journey?"

"Aye," the king nodded, slurping down a large gulp of wine that dribbled into his scraggly beard in a way that reminded Gwyneth of her father. "Food for me and my men."

Gerald joined Gwyneth at her side and volunteered his services to the king. Finishing his cup, Henry gestured for the steward to refill it and said to the seneschal, "My knights would like some wenches to keep them warm tonight." He punctuated the request with a leer and a wink that caused both Gerald and Gwyneth to share a sidelong glance. "No need to find one for me, though." He paused and they waited for him to make some declaration of his loyalty to his wife, the queen. Instead Henry leaned toward Gwyneth and whispered, "I can keep your bed warm since your husband isn't here to do it."

Gwyneth stepped back so quickly she stumbled off the platform on which the head table sat. Fortunately, Gerald caught her before she fell.

"I will see to your further refreshments, your grace," she managed to say.

"And I will look to your men's comforts," Gerald added before they both hurried out of the hall and into the kitchen as fast as they could without breaking into a run.

"God's tears, he's disgusting!" Gwyneth declared in a loud whisper. "That is the man everyone wished to to succeed Stephen? Stephen's own illegitimate son would have been a better choice than that scum!"

She turned and gave quick orders to Cook and then turned back to Gerald who said, "There is no rule that says the rightful heir to the throne must be handsome and good, strong and fair. He's simply the offspring of old King Henry's daughter, and by that right our king. We must put up with him until he sees fit to go."

"Why is he here?"

"I've no idea. I've told you that. Who knows if we'll even be told the reason with the earl absent."

"Can't you ask him? You're John's seneschal."

"Aye, I'll ask. And I'm sending word immediately to Lord John, advising him to return here as soon as he is able."

"Do that." Gwyneth smoothed down her skirt, righted her girdle, and took a deep breath. "Now I'm off to entertain the king—though not in the manner it appears he would wish me to."

"Don't anger him," Gerald cautioned.

"I've lived with a man I found more distasteful than Henry. I know how to avoid conflict. But my husband had better return here soon so that I can make my excuses to avoid our king's royal presence."

Gwyneth returned to the hall as several servants entered carrying trenchers and platters of savory steaming meats and vegetables. Henry patted the empty chair beside his own and urged her to join him.

"Nay, milord," she declined. "It's been but an hour or so since I had my midday meal."

"Sit!" he commanded. "Now."

Obediently, Gwyneth scurried around the table and settled into her chair. Though she steadfastly refused to eat—watching the king and his men would have been enough to ruin her appetite, had she felt any hunger to begin with—it was the beginning of many long hours she would spend seeing that her guests' appetites were satisfied.

By the time of the evening meal, when the trestle tables were set up for the Farleigh men-at-arms and staff, she began to hope John would not return with too many of his other knights behind him, for she feared there would not be enough food prepared to feed them. They were gluttons, she thought as she watched the king and his entourage lick their fingers as well as animal bones clean, and then toss the remains of their repast into the clean rushes on the floor. They were crude, she realized, as Henry himself belched into her face without so much as an apology and the others trumpeted their flatulence up and down the table. They were wicked, she saw, as the royal guards grabbed every wench who ventured too near them, reaching into the girls' tunics to paw their breasts, or under them to pinch their naked buttocks.

When Gwyneth noticed one of the men trying to grab the arm of a little girl who'd come to help her mother serve, she flew out of her chair, off the dais, and gathered the child up, removing her to the kitchen. To both the girl's mother and the other servants she announced, "Not a child, male or female, under the age of fifteen is to enter the hall tonight. Nor is any such child to serve the king or his men for the remainder of their stay here. Do you understand?"

She was so adamant, none of the staff dared question the lady's judgment, not even in whispers among themselves.

When Farleigh's people had eaten and the extra tables were removed, the king and his men stood down from the dais. Henry demanded the earl's chair be put close to the hearth and that Gwyneth join him there, too. His men began disappearing, and though they left the great hall in only each other's company, she did not trust them. So before she reluctantly joined her royal guest by the fire, she told her own guards to pass the word that if any female at Farleigh Castle cried for help, she was to be rescued no matter if the king himself was her companion.

"Gerald, please join us," she said pointedly as her friend hesitated. "A stool for you here, beside me."

"If you've no objections, your highness," he said to the king before sitting. When Henry merely grunted, he did as Gwyneth bade.

"Now," she whispered, leaning close to the seneschal's ear. "Ask him now."

"Your majesty," he began, "could you tell us your reason for coming here? We are honored by your visit, of course, but we should like to know your purpose so that we might better serve you."

"I came to see your lord," he announced, spitting a kernel of something so that it arcked through the air before disappearing in the debris on the floor. Gwyneth winced in dismay.

"The earl is joined with other barons from nearby shires, attempting to rescue the lord of Kurth."

The king turned his absurdly red head in Gerald's direction. "Aye?"

"Yes. That cockshead, Elwood, the baron of Eye, let his men cut the heir to Kurth's throat after forcing the boy's father to surrender the keep. Now Lord John and his neighbors are trying to rescue the family and free the estate."

Henry's countenance was grim as his rheumy eyes

locked on Gerald's. "So I have heard. What think you their chances?"

"Good, I hope. But we've had no word since the siege began."

"You haven't communicated with your lord? He does not know I am here?"

Gwyneth explained that her husband did not expect the king for some days yet, but that Gerald had sent another message to inform him he'd already arrived.

"He'll be here soon, do you suppose?"

"Perhaps as soon as two days' time."

Henry nodded, but if he were pleased or displeased, Gwyneth could not tell.

"Is there anything we might do for you?" Gerald inquired. "Besides extending the earl's hospitality, of course."

"You could tell me more about the situation here in this part of England. I know that Elwood is keenly disliked—I care for him not myself. In truth, he is part of the reason I returned here from Anjou. He had followed me to my homeland and was begging me for an audience I cared not to allow."

"The baron of Eye is despicable," Gerald informed the king a little too eagerly, Gwyneth thought. "He was loyal to Stephen, though even your predecessor seemed not to like him too well. Rarely was Elwood called to Council. And since you disdained his influence for having been so loyal to King Stephen, he seems to have gone a little mad."

"Mad?" Henry pounced on the word. "You mean you think him truly mad?"

"I—I don't know." Gerald seemed a bit flustered by the king's reaction to his comments. "Perhaps the border wars he has initiated, and the random pillaging of inconsequential towns, is simply his cruel and vicious way of retaliating for falling into royal disfavor."

"Madness runs in families," the king was muttering, still dwelling on Gerald's earlier words. "Or so they say. But I do not believe that is true, do you?"

Both Gwyneth and Gerald knew the fear all ruling families had of madness. Too often it occurred among the nobles of highest rank because of close kin bound in marriage. For this reason, no one related to the fourth degree could now wed, by decree of Holy Mother Church.

"Nay, I do not," Gwyneth assured him, feeling a sudden and reluctant sympathy for the man. "Madness comes upon a person because of experience—terrible fears or great losses. It is not passed through the blood."

Henry smiled at her, his crooked, leering smile. Then he glanced at Gerald, seated on his low stool. "Besides the thanes rushing to Kurth's aid, what are the barons here doing to protect their own demesnes?"

"In Sherborne, a town that sits between Farleigh's holdings and Eye's own, they've built—"

"Fortifications," Gwyneth interrupted, not quite certain why she felt it wise to be discreet. "They've dug a trench to fill with water, but I doubt it will be as big an obstacle as a castle moat." Her smile was almost apologetic. "The lord of the manor there even has attempted to teach his villeins to shoot with a trained archer's skill, but who knows? It's little enough, in the face of Eye's trained knights."

Gerald and Henry scowled at Gwyneth, each for his own reasons. She ignored them both.

"And you here? How safe did John of Farleigh leave you when he went off to fight?" the king inquired.

"Quite safe, milord, I assure you. Farleigh's walls

are high and its knights are many, as I am sure your own men will report to you before the day is done."

Again, Henry smiled. What brightened most men's faces, no matter how ugly, made Gwyneth shiver with revulsion. "Clever lady, Gwyneth of Farleigh. A clever lady you are."

"Have you come to help us deal with Elwood of Eye?" Gerald asked his king. "Is that why you wished to speak with the earl of Farleigh?"

"Indeed," he nodded, sipping the last from the goblet he had not set down since he first picked it up hours earlier. "I have come to see that that baron gets what he deserves, and I felt sure your lord would be the one to help me."

Quite abruptly, the king dropped his pewter cup and it clanged on the stones at his feet. Both Gwyneth and Gerald jumped, startled, but Henry did not move except that his eyes closed and his head lolled.

"Your majesty? King Henry?" Gwyneth said as Gerald shook the man's royal shoulder.

"He's asleep."

"He's in a drunken stupor, is what you mean," Gwyneth announced. "Leave him. I am retiring to my room before he wakes and looks for me again."

"Lady Gwyneth," Gerald called after her, following on her heels as she made for the stairs. "Why did you halt me in my answering of his questions? Why did you lie, saying they'd dug a moat when in truth they built a wall? He is our king, after all, and deserves to know what goes on in his own land."

"I don't know," she admitted, stopping to turn to Gerald after placing only one foot on the first step. "But if he is the man decreed by law and the Lord Almighty to rule us for the next several decades, I hope someone poisons his food. I dislike him, Gerald; I distrust him. I'd advise you to be cautious as well. At least until Lord John returns."

She pursed her lips thoughtfully. "Did King Henry send a written message announcing his intended visit?" When Gerald nodded in response to her query she asked, "Are you're certain the message was real?"

"I can read, milady," he assured her. "And I know the royal seal when I see it."

"Very well." Gwyneth let her eyes roam back into the great hall and settle on the sleeping monarch. "'Tis a pity England's got herself such a pathetic and disgusting whelp upon the throne. I'd rather old Arnulf of Sherborne were seated there, instead of this Angevin cur."

Chapter Nineteen

✧ ✧ ✧

Gwyneth was surprised to see neither the king nor any of his men at chapel the next morning. Gerald was not there, either. As soon as she returned to the keep, she intended to look for the seneschal. But before she could begin her search for him, she discovered Bess straightening the bed in her and the lord's chamber.

"Bess, what ailed you this morning? I've grown used to you attending me. You know best how to do my hair," she said conversationally as she removed her cloak. "And you always attend chapel at Lauds—

"God's wounds! What in the name of everything holy has happened to you?"

Gwyneth interrupted herself when the servant, who'd been half hidden by the bed curtains, turned to face her. The girl's pretty face was swollen and both her eyes were black, one closed to a mere slit. As well she had a gash on the back of one hand that seemed to break open with the slightest movement of her fingers—it was dripping blood onto the front of her tunic. "Who did this to you?" Gwyneth demanded, grabbing a cloth from her washing bowl and pressing it against the girl's hand in an attempt to staunch the blood. "It was one of the king's men, wasn't it?" she asked more gently, looking into the servant's pathetically disfigured face. When Bess nodded and tears began to stream down her puffy cheeks, Gwyneth tossed the cloth aside and took her in her arms. Over the girl's shoulder she said, "Why didn't you call out for help? If the devil's bastard was beating you, forcing himself on you, why did you not call out? The castle guard has orders, Bess, to rescue any maid if such a thing should happen."

"From the king's own man?" the girl asked skeptically. "No knight of Farleigh would challenge a royal knight, milady. This house has always supported Henry's claim to the throne, even through all the years of Stephen's reign. Lord John is the king's man, too."

"Lord John is first his own man, and this is his demesne. He would allow no one to hurt a young maid in his household, whether she be gently born or servant. Nor would I, Bess. You should have called for help, screamed your plight—"

"I didn't know." Released from her mistress' embrace, Bess sank down onto the lord and lady's bed, gingerly holding her face in her hands as she cried. "I thought he... he had the right to use me. He is a king's knight, milady, and a guest here at Farleigh." She raised her head to look up, and Gwyneth cringed to see her closed and blackened eye oozing tears much like a weeping sore. "I'm no innocent, Lady Gwyneth. I've known more than a few men. The... the man who had his way with me last night stole nothing precious from me."

"Bess!" Gwyneth made fists of her hands to restrain herself from shaking the girl, shaking some sense into her. "He stole what a woman should only give freely! And he hurt you badly to force you into giving it up. Damn his black heart to hell!"

Turning, she lunged for the door and flung it open. "Bess, get yourself from the keep. Have you family in any nearby village?"

"At Wilkshire, I do."

"It's not far, and not on the way to Kurth where a battle is raging. Go there, Bess. Rest 'til you're well and hide yourself until King Henry and his dogs are gone from Farleigh."

"Where are you going? What are you going to do?"

"I am going to the king, and I intend to say some things I bit my tongue to keep from saying last evening."

"Milady, don't!" Bess jumped up and grabbed Gwyneth's sleeve. "I will recover. The beating was not very bad. But if you speak against the king, and to his face—"

"Bess." She paused and placed one gentle hand over the girl's own.

"I've lived my life. And most of it, I'll admit, was spent in fear of the one man or another who held my fate in his hands. But no more. No man is going to do me and mine injury without accounting for it. Not even the king."

She quit the room and hurried down the stairs, but Henry and his men were nowhere to be found, not even breaking their fast in the great hall with the castle folk. Gerald was still among the missing, too.

"They've ridden off to survey the demesne," one of the men-at-arms finally told Gwyneth. "I heard tell the king wished to see the whole of the castle and its lands."

"Why?"

The knight frowned at his lady. "I confess I wouldn't know. Neither Master Gerald nor the king thought it their business to tell me."

"Gerald is with them, with the king and his men?"

"Aye."

She shook her head. "I suppose, when they return, all of Farleigh's guard is to turn out and give a display of their readiness for battle?"

The man looked surprised. "We are, milady. That's the truth of it."

"Jesu, Mary and Joseph!" she muttered under her breath as she turned away.

Gwyneth was sitting in a gallery room that gave her a view of the hall when King Henry, Gerald, and the royal knights returned to the keep. In an instant she was down the steps and confronting the monarch.

"Your highness, I must have a word with you."

"Certainly, Lady Gwyneth," he said, smiling that disgusting smile of his. "But we've been out since before the sun was up, and I and my men are in need of a meal. Perhaps later…"

"Now."

Gerald, beside the king, blinked in astonishment at Gwyneth's tone. He tried signaling her with his eyes, to send a silent message of warning. But though she knew full well what he was about, she purposely ignored him.

The king himself, however, did not appear ruffled by his hostess' unseemly behavior. Shifting his weight into a more casual stance he inquired, "What is the matter that so obviously upsets you, milady?"

"One of your men," she informed him, glancing at the line of royal knights flanking their king on either side, "beat and raped a serving girl."

Henry's brows arched over his protruding eyes. "That is terrible," he announced. "Griffin? Jake? Do any of you know of this matter?" he demanded, turning first to the left, then to the right, to look at each of his men. When they began, as one, to smirk and chuckle, he declared, "This is no laughing matter!" The startled knights straightened up, each considering his lord carefully. "Did any of you force yourself on an unwilling wench last night?"

The men regarded each other for a few seconds. Gwyneth suspected they were nearly all guilty of such a crime. But finally one admitted, "Aye, I had myself a bitch who made things rough on herself. She did not need to, though. I thought she liked it that way."

"You thought—!" Gwyneth took a step toward the royal guard, but the king himself stopped her by putting himself between them.

"What the lady says is true, then? You beat and raped an unwilling girl?"

The knight's expression was one of disbelief. "She wasn't a noble woman, your—your highness!" he assured Henry. "She was a serving wench, nothing more. And not a virgin, I can swear to that!"

King Henry turned away and gestured to his other knights. "Take Maurice outside. Tie him up and bare his back."

"But you can't do this! I've done nothing wrong! I—"

Maurice gave up his protesting as he was forcibly removed from the keep by his companions. Gwyneth, too surprised by the king's quick and admirable reaction, fell silent as well. "Have you a strap?" Henry asked Gerald. "And a man to use it? Twenty lashes ought to be punishment enough, don't you agree?"

The last remark was directed to Gwyneth. As she had never in her life ordered a punishment of any severity, she had no idea what was appropriate. Mutely, she shrugged.

Though she would have liked to have been almost anywhere else, she was required to watch the punishment delivered. And though she knew it was more than deserved in light of what the man had done to Bess, Gwyneth hated watching the whip stripe his back and the way he danced in agony with every lash.

Fortunately, the soldier was cut down and put to bed almost immediately. Gwyneth sent one of the servants to tend him, to bathe and bandage his cuts. The others returned to the great hall and, at last, to their morning meal. Having no appetite, both Gwyneth and Gerald excused themselves from their royal guests, pleading responsibilities that needed tending to.

She followed the seneschal to his work room and closed the door behind him. "What did you show the king?" she inquired.

"What he asked to see—the keep, the outbuildings, the curtain walls surrounding the baileys…"

"The moat, the bridges, the portcullis and guard towers, the oil pots and the armory—correct?"

"Aye." Seated, Gerald frowned up at Gwyneth. "You don't like it, do you?"

"No." She shook her head. "Why did the king say he wished to see the layout of the castle and all its defenses?"

"Because he suspects Elwood will attack Farleigh. If we can defeat him here, that will be the end of the baron of Eye." Gerald considered his mistress. "You doubt his word?"

"I did," she admitted, "until he took action against his own man. God's teeth, Gerald! You should have seen what that swine did to Bess!" She recounted the girl's injuries and informed the seneschal she had sent the child away for the time being. "If I'd had the power, I would have ordered him executed. But witnessing even what Henry had done to him was too much for my stomach." She sat down at the table. "Have you received word from John? Has he yet been advised King Henry is here?"

"No, no word. But by now he's surely received the message that the king's arrived early. I would think the earl would be returning home within days, if not hours."

"Sweet Mary, but I wish he were here now!" Gwyneth confessed with an exasperated sigh. "As well I wish my sons were with him."

"They will be," Gerald promised. "At least when Kurth is retaken."

"You are so sure—"

"And you are unsure, about the king. Tell me why, milady."

Putting her forearms on the table, she leaned toward Gerald. "Henry is so unkingly."

The seneschal chuckled. "I told you before, Lady Gwyneth. There is no law that says a king must be wise, fair of face, and pure. A king is like any other man, except for his parentage."

"I expected him to laugh at me when I told him what was done to Bess."

"But he did not. He meted out stern punishment, as any goodly lord would do. Now you are confused."

"Aye," she admitted. "My instincts tell me not to trust him, but he did right in the matter of Bess' rape. Though I like not your showing him the castle's defenses, if he predicts a battle between Eye and Farleigh here, then his interest is justified. Still..." Pausing, she chewed her lower lip thoughtfully.

"Gerald, I wish he were not our king. Or that there

was some other claiming the throne, someone whom John could support as so many did Henry's mother, Matilda, against Stephen."

"Well," the seneschal said, arranging some parchments across his table, "he is the monarch Farleigh and most of England has waited for; we must accept him as such. No matter that he is an unpleasant-looking, oafish churl, he is ours and he is against the baron of Eye."

That afternoon, in the outer bailey, the knights of Farleigh castle who were not doing battle with their lord against Elwood of Eye assembled in full armor to show their skills and their might to their king. They engaged in mock battle and displayed their talents as archers with both long and cross bows. At the end they put on a small, impromptu jousting tournament, to the delight of all in attendance.

Except for Gwyneth of Farleigh who, with Gerald and King Henry and King Henry's men, were perched on the parapet to better see the action in the yard. Her eyes kept moving to the land beyond the castle walls, always hoping she would see her husband and, God and John of Farleigh willing, her sons as well. But the road leading to the castle was as barren as an old witch's womb. The men in her life were not yet coming home.

"I see The Dane in Farleigh's knights."

"I beg your pardon?" Gwyneth dragged her eyes from beyond to the king beside her.

"Your husband has instructed his men personally, has he not?"

"Oh, aye. Every day he is home."

"The Dane's reputation was far-spread. He was

known throughout the kingdom, especially on the other side of the Channel, for his daring, his strength, his prowess with the sword and the lance. Imagine my surprise," he said, his lip curling into an ironic smile, "to learn that The Dane was John, heir to the earldom of Farleigh."

She did not know what to say. She simply nodded.

"If he'd been there to defend Kurth when Elwood's men attacked, I suppose there'd have been no contest. Elwood's forces would have been destroyed, and Kurth still in the hands of Neville, its lord."

"Perhaps." Gwyneth watched curiously as Henry's face began to flush.

"He's ruthless, your husband is. Like a lion, he knows no fear. He attacks to kill, and kill he does."

Gwyneth felt Gerald, on her other side, brush her arm. When she turned to him he shook his head almost imperceptibly in a wordless attempt to reassure her. Reading his face as she'd been able to when they were children, she knew he worried their sovereign's words would rekindle her fear for her sons.

When the seneschal protested gently, saying, "Your highness, my lord is neither cruel nor blood-thirsty, simply a brave and chivalrous knight like those of the Order of Templars," she felt as defensive as he. King Henry was so wrong in his estimation of John of Farleigh.

"You speak as if my husband were your enemy, your grace, not your ally," she pointed out, and Henry began to cough and bluster.

"Not so, milady. I only comment on his fame as a warrior. Though he chose to live as a nomad, serving no master for life, among his comrades and the lords he served he was always well known for his savage skill. The Dane survived many battles most did not. I think," he continued softly, clearing his throat as he gazed down at the yard below, "that leading his men in a fair fight against Eye, John of Farleigh would most certainly win."

"That would be best for all of us, would it not?" Gerald asked. "You've no wish to have Elwood among your council, and none of the land-owners on this isle relish him as their neighbor. Were he removed you could award his derelict fief to someone more deserving, a baron with your cause close to his heart."

"That is so," the king agreed, still watching as the Farleigh men-at-arms left the bailey. The tourney had ended. "But naught can be done until a final confrontation. And that, I am afraid, will not occur until this business at Kurth is concluded in some fashion."

"The earl should be here soon," Gerald assured Henry.

"How soon?" he demanded.

"I cannot say, precisely. I've sent word that you arrived earlier than we'd expected. I don't think Lord John would intentionally keep you waiting any longer than he could help. We know a king's time is valuable; he'd not have you waste it."

"I'm not wasting my time here, I promise you that," Henry said, running his tongue over his upper lip as he glanced at Gwyneth.

She shivered in response to Henry's blatant leer, but blamed it on the cold. "The men have finished their exhibition, and it's cold up here on the wall. Shall we climb down and return to the keep?"

"Aye, let's," Henry agreed. "It's accursedly windy and—damn! It is beginning to snow!" he complained suddenly, looking up at the gray sky as though it had personally offended him. Then, as if a fire were licking at his heels, he swung himself over the ladder they had used to climb the wall and descended as nimbly as a monkey.

Henry's knights were a little more gracious, allowing the lady of the castle to descend before following after the king. As she stepped onto the highest rung Gwyneth whispered to Gerald, who was leaning over and steadying the ladder for her, "I still do not like him very much."

"Nor do I," he whispered back.

Chapter Twenty

✥   ✥   ✥

Gwyneth was locked in her room, the chamber she shared with John of Farleigh. He'd not yet returned, though another two days had passed since the day of the knights' exhibition in the bailey. She had pleaded illness yesterday but had accepted all the meals brought her so as not to arouse anyone's, particularly Gerald's, suspicions. But she wasn't sick anymore than she was hungry. She was frightened—of the king.

Unlike his first evening at the castle, Henry had not consumed enough spirits to make himself drunk that second night. His men had, though—all except the one in the sick room in the cellar. They'd been boisterous and bawdy, grabbing the serving women who still had some fairness of face and figure, pulling them onto their laps and slobbering rank kisses upon them that Gwyneth was sure were most foul. But, under the king of England's watchful gaze, some had succumbed to sleep right there in the hall, while the rest had stumbled up to their assigned chambers alone or assisted only by their comrades.

Gwyneth was grateful and, swallowing back her dislike, had been both a gracious hostess and dutiful companion. Even after the castle priest, Father Peter, had retired to his quarters and Gerald had excused himself to work on his accounts, she had remained seated close to the fire with the king. Henry II was not verbose; they spent several hours playing tables and draughts, and he was most often quiet as he concentrated on the board games. It was only when the hour grew late and the great hall fell quiet except for the snoring servants and men-at-arms who, unimpressed with the royal guest still among them, had stretched out on their pallets, that he began to speak with any purpose. His purpose seemed to be to better know Gwyneth.

"You've not been the earl's lady wife long, have you?" he inquired, moving his rectangular checker piece from one square to another.

"Nay. We were wed in the autumn."

"Why?"

"Why?" She repeated the question, looking up from the board where she had been contemplating her own next move. "Because... Lord John and my father desired it. A marriage, I mean. Between us."

"There's no love between you, then?"

She blinked at her opponent. "I—I'm afraid I cannot answer that, your grace."

"You can." His voice was firm. "I am your king. You've no right to deny me anything, certainly not replies to my innocent inquiries."

The short hairs on Gwyneth's neck began to rise, a prickling sensation creeping over her shoulders. She looked down at the board again and admitted, "I did not know my husband before I wed him."

"Nor he you?"

"Nay, your majesty, he did not know me, either."

"Then why did he wish the marriage?"

"Surely you know that." Decisively she moved her piece, blocking one of the king's. "You're familiar with the problems of the barons in this area. The earl —my husband—and my father hoped our marriage would save the town of Sherborne from further strife."

Henry leaned forward, resting his bearded chin on his knuckles. "Sherborne sits on the border between Farleigh and Eye, does it not?" Gwyneth knew it was a rhetorical question; she did not bother to answer but studied the king's absurdly red head. "Your father— Sir Arnulf is his name, yes? Sir Arnulf and his people owe dual allegiance to both Elwood and John."

"Aye, we did. But Elwood demanded my father foreswear his fealty to the earl of Farleigh, as there was no lord here for many years. When he refused, the baron sent his men to plunder the village. They did terrible things. Everything from stealing the manor's sheep to killing innocent babes."

Henry moved his piece and leaned back in his chair. His eyes met and held Gwyneth's. "They were only peasants' children, of no real worth."

"My lord!" Gwyneth felt her original contempt for this man returning. "To a mother, be she low or high born, her babe is the most precious thing in life. Surely you know this. You lost your own son so very recently."

Henry's brows knit for a moment, and Gwyneth thought he seemed confused. Then his already huge eyes widened and he nodded his head. "Oh, aye. William, little William. But he was a prince, Lady Gwyneth, and would one day have ruled all I now rule, had he lived. His loss accounted for something."

With disgust she looked away, picked up a checker, and moved it simply for the sake of moving it.

Immediately the king jumped her, chuckling as he took her piece from the board.

"Forgive me, my lady," he apologized. "I am a man, and men do not feel as women do about children. Not even their own."

"So I have been told," she announced, her tone grim.

"You did not approve of the baron's suggestion that Sherborne's lord renounce his loyalty to the earl?" he asked, returning to his original topic.

"The baron of Eye suggested nothing. He ordered Arnulf to obey his will, and when he would not—when he insisted he must serve Farleigh as well as Eye—men were sent to terrorize the village folk and my own family. In truth, I'd urged my father to do as Elwood wished until the baron's heavy hand forced me to think otherwise."

"Oh? Your move," he prompted before continuing. "But your father and Lord John forced you into wedlock. Did you not think that rather heavy handed? And did it not accomplish the same end, except in reverse? By your marriage to John of Farleigh, the lands of Sherborne are his. Without a formal declaration, Arnulf has relinquished his allegiance to Eye."

"'Tis a pity," Gwyneth said sarcastically, making a purposeful move across the checkered board. "And a shame Elwood wasn't clever enough to think of the same tactic, only earlier." With a flourish she slid her piece onto a square at the edge of the board nearest Henry. "Had he arranged a marriage between Arnulf's daughter and his own son, Sherborne would all be his." She looked up. "King me."

Henry laughed, balancing a second piece on top of the one Gwyneth had just moved. Then, before she could retract her fingers, he grabbed her hand in his own and brought it to his lips. "Now we are equal," he informed her.

A sickening dread rushed into her stomach as if it were some drink she had swallowed down. Snatching her hand from the king's grasp she stood up. "It is very late, your highness, and my day begins before dawn. I am afraid I must retire to my room."

"Let me escort you," he offered gallantly, coming also to his feet. He took her elbow and led her to the stairs.

"Don't trouble yourself."

"It is no trouble, as you well know. My room is just beyond yours."

She could not refuse him, so she endured his touch as they climbed the narrow, winding stairs. How she wished Miles was curled up in his usual spot in the hallway; the young squire would have served as an excellent chaperon. But he was serving his lord along with her sons, at Kurth.

"Good evening, sire. Sleep well," Gwyneth said, forcing a smile as she reached for the latch on her door. But the king did not reciprocate with some light pleasantry, nor did he step back and away. Instead, at the precise moment she lifted the latch he leaned into the door, forcing it open and himself inside the chamber. She gasped as he spun her into the center of the room and closed the door behind him. "Your highness, please!" she exclaimed.

"Please what?" His grin was wicked, and Gwyneth knew only too well what he intended. What she did not know was what to do. She was not required to submit to him, as she'd had to with Ector. She had no desire to be with him as she once had desired John. Yet she could not cry for help as she'd insisted Bess should have done. No, this was the royal monarch. He followed no rules and she had no real recourse.

"Please leave," she begged him, keeping clear of the bed.

Henry laughed. "You don't mean that, my little kitten."

"I do!"

He moved toward her stealthily. "Nay, you do not. It is what all married women feel compelled to say. But here there is no need for pretense between us."

She backed up farther. "I am not pretending, my lord. I wish you to leave my chamber—my *husband's* chamber!"

Indulgently, the king shook his head. "I am not impressed with your protestations. What difference that this is your husband's chamber? He is but an earl and I a king. As my loyal vassal, what is his is also mine."

He reached out with startling quickness and grabbed Gwyneth's arm. She shrieked in surprise but sucked in her breath as he drew her to him. "You are a religious woman, are you, Lady Gwyneth?"

"Aye." She leaned back to put as much distance between her face and his as possible, but Henry kept her pinned to him with a surprisingly strong arm pressed to her back.

"Do not trouble yourself, then, with questions of sin and morality. I am king, chosen by the Almighty," he explained with eager simplicity. "Serve me and you serve God."

With that pronouncement Henry's lips descended to Gwyneth's neck as his free hand groped her bosom. She had thought Ector's touch vile, but it was nothing compared to this king's and she knew why. Her first husband had been corrupt, but she had never known anything else when she knew him. Now she'd had experience with another sort of man. That tender, unselfish experience served to magnify the king's depravity.

Her instinct was to push him off her, and then to hit him with something hard. But she could not do that. Divinely chosen or not, Henry *was* her king! Her mind began racing, searching for some way to end this sickening confrontation.

"My lady, you smell so sweet," he moaned into her neck.

"Certainly Eleanor does, too."

"Who?" he asked, not pausing for breath as he continued to assail her with unwanted kisses.

"Your wife, the queen!" Gwyneth reminded him, exasperated, frightened.

"Oh, dear lady, do not bore me with reminders that I've a wife in—in—Anjou. I care no more for her than you do your own wedded husband." The fingers of one hand were working at the laces on her bliaut. "Do not struggle so. I prefer my wenches willing, not feisty."

"Your majesty!" With a huff she managed to throw him off her. Startled, he backed up a pace or two and sat, with a plop, on the bed. Gwyneth wished he'd landed anywhere but there. The hard, stone floor would have suited her better. She thought his bony ass would have vibrated with pain had he fallen there hard.

Except for her personal revulsion, this scene would have played as a comedy had a band of troubadours performed it—until this moment. Now Henry's complexion ruddied until it matched his hair, and when he spoke his voice reminded her of no one else save her first husband.

"Bitch!" he growled, pushing himself up off of the bed and coming toward her again, menace in his eyes.

bed and coming toward her again, menace in his eyes. "I am the king, and you'd do well to remember it! Women fight to lay beside me in my bed. You've been invited, lady. Do not refuse the invitation, or it shall not go well with you."

Gwyneth swallowed hard and backed up into the table. The washing basin rattled as it jiggled across the surface. "I am the earl's lady wife."

"Neither God nor I care!"

"I do!"

"Your tongue speaks false, woman." He reached out and grabbed her shoulders, though she continued to cling to the edge of the table with her fingers. "You yourself told me you were forced into marriage with John of Farleigh. You knew him not at all before your wedding, and you've not been wedded long enough for any great fondness to have grown between you two. Stop playing the virgin! If you'd been one, The Dane would not have let you so for long. Besides, comely as you are and with the years you wear, there had to have been lovers before your husband took you as his own."

"But he did take me as his own, and I am bound by our vows to be faithful to him!" Gwyneth's words were strong and clearly spoken, but her heart was pounding and her knees were shaking with fear.

Then Henry struck her, hard across the face, and reached into the neckline of her under tunic, ripping it and the bliaut to her waist so that her breasts were exposed. She no longer felt fear. She felt rage like a fire that had first been ignited by Arnulf and later stoked by Ector. Now King Henry was doomed to perish in its heat. Intending nothing less than murder, Gwyneth whirled about and grabbed the heavy metal

But when she spun back to face the highest nobleman in all the land—the skinny, absurdly red-headed and frightfully homely reigning monarch—she was not brandishing the bowl. Instead she held up the bloodied rag she had used to staunch Bess' open wound. "You shame me into admitting this, your grace. A good woman should not be forced to. But I've the flux and am bleeding heavily. Do you still wish to take your ease with me?"

Though she could not fathom how it was possible, once again Henry made his protruding eyes bulge still the more. With a look of disgust he fell away from her. "Nay! Get that thing away from me!" She half expected him to make the sign of the cross as he began backing toward the door, yet Gwyneth continued to wave the soiled rag at him as if it were his standard. As he opened the door and began sidling out of the room he muttered, "That a whelp of Arnulf's would dare treat me as if I were some peasant midwife...!" Then he was gone.

Gwyneth slammed the door closed and bolted it surely from the inside. Except to take in the trenchers of food brought to her and to sneak out to use the garderobe when Nature called, that door had remained shut and bolted in the time since. She did not think that once in all the hours she'd secluded herself in her chamber she had ever taken to bed. Always she paced, or stared out the window, or dozed sometimes in her chair. Always her mind ran about like a hare, trying to find a solution to her dilemma, to plot some fool-proof scheme. But, like a rabbit that tunnels into the wrong hole and emerges lost, forced to scamper about in search of the one that is his, she would discard one notion after another.

Now there was a commotion in the bailey below.

Going to the window again, Gwyneth peered out and saw a strange rider dismounting near the keep. Turning, she was about to open her door and race down the stairs, but abruptly she stopped. She was supposed to be ill and besides, if this was news from John, Gerald would soon come to tell her of it.

The minutes passed with dreadful languor, yet eventually, as she'd expected, there was a scratching at her door. "Gerald, is that you?"

"Aye, milady. Are you well enough to receive me? There's been a message for you."

When the door flew open and he saw his mistress fully dressed and obviously hale, the seneschal's brows arched in surprise. As he stepped inside the chamber he admitted, "I suspected you were not ill, milady, yet I feared you had again fallen into that state that once compelled you to lock yourself in the solar." He closed the door. "I am happy to find such is not the case."

Impatiently, Gwyneth gestured for him to sit in John's chair. "What news?" she demanded.

"Perhaps you, too, should sit."

"Sweet holy mother of Jesu!" With a gasp she crumpled into her chair. "Has something happened to my sons? Are they dead, Gerald? Tell me!"

"No. That is, I've had no word from Lord John or anyone at the siege of Kurth. The messenger—you saw him arrive a short time ago? He came from Sherborne."

"Gwendolyn!" Gwyneth gripped one arm of her chair with both her bands as she leaned toward the table and Gerald. "Arnulf's discovered what she has done—what she and I have done together. Is that it?"

"Nay." With a shake of his head, the seneschal

reached out and patted one of her hands with his own. "Listen now, Lady Gwyneth. I have bad news. Sir Arnulf, your father, is dead."

Her emerald eyes blinked rapidly; she seemed not to have heard what he'd said. "What?"

"Your father is dead. He passed on sometime during the night. It was one of his men who came just now to inform you—to inform Lady Gwendolyn, rather. It is she, of course, whom they all think resides here."

Gwyneth's head dropped and as she looked at her hands, now folded in her lap, she began to laugh softly.

"Milady, are you well?" Gerald asked with concern, moving from his chair and dropping to one knee before her.

She raised her eyes to meet his. "Aye, my friend, I am fine. I was only thinking how well my whole scheme has worked. My sister was not forced into a loveless marriage because I deceived John of Farleigh long enough for her to flee with young Thomas. Now the earl can be free again also, by nullifying his marriage to me. And with Arnulf gone to his Maker, I'll not suffer by his hand for my deceits. I can, as well, return home to my dowerlands to live."

Gwyneth smiled a tight-lipped smile. "But the complications! Gerald, I'm in as much of a stew as I was when I learned Arnulf intended to marry Gwendolyn to John! He's gone off to fight and taken my sons with him, leaving me to deal with that cockshead who calls himself king, and to wonder if they've come to any harm."

"My lady, they are all trained knights, your sons and your husband."

"True." She nodded and stood and walked to the window again. With her back still to Gerald she asked,

"Why, then, do you think there has been no message? No word at all, even in response to the second rider you sent out to advise Lord John of Henry's early arrival here?"

"I do not know." The seneschal pulled himself up and sat again, this time in Gwyneth's chair. "I am sure neither my lord nor your sons have been felled in battle, but I confess I am concerned about Farleigh's messenger. He, too, has failed to return."

"Mayhap he encountered some difficulty along the way," Gwyneth suggested, turning around to face Gerald. "And mayhap the message he carried never reached John's ears."

The man frowned, but he did not gainsay her.

"Something is wrong here, Gerald," Gwyneth said. "I feel it in my bones, just as I feel there is something not right with our King Henry."

"Is that why you've gone into seclusion, Lady Gwyneth? It solves nothing, hiding yourself away," he chided gently.

And she rounded on him. "Nay? Well, if I had not feigned sickness, Master Gerald, I would now be the king's mistress!"

"Nay!" Protesting, he flew up out of the chair.

"Aye!" She nodded her head emphatically. "He tried to force his royal self on me the same as his knight forced himself on Bess."

"The cur—"

"He's worse than that."

"How did you save yourself from him?"

"I put him off," she said cryptically before asking, "He is still here?"

"Oh, aye, as if he were on holiday. He and his men have gone hawking and hunting deer in the forest. He walks the castle grounds, giving orders to our people as if he were the earl. Of course," Gerald added quickly, "I know Henry is the king and his authority exceeds my lord's, but this is Farleigh Castle, not Westminster or Gloucester."

"You dislike him, too."

Gerald nodded. "I am loathe to admit it, but it's true. And I, like you, do not look forward to being ruled by such a loathsome example of royalty for the rest of our lives. Sweet Jesu!" He slapped his forehead with the heel of his hand. "And we thought life under Stephen was torture."

"Where is Henry now?"

"Still sleeping, as are his men. None even roused when the messenger from Sherborne arrived amid much clatter. But then, they drank the best of your beer and Farleigh's wine—I should not expect them to be up until after the noon meal is served."

Gwyneth chewed her lower lip thoughtfully and sat down on the edge of the bed. Gerald asked her, "What of your father, milady? The servants would like some direction. He cannot remain above ground too many days, not even in this cold."

"The messenger is still here?" she asked and he nodded. "Send him to me."

The interview with Dodd, one of Arnulf's long-time men-at-arms, would have been amusing to Gwyneth had she not had so many other, more critical, matters on her mind. He could not contain his shock at finding Gwyneth the lord of Farleigh's wife instead of Gwendolyn, and his scruffy chin had fallen almost to his chest when his mouth gaped open in surprise. But he promised to do as she asked, and set off quickly.

When he was gone, Gwyneth finally sprawled out upon the bed, wondering what she should do next. Hugging John's pillow, still fragrant with the scent of him, an idea formed, at last and quickly, in her head. She had no time to waste so she changed her clothes unaided, slipped carefully down the stairs, and strode to the outer bailey where the stables housed the castle's horses.

Chapter Twenty One

❖ ❖ ❖

Gwyneth was glad for the ease of her escape from Farleigh and King Henry. She worried a little at not having left word for Gerald, but between the two of them, only he could read and write. She could not have risked leaving a spoken message with one of the servants—Gossip traveled among the staff faster than water down a spout. Better to let them all think, for a while, she had gone a little mad again and would not step out of her room.

The road to Kurth was well-traveled in better weather, but in the cold and blustery winds of winter few used it. An occasional wagon lumbered by; once, up ahead in the distance, she saw some riders moving in the same direction as she. Otherwise, Gwyneth journeyed alone. She had been assured by the stable man—whom she'd sworn to secrecy, for whatever his pledge was worth—that the gelding he'd given her was swift and sure-footed. Yet the road and the ride seemed endless.

The winds were biting and damp. The fur rug about her shoulders and the wool cloak under it seemed not enough to keep the cold at bay, especially as the short day wore on and quickly grew dimmer, finally culminating in a black and starless night. She was running on raw nerves, having had little sleep since Henry's assault. Now the endless jogging in the saddle made not only her bottom sore but her limbs and back and shoulders ache. Yet she dared not stop, except infrequently to relieve herself. There was nothing to stop for, actually—she'd not thought to bring any food with her—so going on was her only recourse.

But sleep she did, in the saddle, and it was fortunate for Gwyneth the gelding was well-trained. He plodded along the lonely road, never encountering a fork that offered him a choice of directions, or a deer or a rabbit or even a twitching leaf on a low-hanging branch that could have spooked him into charting a different course.

When Gwyneth woke her heart began pounding in panic, for she did not know where she was. It took her several moments to realize she was astride an unfamiliar horse and alone in the night on an unfamiliar road, and then to remember why. As her hammering heart slowed to a less painful pace, she saw that her mount had found a patch of exposed brown grass that he assumed was a well-deserved reward for his many hours of labor. While he nibbled at it contentedly, she looked around and discovered, thankfully, she had almost reached her destination. A hill rose up beyond the naked tree limbs of the woods lying directly before her. Though the outline of the motte was nearly indiscernible at that distance and in the dark, she could see the campfires scattered on the rise. They seemed little more than blinking fireflies, but she knew what they were even as she knew the dim, glowing rectangles at the crown of the hill were the torchlit windows of a keep—Kurth's keep.

Sliding down from the saddle Gwyneth stretched her legs, waiting a little impatiently for her mount to eat his fill. When he seemed satisfied she pulled herself onto his back again and urged him, at a cantor, up the road.

She did not stay on the narrow path long. Unsure of whom she might encounter, friend or foe, she turned the horse into the woods and picked her way gingerly through the trees. It was not as difficult as she had feared for most of the trees were as naked as tent poles. If it had been daylight, she could have made her way from one end of the woods to the other in a few minutes' span. As it was, it took her a little while to negotiate the distance in the heavy darkness.

"Lord John! Lord John, you asked me to awaken you," Miles said as he shook his master's shoulder. He jumped when the earl sat up on his cot, his hand already on the hilt of the sword he kept beside him. "It's only me, milord, your squire!"

"Miles, I'm sorry," the older man apologized, swinging his legs to the ground as he ran his fingers through his disheveled locks. "I feel as though I'd only just closed my eyes."

"'Tis almost the case. You've slept but a few hours, at most." The young man looked through the open tent flap. "It will be dawn in only a few hours more."

The earl stood and walked outside, the boy following him. He did not seem to notice the hard, frosty ground beneath his thinly covered feet as he raised his tunic, dropped his chausses and relieved himself. A whisp of steam floated up from the small puddle he created.

"There has been no activity, I take it?" he asked, settling his clothing aright.

"Nay, milord, or I'd have wakened you sooner."

"What of my stepsons?"

"The two you cannot tell apart have finished their hours on guard duty and are now asleep in yonder tent," the boy pointed. "The other, Sir Matthew, is preparing for the morning's attack."

"At which fire does he sit?"

"One in the outer ring. He's not too near the walls." Miles followed John back into his tent. "My lord, why do you worry about them so? They're knighted soldiers and men full grown. I'd think you'd keep them hidden in your own quarters, if you could."

John gave the boy a look. "Someday, perhaps, you'll have a wife and family of your own, my lad. When you do, you'll understand. Whether they are four or forty, if it is in your power she'll charge you to protect the children with your life. I advise you not to shirk that responsibility."

"If I have daughters, mayhap that will be true. But my sons I'll raise to be strong men," Miles announced, helping John into his shoes and hauberk.

"Lady Gwyneth's sons are strong men and fine warriors, too. Don't doubt it. But they have a battle of their own they must fight, and I wish them to live to see it through. Besides, my lady wife would despise me if any reached an untimely end on this mission. So, though they are a part of our army against Eye, I intend to see them safe to fight another day."

John shrugged on his fur-lined cloak and fastened it with a heavy pin at his shoulder. As he pulled on his leather gloves his squire asked, "Where are we going, milord?"

"You are going to bed." He pointed to the cot he had just vacated. "You've been awake too many hours already. Sleep until the dawn when I will need you."

"No."

"Now!" Again John pointed and this time, obediently, the squire sat down on the bed.

"I'm not so very tired," he insisted, though his voice betrayed him.

"You are. Not only old men like me need sleep, but growing boys like you." John pushed his shoulder and Miles fell back, curling up inside his own cloak.

"But where are you going, so that I might find you come the dawn?"

"I'll be here," John promised. "But so you'll know, I'm off to check the perimeter of our army's camp. We can afford no surprises if we wish not only to enter Kurth keep, but later, to be free still to leave it."

With that, John ducked through the opening of his tent and let the flap fall back into place. He paused for a moment, looking up at the bailey walls surrounding the keep before turning and heading away toward the woods behind the camp.

If it were only his men who made up the fighting forces, the earl of Farleigh would not have taken this observant walk. He could trust his own knights to both follow his commands and do what needed doing of their own volition. But this army was made up of men serving several lords, and not only were the soldiers unknown to him; so, too, were the barons they served little more than strangers.

John stopped short. Ahead, where the trees thinned on the edge of the grassy hill, John saw a movement, a shape, that did not belong. Stealthily he slipped among the trees and made his way closer.

Gwyneth halted her mount and slid down from him, speaking in soft, gentle tones to keep him still and quiet. She could not help sighing as she considered the tents, the fires, and the countless men awake and asleep among them. How could she hope to find either her husband or her sons in this confused and crowded place? She began to wonder if her impulsiveness had been foolhardy.

"Ah!"

The squeak was all she got out as a muscled arm cinched her waist and a callused hand covered her mouth. "Gwyneth!" John growled as he whirled his wife about so that she faced him.

"John."

For a moment they stared at each other, each startled to have found the other. Then, with a scowl, the earl demanded, "What are you doing here?"

"I need—" she blurted, before catching herself. "Gerald..." she began again before hesitating. Finally she admitted, "I had to speak with you."

"About what? God's wounds, Gwyneth! What could be so important you would ride here alone?"

John's hands were hard on her shoulders. As she looked up into his frowning, bearded face, Gwyneth found she had no answer to his question.

"Well?"

"You are still here," she said lamely.

His scowl deepened as he shook his head. "Where else should I be? The battle's not yet done, though we hope to see it finished with the coming dawn."

"You think to win?"

"Aye." John paused and searched Gwyneth's face. Her eyes sparkled like cut gems despite the absence of both stars and moon. "You're shivering," he realized aloud. "Here." He opened his fur-lined cloak, and when Gwyneth stepped into it, he folded it about her and slid his arms inside her wrap. She sighed a little, John's embrace unerringly providing the only place Gwyneth had ever felt secure.

"So I am here at the site of the siege. Whatever possessed you to come to me here?" he asked again.

"You did not return to Farleigh when Gerald sent the messenger."

"To meet with King Henry?" John peered down into Gwyneth's upturned face. "He's not due at the castle for days yet."

"I'm afraid he's there already."

"What!"

"He arrived a sennight early. Gerald sent a second messenger to inform you of such."

Inside his cloak and hers, John began running his hands up and down Gwyneth's back. She pressed herself closer to him, her belly against his groin, her cheek against his chest. Though it was proving difficult, they continued their conversation as if seated in separate chairs.

"I never received it. I was only told that the king was coming, not that he'd arrived."

"Well, the disgusting swine *has* arrived!" she announced, and her husband frowned disapprovingly.

"My lady, you should never speak thus about our king," he advised softly, resuming the stroking he had momentarily ceased.

"As if half of England did not speak of Stephen in such terms," she exclaimed pointedly.

"I know that's true. But Henry—"

"Henry is a cockshead!" she declared contemptuously. "One of his gallant knights raped Bess, and the spindly-legged beet-head himself tried to do the same to me!"

John stiffened. "He did what?"

"He tried to have his way with me."

"You thwarted his efforts?"

Gwyneth raised her head from her husband's chest and looked up into his face, trying vainly to read his inscrutable expression. "Do you—do you care?" she dared to ask him.

"Bloody hell, of course I care." His reply was gruff, but he jerked her closer to him.

"I thought you despised me." Gwyneth's voice was muffled, her cheek against his quilted gambesons. She could hardly hear herself over that, and the rush of blood in her ears. It took some effort to concentrate on their conversation, as Gwyneth's husband resumed stroking her back.

"Despise you?" he repeated, his words floating over her head. "Never. Though I admit, I was angered by your trickery. You might have been honest with me, Gwyneth."

She let her head drop back and began to explain. "I could not—"

But she was silenced by a kiss that seared her lips and warmed the most private places of her person. Gwyneth could feel the tips of her breasts hardening even as she felt John's manhood pushing against her. Her desire for him was flaming; she hadn't known she could feel such heated yearning without being consumed by it. So she did not protest when John scooped her up and carried her farther back into the woods, under cover of the trees.

He laid her down beneath one of several towering pines that provided shelter from the wind. "Are you still cold?" he asked huskily, and she replied with a quick shake of her head. "Your heat has warmed me," he told her, smoothing beneath her the pelts that had draped her cloak. Then he crouched above her, his own cloak forming a tent around them. "I've missed you sorely, lady wife," he admitted.

She did not reply. To say the same would have been to lie. But now that she was reunited with him—Jesu! But she wanted him now.

She raised her hips so that he could better raise her tunics, and she undid his leggings while his fingers sought the heat between her legs.

The lord found his lady as ready for him as he was for her. He took her quickly, but she met him thrust for thrust and both experienced release within a short minute.

"I behaved like a randy squire," he confessed gruffly when he pulled himself from her and rolled Gwyneth on top of his long frame. They were still snug within the wealth of their cloaks. "You deserve better, my lady."

"I am not displeased."

"We are being reckless." He considered her face contemplatively before exclaiming, "God's bones! 'Twas you who were reckless, coming here! Gwyneth, did you ride all the way to Kurth, unescorted, to seek my protection from the king?"

"Nay." She shook her head and the long, crimped tresses that had escaped her braids tickled the earl's face. "There were other reasons."

"Tell me."

"My sons—"

"—Are fine and well. I can have them line up for your inspection, if you wish."

Gwyneth's eyes searched her husband's face. "None are wounded or—worse?"

"All three fair knights are hale and hearty. Sweet

Mary," John sighed, "even my squire has accused me of coddling them, as though they were mere children."

"They are *my* children," she whispered.

"I know." The earl's voice was tender. "'Tis why I've kept such a vigilant eye on them."

Gwyneth loved him, suddenly. She knew it now, where before she had only guessed, and hoped, and doubted. She also realized he had no intention of dissolving their union. She felt almost giddy with the abrupt and unexpected sense of happiness and contentment that now engulfed her.

But she was not a flighty wench, to be turned from her purposes by a handsome man, not even her own husband. "I would speak with them," she informed John.

"They are not going anywhere." The earl smiled wickedly as he twined a loose lock of burnished hair about his finger. "But as you soon are, I should like to make the most of the minutes remaining to us. And," he added, rolling his wife onto her back as he came up over her, "I should like to improve my performance over my most recent effort."

"Milord!" Gwyneth protested, trying only halfheartedly to squirm away.

"You don't really wish to leave me now, do you?" John asked, his voice all silky seduction as he nuzzled her neck and began touching her in ways only he could.

"I must. Ah! Nay. I mean..." Gwyneth lost her breath between his stroking and his kisses. Soon she lost herself to him again completely.

"Up, up!" John said roughly to his squire, who looked no more than six years of age when he sat up, blinking, and frowned at his lord.

"'Tis dawn?" he asked.

"Nay, lad, but I need you."

"Aye, milord," he mumbled, eyes closing again despite the fact he was still sitting upright.

"Miles, now!"

Finally the squire seemed to find his wits and he jumped up, sticking his feet into his shoes. "What is it, milord?"

"Go out and find Sirs Matthew, Rodney and Richard, my lady wife's sons. She wishes to see them immediately."

For the first time Miles noticed his mistress standing behind her husband. "My lady," he bowed respectfully, though he was backing obediently out of the tent as he spoke.

"That poor child! You are too hard on him, I suspect."

"Precisely why boys are taken from their mothers and sent to foster with men. If left among the womenfolk, you'd have them all twining garlands of flowers and singing ballads. Only men can make boys into men."

"And only men can make war."

Her words hung in the air, and it seemed a chill dampened the warm feelings they had been sharing since Gwyneth's arrival at the camp. John moved toward her, to try and recapture the easy familiarity that had abruptly turned to tension. But before he could speak she asked him, "How goes this siege?"

"We hope to win on the morn. There are far more of us than there are of Eye's men, and we have Kurth's people working for us on the inside," John explained. "Despite their position of strength within the keep's walls, Eye's knights are weakening. They cannot reach the livestock to slaughter for meat—they are all beyond the bailey. Someone within fouled the well, too, so they've no fresh water. And many have died or been wounded during the days of fighting. Today," he said, "they shall be forced to relinquish the barony when we wage an all-out attack."

"But what of Neville and his family?" Gwyneth wondered. "They must be hungry, too. Nor have they any water."

"That cannot be helped. Yet I am sure they would endure any sacrifice to regain what is theirs and to see Elwood humbled.

"Now tell me about Henry," John urged, attempting to veer the subject away from war, for he could see by Gwyneth's expression how it upset her. "I understand from your account he is rude and unchivalrous, but what brought him to my home?"

"He *says* he came to you because he thinks you're the one to see Elwood of Eye cut down to his knees. He *told* both Gerald and me he expects the final battle with that baron to be fought at Farleigh. He *claims* he wishes to be rid of him and award his fief to some lord more deserving."

"That makes sense."

"It does," she agreed, "if he speaks truly. It would explain, too, his keen interest in your demesne and the castle's fortifications. But I think the king speaks with a tongue as forked as a serpent's, and I am not inclined to believe a word he utters."

John cocked an eyebrow, but before he could comment, the tent flap flew open and Gwyneth's sons intruded.

"Mother!"

Richard, the first inside, was quickly joined by his brothers. The three young men halted before reaching Gwyneth and stood, just inside the entrance, looking confused.

"Why are you here?" Matthew asked bluntly.

"A messenger sent to me from Farleigh did not reach Kurth," the earl began to explain.

But Gwyneth stepped between him and her sons and said, "There is a pressing matter that requires your immediate attention."

"What's this?" John demanded, startled by his wife's pronouncement.

But the young knights seemed not even to notice their stepfather had spoken. Rodney said to his mother, "We know. 'Tis why we are fighting against Eye's men with Lord John and the others."

"That's naught to do with why I'm here. I did bring my husband urgent news from Farleigh. But I've brought other news for you three."

"Surely nothing is so important it cannot wait," Matthew decided.

He appeared to Gwyneth very manly—more the nobleman than gangly youth. Suddenly, she sensed a conflict she had not expected.

"Those were my thoughts," the earl admitted.

And Richard rushed on, "This fight is a good fight, and it demands all our attention. Lord John explained to us how Elwood of Eye threatened our grandsire and wreaked havoc on Sherborne. It is one of the reasons Lord John pressed for your hand in marriage, and the main reason why we're here now."

Gwyneth shot her husband another quick glance, this one startled. Returning her gaze to her sons, she explained, "There are other considerations of more import to you than this siege. King Henry is at Farleigh Castle, awaiting the earl's presence. But Arnulf is at Sherborne, awaiting yours."

"What?" Matthew screwed up his face. "There can

be no reason our grandfather requires us immediately. Even the king—"

"Aye, the king can bloody well wait," John interrupted. He walked forward, forming a line with his stepsons. The four of them faced Gwyneth.

Abruptly, she realized they would all stand against her. "Arnulf is dead!" she blurted. "He is to be buried on the morrow. You must come with me to see him in the ground."

"Gwyneth, no." John's tone was gentle but firm. "They cannot go. In less than an hour the call to arms will be raised, and we all shall be there to see justice done, to see Kurth freed from the evil clutches of Eye. And you," he continued, taking a step toward her, "must return fast to Farleigh. Henry shan't like it a bit that I am delayed in meeting him and that you, as well, have run off."

Gwyneth stared hard at John. Where was the tender, concerned husband who'd made love with her minutes ago? Why did he always confuse her, indulging her when she feared his wrath, standing firm against her when she expected his support?

"You wish me to deal with that pig on my own, 'til it's convenient for you to stand as my protector?" she asked him.

John's blue eyes went dark and stormy. "You've handled him this long; you can handle him a while longer. Jesu! There's a keep full of knights and my seneschal—your old friend," he added pointedly, "to help keep you safe from the king's wandering prick."

Gwyneth's glare did not soften. She was alone and out-numbered, and she felt a fury growing within her. Deciding not to spar with him, she looked again to her sons. "You will show your disrespect by keeping absent from your grandsire's funeral rite?"

"Mother, Arnulf is already dead," Matthew pointed out. "As soon as Kurth Keep is retaken, we'll ride out for Sherborne. Grandfather shan't be too disturbed if we pay our respects later than the town's folk. After all, he'll be in the ground a long time to come."

Gripping the fabric of her cloak in her hands, Gwyneth breathed deeply. To a one they were all men, lords, knights. They recognized only their own obligations and remained steadfast to their own sense of honor. But she had her own obligations, her own honor, and though she regretted they could not see the merit in them, she determined not to show it.

"Very well," she said calmly, unclenching her fingers and releasing the material she'd held tight in her hands. "I brought you all the news I felt you needed to hear. I'll be off, then."

The sound of a horn echoed down the hill.

"We must also go now, Mother," Rodney informed her. "We shall be gathering up our arms, now that dawn is upon us."

"Aye," Richard confirmed, stepping forward to brush a kiss across his mother's cheek. "But do not fear for us. We all three are wearing the medallions you gifted us with."

"We shall be at Sherborne soon," Matthew vowed. "God's speed," he added with a dutiful, respectful nod of his head before leading his brothers from the earl of Farleigh's tent.

The flap had no chance to fall back into place again before Miles slipped beneath it. John ordered him to locate Sir Bruno to escort his lady wife home, and when the youth left once again, he turned to Gwyneth.

"There are cookfires near the outer ring of the

camp," he told her. "I'll have a varlet bring you some food. You must be half starved."

"Nay." Gwyneth's lips were set in a grim line as she refused to meet her husband's gaze. "I am not hungry."

"God's wounds!" With that exclamation, John strode to her and grabbed her shoulders in his long-fingered hands. "Gwyneth, look at me."

She refused, and he grasped her chin 'twixt his finger and thumb, forcing her face to tilt toward his.

"Do you think," he demanded, his voice a low growl, "I want to send you back to a man who has tried to defile you? King or no, do you believe I would willingly put you close to him?"

He paused, waiting for a response. When Gwyneth stubbornly refused to give him one, he said, "There is no other way. Even with Henry there—if he is as vile and as sly as you say—you will still be safest at Farleigh. The men Eye has here are not his only men. You know the trouble that baron has caused at Sherborne before. Now, with the old lord of the manor gone, who knows what havoc they will wreak on that village? I must have you safe at my home. Our home."

Gwyneth's jaw was set. Though she continued to look up into her husband's face, she gave him no satisfaction with either words or expression.

"Jesu!" he muttered in frustration. "You did not even care for your sire! You hated him, I think. 'Tis only stubbornness that you insist—"

"Sir Bruno is on his way, milord," Miles announced, bursting once more into the tent. Another blast of the horn echoed in the air. "He is going to saddle his mount before he comes."

The lord released his wife and gestured to his mail and sword near the cot. "Get me dressed," he told his squire. "By the time I am armed, Bruno should be here."

But he was not. And though he was reluctant to, the earl left his lady wife alone in the tent.

She did not stay there long. It was easy enough to make her way through the camp, back to the woods, and elude the knight, Bruno. And soon enough Gwyneth was astride her gelding again, making her way through the forests and across the fields, on her way home—to Sherborne.

Chapter Twenty Two

❖   ❖   ❖

Gwyneth had taken an obscure route to Sherborne, one that involved no roads. She had done so to avoid her husband's long arm, in the person of his man, Bruno. But the terrain she had traversed was not gentle, and the ride had been over-long, so when she arrived at the manor she was in a state beyond pain. There was a soft swirling snow blowing about as she rode into the yard, and for a moment the men-at-arms standing guard thought she was an apparition. Her back was rigid, her jaw set, and she called out no greeting. Only when the first man recognized her did they all run forward to help, to ease her from her horse. Yet when she was on the ground her feet wouldn't hold her. Every muscle in her body seemed atrophied from her hard ride in the saddle, and when the men moved her, they screamed their complaint by shooting pain up her legs and back.

Gwyneth collapsed with a cry, and had to be scooped up and carried inside the house by one of Sherborne's bowmen.

It was only late afternoon, but Gwyneth was put straight to bed. There she slept for many hours.

When Gwyneth woke, late into the night, she discovered she was unable to move. Jean came to her and massaged liniment into her arms, her legs, and her buttocks. She fed her mutton stew and methagline. Finally, they talked.

"My father. I did not see him in the room below. Where...?"

"He's been laid out at the village church," Jean explained.

"Did he die... peacefully?"

The servant snorted. "As peacefully as a nasty old churl like himself could. I think he was in his cups when he went. I'm sure he was feeling no pain."

"I wish I were so drugged I could not feel *my* pain!" Gwyneth complained.

"Drink up. This concoction served your father well. It should serve you well, too."

Obediently Gwyneth took a large swallow of the herb-laced wine in her mug. "From where did you come?" Jean asked her. "Not Farleigh. It's too near to have made you so saddle sore."

"Kurth. And before that, from Farleigh to Kurth. My sons are fighting there, with John."

"Has the earl found out your scheme?"

"Aye." Gwyneth nodded, finishing the last drop in her cup and holding it out for Jean to refill. She then told her old friend, in the barest detail, what had transpired since she'd left Sherborne three months before.

"'Tis a miracle everything came to pass exactly as you planned it would," Jean sighed. "Lady Gwendolyn's safe and wed to Sir Thomas. Even the old lord's gone, and can no longer interfere. But what of you, milady?"

"What of me?"

"How—how goes it between you and the earl?"

Gwyneth's face was pinched and pale as she looked at Jean. "Sometimes," she said softly, "it has been very good. But..." She shrugged and glanced away. "When he learns I disobeyed him to come to Sherborne, he'll wash his hands of me. 'Twill be a perfect excuse to annul our marriage so that he might take a young damsel to wife—one who can bear him sons who shall one day rule Farleigh."

The servant's brow creased in a frown. "Surely Lord John cannot fault you for coming to your sire's funeral rite."

"Aye, he can." Gwyneth's eyes slid sideways to meet Jean's gaze. "For he bade me not to. He deems Farleigh the only safe place for me, what with the baron of Eye's men running amok."

"The earl cares for you, then."

"I thought so," she admitted. "Then I didn't. And then I did again. Oh, Jean!" Gwyneth wrung her hands. "Despite my deception in wedding him, despite the reality I am neither young nor fertile, as a girl of Gwendolyn's tender years would be, I hoped—I believed—we might make our marriage work, the earl and I. We said some hurtful things to one another," she recalled softly, looking down now at her hands, folded in her lap, "after the boys rode to Farleigh searching for Gwendolyn and I was forced, finally, to make a full confession. I expected the worst at his hands, he was so angered. But yester morn, when I spoke with John at Kurth..."

"Aye, milady?" the servant prompted.

Gwyneth looked up at her again, but she shook her head. "If I'd done as he asked me—ordered me, really —to return to Farleigh, then all might have worked out well. But I could not, Jean! Something has happened to me since I came back to Sherborne last spring, and I heard that Ector died. Something... *perverse* in my nature has come to the fore." She took a deep breath and heaved a great sigh. "My whole life, 'til then, I'd been submissive, always obedient and quick to please. But no more." She shook her head. "I speak my mind when I'd be better off holding my tongue. I follow my heart when I should be following orders."

"If you followed your heart," Jean asked softly, "would it lead you back to the earl of Farleigh?"

"Mayhap. I don't know," she replied honestly. "'Twould be lonely without him, now that I've gotten used to his ways."

"And his body in your bed," Jean added with a knowing smile.

"Aye. That, too. But he so readily leaves me to my own devices when I most seem to need him."

"Then you admit you do need him."

"Not so much I'd waste away without him!" Gwyneth snapped defensively. "Besides, I know not why I should put him first in my life when he puts knightly battles first in his. As my sons do as well," she added.

"They are knights," Jean said reasonably, shrugging her shawl-covered shoulders. "'Tis what they all do."

"Then they are wrong, the lot of them—every knighted lord in the kingdom! John should be back at Farleigh, where King Henry is cooling his heels in wait for him. Matthew and the twins should be here at Sherborne, to say their formal farewells to Arnulf, their grandsire. Yet they are all fighting at Kurth, a battle that is none of theirs! 'Tis wrong, and I told them so. But none puts their families first. The oafs lead with their weapons, those they pick up, and those they free from their braies."

"Lady Gwyneth." The womans dark eyes looked gently into her mistress. "Methinks your real problem is that this is all so new and strange to you."

"What is?"

"Having sons that are men, for one thing. Your boys grew up while fostering. When they returned you found them suddenly not small lads any longer. They've minds of their own and no need for your tender nurturing."

"Now, my boys," she went on, "grew up under my roof, right there below, in the town. 'Twas a gradual thing, then, and not so much a surprise to me when the day came I realized, to a one, each was puffed up with self-importance at knowing he was a man fully growed.

"The other thing that's strange to you—if you don't mind me speaking up, milady—is living with a husband you care for. I loved my Nick well and true," Jean admitted, her eyes dimming as an onslaught of memories rushed her, "'til the day he died three winters past." She blinked. "Not that we didn't quarrel. Oh, we did. We shouted and threw things, sometimes. But we made up very pleasantly, we did," she said, her smile broadening.

"Now you told me yourself, Lady Gwyneth, you had a bad time with the lord of Durningham. You did not share a bed most of the years of your long marriage, and you spent most of your time staying out of his way. You did not care if he came or went—in truth, you preferred him to be gone. But it's not like that with the earl, now, is it?"

"Nay." Gwyneth shook her head sadly.

"Don't look so glum. Take heart, milady. You'll learn."

"I don't think there'll be time to learn anything,

Jean. John will be furious at what I've done now. And, truth be told, I'd do it again! It matters not that I detested Arnulf. He was my father, my family, and I owe him his due. 'Tis the last thing I shall ever do for him, now. But my husband cannot understand how I feel about family—how any woman feels about family."

The servant cocked her head to one side. "He has to learn as well, Lady Gwyneth. And there'll be time for the two of you, I'm sure of it."

"Now, lay yourself back down again and get a few more hours sleep before you must rise for the funeral. I'll be up to wake you when it's time."

It was snowing hard in the morning when Gwyneth walked with Jean and the others from the manor down to the village church. It seemed strange to see Sherborne enclosed by a wall. The wall itself was strange, fashioned haphazardly from stones and mortar, tall in some places, low in others. It looked to be the work of children, though it was the work of harried, desperate men. The gates at either end of town were made of wood. Because the community consisted of only one rutted, dirt road lined on each side by daub and wattle dwellings, the gatekeepers were so near to each other they could converse almost without raising their voices.

The gate at the bottom of the path leading to the manor house was opened as Gwyneth approached, and she saw all this as she entered. The church was at the far end of town. As she walked down the center of the street nearly every man, woman and child came out of their houses and followed her.

The little church was quickly filled as the bodies of the town folk pressed inside. But she was nearly unaware of the company as her eyes fell on Arnulf, dressed in his finest and laid in a velvet-lined box. She approached the casket, knelt, and looked at her father one last time. It was impossible to tell what kind of man he'd been, seeing him now.

She thought: Perhaps he was not so horrid after all. Both I and Gwendolyn disappointed him sorely by not being born male and all men, thane and villein alike, want most of all sons in their own image. How he treated us, without caring or tenderness, is how most men would have. Brute force is all they know.

Gwyneth might have gone on for some time, reflecting on the past and her father, but the priest began the final service the lord of Sherborne was ever to attend. When it was done, the casket was closed and nailed shut. Those assigned lifted it and carried it from the church. The priest and Gwyneth followed close behind with the others trailing them, as they left the walled town and headed back up the hill to the manor. Behind the house some distance was the family cemetery, and there a hole had been dug in the hard, cold ground that would serve as Arnulf's final resting place.

"Riders! Mounted knights approach! Riders!" came the cry from one of Sherborne's men-at-arms. He came running toward the mourners as fast as he was able, brandishing his crossbow. "Disperse! Hide yourselves!" he ordered, but before anyone could comprehend the warning and obey, seven mounted riders thundered up the hill and bore down on them.

Everyone save the Sherborne knights and Gwyneth seemed to shrink and cower. The knights poised themselves for battle, their lances, swords and bows at the ready. But Gwyneth stood still and unafraid, for she recognized these intruders. They were not whom she had hoped for when the cry first reached her ears, but she knew them well enough.

"Your majesty," she curtsied when the lead rider came to a halt before her.

"Lady Gwyneth," he replied, swinging himself off his mount. He took her hand and helped her up.

"Good people of Sherborne," she announced, turning to the confused townfolk behind her, "may I present his grace, King Henry II."

They collapsed as if their legs had been knocked out from under them. In an instant the villagers assumed nearly the same prostrate position as their late lord. The men-at-arms, however, lowered their weapons and doffed their helmets.

"Rise," the king ordered with a grand and sweeping gesture. The villagers stumbled up, brushing the snow off their knees and elbows. "Go on," he urged the priest.

The vicar of Sherborne waited until Arnulf's casket was lowered into the ground. Then, sprinkling holy water and tossing fistful of dirt after fistful of dirt on top of it, he intoned the final words directed at the deceased lord.

Finally it was done and Gwyneth turned to the king. "Please, return with me to the manor house."

"Certainly, milady." He tossed the reins of his mount to one of his men and, as the people of Sherborne began to disperse—there would be no work for any this day—Henry addressed Arnulf's men-at-arms. "Why don't you go into town, too? You've as much a right to a day of mourning as any cottar."

"Nay, your highness," the captain respectfully refused. "'Tis our duty to protect our mistress and her property. Elwood of Eye is not dead yet."

"True," the king nodded. "But I've six of my finest knights here. If they can protect my royal person, they can protect Gwyneth of Sherborne and Farleigh. You'll be advised before we leave."

"But, your majesty—"

"Surely there's an alehouse run by a goodwife in town," Henry cajoled. "It will be packed to overflowing soon, so hurry now to get your mug of beer. Go on!"

"Your grace, we cannot—"

"I command you!" the king snapped, all pretense of good humor abruptly gone. The captain and his guards, unwilling but unable to do anything but obey their king, shared a look among themselves. Then slowly, as Henry began escorting Gwyneth to her house, they shuffled off down the path.

Gwyneth, surprisingly, had felt little emotion when she'd first spied King Henry and his less-than-gallant men approaching. But now she was filled with dismay that burned in her chest like bitter gall. She was relieved to see, from the corner of her eye, that Jean had followed them all into the house.

"What are you doing here?" one of the knights demanded of the serving woman. He had done all but slam the door on her to keep her from entering.

"You wish food and drink, don't you?" Jean snapped. "Who would you have serve it, the earl of Farleigh's lady wife? I think not. She has servants like me to do her bidding."

"Let her stay," the king said, his good humor apparently returned. "It would be unseemly, in any case, for the fair Lady Gwyneth to be alone surrounded by men, even though I be one of them."

Everyone removed their cloaks and shook the snow

from them. Henry seated himself in Arnulf's old chair and bade Gwyneth sit beside him. His knights including Maurice, who had apparently recovered somewhat from his beating, clustered on the benches at a single trestle table. Immediately Jean set mugs before each and filled them with some of Gwyneth's fine brew.

"No one at Farleigh realized you had gone until last eve," Henry told Gwyneth, sprawling lazily in his chair as he sipped from his mug. "John's seneschal was frantic, but when I learned old Arnulf had died, I knew you'd come here as any good and obedient daughter would."

She nodded but did not look at him. She kept her eyes on his men, for she had the feeling if they were unwatched they might steal the pewter cups or silver candle holders.

"Have you had word from Kurth?"

"No." She risked a glance at him. "Have you?"

"Nay. I care not much for what happens there, only for what happens at Farleigh."

"Why?"

"Because this business between Eye and the other barons will end at Farleigh, not at Neville's fief."

"You know Lord Neville?" she asked. "You say his name as if he is familiar to you."

Henry shook his head. "Only what I've heard of him. He sounds to me a weak-kneed man, not the sort of baron I'd take into my council."

"He's not then on your council?" Gwyneth inquired, confused. She saw that the snow on the king's head was melting, and wondered how heavy and wet her own hair was becoming.

"Nay—yes—Don't concern yourself, milady." He finished the dregs of beer in his cup and called to Jean to replenish it.

"Would you like some victuals now, your grace?" the woman asked.

"Aye. I'm hungry as a boar." He rubbed his belly in a circular motion.

"I'll be off to the kitchen, then. If you'll excuse me."

Gwyneth gave Jean a longing glance, so with a shrug the woman promised, "I'll be back in a moment, milady."

"I noticed there is a sturdy wall, not a shallow ditch, newly built around the town," Henry observed. He eyed Gwyneth calculatingly.

"I was... misinformed."

"Oh? What will become of the manor now that Arnulf is gone?"

"I do not know," Gwyneth admitted, watching the knights helping themselves to the jug of beer Jean had left for them on the table.

"You'll be returning to Farleigh Castle, I take it?"

"Of course." She spoke with certainty, hiding her own doubt. There was every possibility John would urge her to stay at her dowerlands once he realized she had defied him so openly. Yet she added, "'Tis where I live, with my husband."

"Sherborne will be more vulnerable to an attack by Elwood's men without a lord living in the manor. Mayhap I should award this small fief to some deserving man who will keep it well."

"You cannot!" Gwyneth was startled by her own protest, but continued, "I mean to say, it's come to me, now. It has been in my family nigh on a hundred years."

"But as you said, milady, you'll be returning to Farleigh, and surely the earl has no desire to take up residence in this humble abode."

"Aye, but—" She hesitated before deciding to follow through with the truth. "I have a sister, your grace, who is married to a younger son of Brandywine. Sir Thomas is in line to inherit very little. Mayhap they may wish to return here to live."

"A sister!" That news seemed to gain Henry's attention. "I hadn't heard that. I thought Arnulf had only one daughter and no sons at all."

"I'm surprised you even knew of him, sire. The lord of Sherborne was not a very important lord."

"Except to the people of the town," Henry said.

"And the lords of both Eye and Farleigh," Gwyneth added. She noticed that the king's head was dripping, the melting snow staining his dark green tunic. Instinctively she felt her own head. Even though she had worn a veil outside, her hair was as wet as if she had stood in a downpour.

She rose. "I'll fetch some towels, your highness. We are both wet with snow and if we do not dry ourselves, we'll surely take sick."

Immediately she was up the steps to the bower and soon enough she was down them again. She handed one cloth to Henry.

"Thank you," he said stiffly, and while Gwyneth toweled her long locks vigorously, he gently patted his own, short-cropped hair.

Now the king held her interest more than his men did, and Gwyneth saw something that made her heart skip a beat. His towel, the one he quickly tossed into the fire instead of returning to her, was covered in blood! She opened her mouth to comment but then realized it could not have been blood. Scalps bled when cut but hair did not, and Henry had merely blotted his hair. It was dye, like that she used to change the hue of woolen cloth! Henry had dyed his hair, and that was the reason it looked so unnatural. Now, wetted and toweled, his hair looked less the color of beets and more the color of manure.

His protruding eyes were on hers, and too late Gwyneth realized she had not only stopped drying her hair but was staring, mouth agape.

"Now!" Henry shouted, leaping up from his chair, and before she could ask a question or voice a protest one of his knights had lifted Gwyneth up and thrown her over his shoulder.

"Jean!" she screamed with all the force her lungs would allow, and for that she was slugged with a meaty fist that made her world go temporarily black. Unknown to her, Jean had been just outside the door when she screamed. But when the woman dropped her platters of steaming food and rushed inside in response to her mistress' cry, she, too, was knocked out cold with a single blow and left in a heap on the floor.

Jean was not the only one who had heard Gwyneth's cry. Four of Sherborne's men-at-arms who had lingered not far from the manor came running to investigate. Two met their Maker at the point of their enemy's swords, and two spent some time in a nether world, hovering between life and death until a skilled midwife's nursing brought them back. By the time they could tell what little they knew, their lady Gwyneth was gone with unknown men to an unknown place.

Chapter Twenty Three

✧   ✧   ✧

John knew full well where his wife had gone: Sherborne. Gwyneth had disobeyed him, as he'd hoped she would not. She'd left camp before Bruno came to fetch her, and she'd not been found on the road 'twixt Kurth and Farleigh. So the earl returned to his castle, with his men and his prisoners but not with his stepsons. They, he'd sent to Sherborne to pay their respects to their dead grandsire and, more importantly, to escort their impetuous, stubborn, fool-hardy mother back to her husband's home.

As the earl's troops and their prisoners approached the castle gate, a shout went up; by the time John dismounted before the keep's portal, Gerald and a man whom he deduced to be King Henry were already there to greet him.

"My lord," Gerald said quickly, anxiously, nodding his head in a curt and impatient bow before gesturing to the man beside him. "My lord, may I introduce his majesty, Henry, King of all England."

"Your grace." John bowed formally, appraising the man with a critical eye. Immediately he was confused; Gwyneth was neither foolish nor fanciful, yet this man called Henry of Anjou seemed nothing like she'd described. Stocky and a bit bow-legged, he was nonetheless pleasant-featured and broad-shouldered, presenting a commanding presence. "I apologize for my tardiness. The delay was unavoidable."

"I have not been kept waiting long," Henry said, nodding at John as he climbed the steps to join him.

The earl paused on the stoop outside the portal, and frowned at the king's comment. He also took the time to consider the king again, and his first impression was not altered. In truth, it improved. Close up, Henry, with his short-cropped hair the same color as Matthew's, could be considered handsome. He was young, hardly older than Gwyneth's sons, but there was an air about him that instantly set him apart from others. It was not the short, Angevin cloak he wore that had already earned him the nickname, "Curtmantle." Nay, the young monarch simply presented an aura of strength. John, unlike his wife, was sure Henry would prove to be a good king.

"What do you mean, you've not been waiting long?" he asked as they all, including Gerald, walked into the great hall together.

"I and my men—" the king gestured to two knights standing at ease near the fire— "arrived only this morning."

"What?"

"You received my message some days ago that the king had already arrived?" Gerald asked John.

"Nay, I did not. The only word I had was that his majesty was expected about this time."

Gerald's expression changed. "Then how did you…?"

"My lady wife told me, when she presented herself at Kurth."

"Lady Gwyneth!"

"I take it you were successful there," the king surmised, ignoring the seneschal's exclamation.

"Aye, your grace, we were. Those men of Eye's who survived the siege were divided up among the barons who helped free Neville and his family. I've a few who will be taken down to the dungeon here promptly."

"Where are the boys, if I may ask?" Gerald inquired anxiously. "Matthew and the twins?"

"They've gone to Sherborne to join their mother."

"She is there?"

"I've no reason to doubt it. You must know her father has died."

"Aye, but..." Gerald looked as if he were going to have an attack of apoplexy. John gestured for him to sit but he hesitated.

"I think there is some confusion here," Henry said, taking a seat so that Gerald and John could rest also. "Perhaps you two should talk first and sort it out."

"Thank you, your highness," Gerald said gratefully, accepting a goblet of wine from the steward and drinking from it before either the king or the earl had yet raised their own cups to their lips. "Lord John," he began quickly, "there was another man here earlier, posing as the king."

"What!"

"Aye." Gerald took another swig of wine and nodded his head vigorously. "Your lady wife was suspicious of him and his men—there were six knights he brought with him—from the very first. I did not like him, either. One of his men raped young Bess."

"I know. Gwyneth told me."

"They were put out in rich garb, especially the one who called himself Henry, but they were slovenly and drunkards to a one. They kept surveying the demesne and even had the castle guard put on a display to show their skills and might."

"God's blood!" John swore, slamming his goblet down onto the arm of his chair. The contents sloshed onto his sleeve, but he seemed not to notice. "Your second messenger never reached me," he told Gerald. "Have you had word of him?" When the seneschal shook his head he continued, "No doubt he was murdered to prevent me from returning while the impostor was still in residence. What of the messenger you sent to Farleigh?" he asked the king. When Henry admitted that his own runner had not returned, either, John muttered, "He was probably slain, also, and your royal message, stolen, was delivered here by a cohort of the devil who later arrived at Farleigh, posing as you, your majesty. Sweet Jesu! When I think the damage he could have wrought by slipping behind these walls!" His hard blue eyes turned on Gerald again. "Did you know the cur attacked Gwyneth?"

"Nay!" He was protesting that such a thing ever happened, rather than denying knowledge of it.

"'Tis the truth. She told me so herself."

"That's why she hid herself away again," Gerald muttered to himself.

"Gwyneth hid herself away *again?*" the earl repeated.

"When she's distraught, she hides. My lady retreated to the solar after you and her sons rode to Kurth. 'Tis of no import now, though. Is she fine and well, your lady wife?" Gerald asked concernedly. "We did not know she was missing until only last evening."

"And how could that be?" John demanded heatedly, coming to his feet and looming threateningly over his seneschal. "How could you not know the lady of

Farleigh, your mistress, whom you were to protect in my absence, had ridden off some days ago? She rode unattended all the way to Kurth. Then she slipped away again and went alone to Sherborne for her father's funeral mass."

"I am so very sorry," Gerald apologized with heartfelt remorse. "She claimed to be unwell, but she took her meals regularly so I believed her to be safe in your chamber."

"She could not have been eating when she was gone! Was there someone aiding her in this scheme?"

"Nay, milord. But the servants were not surprised when they began finding her food left untouched beyond her door. 'Tis what she did when you first left. By the time they thought to advise me, it was already yesterday eve, so only then did I find her missing. Upon questioning, one of the stable men admitted Lady Gwyneth had taken a mount two days earlier. He had not come forward because she'd sworn him to secrecy."

"Sweet mother of Jesu—I am surrounded by fools!" John exclaimed angrily, and he began to pace behind his chair.

"Do not be too hard on your people," Henry advised. "They were not looking for danger or deception, and thus they did not see it."

"Aye, you are right, your grace. I'm sorry, Gerald, for my outburst."

"Nay, milord. I am the one who is sorry."

"Whom do you think it was masquerading as me?" Henry asked the seneschal. John paused and looked at him, too, awaiting his response.

"Certainly someone in Eye's employ."

"Aye." John nodded his head thoughtfully and

stroked his beard with his thumb. "Could it have been Elwood himself?"

"I think not. He was not so young as his majesty, but far younger than the baron must be."

"What do you think, if I may ask?" John directed his question to his king.

"It could not have been Elwood of Eye. He's been in hot pursuit of me in recent weeks, as I'll not grant him an audience. I am sure he only returned to England's shores shortly after I did."

"What did this man look like?" John asked Gerald.

"Not very pleasant," he informed his lord grimly. "Thin, stoop-shouldered, with bulging eyes and the most horrid red hair."

"Beet-head," John muttered.

"What?"

"Beet-head is what Gwyneth called him."

"It's true. His hair was the color of boiled beets."

"Dyed," Henry announced with certainty. "It is the one thing about me most everyone would know. So he colored his hair and dressed himself well and announced that he was I." He chuckled. "And his ruse worked. You believed him."

As Gerald covered his eyes with his hand, John clapped him on the shoulder and said gently, "Don't blame yourself, my old friend. You knew the king was on his way here and this red-headed man arrived claiming to be he. You saw what you expected to see, and what you saw was the king of England."

John returned to his chair. "When did he leave?"

"This morning."

"What? Only this morning?"

"Aye. I'm surprised the impostors and the real king's party did not pass each other on the road."

"God's tears! You mean he remained here until it became known Lady Gwyneth was gone?" Gerald nodded in response to the earl's question. "He wouldn't have gone after her, do you think?" he asked both his king and his seneschal. But before either could answer, Gwyneth's sons came bounding into the hall with a great clatter of armor and weapons.

"Lord John!" Rodney and Richard chorused. John stood, an urgent question on his lips. But as all three knights immediately bowed before the king, Matthew uttering a respectful, "Your majesty," he held his tongue.

"Rise," the king said graciously. "May I ask how you knew me? I am not garbed in royal robes today."

"We had the pleasure to see you some years ago, your highness," Matthew explained. "It was before you were crowned king. You'd come into the country on some business and stayed at the home of our foster father, Lord Harold of Becknock."

"Aye, I was there." He nodded.

"I wish you had been here when the impostor pressed himself on me posing as your royal self," Gerald muttered miserably.

"An imposter?" Matthew repeated.

"Was here?" Richard questioned.

"We think one was at Sherborne, too," Rodney announced.

"What?" Gerald leapt from his chair as John grabbed Rodney's shoulders demanding, "Why? And where, dear God, is your mother?"

The younger man explained, "When we arrived at Sherborne, Grandsire was already in the ground. But what we discovered—!"

"Two of Sherborne's knights were dead, and another

two near dying," Richard continued. "Inside the manor, Jean, a woman who's served Arnulf all her life, was confused and dizzy from a blow to the head."

"And your mother?" John asked again, his voice strained.

"Gone," Matthew informed him. "From what we were able to piece together, King Henry and his men arrived at the family cemetery. They sent all of the villagers home and relieved the Sherborne men-at-arms of their duties."

"Certainly I've not been to Sherborne," Henry announced.

"Some of the people thought Elwood of Eye's men had taken you, your majesty, and my mother by surprise," Matthew went on. "It did not seem reasonable to us, though, because there were six men with the king. The man *claiming* to be king, that is. Had Eye's men attacked, there'd have been a fight that would have caused notice, so we were doubtful."

"Finally Jean, the servant, managed to tell us what she had seen," Rodney explained. "She claimed our mother screamed for help and when she rushed into the manor house to aid her, Mother was being carried off by one of the king's guard. Then Jean herself was dealt a brutal blow that left her unconscious for long hours."

"The impostor has taken my lady wife!" John growled.

"Why?" Gerald wondered aloud. "He knows Farleigh Castle better than the rats that sneak into the grain stores. If he is Elwood's spy and intends to attack this keep, he now has an edge that could make him victorious. Why abscond with Lady Gwyneth?"

"Is that not how Kurth was first taken from Lord

Neville?" King Henry asked quietly. "Did the baron of Eye's men not capture Neville's oldest son and hold him for hostage until he surrendered the keep?"

"Aye, that's so," the twins said in unison, nodding their dark heads. "And they slew the lad even after his father had given over his holdings," Rodney added.

"By all things holy, they'll not harm Gwyneth!" John roared.

"Shall we ride to your neighbors and bring together another army?" Matthew asked.

"Shall I alert the castle guard to arm themselves and mount up?" Richard inquired.

"Nay." John shook his tousled head. "The knights who freed Kurth are either still there, burying the dead and tending the wounded, or scattered hither and yon returning to their own demesnes. We cannot wait until they are home and rested and ready to set out again. Besides, we do not know for certain who took your mother or where, exactly, she was taken."

"We must do something—now!" Matthew declared emphatically.

"We will." John's voice was controlled. "But we will do it ourselves. Look how easily this spy of Elwood's slipped into my own keep. Not stealthily, by creeping in under cover of night. No, boldly he did it, and by his brazenness he succeeded. We will succeed, too."

"Where will you go?" King Henry asked.

"Certainly the one who passed himself off as you has thrown in his lot with Elwood, so we will go to Eye."

"But we will never gain access to his keep!" Matthew argued. "They'll shoot us like dogs before we reach the bailey walls."

"The walls are crumbling," John informed him, "as is Elwood's keep. Most of it is still the wooden relic built in King William's day. And how many men can be left to defend it? He has bands marauding, harassing his neighbors who live near his borders. And he lost many at Kurth. Nay, Eye's defenses are weak. We'll get inside, see your mother safe, and destroy the baron once and forever."

"I shall come with you," Gerald announced.

"Nay. I need you here."

"I've failed you here already!"

"Do not wallow in self-pity, Gerald," John ordered him. "You were tricked—I, too, have been tricked. It is embarrassing but not fatal. Besides, you must be here in the event Elwood sends me word that he's holding my lady wife. If you receive such a message at Farleigh, I want you to reply with a message informing him I've been killed at Kurth."

"And me?" King Henry asked, coming to his feet.

The earl looked at him, surprised. "I am sorry, your highness. I'd not thought to include you in this business of mine."

"'Tis not only your business, Lord John. I journeyed here because of Elwood, who is an evil man bent on doing harm to my loyal vassals. He must be mad—why else would he think battling with the lords who hold faith with the house of Plantagenet would bring him royal favor? Damn, I wish the villian dead and gone. I believed you could be an instrument to that end, John, for I thought the final confrontation would happen here at Farleigh."

"But," Henry continued with a wry smile, "it seems the baron of Eye knew the course of my thoughts. He sent his own man here to ferret out the secrets of your castle and to learn the strength of your forces. When his spy confides what he has learned, he will have an advantage neither you nor I wish him to, an advantage that would remain his even if you rescue your lady wife.

"So I will accompany you to Eye's keep. It is there we will have the final battle that should see him in his grave."

"Without an army?" Matthew exclaimed.

The king nodded. "It does not always require scores of armed men to fight a battle, sir. A battle can be waged among as few as two if they have as their weapons quick wits. Such will be our battle with Elwood."

"But how, your grace?" Rodney demanded.

"How did the baron's man get inside this place? Posing as me. Whom does Elwood seek an audience with above all others? Again, me. Thus I shall ride to Eye as myself, and there I will be welcomed, I promise you."

John's face was full of admiration as he looked at his monarch. "A good plan, your highness," he said. "But we should consider the details before we set off." He sat, gestured for the others to join him, and called for food and drink. For the next few hours, then, the king and his vassals put their heads together, weaving a scheme to save Gwyneth and rid themselves of Elwood of Eye.

Chapter Twenty Four

✥ ✥ ✥

Gwyneth dreamt she was at sea, and when she woke she understood from whence her dream had come. She was in a most unusual room, all made of timbers from the floor to the walls to the ceiling above. Wind whistled through the chinks between the boards and she was certain she felt a subtle but unmistakable listing to and fro. Afraid her dream was no dream at all, she stumbled up from the cot she found herself lying upon and hurried to the narrow window that had been created by removing a single width of timber.

She discovered she was not aboard any ship. Though it was fast becoming dark, she could see there was no green water below but only dun-colored mud and drifts of dirty snow piled up against a random pattern of dilapidated outbuildings. Hounds and pigs and chickens went about their business, none taking notice of the others. Only a few ragged-looking peasants, who appeared both freezing and starving, moved with any determination from one place to the next.

Turning away, Gwyneth rubbed her forehead with her finger and thumb, trying to stir her memory. It came to her at once, the last things that she remembered: King Henry's bleeding hair, her own scream, and a hard-knuckled fist slamming into her face. Recalling the hurt, she attempted to move her jaw but quickly ceased such foolishness. The movement made the pain return, almost as vibrant as it had been upon first impact. But she knew, now, where she was: the baron of Eye's keep. His was one of the few in England still mostly made of wood, as it had been when William the Conqueror first ordered it quickly built. But if this was Eye's keep, did that mean the false King Henry was Elwood himself?

Curious but cautious, Gwyneth tiptoed to the door. She was a little surprised to find it unguarded when she raised the latch and opened it to peer beyond. She discovered herself in a gallery that, like the one in Farleigh's keep, overlooked the great hall. Unlike her husband's castle, though, the rooms were set against the outer walls, and only a rail prevented one from stepping off the plank-lined corridor into the room below.

Crossing the threshold, she looked up. The original structure was not very tall and appeared rather squat; there were neither rooms nor a floor above her. Then she looked down. No one, she thought, could ever call the baron of Eye's hall great.

It was large enough and it had been added onto—where a wooden wall must once have stood, was now another section of room built of stone and mortar. It was there the fire burned in an open-pit hearth and there the lord sat in a high, carved chair. He was eating now, tossing bones over his shoulder that the hounds in the keep fought for with snarls and growls and nips. The six men who had accompanied him to Farleigh and a few others more were seated on stools or lounging in the meager covering of rushes on the floor. Some were eating as their lord was, all were drinking, and most had a wench well in hand.

Gwyneth stared. She had never seen such debauchery. The women seemed to have imbibed as much as the men, and they sprawled shamelessly in their knights' laps. Some had their tunics hitched up, exposing more than their naked legs, and they squirmed as rough hands stroked their inner thighs. At least two had bared their bosoms, one allowing her male companion to suckle her and the other leaning back so that her lover could knead and pinch her breasts with his fingers. As her eyes roamed the shadowed, torch-lit hall, Gwyneth was sure at least one couple was copulating in full view of the others.

Sickened by this Sodom and Gomorrah, she turned her head and closed her eyes. Perhaps, too, as she attempted to swallow the bile rising in her throat, Gwyneth made a sound, for the one who had called himself Henry saw her, pointed and shouted, "Get the bitch! Bring her to me!"

Before she could retreat to the room in which she'd awakened, one of Eye's men-at-arms took the nearby stairs two at a time and grabbed her. Unceremoniously, he threw her over his shoulder, carried her downstairs and dumped her, like a sack of peat, in front of his master.

Straightening her shoulders, Gwyneth locked eyes with her captor. "I see your hair is red no longer. A pity you could not have rid yourself of that ugly face as well."

The small table at which he'd been eating exploded as he kicked it aside and stood. Gwyneth gasped, but she could not jump back far enough to escape his cruel fingers when he grabbed her. "You're not the lady of this keep, Gwyneth of Farleigh," he informed her as a gust of cold wind blew through the hall. "But I am the lord here, so you'd best show me the respect I am due."

"You are *not* the master," a voice from behind Gwyneth announced, punctuated by a *bang* as a door slammed open. Turning, she spied an older man, just entered the keep. He was tall, his bones large and his flesh meager, except for a protruding belly visible even beneath his dirt-stained traveling cloak. His thinning hair was gray and his dark eyes flinty. When he reached Gwyneth's side, he said to the man before her, "Remember, Walter, that I am not dead yet."

"Yes, Father."

Walter! Father! So *this* was the baron of Eye, and the man who had posed as King Henry, his son.

"Who is this woman?" Elwood inquired, and after Walter explained he asked, "Why have you abducted John of Farleigh's lady wife?"

"Because his castle is impregnable to attack. We'll never sack it. I know—I've been inside. But by taking her," he sneered, smirking up at Gwyneth, "we'll not only nullify the earl's sovereign claim to Sherborne, we'll sorely prick his pride."

"You've been inside Farleigh's walls?" the old baron repeated. His tone had grown noticeably more amiable. Now he removed his cloak and sat in a chair near the fire. From a servant he ordered food and drink; next he gestured to his son to sit beside him. "Tell me what has transpired during my absence."

With a smug smile that still looked like a leer to Gwyneth, Walter sat beside his sire. "As luck would have it, a messenger from the king himself was intercepted. When I learned Henry of Anjou intended to visit Farleigh Castle, I rode there first and posed as the king himself."

"Really?" Elwood fondled his long, gray beard. "You deceived the earl with your disguise?"

"Nay, he was absent. Gone with his forces to Kurth."

"Which was lost," the older man snapped.

"It makes no difference. The barons in these parts learned a valuable lesson, methinks. The important thing is, I and my men were able to study the keep and the bulwarks, and to observe Farleigh's knights-in-service. We now know for certain his castle is better fortified than any king's."

Another small table was brought to the baron's side. A stringy-haired servant, perpetually stooped to show his subservience, set a full trencher on it along with a flagon of wine and a goblet. As Elwood stuffed his mouth with a large piece of boiled meat he admitted, "You surprise me, Walter. You did far better than I might have expected."

"Thank you, Father."

"But now you're saddled with the woman." Elwood peered at Gwyneth with only one eye. He reminded her of a menacing, black bird—a raven. "What do you propose to do with her?"

"Kill her." Walter's expression was now most definitely a leer, as both his bug eyes locked on Gwyneth's bosom. "After I've had some sport with her, of course."

"You intend only to slay the lady?" Elwood asked calmly before sipping from his goblet.

"Who else?" Walter screwed up his face.

"Fool!" The cup still in his hand, he threw his wine at Walter. The younger man blinked but made no move to wipe the liquid dripping off his chin. "With the eyes you got from your ugly mother, I am ever amazed you cannot see more than you do."

"Do not insult me so before my men!" Walter

shouted. It was more a petulant whine than a demand. Coming to his feet, he finally dried his wet face on his sleeve.

"They are *my* men," Elwood corrected him. "I am the baron here, and I'll do and I'll say as I please."

"Yes, Father." Chastised, he sat again in his chair.

"You did a clever thing, Walter, but only because you were too stupid to know better." The baron turned from his son to Gwyneth. "She will bring us what we want—all that we want, not simply a pitiful show of spite."

Walter frowned as he turned again to Gwyneth. "How?"

With a disgusted snort, Elwood swallowed a piece of bread and then explained his reasoning. "The earl of Farleigh will not ignore what you have done. He will come for his wife and when he does, we shall slay him, too." Ignoring Gwyneth's startled gasp, he continued without pause, "Without a lord again to lead them, and knowing full well there is no heir to come forward and claim the earldom, the knights serving Farleigh will shrink in number. Then we can take it. I will become the earl there, and Henry will no longer be able to turn a blind eye or a deaf ear on me and mine. He will have to give me my rightful place on the king's council, a place you will inherit, Walter, when I finally pass from this earth."

The younger man's frown upended. "I knew that, Father."

With a quick and practiced movement, Elwood backhanded his son. "God's teeth!" he swore. "Be wise enough not to lay claim to that you do not own!"

"But it was my idea to penetrate Farleigh's walls by masquerading as the king! I even dyed my hair. It was

I, also, who took the lady from her father's graveside."

"Arnulf is dead?"

"He is."

"All the better! We shall lay waste to the town. *That* will prick Farleigh's pride before we pierce his flesh with a lethal broadsword."

There was a sporadic cheer from among Eye's men. Elwood turned his head slightly and scowled at those sprawled about the rank and dirty room. "Be still," he ordered. "Go back to your drinking and whoring. Your leisure time here will be short. Soon enough you'll earn your pay by being pressed into hard service."

Gwyneth had no desire to look at the knights and their women, but she heard feminine giggles erupt again and knew the men had gone back to more immediate interests.

Swallowing back a lump in her throat she said softly, "No," and succeeded in gaining both Walter and the baron's attention. "Please, I beg you, do not sack Sherborne town. The people dwelling there are innocents."

"Nay, they are not! By your marriage to The Dane, they became his, and thus, our enemies."

"You savaged the town while my father still lived and was keeping his allegiance to you!" Gwyneth cried.

"But he kept his allegiance to Farleigh, too," Elwood growled.

"It was the treaty since King William's time! You chose to try and alter it, not Arnulf. You cannot blame him or the town's folk for his keeping the faith with both his lords," she insisted reasonably. "Besides," she added, "when you are earl it will be yours again and yours alone. Why destroy it only to rebuild it later?"

"She's right," Walter agreed, to her surprise. But

even as he spoke he leaned quickly in the direction opposite his father, to avoid another blow. When none came he continued, "In any case, the earl of Farleigh will be here soon enough. I've already sent a message to his keep, informing him I hold his wife here."

Elwood's bushy brows knitted over his eyes as he peered at his son thoughtfully. "Perhaps you're not the dunce I took you for," he said as if it were a compliment.

"You're both fools," Gwyneth muttered, shaking her head. "The earl of Farleigh will not come for me. Our marriage was arranged, and I do not carry his babe beneath my heart. He has little use for me. Certainly not enough that he would risk the land his family's held for generations."

"*You* are the fool," Elwood snarled as he jumped to his feet and grabbed Gwyneth's hair. Her breath caught as he said into her ear, "He will come because you are *his!* It matters not what his feelings toward you may be. You are his property, and he will not allow you to be taken from him without a fight."

With a vicious thrust he released her and sent her sprawling to the floor. Gwyneth lay face down in the filth, a gnawed chicken bone piercing the palm of one hand. Raising her eyes, she saw several of the others in the hall looking at her contemptuously—a few even laughed. She wished she were dead.

It seemed as though Walter heard her thoughts spoken aloud, for she heard him say, "Let me have some fun with the slut tonight. When I've had my fill of her, I will kill her."

"Nay," Elwood returned. "I do not wish her dead, yet. Knowing you, there'd be nothing left of the wench to kill, once you'd slaked your lust on her. Bide your time, son. You can have her soon enough."

"Father!" Walter protested.

"Be still. Must you always whine like a cat in heat?"

With those words, the baron grabbed the cloth on her back and hauled Gwyneth up. "You're not a guest here, Lady of Farleigh," he informed her. "While I've still some use for you alive, you will give service to my household."

He called a name and another bowed servant, this one a woman, came forward. "Have Byrdie shackle this one," he ordered, "and dress her in a fashion befitting her new station." Grabbing Gwyneth's chin, he forced her face to his and inquired, "What do they call you?" When she told him, he laughed. "Far too fair a name for one who's fallen as low as you have, woman. I'll call you Gert." He turned to Walter. "I wonder how much you'll still desire her after she's spent some time doing a scullion's work, dumping the slops and serving our men?"

"Don't ruin her for me!" she heard the younger lord complain as she was led away. This was quickly followed by the sound of another blow being struck.

Silently the servant took Gwyneth through a narrow archway set into the far wall of the stone addition. Beyond it was a short enclosure, equally narrow and very dark, that led to the outside. They crossed the yard of frozen mud and manure into a daub and wattle hut. "What is this place?" she asked in French, but the woman said nothing as she began to rout about in a dim corner. Using her own powers of deduction, and judging by the fire, the pots, and the kettles of steaming water, she determined they were in the scullery.

Trying again, this time Gwyneth spoke the tongue of their ancestors. "What is your name?"

"Sheila."

"'Tis a pretty name."

"No use trying to be pleasant. I don't care." From among a pile of rags, Sheila pulled a few which she handed directly to Gwyneth. Disliking even having to touch them, Gwyneth looked up questioningly into the servant's face. "Your clothes," the woman explained.

Grimacing, Gwyneth resignedly scuttled into the corner and pulled off her tunics. Quickly she slipped the coarse, stained, itchy gown over her head. Her own clothes over her arm, she looked at Sheila and asked, "What shall I do with these?"

"Give them to me." With an undisguised smile of delight, the servant grabbed them and fondled them as if they were a household pet.

Gwyneth looked back at the pile of rags balled up on the floor. Apparently, she deduced, some were still considered wearable clothing. She grabbed the item on top and discovered it was a dirty wimple. "Who owns these?"

"They belonged to Mary, who worked here nigh all her life. She died last year."

The man who had first brought Elwood his dinner shuffled into the hut. Sheila hailed him. "Byrdie, the master wants you to shackle this wench."

His sad eyes met Gwyneth's. "She's a lady. Wife to an earl. I heard them talking in the hall."

"No matter what she was," Sheila snapped, "she's one of us now."

"Why do you stay here? Why do you work for him?" Gwyneth asked the woman when the man disappeared through the doorway. "Eye's a wicked lord, and so is his son."

"As if I've a choice." Sheila threw some dirty pans into a kettle of wash water.

"You must have a choice."

"I've no more choice than you!" she barked, turning to glare angrily at Gwyneth over her shoulder. "You're a lady, and look where he's got you!"

That made Gwyneth fall silent, and she waited patiently for Byrdie to return with the chains. When he came to her, he apologized. But still he locked the manacles around her ankles, the length of chain between them providing a sure deterrent to her fleeing.

"What shall I do?" she asked. Both Sheila and Byrdie were busy with chores.

"It's late. Get some sleep. The morn will be soon enough for you to set to work," Sheila advised.

"Where should I sleep?"

"Anywhere you find a place to lie down." Sheila wiped her wet hands on the bodice of her tunic. "Some women sleep in the hall."

"Nay!"

"I thought you'd not much care for that idea." She shrugged. "Well, then, curl up in the corner where you're standing. 'Tis as good a place as any. Better than some, even, because the fire here'll warm you."

The fire did not warm her much. The small structure was drafty with the wind whistling around it, and Gwyneth had neither cloak nor blanket. Taking Sheila's suggestion, then, she settled down in the corner, trying to burrow herself into the scant, ragged clothing the dead woman, Mary, had left behind. But she could not sleep—could not *let* herself sleep—for she had to make a plan. If she did not, John would come for her as the baron insisted he would. Eye was most certainly correct in this matter. Whether or not he cared for her, pride and honor would compel him to try and rescue her. Mayhap, she thought with horror, her sons would even accompany him.

"John," she whispered aloud, hoping that by some wizardry her words would find their way into her husband's head, "do not walk into Eye's trap! Save yourself and the line of Farleigh to come. Save my sons, if you will. I shall endure what I've brought upon myself, so let me go. I'd no business coming into your life as I did; let me leave it now."

Gwyneth ceased her muttering before anyone overheard her and deemed her mad. She knew there was no point to it; she could not will her thoughts into her husband's mind. What she had to do was devise a way to ward off her husband before he rode through the gate or, at least, before he strode into the keep.

With a sigh, she glanced about the filthy hovel where the baron's victuals were prepared. Gwyneth kicked a squealing rat away that tried to sniff her shoes; she felt the damp wind seeping in through the wall against her back; she heard the clank of rusty chain links whenever she moved her legs.

A sense of hopelessness engulfed her.

Chapter Twenty Five

❖   ❖   ❖

Gwyneth could not reason, let alone plan. In Eye's keep, she was truly frightened and fully miserable. By day she spent every waking moment jumping to obey harshly given commands. At night she collapsed, exhausted, into a dreamless sleep. She lived from minute to minute, tense and terrified.

Not the least of Gwyneth's discomfort was her own filth. Her face was smudged with soot from tending the fire in the scullery. The soles of her shoes were thick with mud, manure and straw from crossing the yard between the keep and the outbuildings. Her tunic had fresh stains—food, from that which she served, and human refuse, from the slop pails she emptied. Also, she itched abominably with the vermin nesting in her clothes, She'd had to don dead Mary's wimple to keep the lice out of her braided hair. Her hands were already cut and scraped and blistered, and her breasts and bottom had been pinched and slapped 'til they were bruised and sore, compliments of Eye's mercenaries. Gwyneth thought she could not have endured at all, were it not for Byrdie and Sheila who, albeit grudgingly, advised and protected her. Thus, she did not resent the serving woman wearing her own clean clothes, while she herself remained garbed in little more than filthy rags.

On the morning of her third full day in captivity, the call went up that King Henry was seen approaching. "How far away is he?"

"Half a day's ride, milord," the watch told Elwood.

Everyone, from the hired knights and their doxies to the stable lads, exhibited a certain anticipation. Even the baron and his son behaved like excited children, hurrying upstairs to their rooms to bathe and select the proper clothes to wear for entertaining their monarch.

Ordered to help bring hot water up to their tubs, Gwyneth was disgusted with their self-centered foolishness. If the man approaching was, indeed, King Henry, she doubted he would be much impressed with their costumes once he saw the squalor in which they lived.

Then the full force of the news hit her like a slap awakening her from a stupor. The royal message Gerald received at Farleigh had been legitimate, so if the true king were riding this way, surely the earl would be riding with him!

Toting empty water buckets down the stairs, Gwyneth was suddenly torn as a rush of hope swelled in her breast. Her husband was the only one who might secure her release and see her spared from a miserable existence and a worse end. But he was the hunted, she was the bait—

Her heart constricted again as fear for John's life over her own settled upon her.

"Please, let King Henry come alone!" she prayed softly. Yet, more sure John would accompany the king than not, she found excuses to go into the yard hoping that somehow, some way, she could still warn him off.

In anticipation of the royal's arrival, the hounds

were chased from the hall and their droppings collected and tossed into the fire. The stench was bad, but hardly worse than usual. Additionally, the tables were cleared and three carved chairs set before the fire. In the scullery, the fattest pig was set to roasting.

At last he arrived. Gwyneth, on her way from the kitchen, was outside but behind the keep when she heard the clatter. Already the visitors were dismounting, she could tell, and knowing there was no time to run around the keep, she raised her skirts and ran, instead, inside. She was oblivious to the wine sloshing from the rim of the pitcher she carried, adding to the stains on her tunic. Hiding in the shadows of the shabby hall, her heart hammered anxiously as she watched, with dread, to see whom she might discover in the king's company.

Relief calmed her erratic pulse. Henry had four knights with him, all in full armor and nose-plated helmets, and one hunch-backed, bent-kneed jester in a leather cap that covered nearly all his face, no doubt to hide disfigurement. Gwyneth sized up the royal guards and knew not a one was big enough to be her husband. When the guards removed their helmets, tucking them beneath their arms, she recognized none. Absolved of the worry that her sons might have come to Eye to effect her rescue, Gwyneth looked again at the king, the true king. He was youthful but commanding, and even from her humble vantage point, she sensed that he was honest and fair.

Suddenly, she realized her monarch was the answer to her prayers. All she need do was wait for an opportunity to approach him, to explain, and to ask for his aid.

"Your majesty," Elwood bowed dramatically, "to what do I owe this unexpected honor?"

The handsome, red-haired king snapped his fingers and pointed. Byrdie himself rushed forward and brought one of the lord's chairs into the center of the old, wooden hall, and there sat the king.

"I thought you'd wish to sit nearer the fire," Elwood confessed.

"I'd prefer to sit nearer the open door, where some unfetid air might reach my nostrils."

Insulted, Walter drew himself up to his full, stoop-shouldered height. "We are honored by your visit, your grace, but do tell us why you've come."

"I thought your sire wished an audience with me."

"We—I—of course—"

Elwood stopped his son's babbling with a heel clamped down on his toe. "You know 'tis true," he admitted. "I have tried many times to speak with you. I even followed you across the water to Anjou. But always your majesty was too busy to spare a word with your humble vassal."

"Ah, well." King Henry made a noncommittal gesture before looking toward his men and signaling them to sit. The four knights took seats at a table; the jester plopped cross-legged onto the floor beside his master. "My other business took precedence," he explained to the baron. "But as I was so near to your, ah…" Gwyneth watched as he glanced about the room, his eyes sweeping briefly over her. "… Your abode, I thought I would detour here. Descriptions," he added dryly, "do not do it justice."

"What you've seen is the original grant," Walter informed him defensively. "We've added additional lands to our borders and two or more towns with that. The larger revenues generated will enable us to—"

"Hold your tongue, Walter," Elwood hissed, nodding

at Byrdie, who brought forward the other two chairs so that the man and his son could sit across from the king. "Wine, your highness?" he offered, and when the king nodded, Byrdie began to distribute newly washed goblets. "Gert!" the baron snapped. "Fill their cups!"

Startled, Gwyneth hurried to obey. Only by holding her breath was she able to overcome the sudden shaking of her hands as she poured wine into everyone's goblets. She was still serving the royal guards when Elwood asked, "How come you to be so nearby?"

"I had business with another baron. Your neighbor, the earl of Farleigh."

She jerked, the spout jumped over the edge of the cup she was filling, and wine streamed onto the knight's knee. Mumbling apologies, she tried to dry the stain with the edge of her tunic, but the soldier, whose face was obscured by the hood of his hauberk, grabbed her hand and shook his head.

With a weak but grateful nod, she went next to fill the jester's goblet. As she walked in the hunchback's direction, Walter inquired of the king, "Was your business with him settled satisfactorily?"

"Nay," Henry replied as Gwyneth crouched near his chair, poised to fill the fool's cup. "He is dead."

She dropped the flagon with a gasp, but the jester caught it nimbly. As he filled his own cup, she tried to ignore the pain burning in her chest as if some fiery arrow had pierced her there. *'Tis a lie!* the voice in her mind screamed. *John cannot be dead! Not slain in some trivial battle, not after all the wars and battles he's fought in and survived. Nay! The Dane—the mighty, invincible Dane, cannot be dead!*

"Dead?" Walter repeated as Gwyneth returned to the shadows. Surprise was apparent in his voice.

"Aye," Henry assured him. "The last of Hugh of Farleigh's sons was wounded at Kurth and died enroute to his home.

"Dead," he said again, his eyes searching the hall for Gwyneth until he found her near the far wall. He gave her a taunting look.

"That changes matters, does it not?" Elwood asked conversationally.

"It does," the king agreed. "I never confiscated Farleigh when I knew there was an heir who could still return to claim it. But now, I fear there is no one left."

"Ah... the earl's wife?" The baron spoke softly, his eyebrows raised in question.

"'Tis true he had a bride now, didn't he?" Henry mused thoughtfully. "Well, yes, she could inherit her husband's lands, as there are no children between them. And I could wed her off to a lord of my own choosing who would assume the mantle of earl. But..."

"Aye?" Walter prompted eagerly, leaning forward in his chair so that his watery eyes gazed up at Henry's face.

"She's gone."

"She is?" He glanced again in Gwyneth's direction.

"Aye. Farleigh's seneschal had the news she ran off after her sire, Arnulf of Sherborne, was buried. No one has a clue where she's gone."

"The seneschal has had no other word?"

King Henry shook his head. "Nay, not before I'd left the castle. Only what the messenger from Sherborne told him, that Lady Gwyneth disappeared shortly after her father was laid to rest. But the seneschal did relay to me another curious matter," he added, cocking one brow. "He said some other posed as me and visited with the lady at Farleigh while her husband was occupied with the siege at Kurth. Sherborne's messenger said I had been at the manor, too, having joined the earl's lady wife at her father's graveside." Henry snickered. "I know the earl and the lady were not wed long. No doubt this daughter of Sherborne's had a lover, and it was some elaborate charade. No doubt, too, they've run off together."

"But if she hasn't—" Walter began, and again Elwood silenced him, this time with a backhanded cuff.

"What, then, will you do with the earl's estate?"

King Henry considered the baron levelly. "It seems you could use better quarters."

This time Elwood reacted as openly as Walter was inclined to. Father and son shared a look of unbridled glee before the elder turned back to the king. "You are intimating you would award me Farleigh?"

"Nay, I am saying it outright." Henry held out his empty goblet and dropped it into Byrdie's hands when the servant shuffled forward to collect it.

Seemingly suspicious at his unexpected good fortune, Elwood leaned back in his chair. His dark, flinty eyes narrowed as he asked, "Why, your highness? In the years you've ruled England, you have not once asked me to your council, and you've declined my every request for an audience. I was beginning to assume you had no wish for either my advice or my services. Why now," he asked, "would you honor me with the crown jewel of these southern shires?"

"Because if I grant you what you wish, Lord Elwood, I expect you to give me what I desire in turn."

"And that is?"

"That you leave the other land-lords in this region be. That you cease the unprovoked attacks on your neighbors and return the lands you've stolen from them."

For a long moment there was heavy silence in the hall. Then Elwood of Eye smiled and declared, "Done!"

Respectfully, both he and Walter slipped out of their chairs and onto their knees and kissed the hem of Henry's robe. Rising, the baron announced, "Tonight we shall celebrate! You, of course, shall be our most honored guest."

Henry looked with distaste about the hall, his eyes again glancing over Gwyneth, still huddled near a far wall. "Very well. I suppose it cannot be avoided, though I do hope I'll not find myself infested with fleas for the duration of my travels."

Neither Elwood nor Walter took umbrage at the royal insult. They were both too ecstatic. "As you wish," the baron smiled graciously. "Now would you care to rest awhile?" he offered, gesturing toward the stairs. "You may have my room, the best in the keep."

With a reluctant nod the king agreed. He and his men, including his deformed jester, stood and followed the baron up the stairs. When they were nearly out of sight, Walter's head snapped toward Gwyneth and he sneered, "Oh, Geerrt! Get yourself into the kitchen and help Sheila with the victuals. I warn you, they had better be tasty fare! 'Tis the king himself who'll be dining with us, and I know you know how to provide for a king."

Gwyneth did not move. She was numb with shock over all she had heard—John, dead; Farleigh to be handed over to Eye. It was worse than a nightmare. If true, it was some witch's curse coming to fruition. But it could not be true! John was not dead, and Farleigh remained his own.

Walter was bearing down on her, yet she still had not made a move toward the archway, the exit.

Suddenly the main portal to the keep opened. Walter was distracted, while Gwyneth was roused from her own thoughts. They both looked toward the newcomer, but he was a stranger only to Walter. Gwyneth recognized him from Farleigh.

She held her breath, and in that minute's silence she heard the messenger confirm the king's words. Now there was no denying it: John, earl of Farleigh, was indeed dead!

Frantic, Gwyneth finally turned to flee, but she stumbled. Walter lunged toward her, reached out, and grabbed her shoulder roughly, forcing her to turn and face him.

"Now there's no doubt, is there?" he demanded, a triumphant leer on his lips. "John of Farleigh's dead and no longer a player in this game. Neither are you of any use to us. The earldom is ours without you." Walter chuckled and licked his lips. "Yet still I shall have my way with you, lady. And I vow: The last cock you ever feel between your thighs shall be my own."

Wild with grief and despair, Gwyneth turned again and this time, made good her exit from the keep. She half expected Walter to follow her out, but he did not. He knew she could not get very far. Indeed, as soon as she reached the yard, she sank to her knees, oblivious to the cold of the ground seeping through her thin tunic.

'Twas all her doing, everything, she realized. If only she had not meddled at the very first, when John came to Sherborne to settle on a marriage with Gwendolyn. If only she'd obeyed at the last, and returned to Farleigh as John had told her to. But, nay! She had interfered, she had followed her own head and now everything that had been her husband's was lost—even his own life.

Her shoulders bent with the heaviness of remorse, and Gwyneth knew one thing. She'd not approach King Henry with her tale, beseeching him for his royal intervention. Nay. She'd hold her tongue and await her own end at Walter's hand. 'Twas justice for her to live out her days as Gert, the lowly scullery maid. And justice, too, that her last bedmate would not be her gentle husband, but a villain worse than even Ector.

Gwyneth was freed of her shackles to serve that evening in the torch-lit hall. All of Eye's mercenaries and their women joined Elwood, Walter, the king and his men, two of whom were missing for the meal that night. Together with Sheila, Byrdie, and a few other servants, Gwyneth scuttled about, keeping everyone's trenchers and goblets filled. Though she never failed in her assigned duties, Gwyneth performed them in a daze born of a deep depression.

Henry sat, this night, at the dais table set up for the occasion, but though he seemed good-natured enough, he held himself aloof. Gwyneth wondered, idly, if this was always his demeanor or if he were that offended by his surroundings. She decided it was probably more the latter than the former. Sweet Mary, she sighed inwardly as she replaced an empty tray of victuals with a filled one, if only it had been he, the real King Henry, who had come to Farleigh that fateful day! Then John might have escaped, not only from the bonds that tied him to her, but with his life as well.

"Oh!" she gasped, startled from her solitary musings. She'd leaned too close to Walter as she served him, and he'd grabbed her wrist.

"Looking eagerly forward to this night, are you?" he whispered into her ear as he forced her face nearer his.

"I am indeed, milord," she mumbled dully.

Walter tugged her arm again, forcing her to bend awkwardly over his lap. "I warn you, *Gert,*" he said, "do not dare try and reveal yourself to Henry. The best you could hope for would be to find yourself married to me. Or my sire," he added.

That thought made her stomach curdle. "I'd no such designs, milord."

"Ah, so you do desire me, you lusty wench!" Still smiling, he grabbed Gwyneth's chin between his knuckle and thumb and kissed her, open-mouthed, pushing his tongue forcefully against her lips in an attempt to part them.

He reeked of onions and Gwyneth, nearly gagging, made a half-hearted attempt to pull away. But when Walter responded by grabbing her about the waist and pulling her into his lap, she resigned herself to his public pawing. He did not disappoint her; in an instant his hands were on her full breasts.

"Time for some entertainment, wouldn't you say?" King Henry suggested abruptly, his eyes on Walter's fingers, and Gwyneth's bosom, as he spoke.

The last shred of dignity she'd not yet tossed off caused her to blush in humiliation.

"I am sorry, your grace," Elwood apologized, "but we have neither minstrels nor jugglers to provide a show."

"No matter," Henry said easily. "I have my jester with me. I like my entertainments," he confessed, "so I take Waldo with me wherever I travel."

"Waldo!" he called out, and the fool in the leather cap jumped nimbly up and stood on his bent legs, bobbing his head to and fro like a dim-witted mute.

"Entertain us!"

Obediently the jester began to sing a ribald and bouncy tune, accompanying himself on a lute. He had a surprisingly rich, baritone voice that Gwyneth had not expected of him. As the song was familiar to most in the hall, soon a myriad of voices joined his while clapping hands picked up the rhythm. Gwyneth did not participate. Head hanging, she observed with detachment the fingers pinching her nipples through the fabric of her garb, almost unaware of the pain.

Suddenly she was jerked from her self-contained misery by the jester who, having jumped onto the dais, grabbed her hands. There was no recourse for her but to follow as he pulled her off Walter's lap and down onto the main floor.

Startled, Gwyneth stared with trepidation at the fool's distorted face. His close, leather cap sat low on his brow, encasing his skull and covering not only his ears but his cheeks. It struck her he might be bald, and she wondered if the thin, black scar visible on his hairless chin was only the least offensive of many, too unsettling to allow the world to see. But just then Gwyneth was dismayed to realize the disfigured fool's squinty eyes were actually a striking, cerulean blue. A blue much like—

She closed her own eyes, trying to block out the image of John's countenance. Was she doomed to see him everywhere? she wondered. Even in a cripple's unlikely form?

A tug on her arm forced Gwyneth to look again at the man who'd made her his unwitting dance partner. As he dragged her along, ignoring her shuffling feet while he kept up his own fancy footwork, he winked at her. The quick, secret communication pricked her like a dart. Gwyneth's own lashes fluttered, and when he winked a second time, she nearly swooned.

"Keep your wits about you, sweetling," her husband warned, his voice a whisper in her ear as he caught her up and held her close. "We've much to do before we're through."

So many emotions exploded within her breast, Gwyneth felt only numb. Inhaling a deep breath, she nodded silently and tried valiantly to keep up her end of the dance. By the end of it they were on the far side of the hall, opposite the raised table at which the king and the lords of Eye sat. Most gracefully, considering the stooped posture he'd adopted, John tossed Gwyneth off into the arms of two royal knights who had not partaken of the feast and had only just made their appearance. As they grabbed her arms and steadied her between them, she glanced quickly from one to the other. Her heart would not believe what her own eyes told her—one was Rodney, the other, Matthew!

Her husband, meanwhile, had resumed a central position in the hall, and was still playing his Waldo character. As the fool, he was telling wickedly funny stories that had his audience holding their sides. The joking was immediately followed by a series of magic tricks and then, again, a song. As before, John the jester grabbed Gwyneth's hands and forced her to skip along while he danced the width and breadth of the room.

Walter's eyes did not once leave them. When the singing and dancing ended, he stood and demanded harshly, "Hand the wench over to me."

Gwyneth bit her lip as John, oddly now only a few inches taller than she, put himself between her and the younger lord of Eye. "Nay," he said simply. "Waldo wants her."

"What!"

"Master?" John's head bobbed in Henry's direction.

"She's yours," the king announced.

"Just one moment, your majesty," Walter protested, turning to face the royal guest. "That bitch is mine."

"Oh?" He raised one brow. "But what is yours is also mine, is it not?"

The man scowled. His eyes darted from Henry to Elwood. "Father—"

"Shut up." The baron backhanded his son in the chest, and with a grunt he sat down hard in his chair.

"But you promised!" Walter whined petulantly.

And Henry said, "I, too, made a promise to my loyal servant, Waldo. His back and legs may be bent, but I've heard tell his staff is as straight as my own when a pretty wench attends him."

"A pretty wench!" Walter repeated, as if the words were sour as lemons on his tongue. "She's a dirty, old hag—"

"Then why would you want her for your own?" Henry asked. "I understand why poor Waldo, there, must accept whoever is willing. But you, the new heir to Farleigh?"

"Do keep your tongue in your head," Elwood warned Walter before he could respond. "Henry and his men, including the fool, will be gone on the morn. But *Gert*," he said pointedly, nodding in Gwyneth's direction, "will remain for you to do with as you will."

Walter slumped down into his chair, crossing his legs so that one knee was visible above the edge of the table. The look he gave Gwyneth made her realize that his plans for the morrow were far worse than his plans for this night had been.

"Your majesty." John bowed his thanks before kissing Gwyneth loudly and throwing her over his humped shoulder. The others in the room, Eye's knights and their women, cheered the jester and toasted him with still another round as he carried her off up the gallery stairs.

Chapter Twenty Six

✛   ✛   ✛

John kicked open the first door he came to. It was the mean room in which Gwyneth had awakened at Eye's keep. When he'd kicked it closed behind them, he slowly lowered his wife to the floor. Their bodies rubbed tantalizingly for a long moment, as the earl now stood at his full height.

"John." Gwyneth reached up and pulled the heavy cap from his head. "Dear God, I did not even recognize you."

"Nor I you," John admitted, his hold on Gwyneth tightening instead of loosening. "Christ, when I saw that hag wearing your gown, I thought—I thought—"

She stood on tiptoe, pressing her lips to his so that he need not explain what he'd thought. She knew.

"I am alive," she whispered when that first kiss ended. Suddenly she giggled and reached up, touching the smooth point of John's chin with her fingertips. "I still can hardly recognize you, what with that beard of yours gone."

"Do you like it, my lady wife? Enjoy it while you can. I intend to grow it back immediately."

"Why? I think you more handsome clean shaven."

"Ah, but I cannot tickle you in those places I like

best to tickle you, without hair on my chin."

Both their minds entertained sudden images, erotic images. "God's wounds, Gwyneth," John moaned, "what hell you've put me through!"

She might have tried to explain, to apologize, but before any words came to mind John hauled her up off her feet and backed her to the narrow cot. In a thrice she was tumbled upon it, his mouth pressed hard to hers, plundering, demanding. As his callused hands gently stroked her breasts, made tender and sore by Walter's abuse, Gwyneth reached into her husband's tunic, broke the twine that held his false hump in place, and freed the ball of rags from beneath his clothing. He lay his full weight upon her then, burning off the traces of Walter's unwanted touching with his own heat.

Beneath his broad body, Gwyneth could see nothing but him; above her, John was intent only on removing her headpiece and burying his face in her hair. Thus, when the door burst open behind them, the latch snapping loudly, neither was quick enough to react. Walter stormed into the room and clubbed the earl with a sturdy log, still smoking from the fire in the hall.

Gwyneth screamed when she felt the wind the weapon made as it sliced through the air. She continued to scream when she heard it connect with her husband's skull. She might have gone on screaming even after John went limp and slid, face down, to the floor. But Walter stopped her with a slap that made her ears ring.

"No one steals from me what is mine!" he declared, still whining, as his father had once said, like a cat in heat. Ignoring John's limp body, he sat down beside Gwyneth on the bed. "Certainly not a deformed and dim-witted jester. Not even the king's own."

There were so many thoughts spinning in her head, it may as well have been blank. Wide-eyed and mute, Gwyneth watched as Walter grabbed the neck of her tunic and tore it to her waist. She was rigid when he forced her down beneath him.

"I thought you were anticipating this moment so eagerly, my lady," he chuckled as he straddled her. "Is this not what you wanted?"

Gwyneth knew then, had it come to it, she'd not have submitted willingly to Walter of Eye's raping and slaying her. Alone in the world with no hope for life, she'd have fought this foul cockshead like a mad dog, if need be. As she was not alone, and there was hope of a life ahead, she fought now like an angry cat.

"Damn your demented soul to hell, Walter of Eye!" Gwyneth spat, her chest heaving as she strained for breath beneath the weight of him.

"Walter of Farleigh, you mean," he corrected. Then, running the tip of his finger along the valley between her exposed breasts, he added, "Since you are still Gwyneth of Farleigh, methinks this union between us was destined. Don't you?"

In response, Gwyneth reached up and clawed at his bulging eyes with her cracked, dirty nails. Growling, he fended her off and pushed her arms down above her head. But not before she managed to scratch his cheeks, leaving three bloody trails on each.

"Bitch! You bitch! You bloody, whoring bitch!"

Walter raised one arm, fist clenched, and Gwyneth closed her eyes, bracing for the blow. But it did not come. Instead, she felt Walter go flying off the cot, off her body.

"Matthew!" she gasped when she risked a peek and spied her own son above her. Modestly, she pulled closed the remnants of her dress.

"Mother!" It was Rodney's voice she heard, and soon his face, too, appeared beside his brother's. Before any of them could say more, though, a virtual explosion erupted nearby. The young men jumped aside and Gwyneth came to her knees on the cot, watching as Walter flew up off the floor muttering a string of epithets. It appeared as though the man were bringing the earl up with him, but in fact the opposite was true. John was both holding Walter by the collar and pummeling him with his fist. Though the younger man tried vainly to shield his face with both hands, ducking one way and another, the earl continued to land his blows smartly, all the while steering the object of his rage toward the door. When he reached it, he shoved him out.

Matthew and Rodney made to follow. "Your armor and weapons are there, Lord John," Gwyneth's redheaded son announced, pointing to a trunk near the foot of the bed. "Don't concern yourself with that whelp of a diseased whore," he added contemptuously. "He shan't interfere again. We'll see to it."

Alone again, John and Gwyneth found the intense passion that had earlier flared between them suddenly cooled. Gwyneth could read no emotion in her husband's face as he began pulling off his fool's costume and discarding it on the floor.

She groped for something to say, something that might ease the way for what needed to be said. "I believed," she began softly, "naught in the world could enduce you to shave off your beard."

"God's blood, Gwyneth," he barked, his voice muffled as he pulled his gambesons on over his head. "I'd do anything for you."

"Oh, John." Tears welled in her eyes and a lump clogged her throat, but Gwyneth managed to lift her husband's heavy mail shirt from the trunk and hold it out to him. "I thought you were dead. I wished I were, too."

"I'm sorry to have put you through that." He took his hauburk from her but did not immediately put it on. "'Twas part of our plan, the king's and mine."

"You shouldn't have made any plans to rescue me. It is my own fault that I am here. Don't think I don't know that disobeying you brought all this upon my head. But I would not wish it upon yours."

"We'll not speak of that now," he informed her. "But I vow we shall at a later time." He frowned as he considered her, as if just noticing Gwyneth's filthy appearance. "Put on that tunic I've just thrown off," he ordered. "It's not fresh, but it's clean compared to what you've been wearing."

Obedient at last, Gwyneth stripped off the late servant Mary's tunic as her husband thrust his arms into the sleeves of his hauberk. When she donned John's discarded clothes, however, they hung voluminously about her curves and puddled on the floor.

"Here."

She looked up to find him offering her the piece of twine that had bound the rag ball which had served as his hump.

"It should at least hold up the hem so that you don't trip."

Gwyneth knotted the string about her waist and bloused the upper part of the garment over it so that the tunic fell only to her ankles. "Thank you," she mumbled, discovering that a bit of cleanliness buoyed her spirits drastically. "Do you need any help?" she inquired as she watched John slip his baldric over his shoulder and reach for his sword.

"Nay." He shook his head and Gwyneth shook hers, free at last of the wimple and tight braids. She raked her nails through her long, crimped tresses, and her scalp tingled delightfully.

"I'm sure you and King Henry have a good plan," she went on eagerly, hopefully. "I presume it includes killing both Elwood and Walter?"

"Aye." John was sitting on the cot now, tugging on his heavy leather boots.

"I should like very much to help."

The earl had been bent over. Now he straightened, his head snapped up, and he faced his wife aghast. "You'll do naught—"

"Milord? Mother." The words were whispered as the door opened a crack to reveal a dark head. The intrusion forced John into silence as Rodney and his older brother entered the small room. It allowed Gwyneth the opportunity to avoid whatever it was her husband had intended to say.

"Have you two been here all the while?" she asked her sons.

"We came with King Henry and Lord John, Mother," Rodney replied. "You spilled wine on my knee, but you did not even know 'twas I."

"Where's Richie?"

"Outside the keep, but within the walls."

"And the others?"

"What others?" John demanded tersely, one eyebrow raised higher than its twin.

Gwyneth turned to him. "Lionel. Bruno. All your knights."

"There are no knights with us other than your sons and the king's two guards."

She gasped. "What? Oh, John, you cannot expect to defeat Eye with just the handful of you against him. Have you seen the number of men he keeps here?"

"King Henry says a war may be waged with as few as two," Rodney explained to his mother. "That's our intent here."

"Oh, no." All the hope that had filled her heart dribbled out, like wine from a torn goat's bladder; she could almost feel it puddling on the floor at her feet. "It shall never work, and I would not have you all rush hell-bent to death, because of me!" Her tear-glittering eyes moved from Rodney to Matthew to John.

"You should have thought of that before you put yourself in harm's way by riding alone to Sherborne," he suggested as he came to his feet.

"I am sorry for that!" Gwyneth lunged forward and grabbed the earl's muscled forearm. "Yet I cannot undo it. And 'tis no reason for you to sacrifice yourselves—"

"We are not sacrificing ourselves," John informed her, removing her hand from his arm. "Besides, this fight between Elwood and me has been destined for some time. Better here than at Farleigh, methinks."

Blinking rapidly, Gwyneth tried to force her tears back instead of allowing them to stream down her cheeks. She was only partially successful in her efforts.

"Please. Tell me what the plan is," she begged, "and let me assist you. Since there are so few of you, 'twould be better to have eight against Elwood than only seven."

The lord glared at his lady but said nothing. Still, the tension crackled between them like sparks between burning logs in a hearth. Matthew dared to speak up, to break the silence, by announcing, "Rodney and I shall return to the hall, as you seem to have no need of us at the moment. We'll keep an eye on Walter. When last seen, he was hiding his battered face in a large cup of mead."

"And a fat slut's over-sized tits," his brother added, attempting a lame jest that brought no laughter, nervous or otherwise, from his parents. Sharing a look with Matthew, then, they both quit the room.

John still did not look away, but he did not speak, either. In desperation Gwyneth said quickly, "I understand you've no wish for my help, then. Obedience. Obedience is all you want from me. Well, fine and good, I owe you that much, don't I? So I shall do as you say. Whatever you say. But, John, please tell me what's to happen so I am not conjuring things in my mind. I should like to know your intentions. The intentions that you believe will see the lords and knights here overpowered and you—you, the king, my sons—safe and victorious. Please tell me!"

She reached out, intending to touch him again. But Gwyneth immediately recalled that he'd disdained her touch moments earlier. She dropped her hands then, and let them hang at her sides. Her arms suddenly felt very awkward appendages, as if they did not belong attached to her shoulders.

The earl blinked very slowly. He shifted his weight, righting his shoulders. "Richard," he told Gwyneth, "is hiding in the bailey. Later, Rodney will come to you and take you to him. Richard will then see you safe away."

"And you?"

"I intend to see this foul keep burned to the ground, its masters and all those who served them still inside it."

"Everyone?" Her voice was thin and reedy.

"Everyone." The tone of his voice alone was a dare.

He was daring her to question him, to argue with him, to defy him.

She dared not. Folding her hands in front of her waist, she looked down, afraid to face her husband lest he read her thoughts.

"Get some sleep." John's voice had changed again. Now, it was gentle. "You look ready to drop, and there's a few hours yet before the beginning of the end of Eye."

Gwyneth nodded. Suddenly, impulsively, she threw herself at him and wrapped her arms about his waist. It was impossible to span his girth with her arms, what with his armor and belts and weapons. But he leaned over, splaying his fingers against her back. And he rested his chin on her head.

"'Tis imperative," he whispered, "you keep the pledge you just made me. I need your obedience now, milady. There is a plan, and all must go accordingly. Should you dare to interfere…"

His voice trailed off. There was no need to name the consequences.

She woke with her son, Rodney, shaking her gently. "Mother, 'tis time to rise. The hall below is quiet, all of them asleep, most of them drunk. We must move quickly."

Gwyneth came to her full senses in a second. "Where is Matthew? And—my husband?"

"They slipped outside into the bailey some time ago. There, with Richard, they intend to eliminate the keep's waking guard."

Mutely she nodded and followed Rodney out of the room. Viewed from above, the great hall was shadowed in darkness. The fire in the hearth had burned low, most all the candles were guttering out, and even the torches mounted on the walls cast off more smoke than they did light. As they descended the stairs from the balcony above, Gwyneth heard a cacophony of snoring from the men curled up on the tables, slumped on benches, and sprawled among the rushes on the floor. King Henry and his men were not among them, awake or asleep; neither were Elwood nor Walter.

There were others missing, also. Others Gwyneth wished to warn, so that they might not perish. Others who were guiltless of Eye's crimes, others who were as much captives as she.

Despite it all: the honest pledge she'd earlier given her husband, the consequences of similar actions, and her most earnest wish that she might be obedient, Gwyneth could not.

"Mother!" Rodney hissed, grasping for but missing her sleeve as she darted into the great hall. "Where are you going? The door is here," he informed her, pointing to the main portal.

For a moment she hesitated. But Byrdie and Sheila and the others—

"I must go out the back way," she whispered in turn. "There are people here who do not deserve—"

"What! What the hell is going on?"

Gwyneth froze as one of Eye's knights sat up with that exclamation. In another moment he was on his feet and fumbling for the sword at his side. But before he could draw the weapon, Rodney sprang forward with his own at the ready. He stabbed the knight cleanly, his withdrawn blade sheathed in crimson.

"Mother!" he shouted now, still beckoning her to his side. Yet as he called out, the knight he'd slain fell back onto one of the trestle tables, a great racket erupting as metal plates and ewers and mugs crashed to the floor. Immediately the others who'd been sleeping at that table began to waken, and Eye's surviving men took up the fight their fallen comrade had begun.

Rodney could not take them all alone, even though their eyes were bleary with sleep and drink. Fortunately the sudden noise brought the royal knights and the king himself charging down the gallery stairs, all well-armed and dressed in mail. Gwyneth hesitated until one of Eye's men made to grab her. Two screaming women darted past at that same moment, so as they fled she fled, too, through the archway and into the yard behind the keep.

"What are you doing?" she shrieked, spying Richard setting the hut that served as the scullery to flame.

"Mother, come," he urged as his twin brother had minutes before. The thatch was already burning brightly. "I've horses tied for us near the gate, which is now unbarred and unguarded."

"Go help your brother inside the hall!" she commanded as she ran toward him. He looked surprised when she ignored his offered hand. "The knights of Eye were alerted—King Henry himself is fighting them."

"But you—I'm to take you—"

"Do as I say!" She paused just outside the doorway of the small, burning structure. "I can get myself away, but your brother and the king's men require your sword arm!"

Richard needed no more urging. He pitched the torch toward another building and it, like the scullery, began crackling and popping like dried leaves. He loped with the long, strong legs of youth toward the keep and the battle within.

Gwyneth ducked into the scullery. "Byrdie!" she called, coughing on the already thick smoke caught inside the walls. "Sheila!"

They answered her with choking sounds and she found them through the haze. "Come," she urged, pulling them up from their sleeping places. "Elwood is doomed, and his keep will soon be ashes. Hurry!"

Together, the three stumbled outside and fell, catching their breaths as they lay in the snow-dusted yard. "Where are the others?" Gwyneth asked when she could speak again.

"Some sleep in the stable, some where the stores are kept."

With Byrdie's help, both women found their feet again. A glance behind confirmed the scullery was almost gone; the roof had turned to ash with the quickness of a lighted piece of parchment. Now the walls were going.

A glance ahead and they saw the other building Richard had torched was burning as much from within as without. If anyone living had been inside, he was no longer.

"Come!" Gwyneth shouted, and the three found the buttery still intact. Rousting the sleeping servants from within, she retrieved Richard's discarded torch from the dirt, and set the structure to flame.

"The stables, the horses!" she cried. But as she turned she stumbled over the prone body of a fallen knight. Scrambling up, at first she thought the soldier was grinning. It took a second to realize it was another mouth he had, where his throat used to be. Horrified, Gwyneth thrust a fist in her own mouth to keep from retching.

"He can't hurt you now, milady," Byrdie told her, taking the torch she still held in one hand. "Come."

"Nay." She shook her head, her wild hair gleaming red in the firelight. "Rouse what other servants there be, and see them safe. The beasties, too. The gate is open and unmanned—get you gone from here. But Byrdie, Sheila, use that torch. Fire everything in your wake. Before the night is done Eye, its lords, and all its holdings should be naught but cinders."

They nodded, lurching on, and Gwyneth turned back to the keep. How many animals there were within this barony's wooden walls! Before she'd taken no real notice, but now they surrounded her, running blindly to and fro. Rats and mice were scurrying from what had been the kitchen and the granary. Dogs were yelping, pigs squealing, chickens clucking. All the animals darted around the yard, circling in panic, whining in dread, so that walking a straight course became impossible. Yet she managed to return to the keep and entered as she had left it.

Chapter Twenty Seven

✧   ✧   ✧

Back inside Eye's shabby hall, hidden in the shadow of the arch, Gwyneth took in the room: Bodies littered the floor, none asleep any longer, and all were male—the soldiers' whores had, or were still, fleeing. Yet several knights remained afoot, their swords clanking as they fought man to man. A yell caused her to look in the direction from which it had come. She gasped as she saw a gush of blood spurt from Matthew's shoulder. She wanted to run to him, but instinct kept her still until she witnessed her son counter the blow that had wounded him with an angry roar and his own weapon. He pierced his opponent so that the man's life escaped as he fell to the floor. Immediately, Matthew turned to engage another.

The twins were fighting, each on opposite sides of the wide room; one royal knight was also waging battle but the other, Gwyneth saw, was dead nearby him. The king, though, was holding his own. He was even smiling, though his smile was grim, as if this exercise were merely rough sport.

Gwyneth caught some movement near the keep's main door, and she spied a few of Eye's knights and their women escaping. There was a limit, it seemed, to their loyalty. Next an angry curse, muttered by a voice she knew quite well, caused her to look at the top of the stairs. At that very instant her husband plunged a dagger into Elwood's chest and the baron fell, like a straw doll, down the steps. A single twitch and he moved no more.

"John!" she called out, but fortunately he did not look down at her. Instead he twirled, unsheathing his sword, and deflected Walter's weapon when he suddenly appeared on the gallery, lunging forward menacingly.

Gwyneth was frantic, but there was nothing she could do. All around her was carnage. The smoky room made her eyes burn, and the clank—clank—clank of metal striking metal as the knights thrust and parried with their swords matched the pounding rhythm of the pulse beating in her temples. Frozen in anxious terror where she stood, her eyes searched above as she strained for a glimpse of her husband. But he and Walter had disappeared into the dark recesses. Holding her breath, Gwyneth waited in suspense to discover who would appear, the victor over his enemy.

John came first into her line of vision. With a splintering crash he broke through the gallery rail, falling backwards, his bare head cracking audibly as it made contact with an over-turned stool in the hall below. A sickening thud accompanied his landing; John did not move. He looked dead as his clanging broadsword skittered free of his open hand and came to rest some distance away.

Opening her mouth to call out his name again, Gwyneth placed one foot forward. But she neither uttered a sound nor ran to him. It was good she did not, for Walter quickly followed John, fairly flying off the gallery as he landed, feet first, on a trestle table in the hall. Next he jumped the shorter distance to the floor and straddled the earl, who remained as still as a corpse.

Her eyes darted quickly as she took in everything in the hall. What Gwyneth saw was that every man who was on her husband's side was engaged in mortal combat. Even King Henry was breathing heavily as he parried with his opponent. Unthinking, she rushed forward and picked up John's own sword. The weight was fierce, but she grabbed the hilt with both hands and pressed the handle to her stomach to better support it.

"I'll have Farleigh yet!" she heard Walter declare, and saw him raise his dagger high above his own head.

Rage and revenge swelled within Gwyneth as if they were palpable, living things. She could not allow Walter to take from John all she had once thought he'd lost to Eye already: his life, his lands, his legacy. With a piercing yell, she screamed, "You'll not!" and charged toward the lord of Eye as if she were mounted on a cantering destrier.

She plunged the sword into his back. The sharp steel blade made contact, but she kept pushing, ignoring the sounds of rending flesh and crunching bone until she had run him through. For a long moment, her hands petrified in their grip, Gwyneth clung to the haft until Walter's crumpling weight forced her to release it and he fell lifelessly off of John and onto the boards beside him.

Like Elwood his father, Walter was dead. Eye was no longer a threat to Farleigh. But John, Farleigh's earl—

Gwyneth fell to her knees beside her husband and raised his head into her lap. When he inhaled a ragged breath and opened his eyes a crack, her relief was all-encompassing. "John?" she whispered, his scarred and rugged face all she could see despite the distracting chaos surrounding them. "Are you sorely hurt?"

"Nay," he responded, though he coughed and winced. "Why... why are you here? You were to be gone before the fighting started."

"I—" She glanced up to see that one by one, Eye's mercenaries were falling beneath the swords wielded by the king, his knight, and her own sons. "I fear I disobeyed you again," she admitted with a sigh.

Once victory over Eye's forces became inevitable, it came about quickly. Immediately Gwyneth tended her sons' wounds, both major and minor, and bandaged the bleeding cut on the back of her husband's skull. Once he gained his feet, John shook off her queries regarding both his labored breathing and his limp. Leading her and the others outside, he personally put a torch to Eye's decrepit, wooden keep. Joined by the few servants who'd toiled in terror under the tyranny of the lords of Eye, the Norman king and Saxon earl watched as the structure became a bright inferno before choking on its own smoke and crumbling inward on its former lords.

"Richard, the horses!" John commanded, and immediately Gwyneth's son departed, returning with mounts for them all. "Assist your mother," he ordered next, and as Richard knitted his fingers together so that Gwyneth might step into hands and boost herself into the saddle, she watched her husband climb laboriously onto his own warhorse.

Immediately she was off the palfrey she'd been provided. "You're hurt!" she declared accusingly as she came to John's side, causing even the king to turn toward the earl. Touching one of her husband's limbs and seeing his grimace of pain, she announced, "Your leg is broken!" And, as her eyes widened with dawning understanding, she added, "You no doubt cracked your ribs as well, when you took that plunge. Damn you, John of Farleigh!" she muttered fretfully beneath her breath.

Turning, Gwyneth glanced around. Spying Sheila, she inquired, "Do you know of a cottar's hut nearby? Somewhere the earl of Farleigh might take refuge 'til he can recover?"

Before the serving woman could reply, John slid down from his destrier and placed a firm hand on Gwyneth's shoulder, mostly to restrain her, but also for support. "Woman," he growled, "I'm going nowhere but home to Farleigh."

"Soon enough," she informed him crisply. She knew what was best for him, even if he did not.

"Now! Tonight!"

"Nay." Gwyneth shook her head and stood her ground, unaware that Henry, his man, and all three of her sons had urged their horses off at a silent walk so as not to be unwilling witnesses to the inevitable confrontation already brewing.

"Gwyneth, I will no longer tolerate either your headstrong stubbornness nor your willful disobedience! I've had a belly full."

If he'd slapped her, John could not have more effectively brought Gwyneth to her senses.

"Forgive me, milord," she begged, her eyes downcast. A crashing timber and a shower of sparks caused her to jump, but she continued, "Again, I did not mean to be willful. 'Tis only that I am concerned for your health."

Gwyneth swallowed hard and risked a glance up at her big, burly husband. The fire in the distance caused his hair to gleam more red than yellow, and even his flesh had a crimson cast. He looked like a great, fierce demon come to life, but she determined not to cower timidly. It was not the way she wished him to remember her. So she raised her chin a notch and squared her shoulders.

"Milord," she said, "I know you are determined to set off for home this night, and I know it's not my place to thwart you. But I beg you, let me at least set your bones and bind your ribs before I go."

"Before *you* go?" John repeated, his eyebrows becoming one as he squinted down at her. "God's tears, Gwyneth! I am a simple man. Speak plainly when you speak to me, I beg you."

It was hard for her, this parting. Why couldn't John just let it go, just let her go? Gwyneth wondered. But she took a deep breath and explained, "When you ride to Farleigh Castle, I shall ride to Sherborne Manor."

"Why in heaven's name would you wish to ride to Sherborne? You've already been there recently, as I recall." He folded his arms over his broad chest.

"'Tis my home," she explained impatiently, "my dowerlands. As Ector's demesne is lost to my eldest, I shall reside at Sherborne."

The earl inhaled deeply and looked up at the blinding blaze behind Gwyneth's head. His own patience wearing thin, he growled, "Farleigh Castle's your home."

Gwyneth's heart spasmed. He could not mean it. "But—but—"

"But what, sweetling?"

She blinked. Tears streamed down her cheeks in an endless flow unleashed by John's endearment. "I—I've been naught but a trial to you," she reminded him. "Earlier I pledged to obey you, to go with Richard to safety. You spoke of consequences, and I know full well what they be. Surely you are done with me, now.

Surely you intend to annul our marriage—"

John of Farleigh stepped forward and placed his hands on Gwyneth's shoulders, effectively holding her in place before him. "I have never considered annulling our marriage, lady wife," he informed her. "You are the one who entertains this thought and keeps suggesting to me."

"I've done you naught but wrong," she insisted weakly.

"Holy mother of God!" John shook her, though he winced at the effort.

Immediately she reached out to support him. He glanced at her hands bracing his elbows. "See? I know that everything you do, Gwyneth, you do to protect and care for those you love. Your sister, your sons. Me." His eyes locked on hers. "It may annoy and irritate me, but do you think it makes me care for you any less?" He shook his head, answering his own question. "I am not angered that you disobeyed my order to leave this keep. Jesu, Gwyneth, you saved my bloody neck! I owe you my life." He drew her closer and whispered, "And that life I pledge to you. I love you."

John drew her closer still and kissed her. When he raised his head again, she searched his face. "I love you, John. I vow, you're my first and only love. But even that love cannot ensure I'll give you children."

He smiled. "You brought three fine sons with you into marriage. I've no fear we cannot make babes of our own—I intend to work at that effort most vigorously," he added, his smile broadening into a grin. "But should we fail there, I would be proud to make any or all of your sons my heirs to Farleigh."

Gwyneth's heart felt as if it were bursting open, like flower petals unfurling rapidly in the warmth of the bright sun. Overjoyed to still be alive, to be free of her captors, to be with her husband again, she flung her arms about his neck and kissed John desperately, gratefully, lovingly.

"Let's be home to Farleigh Castle," he suggested when finally he released Gwyneth from his embrace. "I long for my own bed, and you beside me in it."

"Nay."

"Nay?" John dropped his horse's reins, which he had just picked up again. He turned back to his wife, his expression incredulous.

"Your leg," she explained.

"My leg?" he repeated. "What of it? I've ridden with far worse injuries."

"Not while I've been your lady wife."

"Woman, I refuse to spend weeks healing in some humble serf's cottage!" the earl roared.

"There's no need for that," Gwyneth explained hurriedly. Turning, she called out into the darkness, "Richie! Roddy! Find a length or two of wood that will make a decent splint for your father's leg. Sheila? Byrdie? Are you still about? I need some cloth, too, to bind my husband's ribs. Be quick about it."

Henry emerged from the shadows into the glowing firelight where Gwyneth and John stood—she, steadily; he, leaning again on her shoulder for support.

The king considered them both for a long moment before asking, "Is what your lady wife says true, John? You're a broken man and we must delay still longer while she mends you?"

"Aye, 'twould seem so," he replied with a scowl that seemed determined to quirk into a crooked smile. "And as she's a willful woman who, as we've seen, has a certain skill with a sword, I suggest, your highness, you not attempt to sway her from her purpose."

"Not I!" Henry chuckled, raising both his hands in a gesture of defeat. "As husband to Eleanor of Aquitaine, I know when to defer to my lady—and yours."

"Do you?" Gwyneth inquired of her husband.

"Do I what?"

"Know when to defer to me."

"Oh, aye." He was smiling now as he kissed the tip of her nose. "Whenever it suits my purposes."

THE END

Keep on reading for a delightful preview of
Candice Kohl's next book *Destiny's Quest*
the second in her medieval trilogy.

Destiny's Quest

Chapter 1

❖   ❖   ❖

The South of England, Springtime, 1162

He saw the darker wench first. Lounging against a tree trunk, he took respite from the uncommonly hot morning sun by slaking his thirst with a cup of Farleigh's finest brew, made from his own mother's recipe, as he idly surveyed the crowd. The girl caught his attention because, despite her drab peasant garb, she was obviously fine, of form and feature. He enjoyed his talent; always he was able to pick out the comeliest wench in a crowd, be it in a humble village or at a banquet attended by King Henry's court. As was his habit, he amused himself with wondering who she was, cottar's wife or freeman's daughter, married or maiden, virtuous or wanton.

He watched her speak to someone blocked from his view by the corner of a large vendors' tent. Now her arms went out, her hands disappearing behind the brightly colored fabric that billowed and rippled in the breeze. He could not easily determine what it was she was doing, so he took a step away from the tree to get a better view. At that moment *she* appeared.

Matthew went still, though he blinked rapidly, sure his vision had abruptly gone faulty. No wench, he thought, be she princess or peasant, could look as this one did.

She was garbed in a hooded white cloak that glittered with threads of spun silver. Then she turned so she nearly faced him, and Matthew saw she was wearing only coarse tunics of faded blue, and no hood at all. Her head was uncovered, and the mantle floating down over her shoulders, past her hips, and nearly to her toes, was the most glorious wealth of hair he had ever seen. Pale as moonlit snow, it sparkled like silk embroidered with strands of silver. And the face beneath it—

"Christ."

Matthew gulped the dregs in his cup before thoughtlessly tossing the empty vessel aside. Impatiently he stepped to one side so that no passers-by could obstruct his view. His continued perusal only confirmed his first impression. The wench was beautiful. Her face was small and heart-shaped, her lips lush, her cheeks rosy. And her eyes—they were blue, cornflower blue. Her eyes were startling, not only because of their deep hue, but because they were framed by thick, sooty lashes and above them arched two fine, black brows, in contrast to the pale blondness of her glorious tresses.

"You ought not to unplait your hair."

It was the dark-haired wench, the one Matthew had spied first, that he overheard now speaking. He stepped closer to better eavesdrop on their conversation, and could finally see what it was she'd been doing: running her fingers through the other's mane, using her nails to comb out the waves left by the braiding.

"'Tis unseemly."

"It is not!" the fair beauty protested, though a smile played on her lips. "I've barely ten and eight years to my age, and I'm a maiden in the bargain. There's no sin in letting my hair hang free."

"But... you've so much of it."

"Tsk, tsk, tsk."

Matthew saw the blonde goddess wink impishly at her companion.

"Don't behave like a stuffy old abbess, Charlotte" she chided her friend. "Besides, I only took the braids from my hair so that the hair pieces I try on are set off to full advantage."

While he continued to observe them, the two young women stepped into the tent they'd been standing near. With a slow, casual stride he followed them in, finding them easily as they patronized an old woman's stall and examined her goods. The aged crone was grinning as she set a circlet of flowers on the fair maid's head and began to fan out the strips of embroidered cloth that flowed from it.

"'Od's blood, she's made herself more beautiful," Matthew muttered to himself. On her, the chaplet of flowers with its many-hued ribands was more dazzling than a crown studded with jewels. The streamers of bright colored silk against her shimmering stresses made the damsel stand out among the crush of peasants surrounding her like a glittering gemstone nestled in a handful of rough pebbles.

While he watched, the maid twirled about, pleased, and looked at Charlotte expectantly.

"It certainly suits you Adrienne," the other girl admitted. "But the flowers will die."

"They are woven through grape vine," the vendor explained, "and may easily be replaced by strolling through a summer meadow."

"But the cost!" Charlotte persisted. "A headpiece as unique as this one you've crafted."

"What can you afford, mistress?" the woman asked Adrienne.

She responded by digging her slender fingers into the small leather pouch tied to her belt. Pulling out nearly all the contents, she showed the vendor the short-cross pennies in her palm.

"This'll do," the woman declared, taking all but a few.

"Surely, it's not enough?" Adrienne questioned

"'Tis, if you pledge to tell all who admire that chaplet where it is you got it. I'll make up in extra custom what I lose on my sale to you."

"Truly?"

"Aye." She nodded, squeezing the girl's pale fingers in her own spotted hand.

"My thanks, then. I vow to tell anyone who asks, and even those who do not!"

With a beaming smile, Adrienne went off with Charlotte.

Matthew approached the narrow stall and announced without preamble, "I'll make up the difference."

The old woman squinted up at him, though her eyes were as clear as her fingers were nimble. "That you, Lord Matthew? Lady Gwyneth's son?" she asked, and he nodded. "Thought so." She turned her gaze toward the opening in the tent where Adrienne and Charlotte had exited. "D'you know her, the one with all that fine, white hair?"

"Nay, not yet. But I intend to."

"Then go off and seek her out. Don't worry about the cost of her trinket. I tell you truly, I'd have given it to her for the price of a smile. She's a grand one, she is, and probably the only one here at the fair to do me work justice."

Undeterred, Matthew tossed a few coins onto the splintered board that served as the womans trading counter.

"Do you know anything about her? Is she from the area Sherborne, Wexley, Kurth?"

"Can't say I've seen her or her friend before, milord. Her dress confirms her lowly station, but her looks…" The crone shrugged her stooped shoulders. "She must be a bastard sired on a local village wench by some fair-faced lord."

Matthew nodded thoughtfully. Certainly she was just that, the fruit of an intense passion between a peasant and her nobleman lover. He liked that romantic notion, and he savored it as he followed the path she had taken from the tent. Her liked the idea so well, in fact, he determined to continue the tradition the girl's own mother had begun.

❦

THE LIONHEARTED STORY

Dear Reader,

We hope you enjoyed this LionHearted novel. You may have already noticed some differences between our books and many others, beginning with our covers. I was always embarrassed to read books with 'bodice-ripping' covers in public, so I had our team of artists create covers I wouldn't even hesitate to recommend to my male friends.

You may also notice that necessary violent scenes in our novels have been toned down or take place out of view of the reader. I personally enjoy empowered heroines and heroes who show that honesty, integrity, high values, persistence and love will ultimately triumph over adversity.

We have a different vision of what constitutes excellence in romance fiction, and hope you agree. It takes authors with talent, skill, and imagination plus a diligent and caring editorial staff to produce entertaining and memorable stories. And it also takes *you!* Please write and let me know what you like so that we can keep providing quality and entertaining stories. And, don't forget to tell a friend about our books.

Mary Ann Heathman
President & CEO
LionHearted Publishing, Inc.

The LionHearted Story

♥ ♥ ♥

When forming LionHearted, we discovered that approximately 50% of all paperback books go unsold and are destroyed, often being dumped into our oceans as wastepaper. Yet more book titles are being released each month than there is space for on book store shelves. As the number of books increases, their shelf life decreases, severely limiting their exposure time to customers, and limited exposure means limited sales and lower author royalties. Also, many books being released now are actually re-issues of earlier titles that consumers have already read.

It appeared to us that there was a need for an alternative approach to the marketing and distribution of paperbacks, and in the methods of author compensation in the publishing industry. So we chose to create an environment where authors can earn better than average royalties and receive them sooner, and readers can turn their romance reading into an income producing activity by simply telling their friends about LionHearted books!

The LionHearted Story

How often have you recommended a great movie, an excellent restaurant, a good book, or even a brand name you liked? All the time! But has any restaurant, movie theater or author ever reimbursed you for the highly effective "advertising" you did on their behalf? LionHearted does!

We will publish six new romance titles each month, and readers can purchase the books at discounted prices saving $1.00 or more per book over what they would expect to pay in stores.

Customers purchase their monthly six-pack from the LionHearted Romance Network (LRN), LionHearted's marketing division. Each six-pack will contain an entertaining and memorable variety of romance sub-genres such as contemporary, historical, Regency, time-travel, suspense, intrigue, and more.

By selling and shipping the books directly to our customers, the money that would otherwise be paid to large book distributors, wholesalers and stores can now be paid to you. Independent LRN Representatives can turn a favorite leisure activity from an expense into a profit making business, and write off any business related expenses.

As a LRN Representative, each month you purchase a six-pack from LRN, you qualify to earn a referral fee on the purchases made by all of the customers you personally refer, and on all of the customers those customers refer, etc. extending to five levels of customers.

LRN Representatives are not required to maintain

an inventory, and there are no required meetings or trainings to attend. LionHearted wants you to spend quality time with your family and do what you love most. We hope that includes reading and telling your friends about LionHearted so they can get their own books—and we will pay you to do it!

This marketing approach presents an interesting opportunity for authors. By building a network of readers, they can now earn more than the royalties on their own books. They can earn referral fees on the sales of LionHearted's books, and the referral fees will not run out as royalties eventually do, they will continue year after year with the release of each new monthly six-pack.

Since LionHearted does not withhold royalties in reserve against returns, we can also pay authors their royalties monthly right along with the referral fees paid to our Representatives.

Our humanitarian project is a literacy video that can teach people how to read in the privacy of their home. One out of five adults in this country can't read, and illiteracy has been found to be the biggest link to the rise in crime. Unfortunately, many adults won't attend public reading programs because they don't want others to know they can't read. Let us know if you are interested in this project, or know others who would be.

Whether you are an author, an avid romance reader, or know someone who is, we would like to hear from you.

The LionHearted Story

To receive more information on LionHearted Publishing, The LionHearted Romance Network, becoming a LRN Representative, or to request our author guidelines, contact us at:

LionHearted Publishing, Inc.
P.O. Box 618
Zephyr Cove, NV 89448-0618

888-LION-HRT (546-6478)
702-588-1388
702-588-1386 fax

admin@LionHearted.com
LionHrtInc@aol.com
75644.32@Compuserve.com

Visit our Web site on the Internet at http://www.LionHearted.com

Or fill out one of the information request pages that follow and mail or fax to the above address.

Note

If you don't subscribe to *Affaire de Coeur*, a popular romance industry trade magazine that reviews novels from publishers of romance, you have likely missed their reviews of our books. They have given LionHearted the highest rating awarded any romance publisher.

Affaire de Coeur
3976 Oak Hill Rd.
Oakland, CA 94605-4931
510-569-5675, 510-632-8868 fax
SSeven@msn.com

LionHearted Romance Network

___ Please send me your six-pack of romance novels for $29.95+$3.55 s/h. I am enclosing a check, cashiers check or money order for $33.50 (+ 6.5% sales tax if purchased in Nevada).

___ Please send me the following number of copies of book #1___, #2___, #3___, #4___, #5___, #6___, + 6.5% Sales Tax in Nevada + $2.00 s/h for one copy and $1.00 s/h for each additional copy.

PLEASE PRINT CLEARLY

Name_____

Addrs_____

City_____

St/Zip_____

Phone1_____

Phone2_____

eMail_____

I was referred by:

Name_____

LRN PIN_____

Personal Identification Number is the last 7 digits of SS#, or Employers Identification Number (EIN) if a business.

Mail to: LionHearted Romance Network
           PO Box 618
           Zephyr Cove, NV 89448-0618

Or call: 888-LION-HRT (546-6478)

Six-Pack #1
Order all six books for only $29.95 + $3.55 s/h

1) UNDERCOVER LOVE — Lucy Grijalva (1002) $5.99
The last thing undercover cop Rick Peralta needed was a tempting but off-limits school teacher poking around in his business. The rough biker low-life was everything Julia Newman disliked in a man. He was dangerous but irresistible. Soon she found herself in deeper trouble than she—or he—could handle.
"Way to go Lucy! You have a winner." — *Affaire de Coeur*

2) DESTINY'S DISGUISE — Candice Kohl (1006) $6.99
Lord John, the earl of Farleigh, never expected to inherit title or lands. He arranges to marry the youngest daughter of a neighboring lord. Lady Gweneth is the eldest daughter, a widow bitter toward men. She saves her younger sister from the warrior's hands by impersonating her sister and marrying him herself. John doesn't discover her lie until after the wedding.
"A deliciously convoluted romance. Believable characters and true to period situations." — *Affaire de Coeur*

3) FOREVER, MY KNIGHT — Lee Ann Dansby (1007) $6.99
It is 1067 and Cameron d'Aberon, a Norman knight, is in service to William. He does not need or want another wife, his first having betrayed him and caused the death of his son. Kaela of Chaldron hates the Normans almost as much as she hates and fears her evil and lustful Saxon cousin, Broderick. Now she is the King's ward. Cameron's duty is to escort her to court where the king will choose a husband for the spirited young heiress.
"Tension filled... pulls the reader forward to the end." — *Affaire de Coeur*

4) IF WINTER COMES — Millie Baker Ragosta (1003) $6.49
Her husband's deathbed confession shatters Laura Fortunato's world and begins a journey of self discovery, forgiveness and the power of healing love. Ian McMurtry pursues the reluctant Laura as she battles the lingering ghost who must make things right before he can go on to The Light.
"Truly remarkable. Charming. A keeper." — *Affaire de Coeur*

5) THE MARPLOT MARRIAGE — Beth Andrews (1004) $5.99
Widow Lady Phoebe Bridgerton wakes up in bed next to her cousin by marriage, the last man she'd ever want to marry. Charles Hargood believes her late husband fortunate to be dead rather than alive and married to her. Caught, then jilted by his current fiancée he now has a new fiancée: Phoebe.
"Pure enchantment from cover to cover." — *Affaire de Coeur*

6) THE SIPÁN JAGUAR — Joan Smith (1005) $5.99
A week before the wedding Cassie Newton is unexpectedly invited by her fiancé to join him in Canada. John Weiss, an insurance investigator, has traced a stolen art object and is in deadly pursuit of the thief. But something has gone wrong with the case, and he fears he might not survive.
"Inventive. Delightful. Bright, witty and loving." — *Affaire de Coeur*

LionHearted Romance Network Representative

Name_____

LRN PIN_____

Write: LionHearted Romance Network
PO Box 618
Zephyr Cove, NV 89448-0618

Call: 888-LION-HRT (546-6478) or
702-588-1388

Fax: 702-588-1386

eMail: admin@LionHearted.com

Web site: http://www.LionHearted.com

Candice Kohl

Candice was born and spent most of her life in Milwaukee, Wisconsin. There she worked as a copywriter in advertising and public relations. She also performed as an actress at the Sunset Playhouse, a major midwest community theatre that has also spawned the likes of Anthony Crivello, a recent Tony award winner. In her spare time, she taught English as a second language to recently arrived immigrants. As well, she and her husband, Phil Brabant, raised two sons. Christopher is now a jazz musician in New Orleans, and Dustin remains a student in Milwaukee.

Meanwhile, in late 1992, Candice relocated to the Atlanta, Georgia area with her husband. They now live on five-plus forested acres with her horse, Miz Ed—who has yet to learn to speak as her namesake did. In 1993, her first book, *The String On A Roast Won't Catch Fire In The Oven—An A to Z Encyclopedia of Common Sense* was released to excellent reviews, including one by the American Library Association.

Candice has had numerous articles published in periodicals and newspapers, and is even writing a book about her husbands ancestors, King Leopold I of Belgium and the natives known as Brabanters. But her great passion has always been the historical romance. In addition to *Destiny's Disguise*, she has written two sequels, *Destiny's Quest* and *Twin Destinies*. The medieval trilogy will be published by LionHearted Publishing, Inc.